Final Ascent

8-Bit Syndicate Series - Book 2

April Orion

Print ISBN: 979-8-9863574-1-6

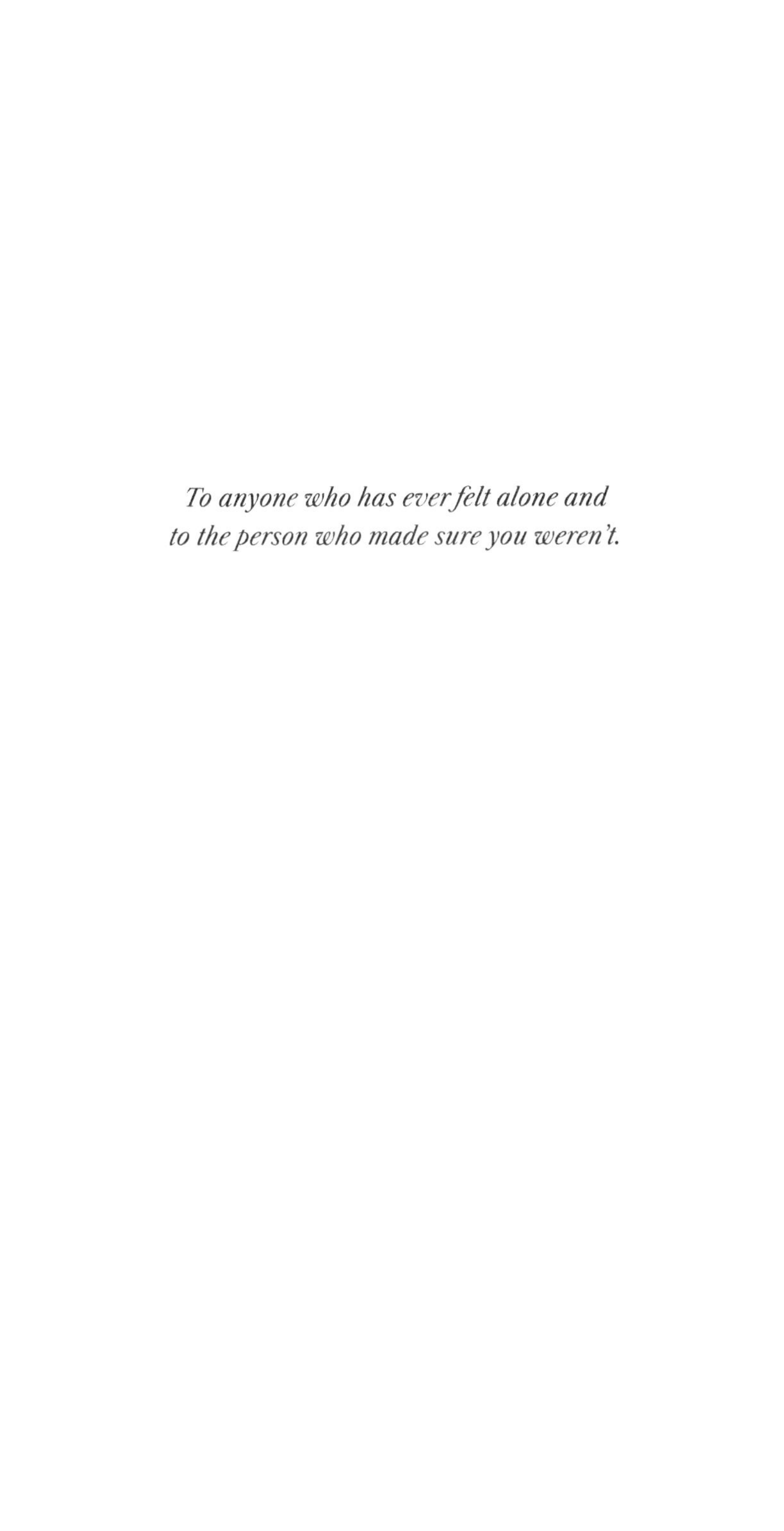

*To anyone who has ever felt alone and
to the person who made sure you weren't.*

Contents

Prologue

Ash

I can count on one hand the number of times I have felt utterly helpless: losing my mom, ditching Wren at her apartment, and watching Robbie die. Now, I get to add being on trial for a murder I didn't commit.

Lucky me.

I'm standing on a raised platform in the Academy atrium. Trials are usually held behind closed doors in a courtroom, but I guess being accused of murdering the director gets you special treatment. My hands are secured in front of me, the cuffs fastened so tightly my fingers start to numb. Thick shackles bind my ankles together, the center of the chain looped through a metal ring connected to the platform at my feet.

I don't know where they expect me to run. The place is packed with enforcers. I wouldn't make it ten feet.

The media crews have set up their cameras so the two-story waterfall is visible behind me. I'm centered under the chandelier of broken glass that is the defining architectural feature of the building. Each shard hangs from a clear string, making it appear as if they were frozen mid-fall like a deadly rainstorm. The foyer is open for at least ten stories with enforcers hanging over the railings watching the proceedings in silence. I'm not sure I've ever heard a crowd of this size be this quiet. It's disconcerting. The Council members are seated at the base of the platform, but even they're not speaking. The only noise comes from the crowd of elites gathered outside where my trial is being projected on the side of the Academy.

I guess everyone loves a good execution because that's what this is. I have no delusions my trial will end any other way. The verdict was reached before Jace pulled the trigger and ended his father's life. Jace planned his takeover for months. There's no other explanation for how smoothly he was able to assume the director's seat. My stepbrother was playing the final moves in a game I had just started. Byron Axton was the director, my stepfather, and a royal pain in my ass...that doesn't mean I wanted him dead.

Jace had a different opinion.

I see Jace sitting with the rest of the Council members at the base of the platform, his chair directly in my line of sight. He's dressed in the uniform of an Enforcer general with the gold epaulets and red ceremonial sash he last wore to the Ascent Day celebration at the Axton mansion. He probably laughed when he put it on this morning - the true culprit dressed as a man of law at trial for the person he framed.

Jace inherited his father's aristocratic nose and short stature. His dark hair is slicked back from his face and styled. He's wearing a somber expression that's nothing more than a curated mask - a mask I wish I had seen through sooner. Every time I close my eyes, I relive Byron's murder at the Axton mansion.

The sound of the gun. My stepfather's chair toppling over. Chaos.

It plays on repeat in my mind. I go over every moment, every interaction that could have indicated Jace was about to flip the world upside down. Every time I come up blank, but that doesn't stop me from blaming myself. I failed as an Enforcer and as a son. I knew Jace was sick, but I underestimated him.

It won't happen again.

Jace stands. He flattens his hair and straightens his suit in preparation for his speech. He studies me, as if looking for a weakness he can exploit in his testimony. I wonder if I'm the only person who can see the smirk he's trying so hard to hide. Camera crews get into position to film us as Jace delivers my sentence.

The whole thing is like a train wreck you want to look away from, but you can't because you're on the train.

I throw my shoulders back and try to look as dignified as possible. I don't remember the last time I had a decent meal or a shower. I'm wearing an orange prisoner jumpsuit and my feet are bare. I'm sure I look terrible, but that doesn't mean I have to sit back and accept my punishment.

I've done nothing wrong and I've got nothing left to lose.

I'm the one with the power in this situation even if it doesn't feel like it. The thought makes me stand a little taller. Wren and Ariel are safe with Miles. She probably blames me for Robbie's death, as she should. I could have prevented it if I had moved faster and been a better enforcer. I look into the camera, wondering if Wren is watching.

I failed her. Again.

I left her to take my place as the director's successor. I couldn't save Robbie, but I thought I could save others like him. I wouldn't have left her if I didn't believe I could make a difference. Maybe I was naive. It doesn't matter. I won't get the chance to find out. Jace addresses the crowd, babbling on about how much he loved Byron and how well-respected he was as a leader and a father. Prisoners usually get to make a statement at their trials, but I doubt Jace will offer me that courtesy.

Screw it. What's the worst he can do if I interrupt him? Kill me? I almost laugh.

"Jace Axton killed the director," I speak over Jace, staring into the camera. He cuts off mid-sentence. "I watched him shoot Byron in the chest four times in cold blood. Before he died, Byron made me the designated successor."

There are a few gasps from the crowd. Some Council members watch me with guilt-stricken faces because they know I'm telling the truth. They were there when Byron made me his successor. They have known Jace and I since we were children. I'm sure they've connected the dots by now; they're just too afraid to say anything.

My eyes land on Elle, my best friend. She sits with the other Council members, her hands clasped in her lap. Her straight blond hair is tied in a high ponytail, her blue eyes giving nothing away. She looks the part of an Enforcer lieutenant with her dress uniform and straight posture. Unlike Jace, she isn't wearing the traditional sash and epaulets. It makes the uniform appear more pragmatic and less like a costume. It suits her. She meets my gaze and nods, encouraging me to keep going.

I stare at her.

Elle has always believed in the Council. Their mission. What they stand for. She arrested me when I let Wren and Miles escape. Speaking out against the director on a televised broadcast is treason. The fact that she's supporting me now means a lot.

She believes in the Council, but she doesn't believe in Jace.

I wonder how many Council members share her sentiment?

"Kill the feed," orders Jace. Most of the camera operators obey his command, but there's one man who doesn't budge. He mouths, "keep going." There's determination in his eyes, an understanding of the gravity of this moment. He knows he'll be arrested for this, but he's deciding to stand up and fight. I swallow the lump in my throat and continue.

"The Council was present for the announcement. They can confirm I am telling the truth," I say.

I stare at the rows of chairs at the base of the platform. The Council members fidget. They avoid my eyes. All the while, the camera captures their response to my accusation. They don't need to say anything at all. Their guilt is evident.

"They're afraid of what will happen to their families if they speak against their director. Jace Axton is corrupt. He plotted with the Syndicate to assassinate his father," I say.

The enforcers above us break their silence, shouting accusations from above. It's hard to pick out a single voice - it all blends together in a cacophony of dissent. They've sacrificed so much for this city. They trusted the Council and the director to make the right choices.

Jace betrayed that trust and, in doing so, showed them that their sacrifice meant nothing.

"Are you going to support a leader like that?" I yell, yanking on my chains. A shot echoes in the chamber. The cameraman topples over, his equipment crashing to the floor. Jace stands over him with his gun raised. He slowly turns until the barrel is pointed at me.

"The Council finds you guilty of treason. Your punishment is execution," says Jace. He looks unhinged, crazed. The exact opposite of what a director should look like. I smirk at him because the damage is already done. I knew my outburst wouldn't force the Council to take action. They've had the opportunity to remove Jace from power for weeks. They haven't acted and, chances are, they aren't going to. I wasn't even speaking to them. I was talking to the people. I consider it a win if I can get even one person to question Jace's right to the director seat. My trial was being broadcast live across the nation. Someone will finish what I started, even if I'm not around to see it.

"Let him live," Elle yells, standing up. The other Council members stare at her in horror. The atrium is silent for a heartbeat, before someone in the crowd of enforcers mimics Elle's words. My eyes shoot up, but I can't locate the person who spoke. One by one, the other enforcers join in until a steady chant fills the room. A few Council members have joined in, standing in solidarity with Elle.

"Let him live. Let him live. Let him live." Their chant echoes through the atrium.

I stare up at them in shock.

I didn't expect my best friends, let alone the enforcers, to stand by me when I was arrested. This is my home, my family, coming to my aid. It's more than I could have asked for. I return my eyes to Jace, giving him a little smirk. Jace grits his teeth in frustration. He may be the director, but Elle has the loyalty of the Enforcers and the Council. By standing up to Jace, she showed him just how flimsy his throne is. He lowers his gun, glaring at me.

"Very well. I sentence Asher Axton to indentured servitude to the Council for life," growls Jace. He tries to make it sound like his idea, that this is the worst he could have done to me.

Everyone here knows the truth - Elle forced his hand.

For the first time since Byron died, I allow myself to hope because this is how revolutions start - with one person who is brave enough to say no.

That enough is enough.

Chapter 1

Wren

I find comfort in inevitability. There are no surprises, no sudden shock or anger when everything goes to hell - just the courage and sense of control that comes with acceptance. Right now, I'm not in control. Unless you count hyperventilating as meditative breathing, I am completely losing my shit.

I'm usually pretty stoic about my lot in life.

Orphaned? No problem, I'll take care of my family.

Broke? No worries, I'll find an illegal source of income so we can eat.

But when it comes to finding out everyone in my life has been lying to me, that's where my composure jumps ship.

The fire crackles at my feet, giving off a warmth that's only skin deep. I lay back, crossing my arms behind my head to look at the night sky. The number of stars is overwhelming. I didn't realize how many were visible outside the city away from the light pollution. You'd think acknowledging the size of the universe would make everything else seem small in comparison, but it just makes me feel insignificant and my problems insurmountable.

I've never felt so completely lost.

There are a million things I should be doing, but nothing that motivates me to get out of bed in the morning. I feel like I'm drowning. I know some people have it worse than me. My family is safe. We have food, water, and shelter. We're together, and we're comfortable. It's more than I could have ever hoped for, but that's the thing about drowning.

It feels the same whether it's in the bathtub or the ocean.

Three months have passed since I left the city with my family to hide out at the Syndicate headquarters. It sounds more official than it is. In reality, the Syndicate is based out of a two-story farmhouse in the countryside. Things have deteriorated back home. Jace Axton was appointed the new director following his father, Byron's, assassination. Jace exceeded all my expectations of his ruthlessness as a leader, his atrocities laid out in the reports coming out of the city like some alternate reality.

Discrimination against grunts.

The systematic slaughter of political opponents.

Strict imposition of martial law.

It's not like the disparity between the grunt neighborhoods and the elite sector is a well-kept secret, but the Council used to pretend to care. Needless to say, that facade has been destroyed by Jace. My home is a war zone with only one side capable of taking up arms. If Jace keeps up his reign of terror, I'm not sure there will be anyone left for him to order around.

I take a few deep breaths and close my eyes. Max whimpers beside me, sensing something is off. I stroke his head until he settles down. Max is a German Shepherd. He's missing part of his left ear and walks with a limp. He was my mom's dog back when she was part of the police force that preceded the Enforcers. After she died, he came to live with us. He's better company than most people I know.

Ash's trial was broadcast a week after we left the city. He was accused of murdering the director. I don't believe for a second that he did it. Byron and Ash had their differences, but that doesn't mean he wanted him dead. That's not who Ash is. I have no doubt Jace was the one to pull the trigger. We set up a giant flat screen in the farmhouse living room to watch Ash's trial. Every Syndicate member in the compound gathered to see it. There must have been forty people crammed in the space.

It was surreal seeing Ash again. They had him in chains on a platform in the Academy atrium. I've watched Council trials on TV before. None were held in a public space, and there weren't as many people. They're using Ash to send a message, to show people what happens when you cross the Council. Between the cramped living room and my fear for Ash, I was on my way to a panic attack.

Ash looked terrible. He was wearing an orange prison jumpsuit. His hair was greasy, and he looked like he had dropped a few pounds since we parted ways. Then, the camera zoomed in to give a close-up of his face. That's when I saw his eyes. Ash didn't look like a man about to be executed.

He looked like a cornered animal ready to fight to the death.

"Jace Axton killed the director," Ash said. He stared straight into the camera, addressing more than the people in the room. He was speaking to the nation. "I watched him shoot Byron in the chest four times in cold blood. Before he died, Byron made me the designated successor."

"Kill the feed," Jace ordered, but the broadcast didn't cut out. The screen stopped switching between multiple views, as if only one person was still filming. The Syndicate members gathered in the living room started whispering.

Someone disobeyed a direct order from the director while the entire country was watching. That had never happened before.

"The Council was present for the announcement. They can confirm I am telling the truth," says Ash.

The camera swept to the Council members seated at the base of the platform. They wouldn't meet Ash's eyes. They looked...guilty.

"They're afraid of what will happen to their families if they speak against their director. Jace Axton is corrupt. He plotted with the Syndicate to assassinate his father," Ash continued.

The feed was interrupted with shouted accusations from the crowd gathered on the balconies above the atrium floor, the camera sweeping up to the Enforcers hanging over the railings.

"Are you going to support a leader like that?" Ash yelled.

That's when the broadcast cut out.

There was something that sounded a lot like a gun going off. The camera toppled over and hit the ground before the screen went dark. I lost it. I was sure they killed him. I bolted from the room and ran into the woods behind the farmhouse until I reached the fence surrounding the compound.

You don't disobey the director and walk away from it.

Later that day, the Council released a statement apologizing for the technical difficulties viewers experienced during the trial broadcast and listed Ash's verdict as a "life of servitude to the Council."

Whatever that means.

That was three months ago.

I'd give anything to know what Ash said that changed Jace's mind. I'm sure the rest of the world would too. I know Ash didn't kill the director. I have zero proof other than his word, but that's enough. I can't reconcile the man I know with the murderer the Council broadcasts make him out to be. Ash hasn't been seen or heard from since his trial.

I even broke my silent treatment to ask Glitch for help, but she couldn't find anything either. It kills me to know the once proud enforcer was reduced to a public punching bag, a scapegoat for the Council agenda. He was the unlikely friend who was there for me when no one else was, and I abandoned him. Ash and I were many things: enemies, reluctant partners, and then friends.

In the end, I'm not sure what we were.

He told me he loved me. Or at least that's what I think he was going to say before I cut him off. Either way, I didn't say it back.

I wanted to. God, I wanted to, but what good would it have done?

I asked Ash to come with us. He told me no. He wanted to take his place as the designated successor. He told me he would work with the Council to make the nation a better place for grunts - for people like Robbie. My gut twists painfully, the memory fresh enough to cut deep. Robbie was like a little brother to me. He was twelve, loud, and a generally cheerful person. He had a heart of gold and was always willing to help others. It's what got him killed.

His blood is on my hands.

If I hadn't joined the Enforcers to rescue his older brother, Miles, things might have turned out differently. The Syndicate wouldn't have come around asking for protection fees, and Robbie wouldn't have started working for the surge crew in the first place. Even as I have the thought, I know leaving Miles with the Enforcers was never on the table.

Miles was my best friend...is my best friend. We grew up together. He helped me run my dad's auto body shop, Jimmy's Auto after he died. We were there for each other.

At least, I thought we were.

When Miles was released from the Academy holding cells, I realized he had been lying to me for a long time. It turns out that my mom faked her death so that she could run the Syndicate. I understand why she did it.

The technology giant Axton AI, and companies like it created software bots and robots that mass automated jobs once done by humans. Blue-collar jobs. White-collar jobs. It didn't matter. They disappeared over a decade, leaving millions unemployed. People protested. My mom created the Syndicate to provide an alternative job market to the one Axton AI destroyed. She did it to bring relief to people who were left behind by the evolving economy.

That's the key.

This wasn't happening to strangers; it was happening to people she knew: friends, family, and neighbors. She decided to do something about it, but she didn't want her actions to fall back on dad and I, so she faked her death.

Dad, Grams, and Miles knew the truth while I was intentionally left in the dark. Miles worked with my mom to build the Syndicate into what it is today. He created the 8-Bit app. At face value, 8-Bit is a phone app featuring a vintage video game collection. They're all playable, but that's not why anyone uses 8-Bit. The digital marketplace allows Syndicate members to list jobs or apply for them. You can buy goods or services using credits, the digital currency backed by the Syndicate and linked to your Axton AI chip implant.

Got laid off from your accounting job? No problem, you can run drugs for the surge crew.

Don't have enough money to buy food? No worries, you can trade your hacking services for rations.

8-Bit is the currency of the shadow economy the Syndicate created. It was all working perfectly until Rook decided to sell them out. Rook runs the most extensive and best-equipped crew in the Syndicate - the surge crew. They deal in the manufacture and distribution of the most popular street drug on the market. As Miles explains it, Rook had been butting heads with my mom for years. She wanted more say in Syndicate leadership decisions and more territory. My mom wouldn't hear her out, so she went to someone who would - Jace Axton.

Bryon had recently told Jace he was making Ash his designated successor for the director position, a title Jace had assumed he was getting. Furthermore, Byron decided to split the director seat and his shares in Axton AI between his two heirs. Jace would become the new managing partner of Axton

AI alongside Carl Bronxton, while Ash would head up the Council as the director. Byron believed the two positions had become too powerful for one person. Jace didn't take the news well. He agreed to help Rook overthrow my mom as leader of the Syndicate in exchange for her help getting rid of Ash. She agreed.

So, Jace organized a meeting with my mom, resulting in her death. At the same time, Jace dropped a tip to the Enforcers that led to Miles's arrest. Jace took out the two most essential Syndicate leaders in one night. That should have been the end, but he didn't plan on Ash and I making a deal. I agreed to help Ash take down the surge crew leader in exchange for Miles's freedom. We derailed the plan Jace and Rook were executing. Not that it mattered. At the end of the day, Jace is still the director and Rook has expanded her control of the Syndicate. They both got what they wanted and Miles is left fighting an internal power war I'm not so sure he can win.

To summarize, I'm living at a Syndicate stronghold outside the city, preparing for a gang war.

I don't know where Ash is or if he's still alive.

The country is burning under Jace's reign.

There's nothing I can do about it, which explains my generally bad mood. You know, that and being lied to by my family for years.

Yep, that's the clincher.

It flipped my world upside down, erasing everything I thought I knew. I've been avoiding Grams, my paternal grandmother, for months now. I've said ten words to her since we arrived at the farmhouse. She practically raised me. She watched dad lose himself in a bottle and didn't try to get my mom to come back to stop him. Logically, I know it wasn't Grams's choice. There was probably nothing she could have said or done to make the situation right, but that doesn't mean I'm any less angry.

Maybe one day I'll be able to forgive her, but it won't be any time soon.

I think depression is a natural response to finding out your mom faked her death to found a criminal organization, and everyone in your life - your best friend, your grandmother, and your dad - knew about it and didn't tell you. I miss the chaos of living in the city. The constant stream of people, the customers at Jimmy's Auto, and the general noise of existing.

I want to go home. The country is too quiet for a loud mind.

I wish I had something to distract me from the torrent of emotions eating me from the inside out. I feel like a passenger inside my head. Like I'm not in control of my life or my decisions. I just keep making them, because that's what people expect me to do.

I'm not okay.

Even admitting that feels like defeat. I've always put on my mask. I've always been the one to keep myself together when everything else falls apart. I took pride in that.

I'm not okay.

I haven't been for a while now, but it's becoming harder to ignore. I'm depressed. I don't sleep well. When I do sleep, I feel like every day is a battle to get out of bed. I should be rewarded for getting dressed and taking a shower like a normal human, but that's not enough. I have a daughter who means the world to me.

I hate that I can't be there for her the way I want to be right now.

I hate that I can't be there for Ash the way I want to be right now.

I hate talking to Miles and feeling like garbage because talking to my best friend feels more like talking to a stranger. I hate that I lost my confidant and gained an employer because that's what my relationship with Miles has become, hasn't it?

I'm trading my principles for Syndicate protection.

I cross the days off and watch the minutes tick by, hoping Miles will give us the green light to search for Ash.

Hoping one day, he'll care.

Hoping one day, I'll care.

Because the apathy is slowly killing me.

"Can I join your pity party?" Roy asks, interrupting my internal spiral. I lift my head just enough to see him standing at the end of the truck bed. He has two soda cans clutched in his right hand and his camera in his left.

"It's only a pity party if you celebrate alone," I say because that's what I do when my life is in shambles. I make a joke and laugh it off. I pretend like everything is fine when it's not. I crunch up into a sitting position. Roy sits cross-legged beside me. He gives me a look that tells me he sees right through my lie, but he doesn't call me on it. That's the best part about Roy. His friendship is like a coat of lacquer applied to dull wood, restoring your color and adding vibrancy to your mood that wasn't there before.

"What are we commiserating about today?" He opens one of the cans and hands it to me.

I take a sip. "Do I have to pick one thing?"

He chuckles. "You sound like Glitch." His face screws up when he says her name as if recalling an ugly memory. Glitch joined the Enforcers with me at the Ascent Day bid. We became fast friends. At the time, I didn't know she worked for Miles and joined up to rescue him. She hacked the Ascent Day lottery to get me a winning ticket at Miles's request. It was my best friend's way of taking care of me when he discovered my mom was killed and realized he had a target on his back. He didn't expect me to use it to try to rescue him. He had Glitch for that.

Roy takes a sip of his drink. Roy and I began our friendship at the Academy, but we didn't hang out one-on-one until we left the city. He had the hots for Glitch, and I was undercover with Ash. We bonded over our mutual frustration at being lied to by people we thought we knew. In some ways, he's the only person I feel like I can trust right now. Maybe that's because he's the only one who hasn't betrayed me.

Roy is boy-next-door cute. He's tall, bordering on lanky, with wavy red hair and a narrow nose dotted with freckles. He's...nice. Charming even. I try to imagine loving someone like him for a moment, but I can't. The image quickly gives way to haunted charcoal eyes, sharp cheekbones, and dark hair. I sigh. Why can't I be normal?

"You talked to Miles again," Roy states. It doesn't take a genius to deduce the reason for my terrible mood. I've had the same conversation with Miles every day for months, and it always ends with us screaming at each other and Miles refusing to help. Then, I hide out by the fire with Max and try to psych myself up to go another round in a futile fight.

I wish I could get Miles to understand it's in our best interest to find and rescue Ash. Ash is the true designated successor. He has the power to usurp Jace. He could work with the Council to make changes to bring peace to the city and to find a balance for both grunts and elites. Miles doesn't see it that way. He has spent most of his life building the 8-Bit app and was my mom's second in command.

Now that she's gone, he's leading the entire operation. At least, he's trying to. Rook gained quite a loyal following while Miles was locked up. She has gone to ground and no one is ratting her out. Miles has been expending all of his resources trying to find her. He says it's because he has to regain control of the Syndicate, but I know that's not the only reason.

Miles blames Rook for Robbie's death.

Axton AI bots killed Miles's little brother after the surge crew took him hostage. Rook was responsible for Robbie being there, but I don't think she killed him. I saw the look on her face when the bots started firing. She lost people that day too. Someone else was controlling those bots. I've tried to tell Miles my suspicions, but he shuts down and gets angry.

He thinks I'm trying to get him to stop looking for Rook so he can focus on helping Ash. He's unwilling to use his resources to rescue "my enforcer boyfriend" when the Syndicate has enough problems internally.

His words. Not mine.

"Yep," I say, popping the "p." Roy rolls his eyes. He's as irritated with Miles and Glitch as I am. He knows better than to ask for details.

"Have you talked to Glitch?" I ask.

"Sort of," Roy sighs. "I care about her, but as much as I want things to go back to the way they were before, I don't think it's possible."

He stares into the flames crackling at our feet. We both know what it's like to have someone we trust and care about lie to us. I get that it's hard to work through. I still haven't patched things up with Grams and Miles, so I don't have any advice to offer him on letting things go.

I'm still unreasonably angry at my mom for all of this. Sometimes, I wish she was still alive so that I could scream at her. I could air all the lies, pain, and hurt I'd built up over the years. We would get everything out in the open in one massive fight, patch things up, and then move on. I'll never get that chance. I'll never get to have that fight. I'll never get an apology or a second chance at a new relationship. All I'm left with are unanswered questions.

"Take any good pictures?" I ask to break the silence. Roy glances at the camera lying on his lap.

"It doesn't matter," he says. He finishes his soda and sets it beside him, leaning back on his hands so he can look up at the stars. "It's a coping mechanism more than anything."

I shrug but stay silent, giving him room to speak.

"I've been taking pictures of people I know again," he says quietly after a few minutes. I raise an eyebrow. For as long as I've known Roy, he has only taken pictures of landscapes or inanimate objects. Glitch made him take his camera the night we went out dancing. He took some group photos, but I haven't seen Roy initiate anything since.

"When I take a picture, I can make sure everything is framed just right," he says. "I can take my time and capture things in the moment. Do you remember the one of my little brother, Jake?" I nod, recalling the picture of the little boy with red hair Roy showed Glitch and I at the Academy. "After Jake died, I was so concerned anyone I turned my camera on would end up like him. I didn't want to be responsible for taking the last picture of anyone."

"So, what changed?" I ask, setting my drink aside.

"Nothing. Everything," Roy sighs. "Jake died in an enforcer raid just before I won the Ascent Day lottery. When I won, I told myself if I could take down a few enforcers, it would make the pain go away. When Ash introduced himself in the virtual reality arena, I thought it was luck. The director's son! If I could kill him, then I could avenge Jake's death. That's why I tried to shoot him the first day we met."

"I didn't know that," I say.

"I was wrong about Ash, you know. He put himself between you and those bots. He chose to protect the leader of the Syndicate and a grunt mechanic despite the position it would put him in. He chose justice." Roy glances at me. "Did you know Glitch and her team have been circulating footage of Ash's trial and the truth about the rogue bots that killed Robbie? People are rallying behind Ash from both sides - grunts and elites. They see him as a revolutionary, a leader they are willing to follow," Roy says wistfully.

He shakes his head. "I decided change isn't always bad, and a reminder of who we used to be isn't either. If grunts and elites see a common leader in Ash and a picture is what gets people to see that, then it's my duty to document what we're doing here." He raises his camera and snaps a picture of me. I roll my eyes, but I don't swat the camera away.

"I wish we could save him," I say.

"Then, we'll do it ourselves."

"How? We don't have any resources. Miles won't help us. We're probably going to get ourselves killed."

Roy shrugs. "Or we can sit here and watch the country burn while we ride it out and do nothing. Can you live with that? I can't."

He's right. I hate that he's right. I have everything I ever dreamed about right here in the Syndicate compound. I could turn my back on Ash and the rest of the city and live out my days in peace, but that's not who I am. It never was.

"No, I can't," I say.

Roy gives me a sad, crooked smile. "Then let's do something about it."

Chapter 2

Wren

"We don't have to talk to her tonight," says Roy.

Glitch and her team are holed up in one of the outbuildings on the property. It's a sheet metal barn that looks one windy day from collapsing. Roy is rocking back and forth on his heels with his hands tucked in his pockets. He might be less thrilled to talk to Glitch than I am, but I've already decided I'm going to ask her to help rescue Ash.

I don't care what Miles says.

I take a deep breath and knock. I hear light footsteps inside before Viper yanks open the door. He glares at us - not that I'm surprised. I don't think the guy is capable of any other expression. If I had to guess, I'd say Viper is in his early twenties. He's tall and slim with severe cheekbones and a silver hoop through his left nostril. His dark eyes are made more menacing by thick eyebrows. Viper tucks his shoulder-length black hair behind his ears, revealing a pair of black stud earrings.

The guy is the definition of intimidating. His menacing demeanor doesn't seem to phase Max. He trots forward and nudges Viper's leg with his head before sitting on his haunches with his tongue lolling out of his mouth.

"Sorry," I mumble. I squat down and stroke Max's head. "Go find Ariel," I say. He licks my nose before taking off in the direction of the farmhouse. I wince and swipe my sleeve over my face to dry Max's kiss. Viper is still standing at the door staring at me. I clear my throat. "We're here to see Glitch."

He stares at us for another beat before grunting and stepping aside to let us pass. He's said maybe two words to me the entire time I've been here. I don't take it personally. He's not shy, more selective with his words. Viper only speaks up when he has something important to say and people always seem to listen. I step past him before I can change my mind about approaching Glitch.

Despite living on the property for three months, I haven't been inside this building. There are rows of servers lining the back wall. The air conditioning runs full blast, causing goosebumps on my arms. Glitch sits at a desk in the corner in front of three monitors. She's so engrossed in her work she doesn't realize we're here. Viper walks to the other side of the room and sits at his desk. He goes back to typing as if we had never interrupted him. I glance at Roy. He shrugs, appearing as uncomfortable as I feel. I guess that means I'm leading this conversation. I walk over to Glitch and tap her on the shoulder. She jumps almost a foot off her seat before spinning her chair around.

"Don't scare me like that," she gasps, clutching her chest.

"I need your help," I say, ignoring her dramatic response. Glitch stretches her hands above her head, groaning when her back pops.

"Sure, what's going on?" she asks.

"We need your help finding Ash," I say.

Glitch quirks an eyebrow. "I thought Miles told you he wasn't going to use Syndicate resources to help you."

"But you haven't told us that," says Roy. Glitch's eyes snap to him. I see a flash of pain in her expression, but she schools her features. They aren't on speaking terms most days, and it looks like it's impacting both of them negatively. I wish they would just apologize and move on. As soon as I have the thought, I kick myself for being a hypocrite. It's not that easy. If it were, I would have patched things up with Miles and Grams weeks ago.

"No," she agrees. "I haven't."

"So, you'll help us find Ash?" I ask.

"I already found him," says Glitch.

"Why haven't we sent in a team to help him?" I ask, raising my voice. I promised myself I would keep my cool. That I would be able to convince Glitch to help us with a rescue attempt, but my resolve is quickly failing. This isn't a social call. This is a negotiation.

"Because Miles hasn't given the order, and I don't have the authority to do it myself," Glitch sighs. "Look, Ash is being held at the Academy. It's going to take a small army to bust him out. From what I can gather, Jace is doing whatever he can to humiliate him and destroy his reputation."

"Like what?" I ask, even though I'm afraid of the answer.

"Like serving food at Council parties or making him a punching bag in Enforcer training demonstrations," says Glitch. I wince.

"Why not just kill him?" Roy asks. I glare at him. He gives me an apologetic shrug. "What? It's a fair question."

"Killing him without destroying his image would make him a martyr," says Glitch. "It'll make more sense if I show you something." She turns around and pulls up a video on the monitor. I immediately recognize the footage from Ash's trial, but it's not the broadcast we watched. "Someone recorded the trial on their phone after the public feed cut out," she explains.

The video is of poor quality. It was taken by someone standing on an upper level looking down into the atrium. Ash is centered in the frame, chained to a raised platform in front of the Council. The view is partially obstructed by the glass shards making up the chandelier.

"Are you going to support a leader like that?" Ash's voice comes through the recording.

Jace shoots the cameraman.

Roy and I both jump.

The action is fluid and practiced. If there was ever a doubt in my mind that Jace killed Byron, there isn't now. Jace has killed before. The cameraman topples over, his equipment crashing to the ground. Screams erupt in the background. I can't tell if they're coming from the Council members gathered at the base of the platform or the enforcers above. It's probably a mixture of both. The other media crew members rush to move away from the platform, terrified Jace will come for them next. Some Council members stand up, but no one tries to stop Jace.

The guy holding the phone curses. The frame shakes a bit, and the image blurs before returning to focus. I see a piece of fabric in the corner of the shot as if he's holding his phone under his coat to keep people from seeing that he's still filming. I hear whispering around him and shuffling like some enforcers are leaving before things get ugly. Jace gestures for the Council members to sit. They glance at each other before obeying his orders. I'm surprised none of them tried to bolt.

"The Council finds you guilty of treason. Your punishment is execution," says Jace, leveling his gun at Ash. I clench my teeth. I know Ash is still alive. Glitch told me as much, but that doesn't mean I like the reminder of how close he came to death.

That's when Elle stands up. She's Ash's best friend and an Enforcer lieutenant. I met her once when she told Jace to back off after he broke into my compartment at the Academy. From what the other enforcers say, she's an elite loyalist through and through. She believes in the Council and follows the rules, so it's surprising that she broke protocol at a public hearing by standing during a verdict.

"Let him live!" she yells. The other Council members stare at her. No one moves from their seat. Then, the guy recording this on his phone echoes her chant, his voice coming through clearly in the video. The other enforcers join in one by one until the sound is overwhelming. Jace looks like he's about ready to go on a rampage. I watch the screen in shock. To my knowledge, no one has ever opposed the Council or the director at a public hearing. It doesn't happen.

"Very well," Jace grits out. "I sentence Asher Axton to indentured servitude to the Council for life."

Commander Harper and another guard I don't recognize unchain Ash from the stage and haul him away. They're more aggressive than they need to be. Ash isn't fighting them. He's still looking up at the enforcers in shock. I realize he didn't expect anyone to come to his aid. I swallow the lump in my throat as the video feed stops.

Roy told me Ash was a symbol of the resistance, but I didn't know exactly what that meant until now. The Council and the Enforcers turned against their director. They asked for mercy, and it was granted. No, that's not quite right. They demanded it. Elle's chant and Jace's response showed everyone in that room that the director is only as powerful as the people allow them to be. Together, they revealed Jace's vulnerability to the public.

"I managed to post this video on the Council website for thirty minutes before it was taken down," says Glitch. "People are rallying behind Ash. Our director killed a member of the media in cold blood. Then, the crowd saved the life of a man who claims to be the true successor to the director seat. We haven't seen a public reaction like this since before the Council was created. Ash has become an unintentional symbol for the revolution."

"Then why aren't we trying to rescue him?" I ask. I feel like I'm stating the obvious.

Glitch sighs, her shoulders drooping. "I've shown Miles all of this, but he's still focused on taking out Rook. He blames her for Robbie's death and will not back down until he finds her. I get it. I do, but we need to act on this. Ash allowed us to rally support to overthrow the Council. We haven't seen an appetite for this in years. We've never had elites and grunts agree on a candidate like this. For the first time, we have a political figure both sides are supporting. We have to act now before we lose that momentum. Or worse, Jace decides keeping Ash alive is too big of a risk and kills him anyway."

"So, you're going to help us?" Roy asks. Glitch gives him a small smile.

"Absolutely. I've already got a contact inside the Enforcers."

"The guy who was filming Ash's trial?" I ask.

"Better," Glitch grins. "Elle."

I blink. "How?"

"A few weeks after Ash's trial, she stopped by your old apartment. I had someone keeping an eye on the place just in case Ash showed up. Elle gave my contact the trial video and told him she was trying to find a way to bust Ash and Liam out. She's quietly gathering support within the Enforcers and the Council. Most of them hate Jace, but only a few are willing to admit it publicly," says Glitch. She presses her lips together and watches my reaction. She opens her mouth to add something but stops.

"Whatever you're thinking, you should go ahead and say it," I grumble.

Glitch sighs. "Liam was controlling the bots when Ash and Elle arrived to help extract Robbie from the surge crew."

My jaw drops open. "Liam...he didn't..."

Before I can stop it, the image of Robbie's body comes to mind. His too-small frame sitting limply in the chair. The bullet wounds. The blood. I dig my fingernails into my palms to ground myself.

The bots killed Robbie.

Miles suspects Rook was behind it, but I doubt it. Why would she kill her people and put herself in danger if she was in control? If she wanted Robbie dead, she could have killed him herself. No, it's more likely there was someone else in charge of the rogue bots. But Liam? That doesn't make sense, either.

Liam is the head of covert operations for the Enforcers and Ash's best friend. The first time I met the man, he put himself between Jace and my family to de-escalate a situation that could have been much worse. He warned me against going undercover with the surge crew and went toe-to-toe with Ash to keep us both safe. I think about his friendly face with laugh lines etched around his warm brown eyes. I refuse to believe Liam was behind the controls.

Glitch shakes her head, confirming my suspicions.

"Elle said Liam was arrested mid-raid, and Commander Harper took control of the bots. He was the one who killed Robbie." My fingernails bite into my palms, drawing blood.

I'll kill him.

It's not a threat. It's a promise.

I was so concerned about Ash I didn't know about anyone else. How many others were arrested alongside Ash for allowing Miles and me to escape? I swallow.

"Have you told Miles that Rook wasn't responsible for Robbie's death?" Roy asks. He's been quiet through most of this, taking in the situation and silently assessing the options.

"I have, but he's convinced Rook is at fault. Nothing I say or do will prove that to him until he finds her."

That sounds about right. Miles is one of the most stubborn people I know. When he gets something in his head, it's nearly impossible to change his mind. It can be a good characteristic. It's what gives him his drive. He spent years working double shifts at Jimmy's Auto and then going home to develop the 8-Bit app for the Syndicate. He did it all without complaint and with such discretion that I never guessed the truth. If he could find Rook with sheer determination, I have no doubt he would do it. But that's not how the world works; believing someone is guilty doesn't necessarily mean it's true.

"I'll talk to him," I say.

Roy crosses his arms and leans against the desk beside Glitch. "You've been talking to him. Do you really think talking to him again will make a difference?" he asks.

"Yes...no...I don't know," I say, raking my hands through my hair. I wish we could rewind to a few months ago when I was back at the apartment with Grams and Ariel. To a time when I was ignorant about Miles's involvement with the Syndicate, I hadn't met Ash, I could trust my best friend, and I had a job that I loved. To a time when I hated elites and Enforcers with every fiber of my being. To when things were simple.

But I did meet Ash. I joined the Enforcers. I found out there are good people on both sides that have the same desires, goals, and basic needs. That complicates things. Ash humanized the elites for me. He showed me that while the Council and our system are broken, they aren't beyond repair.

If I was given a chance to go back to before Miles was arrested, I'm not so sure I would take it.

Everything would be the same, but I would still be in the dark. Miles would still be working for the Syndicate behind my back. My neighborhood would still be suffering. Ash and the Enforcers would still be my enemy. The cycle started by Byron Axton and perpetuated by both sides would continue.

Ignorance may give you the illusion of peace, but a cage is a cage even when you can't see the bars.

An earsplitting siren accompanied by a white strobe light illuminates the building. Glitch curses and turns back to her computer. The monitors change to a security feed of the gravel road leading to the farmhouse. Armored trucks are roaring up the path. They aren't like the Pods the Enforcers use in the city, but I'd recognize those white uniforms anywhere.

"I have to find Grams and Ariel," I say, already sprinting for the door.

"Find them, then meet me at the back exit. I have to take care of the servers," says Glitch. She joins Viper, who is already working on destroying the equipment closest to his desk.

"I'm coming with you," says Roy, catching up to me.

I shove open the door and exit into chaos. Syndicate members are rushing everywhere, trying to find weapons and get organized. It's the middle of the night. Half of them look like they just rolled out of bed. The Enforcers caught us completely unprepared.

How did they even find us?

The Syndicate has used this place for roughly six years without any issues. So, what changed? I run for the farmhouse, my breath coming out in heavy pants. I'm out of shape. I haven't been exercising like I should have been the last few months, and the muscle I put on from my enforcer training is gone.

Almost everyone in the compound sleeps in an old barn converted into a bunkhouse. Grams and Ariel are the exceptions. Miles let them use a bedroom in the farmhouse so Grams would be more comfortable. I decided to have Ariel stay with her at night, so she wasn't sleeping in a room full of strangers.

As the first truck crashes through the gate, I sprint across the open field. The twelve-foot high chain-link fence surrounding the property is topped with barbed wire. It was built to keep people from sneaking up on us, but it wasn't made to withstand the force of a vehicle ramming it at full speed. I wish my mom and Miles had planned for this scenario.

The vehicle skids to a stop and enforcers pile out. They start shooting. Roy grabs my arm and yanks me behind a parked car. I hit the ground with enough force to expel the air from my lungs. The bullets slam into the side of the car and the windows shatter. I throw my hand up to shield my face from the glass.

We can't stay here.

I stay low, running in a crouch to the back door of the farmhouse. Roy follows closely behind. Inside, Syndicate members are running around, grabbing weapons, and destroying the computers. Despite being caught off guard, everyone seems to have a job. They must have planned for this to some extent, even if it's complete chaos outside. I head for the stairs, but Miles is already on his way down, carrying Ariel. His dirty blond hair, usually tied back in a bun, hangs loosely around his shoulders. He looks like he just woke up. Grams and Don, Miles's dad, are right behind him. Max weaves around their legs until he's standing by my side.

I take Ariel from Miles, cradling her head against my hand. Her body is shaking. She buries her face in my chest, and her small fists grab onto my shirt. Miles grabs the rifle and checks that it's loaded. He hands it to Roy and holds a second weapon.

"Glitch said to meet her at the fence; she has a car ready to go," I say.

"Stay low and follow me," says Miles. "Whatever happens, don't stop." He opens the back door and runs down the stairs, taking out two enforcers to clear the way. I run down the stairs after him, sprinting for the woods.

The yard is a war zone.

There are enforcers everywhere. Bodies from both sides lie in the garden and near the entrance. Luckily, the battle has tied up enough enforcers that not many of them have made it to the back of the house. I hold Ariel tight to my chest and push myself to run faster than ever. I make it to the trees just as bullets slam into the trunks around us, showering me with splinters. I curse and pump my legs harder. I hear yelling behind me and guns going off, but I don't stop. I can't stop.

I have to get Ariel to safety.

Finally, I see the old green minivan we arrived at the farmhouse in. Glitch is sitting behind the wheel with the engine idling. Viper is standing by the open door. He doesn't acknowledge our approach. I watch as he pivots to take out the enforcers with precision before they can get near the van.

Despite Viper's accuracy, the van will be overrun if we don't leave in the next thirty seconds.

I'm almost there when an enforcer barges through the brush to block my path. He aims his weapon at me. I cradle Ariel closer and turn my back on him, clenching my eyes shut. A ferocious growl rips through the clearing. Someone screams. I risk a look behind me. Max has his jaw clamped around the enforcer's wrist. The man is trying to throw him off, but Max holds on. I use the opening to get to the van. I half dive inside, still holding Ariel against my chest. I get in the back seat and set her down. She looks up at me with watery eyes.

"I know this is scary, but I need you to stay on the ground as low as you can. Can you do that for me?" I ask, trying to keep the fear out of my voice. This situation is so screwed up. I'd give anything in the world to transport her away from here. Ariel nods and sits on the floor at my feet, curling into a ball. I lean over her, shielding her with my body. Grams and Miles get in the car just as the back window shatters, sending glass onto my back and hair. Max hops in after them, his muzzle covered in blood. He weaves his way through the seats and jumps up beside me.

Viper throws himself back into the car so that he's practically laying across Miles and Grams' legs. "Go," he barks, firing out the open door. Glitch slams the gas, and the car lurches forward. Viper braces his feet on either side of the door, so he doesn't get tossed out. Glitch floors it, breaking through the fence with a crash. The van shutters, but Glitch straightens us out and keeps going.

Glitch called this the "back exit," but that's generous. Miles cut a few links in the fence surrounding the compound to make it easier to drive the van through and Viper cleared out some of the bushes and logs to create a winding path through the woods. There isn't a road. They also had to leave enough debris to hide the weakened fence from enemies.

Miles created the back exit shortly after we arrived at the farmhouse. After the enforcers attacked Jimmy's Auto, he thought having more than one escape route would be best. I've never been more thankful for my paranoid best friend.

Glitch hits a bump that makes my head collide with the ceiling, and then we're on a paved road. She floors it. Viper sits up and forces the door closed. Ariel is still crouched on the floor. I run my fingers through her hair, gently untangling the knots and trying to soothe her. I pray to anyone that could be listening to help us make it out of this alive. Headlights illuminate the inside of the van and I hear the roar of an engine behind us.

I turn around. There are three cars behind us. An enforcer leans out the window with a gun and I just manage to duck before they start shooting. Viper curses and scrambles into the back seat next to me. He kneels on the seat, keeping his head low. He fires out the rear window. There's a second handgun strapped to his waist, so I grab it from the holster and kneel next to him.

There are only two cars behind us now. Viper must have handled the third already.

He sends a bullet through the driver-side window of the car on the right. It jerks wildly before crashing into a tree. After a couple of shots, I hit one of the front tires on the final car. It crashes into the car on the left. After one last look out the back window to ensure no one is following us, I hand Viper's handgun back to him. He accepts it and gives me a look that could almost be interpreted as approval before climbing into the row of seats in front of us.

"It's okay, baby girl. You can come up now," I say, reaching down to help Ariel into the seat beside me. She's still sniffling, but most of the tears have gone away. I sit her on my lap and hold her close to my chest. This is something no kid should ever have to go through. Miles is sitting on the floor with his back against the driver's seat. He has tears running down his face. Grams sits in front of me, but the front seat is empty.

We're missing people.

"Where are Roy and Don?" I ask.

Glitch slams on the brakes. "What?"

"Roy and Don aren't here," I say.

"Don betrayed us," chokes Miles. "He called in the Enforcers. They got Roy."

"We have to go back," says Glitch. She puts the car in reverse, preparing to turn around, but Viper rests his hand on her shoulder.

"If we go back, they'll arrest us, and we won't be able to rescue Roy. Not to mention, the Syndicate and the 8-Bit app will be finished. This is bigger than one person, Lauren."

Lauren. Is that Glitch's real name? I want to ask but now isn't the time.

This is the most I've heard Viper say since I met him. Glitch doesn't correct him. She swears and pounds her fist into the steering wheel. Viper releases her shoulder and sits back in his seat. Glitch slams the car back into drive and continues down the road. We're in the middle of nowhere. On our way to the farmhouse, we passed through a ghost town. Miles explained that commercial agriculture conglomerates had bought up the farms in the area. We could try to find somewhere to hide, but I have no idea what we'll do for food or clean water.

Miles finds a water bottle and uses his jacket to clean Max's face. As soon as he's clean, Max shoves his way between the seats and hops up next to me. He nudges Ariel's leg and whines, curling up beside her. He was waiting for someone to clean him up before he could check on Ariel. He's a good dog. I scratch behind his ears, his eyes slowly closing. He rests his head on his front paws and flicks his tail.

"Where are we going?" I ask.

Glitch glances in the rearview mirror, exchanging a knowing glance with Viper. "Home."

Chapter 3

Ash

I cross my arms and glare at the staff member trying to hand me a tray piled with hors d'oeuvres. There's a small army of enforcers watching our exchange. Liam is standing next to me, but he doesn't interject. He's just as annoyed with this situation as I am. This is the first time he has been in the Axton mansion kitchen. It's not a room guests visit. Byron installed commercial appliances and hired enough cooks and wait staff to host banquets for hundreds of people.

They don't need our help to serve a small dinner party.

We're here because Jace wants us to be. It's as simple as that.

When I don't move to take the tray, the poor waiter's face turns the same shade as the shrimp he's trying to hand me. He gives me a pleading look that almost makes me feel bad for him. The other staff members are doing their best to pretend we don't exist. It's not like it was our idea to serve dinner to the Council members seated in the dining room. That was all Jace.

My stepbrother is acting like my sentence was some great act of charity on his part. Anyone with eyes can see that "indentured servitude to the Council" translates to being Jace's punching bag.

I may not be well-loved by the Council, but they respect me enough not to use me as a serving bot. If Jace wanted to be altruistic, he could admit to murdering Byron. There's no way he's ever fessing up to that. Instead, I get to bow to his every whim like the show pony I've become, biding my time until Elle can get us out of here.

Right now, I wonder if execution would have been the easier way out.

Besides, it wasn't Jace's mercy that led to my new gig. Elle and the other enforcers forced his hand by publicly pleading for my life. Jace only relented because he was worried about losing the support of his army. I thought that moment would lead to something more, like a coup or a public revolt. At this point, I'd even accept an email complaint to the Council.

Nothing has changed.

Jace is still in charge and I'm stuck in a cell.

The waiter sighs and offers Liam the same tray. Liam mimics my stance, crossing his arms. He rolls his eyes, but the action is almost lost behind his long hair. I've never seen his hair longer than a buzz cut. After a few months imprisoned in the Academy holding cells, he looks more like the frontman for a rock band than the head of Enforcer operations. The last few months have aged him. We're both worn out from lack of food, sunlight, and proper hygiene. They let us shower before coming here tonight because Jace has an image to maintain.

"Take the tray." One of the guards steps up behind the waiter and glares at us. He taps his wristband threateningly. I resist the urge to flinch. A tracking bracelet clamped on my right ankle broadcasts my location to every bot in the area. It also has the added benefit of being a personal tasing device.

Thank you, Byron, for developing that one.

"No," I grind out.

The guard taps his wristband. Liam goes down, his body convulsing. My lips part in shock. I didn't expect the enforcer to go after my friend. I've been harassing the guards for weeks.

It sucks to get zapped, but if I don't do something to rebel in some small way, I will lose my mind. I'll take the pain any day to maintain my sanity, but I won't make that choice for Liam. I'm the reason he's in this mess to begin with. I won't make this more challenging for him than it already is.

I take the tray from the servant.

"Good boy," says the guard. Liam is still shaking on the floor and the guard isn't doing anything to stop it.

"Turn it off, I did what you asked," I snarl. The guard waits a few more seconds before slowly tapping on his wristband. Liam heaves a sigh of relief at our feet. I glance down at him. His chest is heaving, but when his eyes meet mine he gives me a weak smile.

"You good?" I ask.

"Never better." Liam attempts a dry chuckle, but it turns into a coughing fit.

The guard grabs my arm. "Time to go."

I glare at him, memorizing his face. He has ice blue eyes and short blond hair. The name tag on his uniform says "Hawkins." I'll pay him a visit the second I get this tracking bracelet removed. I let Hawkins lead me toward the dining room door.

"Try anything and I'll take it out on your friend," he says. I nod because I don't trust myself to open my mouth. I shake off his hold when we get to the door leading into the dining room. I take a deep breath. If I do this, I'll do it with my head held high and a cocky smile. I won't be dragged into that room by a guard. I push open the door.

The dining room of the Axton mansion is as extravagant as the rest of the house. It sports four chandeliers, a colossal mahogany table adorned with enough candles to heat a jacuzzi, and mirrors lining every wall. The mirrors make the room appear larger than it is, replicating the gold chandeliers until it looks like you're staring down an endless hallway.

I take in my reflection. My black hair, once shorter on the sides than on the top, has started to grow out. I look like the guy who wears a bathrobe and boxers to the corner store to pick up a six-pack. I've lost weight over the last three months. Not a ton, but enough that I've dropped a pant size and my cheekbones are more prominent. There are dark circles under my eyes. I look like trash.

The room falls quiet as some Council members try to hide their shock at my appearance, while others cover their mouths in disgust. I throw my shoulders back and walk into the room with my best I-don't-care swagger. Jace is seated at the head of the table like the powermonger he is. I wonder if anyone on the Council believes anything he says. I heard he attended Byron's funeral and even shed a few tears. He's an authentic actor and a phony human being. Jace leans back in his chair and gives me a sardonic smile, clearly enjoying my misery.

Carl Bronxton, my father's business partner at Axton AI, sits beside Jace. He's staring at the empty plate in front of him, appearing uncomfortable. Carl and I have never been close. What little relationship we had was destroyed when I publicly rejected his daughter, Penny, by proposing to Elle. It was a fake proposal, but he doesn't know that. All he saw was the snub to his reputation. Still, I can't help but feel some respect for the man at his refusal to kick me when I'm down. That means something.

My eyes land on Elle. My best friend is sitting at the other end of the table, directly across from Jace. She's wearing an enforcer dress uniform instead of her everyday formal attire. Elle doesn't flaunt her position in the Enforcers. She usually wears a dress or a pantsuit for important occasions. She told me it makes it easier for the people who report to her to approach her. She doesn't like the distance decorum creates between her and her subordinates. Tonight is different. Tonight, she's making a statement that she belongs at this table and will put anyone who says differently in their place.

Wearing the uniform to my trial was the exception to her rule, but I'm beginning to think that was the start of a new norm.

I'm proud of her.

Elle has spent years catering to the Council's every whim. She has sacrificed everything to get where she is. The Enforcers and the Council respect her. Elle would be a strong candidate if the director succession wasn't hereditary. She knows how to navigate politics and bureaucracy to get things done without offending anyone. If anyone can stand up to Jace and succeed, it's her.

We haven't had many opportunities to speak in the last three months. Elle arranged a discreet burial for Robbie O'Reilly behind Jace's back. I know she started the chant that convinced Jace to stay my execution and opt for serving the Council instead. There's a reason Liam is in prison with me and Elle walks free - Jace needs her because Elle is the golden girl of the elites. You can't eliminate her and expect the Council and the Enforcers to fall in line. Jace's black heart may pump the lifeblood of governmental power, but Elle is a blade poised to sever the artery. His rebellion won't last without her. I wish she would do more to wield that power.

Since the trial, Elle has been keeping her head down. She has always believed that the Council and Axton AI can create a better, safer world. She believed in Byron's vision. I can't say I blame her. It's an attractive reality that, if carried out correctly, could have been everything it promised. However, with Jace heading that dream, it will not come to fruition. I can see her slowly coming to that realization. Wearing her uniform is the first step. She's never liked Jace, but now that he's attached himself like a leech to the office she has always respected, she's being forced into a confrontation she never wanted.

It sucks. I know, I've been there.

I went through the same existential crisis when I let Wren and Miles escape. I thought the Syndicate was our enemy. They are, to an extent, but we've been so focused on the obvious villain that we failed to see the one we created in-house. I may not be in touch with the world from the prison at the Academy, but the guards talk. The servants in the kitchens talk. Jace is waging a personal war against the grunts. He's executing Council members and broadcasting it - Council members who are respected and have stood at Byron's side for years.

You can only stab the beast so many times before it decides to fight back.

I wonder when the Council will reach its tipping point.

"Anyone want shrimp?" I ask, still standing at the end of the table. A few people clear their throats. No one will make eye contact with me. I shrug and turn around to head back into the kitchen. I did what Jace wanted. Now, I can get out of here and hide in my Academy cell until we have an escape plan.

"Don wants one," says Jace, stopping me. I freeze. I didn't notice Don sitting at the table. I didn't even know he was back in the city. When I was arrested, Elle told me not to trust Don. She didn't know he had already left the city with Wren and Miles.

I thought Elle was wrong. I assumed Don had changed his mind about working with Jace. That he realized his family is more important than maintaining ties to the director seat and decided to escape with them. My stomach churns.

If he's here, his allegiance was always with the Council.

I'm not sure what that means for Wren and Miles. I just hope they're alright. I grind my teeth and plaster a fake smile before turning around. Sure enough, Don O'Reilly is sitting on Jace's other side, across the table from Bronxton. He tenses up, his eyes coming to mine in the mirror. Now that I know he's related to Miles and Robbie, it's easy to see the resemblance. He has the same, sandy blond hair and blue eyes as his sons. There's a hardness in his expression I haven't seen before. After my mom died, Don was like a father to me. He served in Byron's household as a butler, but his role was more important than that. He made me feel like I belonged in a world that would rather I didn't exist at all.

I have to remind myself that they're holding Liam in the other room.

His well-being depends on my ability to behave when all I want to do is drag Don to the Academy interrogation rooms to ask him about Wren and Ariel. I take a few calculated steps toward Don and lower the tray for him to reach. He picks up a shrimp and tosses it onto his plate, but I don't walk away. I just keep staring at him as if that will clarify the situation. I thought Don had changed his mind about working with the Council, but his seat next to Jace makes it hard to continue lying to myself.

Over the last three months, I've managed to piece together how Jace came to power, like the pages of a book scattered across a room slowly being reassembled into a story. Byron decided to divide the director's responsibilities into two separate roles - head of Axton AI and leader of the Council. He wanted me to lead the Council and Jace to take ownership of Axton AI. Of course, he told Jace about his plans long before he told me. Jace was pissed, so he decided to force Byron's hand.

Enter Don.

The man who hates that his son is part of the Syndicate leadership.

The man who was a Council loyalist before he was a parent.

The man who only cares about himself.

I can't believe I didn't see him for what he was when I was younger. I was starstruck by his friendly smile and the scraps of affection he threw my way. I wonder if any of it was real or if he was just digging for his meal ticket to a better life. Sometimes I wonder if he is truly loyal to the Council or if he just wants the lifestyle they can give him.

I have so many questions I need him to answer, but I have to be alone when I do it. Jace enjoys keeping me in the dark. It's safer for him and it protects me, to an extent. The moment he thinks I have the upper hand Elle won't be able to placate him anymore. He'll have my head and Liam's. Don takes a second shrimp from the platter and sets it on his plate giving me a look that can only be interpreted as a dismissal.

Jace leans back and crosses his hands behind his head. "Don is our guest of honor tonight. Do you want to know why?"

"No," I deadpan. Jace frowns. He drops his hands to the table and leans forward.

"Don led us to the Syndicate headquarters. They were hiding out at some farm in the countryside. We wiped out the whole operation, including your girl. What was her name?" Jace pretends to think about it for a moment while the pounding in my temple intensifies.

"Wren," Don answers automatically. He pauses, moving the shrimp around his plate with his fork.

Who eats shrimp with a fork?

He doesn't look sympathetic or sorry for his actions. There isn't any emotion there at all. It was like he finished making a mundane, everyday decision like which brand of toilet paper to buy or what to eat for lunch.

I haul Don out of his seat and slam his back into the mirror before I'm conscious of my actions. The glass cracks behind him. Some of the shards fall to the ground. I pry a piece off the wall, barely noticing when it cuts my hand and hold it to Don's throat. His pupils dilate with fear.

Finally.

I was beginning to think Jace had replaced the man with a robot. I guess Don does have feelings, but only when they pertain to his well-being. I press the blade down until a line of red appears across his jugular.

"What happened to Wren and Ariel?" I growl. "Is Jace telling the truth?" I let up the glass shard just enough to allow him to speak without cutting him deeper. Don's eyes are wild.

"I...I don't know."

"What do you mean you don't know?"

"There were guns and trucks everywhere. They didn't get Miles."

"I didn't ask about Miles," I say.

I increase the pressure on the glass.

"No one cares about Wren. She's not in charge of anything," Don stammers.

Wrong answer.

I like to think I'm a level-headed person. I handle pressure well. I'm good in a fight and I rarely lose my cool.

Right now, that's not the case.

I'm about to murder someone in the Axton family dining room.

A strong hand wraps around my bicep. I turn to swipe at the person. I'm mid-swing when I realize it's Elle. She redirects my arm before I can make contact and slams a fist into my stomach, driving the air from my lungs.

Damn, she can pack a punch.

Elle kicks the glass shard away before slamming my chest against the wall. I manage to turn my head at the last second, so I don't crush my nose. She draws my hands behind my back, and I feel handcuffs snap into place. I try to push back, ready to continue my conversation with Don. She slams me into the wall a second time.

"Stop fighting me," Elle hisses, "I'm trying to save your life." She grabs my arm and hauls me towards the kitchen.

"I'm taking him back to the Academy," says Elle, raising her voice. Don is still standing by the wall rubbing his throat amidst a full-blown panic attack. Jace is drinking from his glass with a Cheshire grin on his face. The other Council members are watching with wide eyes, their food left forgotten on their plates. I doubt any of them have seen someone get punched in real life. They're sheltered, and it shows. No wonder they haven't stood up to Jace. Elle shoves open the door to the kitchen. Liam and the guard are sitting at a table in the corner. There are a few servants preparing food.

"Go get the transport. I'll bring Ash out in a minute," orders Elle. Liam's guard jumps to his feet and rushes to obey her order.

"Do I need to shock the prisoner? What did he do?" asks Hawkins. Elle glares at him, and he winces when he realizes his mistake.

You don't ask questions after being given a direct order from a superior.

Elle usually doesn't mind, but she's not in a joking mood right now. Liam studies my rumbled appearance and gives me a look that says we'll talk about this later. They disappear through the back door.

"Everyone else, get out," Elle addresses the remaining servants. Pans clatter as the servants hastily obey her orders. She turns to face me with an expression that tells me I messed up. "Do you have a death wish?" she demands.

"He said Wren is dead-"

"Yeah, Jace says a lot of things. That doesn't mean any of it's true," Elle seethes. "I know there was a raid on a Syndicate compound outside the city that was called in by Don. People were killed on both sides. We took some prisoners. But," Elle holds up her hand to stop my outburst, "a lot of people escaped too. We know for a fact they didn't capture Miles. That means there's a good chance Wren made it out too." I hear what she's saying. Don confirmed as much himself. I know Jace was trying to get a rise out of me, and it worked, but that doesn't mean I'll be able to breathe easily until I know Wren and Ariel are safe.

"Can you find out?" I ask. Elle presses her lips together and sighs.

"I'll do my best. In the meantime, I need you to stay calm. I'm still working to find a way to bust you out, but you have to stay alive until I can do that. Stop making my job so damn difficult."

"Then work faster," I say.

She growls, stabbing her finger in the center of my chest. "I'm doing more than you realize, but I'm being smart about it. I'm not going around starting fights in the middle of Council dinners or calling out the director on a live broadcast. Most elites don't agree with Jace's leadership style, but if their other option is the director's unhinged stepson, they will be harder to convince."

"So, I'm supposed to sit tight in prison and wait for them to come to their senses?" I ask.

"You're supposed to set an example for them. They don't need unhinged. They need a leader. Someone who takes all the insults Jace throws at him in stride and continues to do better. You need to be that person for them, Ash. Don't give them a reason to question you. Did you see that idiotic grin Jace had when we were leaving? He put you in Don's path on purpose. He wanted you to start a fight. He wanted to show the Council that you can't be trusted, making it easy for them to side against Jace. He played you. I'm not asking you to be okay with rotting in a cell. I'm telling you there's a time and a place for everything, and tonight isn't it."

Well...damn. When she puts it like that, it makes a lot of sense.

"I'm sorry for being a jerk," I say.

Her wristband lights up with a notification. "The Pod is waiting for us." She takes her place beside me and grabs my arm. I don't fight her this time, because I know she's looking out for me. Elle stops beside the back door. "There are reporters outside. Are you ready to do this?"

I figured as much. Whenever Jace allows me outside the Academy, I'm swarmed by reporters who are friendly to the Council. I can only imagine the image they're creating for me to the rest of the nation. I nod, and Elle opens the door. The sun set hours ago, but the lights on the camera equipment are bright enough to emulate daylight. I know the drill. No matter what, keep walking. Do not engage. It's better if you don't listen to the questions at all. There are the usual culprits regarding my relationship with Elle or asking why I killed the director.

I focus on the prisoner transport instead. It's parked on the circle drive in front of the Axton mansion. My childhood home makes a statement. It looks more like a castle that belongs in a storybook than in a wealthy neighborhood. There are tall towers on each side of the stone building. The front entryway is arched and framed by a pair of seven-foot-tall dragon statues. It's ridiculous for the CEO of a technology company to live here, but I guess it does its job.

The Axton mansion has become iconic. It's a symbol of the Council's power.

Love it or hate it, it's impossible to ignore.

Elle and I force our way through the reporters, maintaining a brisk pace until we reach the prisoner transport. It's a black Pod with blacked-out windows. When we step inside, the doors slide closed behind us, muffling the sound from outside. The back half of the vehicle is fenced off with floor-to-ceiling bars to create a makeshift holding cell. Liam is already inside, sitting on the floor against the wall. There are more comfortable seats for the guards taking up the rest of the vehicle. There are no seats behind the bars.

Elle guides me to the cell, and I step inside. She locks the door behind me before joining the other guards. I feel the Pod pull away from the Axton mansion. I squat and do my best to sit without falling, because my hands are secured behind my back. I'm sorry to say it's a skill I've developed over the last three months. I prop myself up against the wall opposite Liam. He studies me quietly, glancing at the guards to see if we can get away with talking. They're caught up in a conversation with Elle. She's practically a celebrity among the elites. They're all vying for attention which means their focus is off us for a few minutes.

"Are you going to tell me what happened in there?" Liam asks.

"Don's home," I say.

Liam leans his head back against the wall and closes his eyes. "Did you kill him?" he asks, making the same connection I did.

"Almost. Elle stopped me."

"Did he say anything about Wren?" Liam asks warily.

"He confirmed Miles escaped, but he didn't know what happened to her. She wasn't the target," I grumble.

"I'm sorry," says Liam. He knows how much Wren means to me. We've had a lot of time to talk over the last three months. That tends to happen when you're locked in a cell with someone all day with little entertainment.

"She escaped. I know she did," I say, because there isn't another option in my mind. I feel worthless sitting here when I should be looking for her. It's hard to accept that sometimes taking no action is an action. As soon as Elle can bust us out, I will find her.

I just hope I can stay alive and sane until then.

Chapter 4

Wren

When Glitch said she was taking us home, I assumed that meant returning to the city. We've been driving for about three hours, and I haven't recognized any landmarks. Then again, it's not like I had a great view during my trip to the Syndicate compound.

I spent most of it stowed away in a shipping container.

We could be retracing our steps, but I doubt it. The drive to the compound was smooth. There weren't any potholes, and there were only a few turns. When Viper picked us up, we were under a highway overpass. These roads are rural and covered in debris. My body would remember going down a road like this. When we hit a mini crater, I grab the bar by my head and say a silent prayer that we don't blow out a tire.

Miles is sitting in the row of seats in front of me. He has his head leaned against the window, his warm breath creating a fog ring on the glass in his sleep. His head bounces against the window with every bump we hit. I have no idea how he's sleeping through that.

Grams is asleep in the seat beside me. She moved back a row after we got away from the compound. Ariel is sprawled out between us with her legs on Grams's lap and her head on my thigh. Her arms are draped around Max, snuggling into him like a giant stuffed animal. I brush her brown curls away from her face. She shifts in her sleep before her breath evens out. She's been through a lot today and is clearly exhausted. We all are. Even so, I can't sleep. I don't usually get car sick, but my stomach is roiling.

"Where are we going?" I ask Glitch, hoping for a distraction that will keep me from tossing my cookies in the backseat.

"Home," repeats Glitch, her eyes coming to mine in the rearview mirror.

"I know. You said that before. Where are we going once we get back to the city? We have to go somewhere where Jace won't be able to find us."

"I didn't say we were going to your home. We're going to mine," says Glitch. "There are organized communities outside of the cities. Viper and I grew up in one of them. Our people are good about taking in strays. They'll give us a place to lay low to figure out our next move."

Before traveling to the Syndicate compound, I didn't think anyone lived outside the cities. Grams grew up in the country but moved when Axton AI started eliminating the jobs. It wasn't just her. Everyone flocked to the cities looking for work, and rural living became a thing of the past. I didn't know anyone had stayed behind.

I always assumed Glitch grew up in a grunt neighborhood like Miles and I did.

It was easy for us to bond over the excessiveness of the elite lifestyle and our experiences with the Enforcers. I thought it was because we came from the same place.

I guess I have a lot to learn.

Glitch glances over her shoulder at Viper. He's sitting beside Miles in the middle aisle. He hasn't said anything since we ditched the Enforcers, but that doesn't mean he has slept or let his guard down. I don't miss the gun laying across his lap or how he constantly scans our surroundings for threats. Luckily, there haven't been any. I remember the way he took out the Enforcers storming the van.

He was like a machine...a one-person army.

I've seen Ash and some of the senior enforcers at work, but this was different. I wonder what Viper does for the Syndicate. I know he helps Glitch on the technology side, but he didn't hone that skill set by sitting behind a computer. I'll never ask him and I know he won't offer that information freely.

Glitch has stuck to the back roads, avoiding highways that cater to autonomous trucks that are heavy with surveillance. So far, we haven't seen another car or person.

"I didn't realize so many people lived outside of the cities," I say, summarizing my thoughts. "How do they survive?"

"Most of the people in the communities come from the cities. Some of them are ex-Syndicate members looking for a new start. Others refuse to take sides and opt for a third choice outside the Syndicate and the Council. The point is that they attract people from all walks of life with unique expertise. They move between abandoned towns and temporary settlements in the country to make it harder to find them. The communities get most of their supplies by looting shipments. The trucks that run the routes between cities are autonomous. We can hack in to determine which trucks to target and redirect them. It's a similar process to how we escaped the city before."

I think back to the autonomous truck Miles stashed us in. The Syndicate hijacked it, so it drove off the highway and under an overpass, where it stopped to let us off discreetly. The move was so practiced, I knew they had done it before. It makes sense they would use the same process to transport cargo.

"The best way to avoid detection is to understand the technology the Syndicate or the Council would use to find us. The communities are known for having some of the best hackers in the country. Most of us aren't loyal to any one party," says Glitch.

"Then how did you and Viper end up working for the Syndicate?" I ask.

Glitch shrugs. "When we were kids, our community was attacked by the Enforcers. Our parents and a lot of people we cared about were killed. I'm not saying the Syndicate is better than the Council. I don't agree with everything the Syndicate stands for, but they're the lesser of two evils."

I stare at the back of the driver's seat. There's so much I don't know about Glitch. We were friends at the Academy. Given how she acted around the other elites, I assumed we had a similar history. That we both grew up in the grunt neighborhoods and bonded over our mutual distaste for the elitist lifestyle. The more I learn about Glitch, the more I realize I never knew her. It's easy for me to understand why Roy was so upset with her. I'm angry too.

Angry at Glitch. Angry at Miles. Angry at Grams.

Roy understood that anger because he shared it. He was a friend to me when I had no one else. We have to get him back, I owe him that much.

Glitch curses. "We're almost out of gas."

Viper stiffens, instantly on high alert. He climbs over the center console and takes the passenger seat beside Glitch. Opening the dash, he pulls out a crinkled paper map. There are so many pen marks on it I'm surprised it's even usable.

"We're close to Jericho. If we're lucky, we'll run into a community. We can trade for supplies," says Viper.

"What's Jericho?" I ask.

"It's an abandoned town," explains Glitch. "Most of them aren't worth visiting, but there are a few that the communities pass through more often than others. Jericho has a fire station the communities keep stocked for travelers."

The more Glitch talks about the communities, the more I realize they have their own system. I suppose they're not unlike the Council or the Syndicate in that way. I wonder if they're organized or if it's more of individual groups traveling the countryside like nomads? I have so many questions, but Viper starts giving Glitch directions. I don't want to distract them when we're running out of gas, and a detour could leave us stranded beside the road. Glitch drives for another mile before taking a right onto a minor road. We drive another few miles before the town comes into view, just as the sun rises.

There's not much here.

I see a gas station missing the advertising strip above the pumps, long gone to some windstorm. Electric vehicle charging stations are set off to the side, but they look dead. There's a bar on the corner and some squat brick buildings that were probably businesses at one point. At the end of the block, I see a church with peeling white paint and broken stained glass windows.

Behind the main street, I can make out modest homes that have fallen into disrepair. The lawns have returned to nature supporting wildflowers and grass as tall as the first-story windows. On the main street, there's an abandoned truck that's more rust than metal parked in front of what used to be a pharmacy. The front door is hanging off its hinges and the shelves are empty, their contents were stolen long ago. This entire town is a window into a life that doesn't exist anymore.

It's eerily quiet, like a nuke town before a bomb goes off or the last remaining human stronghold before a zombie army overruns it.

"I'm not optimistic that the gas station has gas or electricity," I say. I think this van is an older hybrid model that can run on either. We still need to find fuel. It won't run on hopes and curse words.

"Worst-case scenario, we have enough gas to get to the closest Axton charging station. Best case scenario, there's a community in town we can stay with or trade with. If we go to the charging station, the Enforcers will know where we are.

We'll have to be prepared to run, so we need to decide where we're running to," says Glitch.

She parks in front of a brick building at the end of the street. It has two massive garage doors with "Jericho Community Fire Station" spelled above them. At least, that's what I think it says. It's missing most of the letters, including the majority of the town name.

Viper gets out first, his weapon at the ready. He jogs to the door and presses his back against the brick wall so he can look through the window. Seemingly satisfied that there isn't an immediate threat, he disappears inside. A few minutes later, the garage door opens. Glitch drives into the building and kills the engine.

"Where are we?" Miles yawns and stretches...or what passes for a stretch in the confined space. His blond hair is mussed up on one side, and he has a red circle on his cheek from where it was resting against the window.

"Jericho," says Glitch.

Miles sits up, instantly more alert.

"Why? We should circle back to the compound to regroup with our people," says Miles.

"What people?" Glitch scoffs. She gets out of the car before Miles can say anything else, slamming the door harder than necessary.

"What's her problem?" Miles asks.

"I think she blames you for Roy being taken," I say. Miles turns around to look at me over the back of his seat.

"How is that my fault? If I had known the Enforcers were coming, we would have evacuated or been more prepared to fight them off. They caught us totally off guard."

"Yeah, because Don decided to betray us," I say, crossing my arms. "You should have seen that coming."

Miles snorts. "Right, just like you knew I was involved with the Syndicate while working together at Jimmy's Auto."

I glare at him. Grams clears her throat. Our argument must have woken her up. Her hair is rumpled from sleep, but she's sitting on the edge of her chair like she'd rather be anywhere but in the middle of our argument. Ariel is still asleep on my lap. I gently pick her up and make my way into the next row of seats. Max whines before hopping down to follow us outside.

"We'll talk about this later," I say. I get out of the van and stop to stare.

There's an old-school fire engine in the other garage bay. I recognize it from old movies, but the new Axton fire engines look nothing like this. Where this truck is red, the Axton AI emergency vehicles favor sleek black and white designs similar to the Pods. They don't have the emergency lights on the top. Most vehicles downtown are autonomous, so they simply move out of the way when they detect an Enforcer Pod or fire services nearby. They don't have to announce their presence.

We prefer that they don't because it tends to cause panic.

The red paint on this engine has faded to more pink, but it's still a stark reminder of a different time. There are bunks against the back wall and what looks like a kitchen through a side door. Viper set up some kind of flood light that must run off batteries. It's completely silent but produces a surprising amount of light. It's a box contraption sitting beside the van with an illuminated dome.

The garage door squeals behind me, the sound of rollers moving down a track in need of grease. In the corner, I see Viper lowering it by hand using some kind of crank. Someone made the door functional with or without electricity.

Ariel stirs in my arms. Her eyes bat open, and she looks up at me with her brilliant green eyes. She presses against my chest to get down. Her eyes widen when she sees the fire truck. I set her on the ground, and she makes a beeline for it at a breakneck, unsteady sprint toddlers have mastered. Max takes off after her, and I follow. Ariel stares up at the machine in awe. She tries to climb onto the first step leading up to the cab but can't quite get it.

Max jumps up onto the first step and launches himself onto the seat. His tongue flops out of the side of his mouth, and he cocks his head to the side as if to ask, "Are you coming, or what?"

"It's safe." I jump when I realize Viper is standing right behind me. He steps up onto the fire engine and opens the door. "The battery is disconnected. The community kids like to play in there."

"Up!" Ariel says, jumping up and down and holding her arms above her head. Viper raises one eyebrow.

"Sorry," I say, stepping forward. Then, Viper smiles. I'm surprised it doesn't break his face. The man is so damn stoic he makes Byron Axton look like a study in emotion. He picks Ariel up and sets her on the seat inside the fire engine while my jaw is still on the floor. Ariel immediately stands on the seat and tries to turn the wheel. Viper remains on the step, blocking the doorway, to ensure she doesn't fall out.

I have no idea what to make of the whole interaction.

"He's a marshmallow, he just doesn't let many people see it," Glitch says quietly, standing beside me. Viper flips her off behind his back, but Glitch just laughs. I vaguely wonder what they are to each other. Glitch mentioned they grew up together. I don't miss how Viper watches Glitch when she's not looking, but I always thought Glitch had a thing for Roy. Maybe he's just protective of someone he considers family.

Grams makes her way over to me. She's still wearing her pajamas but now has a coat slung over her shoulders. It's much too large for her, hanging down to her knees. She pulls the two sides together and crosses her arms to cinch it in to trap her body heat. We're going to have to find her some real clothes soon.

"Where did you get the coat?" I ask.

"Miles gave it to me. He said there are people who stock this place for travelers."

"We need to decide what we're doing next," I say, stating the obvious.

"We rescue Ash and Roy," says Glitch. Her face twists when she says Roy's name. Viper could barely stop her from turning around when the compound was being raided. I'm surprised she's keeping it together as well as she is. Glitch eyes each group member as if daring them to have a different opinion.

"No," says Miles, approaching our group. "We find gas. We start looking for the other Syndicate members. Then, we go after Rook and the surge crew."

Viper snorts. Miles glares at him. "You got something to say?"

"I doubt you have many loyal followers after the raid," says Viper. Miles's fists clench, but Glitch intervenes before it can escalate.

"Viper is right. We lost people to Rook and the surge crew before the farmhouse was compromised. It's not going to sit well with your people that the Enforcers raided the Syndicate headquarters. People have lost faith that you can keep them safe. Which makes sense, considering you let them take Roy," says Glitch.

"I didn't let them do anything," snaps Miles.

"You should have been more concerned about guarding our headquarters than searching for Rook," yells Glitch.

"You should have done a better job setting up a monitoring system for the road into our compound to give us more time to prepare for an intruder," screams Miles.

Viper hops down from the fire engine, putting himself between Glitch and Miles. I take his place to make sure Ariel is supervised. She's still messing with buttons in the cab, unaware of the grown-ups arguing outside.

"You need to back up," growls Viper, staring down Miles. Glitch grabs Viper's arm and says something to him. Her voice is too quiet for me to make out, but it seems to calm him down. Viper backs up but doesn't take his eyes off Miles and stands at Glitch's side, ready to intervene.

"We should take a vote," says Glitch.

"This isn't a democracy," says Miles.

"It isn't a dictatorship either. I respected you as a leader and refused to rescue Ash without your consent, but the game has changed. Don betrayed us. Roy is gone. Our headquarters is compromised, and you don't have an army backing you. We need to go on the offensive. What do you think?" Glitch asks. It takes me a moment to realize she's asking me.

"I want to rescue Ash and Roy, but my priority is keeping Ariel and Grams safe. If that means finding a community that can take us in, then that's what I want to do," I say.

Glitch nods once. "Grams?"

"I'm with Wren and Ariel. Wherever they go, I go," Grams says.

"We already know Miles wants to regroup with the Syndicate to go after Rook. I want to rescue Ash and Roy. What about you?" Glitch looks at Viper.

Viper thinks about it for a moment before responding. "I propose a third option. We find somewhere safe for Wren's family. Then, we break into the city and contact the surge crew. They can help us bust Ash and Roy out of the Academy."

"No!" Miles throws up his hands. "We're not working with the surge crew. Rook killed Robbie. They're murderers. Why would they want to help us rescue an ex-enforcer and the director's successor anyways?"

"Rook didn't kill Robbie," I practically whisper, but they still hear me. Miles looks like he's about to explode, so I hold up my hands. "Hear me out. Rook froze the bots for a few seconds, but something overrode her. The bots went after her people too. Why would she do that?"

"Commander Harper took control," says Glitch. She keeps her tone gentle. I can tell this isn't the first time she has tried to broach the subject with Miles. "Elle confirmed it."

Miles scoffs. "That's a lie. Rook killed Robbie. End of discussion."

"The question of Rook's guilt aside," Viper intervenes, "she might be willing to help us to get back at Jace. We know Jace and Rook had some sort of agreement. So far as we can tell, Jace didn't deliver. Rook still has the same territory and power as she always did."

"What if she says no?" Glitch asks, ignoring Miles's murderous expression.

"Then we sweeten the deal. Miles officially agrees to join the surge crew, and we turn over management of the 8-Bit app to Rook's people. In exchange, Rook helps us bust Ash and Roy out of the Academy," says Viper.

"Rook could still be working with Jace," I say.

"We know she isn't," says Glitch. "Rook sent us a message a few weeks ago. She claimed that your mom hired an assassin to kill her." Glitch gives me an apologetic look. "She said other crew leaders were targeted over the years. Some were successfully eliminated. Others got better at hiding and lived to tell their stories. According to Rook, when crew leaders gained too many followers, your mom tried to take out the competition."

I want to tell Glitch she's wrong, but I can't. The woman I knew wouldn't have allowed her daughter to believe she was dead. She wouldn't have left her family to run the Syndicate without a goodbye. The more I learn about Marcia, the more I realize I never knew her. So hiring a gun to take out the competition? Sounds reasonable to me.

"She's lying," says Miles.

"Do you know that for sure?" I ask. Miles meets my eyes, but his gaze drops to the floor. Despite our differences, he's still easy to read. I bet he doesn't know about half the stuff my mom did before he took full ownership of the Syndicate. Miles is a geek at heart. He spent most of his time on the 8-Bit app. I doubt he was involved much in the day-to-day operations of a criminal organization.

"So my mom ordered a hit on Rook, then Rook decided to help Jace to keep herself safe?" I ask.

"Pretty much," says Glitch. "She also apologized for Robbie's death and claimed that the remote she had for deactivating the bots stopped working. Someone changed the bot configuration and locked her out. She lost her right-hand man in the attack on the warehouse. She thinks Jace is responsible."

"You should have told me," I say. Glitch has the decency to look guilty, but I know it wasn't her call. She has made it clear that up until recently, she was following Miles' orders.

"Why?" Miles scoffs. "She's lying to cover her tracks. She knew we were close to finding her. She's just saying that to save herself."

"We weren't even remotely close to finding her," says Viper. "She sent that message because she came to the same conclusion I did - we can help each other."

"You're asking me to turn over the 8-Bit app in exchange for what? Releasing a couple of enforcers? No offense," says Miles, glancing at Glitch. She scowls.

"One of those Enforcers is the legal director," I say. "Ash isn't like Jace. If he became the director, I think he'd be willing to hear us out. It would be the first time grunts and the Syndicate have a seat at the table."

"Let's take a vote," says Glitch, cutting off Miles's rebuttal. All those in favor of Viper's plan, raise your hand."

I raise my hand along with everyone else. Miles is the only person left with his hand down. He curses.

"You're making a mistake," he says, storming off towards the back door. For a half-second, I wonder if I should go after him.

In the past, I would have.

I would have listened to his side of the story. We would have come to a compromise that made us both happy, and we would have moved past it. I wonder if we'll ever have that kind of relationship again.

"He'll get over it," says Glitch, as if reading my mind.

I sigh. "Where can we go where Grams and Ariel will be safe?" I ask, deciding to focus on the plan. "I don't have any relatives they can stay with."

"Hold that thought," says Viper. He tilts his head to the back of the firehouse. I see a blur of movement, but that's all. He readjusts his grip on his gun. "We've got company."

Chapter 5

Ash

I'm bored out of my mind. I guess I should be thankful that I have the opportunity to be, but at this point, I'm almost willing to serve another meal at the Axton mansion if it gets me out of my cell.

Almost.

What? I have standards.

Maybe it's for the best. I'm not sure I can make it through another conversation with Don or Jace without throttling one of them. Elle told me to keep my head down and bide my time. Throat punching the new director is the exact opposite of laying low, but she's not the one locked in the Academy basement with nothing to do.

Our cell is six feet wide and eight feet deep. Trust me. I've had the time to check.

More than once.

The walls are a suffocating beige that makes you question if color ever existed in the world. There is a built-in shelf meant to double as a desk, but Jace had the stool removed before we were brought in. A bunk bed is mounted on the wall with the two platforms so close together that the person on the bottom bunk can't sit up fully without whacking their head on the underside of the upper bunk. The sheets were stripped off and the blankets removed before we got here, compliments of Jace.

Liam is lying on the top bunk with his arm slung over his eyes, but I don't think he's asleep. We've just run out of things to talk about. Across from the bunk beds, there's a tiny sink bolted to the wall next to a toilet.

There's no privacy. No entertainment. No purpose.

I can't remember the last time I took time off. I haven't had a vacation or a personal day since I enlisted with the Enforcers. My weekends were spent training or working extra hours to identify Syndicate targets. There wasn't time for hobbies or relationships. Elle and Liam practically forced their way into my life. I wouldn't have given them the chance to get to know me otherwise. It's hard to go from a grueling schedule fueled by a personal vendetta to sitting in a cell with nothing but time to think.

Thinking is the last thing I should be doing right now.

I dedicated my life to a cause I ultimately turned my back on. I can admit I'm twisted up about it.

Do I believe I made the right decision? I'm not sure. I know I wouldn't have been able to forgive myself if Wren had been captured. I wish I didn't have to let the leader of the Syndicate go to ensure her freedom.

Then again, the Council and Enforcer leadership weren't strictly honest with their people. Maybe that makes my loyalty a moot point. If you believe everything the Council says, you'd think the elites are doing grunts a favor by allowing them to exist in our world. They present them as criminals and mooches - the scum of society.

After spending a few days with Wren at Jimmy's Auto, I know better.

I saw families trying to make ends meet. Neighbors who looked out for each other. People who were just doing their best to get by turned to the Syndicate only when they didn't have another option. The Council failed them. Byron failed them. I came back to make changes to help people like Wren, but now I'll never get the chance.

Does any of it even matter?

What if I had simply arrested Miles and Wren?

The Syndicate would be leaderless, and my worst enemy would be a thing of the past.

As soon as I have the thought, I know it isn't true. You can't beat an organization that has the backing of the masses. Eliminate Miles and another leader, like Rook, will take his place. I saw that power firsthand when the Enforcers forced Jace to spare my life. The people have power regardless of how much the Council and the Enforcers try to downplay it.

I wish they would wield it more often.

Then again, what's obvious to me may not be evident to those who didn't grow up around the Axton family. I heard the discussions at the dinner table. I got to know Byron as a person, not his title. If you believe what you see on the Council broadcasts, you'd think Byron Axton was a God. I suppose it's easy to get drawn into the Council propaganda when you don't have a reality to benchmark it against.

I made the right call. I know I did.

If we want peace, we have to find a way to bring the Syndicate and the Council together. We have to start a conversation about how to help people in this city. That includes all people - not just the elites. Every story has two sides, and for the last decade, the Council has only focused on half the picture. That needs to change, but someone has to force them to see it. I doubt the Council will be okay with Miles waltzing into a meeting and demanding a seat at the table. Someone will have to facilitate that.

It'll be messy. It'll take some time, but I think it can be done.

I just have to get out of this cell to make it happen.

I lean my head against the cool cement. I'm sitting on the metal desk with my back against the wall and my knees drawn up to my chest. The desk isn't deep enough to fully stretch out my legs. I could sit on the concrete floor, but I felt like switching it up today.

You know me - I like to live life on the edge.

I wrap my arms around my legs tighter to ward off the chill. I'm not sure how the Enforcers managed it, but this place always feels cool and damp. It's soul-sucking. I'm not sure I even remember what my skin looks like without goosebumps. When I get out of here, I'm going to bundle up in a king-sized bed with a cheeseburger and a thousand blankets.

Oh, and I want a shower.

A long, scalding shower to wash this whole experience away. And I want to take a dump behind a closed door. I thought that fell in the category of fundamental human rights. I didn't know it was something you could wish for until it was taken away.

Maybe I need to stop whining but screw it.

Anyone who pretends this situation is normal is fooling themselves. In some ways, I think complaining is a way to keep my sanity intact. It reminds me that I don't belong here. It gives me something to look forward to when we bust out.

When, not *if*, because there's no way this place is where my story ends. I drape my arms around my legs and rest my head on my forearms. Elle told me to wait until she could find a way to break us out, but I will lose my mind if I don't do something. I try to slow my breath and calm my mind, but I've always been terrible at meditation. Shutting down your thoughts sounds easy enough until you try to do it for more than thirty seconds.

"Did you know the platypus is a mammal that lays eggs?" Trip asks. I groan and keep my chin tucked against my chest. If it's between losing my mind to boredom and a conversation with him, I will choose insanity any day of the week. Trip's real name is Evan Murphy, but I can't bring myself to call him that. His given name doesn't fit him. He's about our age with pale blond hair, light blue eyes, and a smile that makes me want to sink my fist in his face.

Before I arrested him, Trip was a runner for the surge crew. The surge crew is a Syndicate group that deals exclusively in the highly addictive street drug that gave them their namesake. Liam infiltrated their ranks a few years ago to disrupt and eventually stop distribution. He discovered first-hand what happens to moles. They tortured him by pumping him full of surge and then taking it away. They repeated the process for weeks - growing his addiction, then watching him withdraw over and over again. When we finally rescued him, he was in rough shape.

It took him a week to keep solid food down and a month to start talking again.

Until three months ago, Liam still relied on medical adhesive patches to help keep the cravings in check. Liam hasn't been allowed to use them during our imprisonment at the Academy. He had withdrawal symptoms the first week. Luckily, it wasn't as bad as it was the first go-around.

Don't get me wrong. It was about as pleasant as being locked up with a bear. It was hard on him, but he pulled through it. If nothing else, the silver lining of this situation is that it broke my friend's dependence on the medical patches.

"Bro, did you hear me? The platypus is a mythical creature," Trip repeats. If we weren't trapped here, I'd think the guy was high out of his mind. It turns out that Trip doesn't need substances to fuel his brand of crazy. I lift my head to glare at him.

Jace decided it would be a good idea to give Trip a TV. The problem is he only has access to two channels. There's a history channel and then some animal or nature show he watches sixteen hours a day. I don't think Trip is interested in the content so much as annoying us with random facts.

"I don't care. Shut up," I say. Trip gets off his bunk and saunters to the cell door. He's across the hall from us, so he can see me sitting on the desk. He loops his arms through the bars and presses his forehead against them.

"What? You busy staring at the floor again?" Trip asks. I grind my teeth. I know if we didn't have bars between us, he wouldn't dare push my buttons, but he knows there's nothing I can do to get him to shut up. I wonder if he sees this as punishment for punching him during his interrogation.

To be fair, he deserved it.

I tap the toes of my shoes together. I wonder if I can throw one through the bars with enough accuracy to nail him.

"He's not worth it," snickers Liam as if reading my thoughts. My friend is sitting up in his bunk, watching our exchange with amusement. Unlike the bottom bunk, the top bunk has generous head space. Liam offered to play a game of rock-paper-scissors for it, but I told him he could have it. It's my fault he's locked up here to begin with. The least I can do is not be a jerk about sleeping arrangements.

I shrug and relax against the wall. He's right. I would be down a shoe, and the guards would probably come in and rough us up. They don't need to, but I think Jace has instructed them to be hard on us even for minor infractions.

I wonder how Jace would hold up if our roles were reversed. He would probably try to bribe one of the guards or ask for special privileges. I snort. My stepbrother hasn't roughed it a day in his life. I find great joy in the image of Jace locked in a prison cell for a few moments before a buzzer sounds, indicating the door to the cell block is opening.

Someone is coming.

I stand up and try to shove my head through the bars, like an eager dog, to get the first glimpse of the new prisoner.

Oh, how the mighty have fallen.

Liam jumps down from his bunk to join me. We've seen our fair share of people pass through here, but no one stays for long. There have been a few Syndicate members, grunts, and the occasional low-level elite. They're held here temporarily until they're transferred to another holding location or executed. Jace tends to make an example out of prisoners.

I wonder what is being said in the press releases from the Council. Do they try to make Jace sound good, or have they stopped pretending to care?

Two guards come into view dragging a limp body between them. Hawkins, the enforcer who zapped Liam at the Axton mansion, is one of them. The prisoner they're escorting is in rough shape. His brown hair is matted with blood, and his face is discolored with bruises. His t-shirt is torn and his jeans look like he wore them sliding down a hill covered in mud and thorn bushes. He's missing his shoes.

The guards stop in front of Trip's cell.

"Stand back," Hawkins orders Trip. He obeys, backing up against the wall. I haven't seen him disobey a guard once since we got here. Maybe he's smarter than I give him credit for. All Liam and I have to show for mouthing off are cuts and bruises.

"Roy," Liam murmurs, speaking softly so only I can hear. My eyebrows shoot up. I study the new prisoner's face more closely.

Sure enough, it's my old recruit.

Elle said he disappeared along with Glitch when Wren and Miles escaped the city. Wren was close with them, so I assumed they skipped town together. I'm shocked Liam recognized him.

Roy's eyes open slowly, and he seems to realize where he is. He thrashes, trying to throw the guards off of him. Even I can see it's hopeless. He's too weak. Hawkins delivers a quick hit to his gut, leaving him heaving on the floor. It gives me one more reason to hate him. The other guard opens the cell door and Hawkins drags him inside, dropping him unceremoniously on the floor. Roy barely manages to get his hands out in time to prevent himself from face planting. The guards lock the cell door and disappear down the hall again.

"Hey man, are you okay?" Trip asks, moving forward to help Roy up.

"Stay away from him," I growl. Trip holds up his hands and backs away, his eyebrows raised.

"I take it this is a friend of yours?" Trip asks. Roy uses the wall to walk himself up to his feet with a groan. He limps over to the bars and looks at us, looping his arms through them for support. One of his eyes is partially swollen shut, and there's dried blood on his shirt.

"You look terrible," I say. Roy chuckles, then winces.

"I feel terrible. Wren got away," he says, answering my unasked question. I feel a weight lift off my chest with the news.

"What about Ariel and Ms. Parker?" I ask.

Roy starts to answer before breaking into a rattling cough that leaves him clutching his side in agony. Trip takes a step forward, concern etched on his face, but Roy waves him off. "They got out too."

I laugh. Maybe it's not the appropriate response given our situation, but I'm so relieved Wren and her family weren't captured.

"What happened?" asks Liam.

"The Enforcers attacked the Syndicate compound we were staying in. There were too many of them for us to take. I was covering our retreat with Miles and Don. Don tried to stop Miles from escaping. It turns out that he was working for Jace the whole time. I couldn't let him get Miles, so I attacked Don to give him a chance to escape."

Roy gives me a look. I know he's silently asking if I know that Miles leads the Syndicate, but he's being smart about it. I have no idea what kind of surveillance equipment Jace had installed here. I look at Roy's wounds. Neither of us wants to give Jace information for free when one of us has already paid in blood.

"Jace already knows about Miles leading the Syndicate," I say.

Roy frowns. "After I tackled Don to stop him from shooting Miles, the enforcers arrested me. The van Wren and Miles were in got out of the compound. I heard some of the enforcers talk about organizing a search party. I recognized Commander Harper. I think he stayed behind to round up anyone who escaped. They interrogated me to see if I knew where the others had gone, but I have no idea. Honestly, I'm glad I don't know."

Roy shifts from side to side before settling against the bars again. "Wren never gave up on you. I thought you should know. Miles wouldn't give her the resources to come and rescue you, but she never stopped trying. On the day of the raid, she went behind his back to enlist Glitch's help. We were going to come after you."

Wren wanted to rescue me.

Roy's words warm me from the inside out. I thought Wren blamed me for Robbie's death. I didn't know she would want to see me again.

I've never been so happy to be wrong.

"How is she?" I ask.

Roy frowns. "She's hurting. Her best friend lied to her. Everyone in her life knew about Miles's ties to the Syndicate, including her grandmother and Glitch. She doesn't know who to trust anymore. I tried to be there for her. Glitch lied to me too, but it's not the same. I only knew her for a few months. Miles was Wren's person. He was there for her through everything else. Something inside her broke when she found out he lied to her for years."

"That doesn't make what you went through any less horrible," interjects Liam. I nod in agreement, processing what Roy is saying. I'm glad someone was there for Wren when I couldn't be. Roy's a good guy. He did well in training after our initial rough start. Anyone could see that he and Glitch had something going on. I don't know if it was friendship or more, but it was obvious to anyone who spent time with them. Roy gives me a sad smile that doesn't reach his eyes.

"Yeah, I guess so. There's something else you should know. Glitch showed us the video of what happened at your trial. Someone in the audience kept recording after the main cameras cut off. They leaked the footage to the Syndicate. The video showed Jace executing the rogue cameraman and the enforcers pleading for your life. More importantly, it showed Jace giving in to the enforcers' pleas after he delivered the guilty verdict. The Syndicate has published that video on every platform available to them. Before you ask, the Council knows about it. Glitch hacked into the Council website and posted it. They took it down, but not before a bunch of people saw it."

Liam chuckles beside me. "If I had known Glitch was that good, I would have poached her for my team."

"Then the Syndicate would have all of our data," I point out.

Liam shrugs. "Fair."

"Like it or not, you've become the face of a movement," Roy continues. "According to Glitch, more grunts and elites are calling for change now than there have been since before the Council rose to power. You did that." He gives me a weak smile. "I guess I should apologize for trying to shoot you during training now that you're important and stuff."

I laugh because, honestly? After going undercover with the surge crew and being put on trial for a murder I didn't commit, Roy pulling a gun on me during training feels insignificant in comparison. That was a lifetime ago.

"Forget about it," I say.

"The protesters won't get very far without the surge crew," Trip interrupts. My eyes go to him. He's sitting cross-legged on his bunk, watching the TV just out of view. It's illuminating the floor, painting the concrete with different colors as the image changes.

"What is that supposed to mean?" Liam growls.

Trip yawns so wide I can see his tonsils. He gets off his bunk and stands beside Roy. He loops his arms through the bars and bumps Roy with his shoulder. Roy eyes him suspiciously but doesn't shove him away.

"It means that Miles only controls part of the Syndicate. If the headquarters compound was raided, it's only a matter of time before more of Miles's people defect. They have two options: the Council or the Syndicate. Most of his people are too dirty to go to the Council without getting arrested. That means they'll be in the market for another Syndicate job. The surge crew is powerful and looking for new blood. They're the obvious choice. There's a power war within the Syndicate and Rook is in a good position to win."

"You seem to have good insight for someone on the ground floor," says Liam, observing Trip.

Trip holds up his hands. "Look, I'm just telling it like it is."

Liam continues to banter with Trip, but I tune them out.

The Syndicate.

The Council.

Trip presents the two options as black and white with no gray area in the middle. You're either with the Council, or you're with the Syndicate. You can't be neutral. You can't belong to both.

How did we get here as a society?

I wish we could go back in time and start over so that we could wipe the slate clean with a new version of the Council that's better suited to the needs of all of our citizens, not just the elites. I sigh, pressing my forehead against the bars. I wish we could go back to before Axton AI created a monopoly and the Council rose to power. Back before the Syndicate and the 8-Bit app existed.

It would be so much easier to start from a place where there aren't any loyalties to any organization, and neither side has committed any atrocities. It's like we spent so much time making a mistake we keep committing to it repeatedly to reassure ourselves that we made the right decision. We need to break the cycle.

"We need to move up our escape plan if we want to take Roy with us," Liam whispers behind me. I step away from the bars.

"Next time we see Elle, I'll mention it," I grumble. I feel useless. There's nothing I can do from here. I know we can trust Elle, but I hate that we have to rely on her. She doesn't deserve that burden. Liam squeezes my shoulder before retreating to his place on the top bunk. I go back to my seat on the desk.

A few minutes later, Roy takes the bottom bunk when his conversation with Trip dies down. He throws his arm over his eyes to block out the light. It's mid-morning and the lights won't go out until after dinner. For the first time in days, Trip isn't chattering away. He watches his show in silence, either zoning out or deep in thought.

Probably zoning out. The guy is about as deep as a puddle.

Lunch is dropped off. I pick up my tray and return to my seat on the desk. I use the term "lunch" loosely. It's a colorless gray slop that tastes like burning rubber smells.

Trip breaks his silence to tell me about the Tasmanian Devil.

I tell him to eat a dick.

Just another day in paradise.

Sometime in the early afternoon, I hear the buzzer at the end of the hall sound. Elle appears first. She gestures for me to come to the bars, glancing behind her to see how far the other guards are. I scramble off the desk to get closer to her. Her blond hair is duller than it usually is, frazzled even. There are dark circles under her eyes. She looks exhausted. From what I can tell, Jace has been running her into the ground. He knows she's friends with Liam and me, but he can't prove she's trying to help us. Technically speaking, Elle hasn't done anything illegal yet. I hope we can find a way to escape before Jace gives an order she can't follow.

"Whatever happens, don't agree to Jace's demands," Elle whispers.

That isn't ominous at all.

I want to ask her what's happening, but Hawkins and a few other guards come into view. I take a few steps back and cross my arms, appearing as standoffish as possible. Eight guards in total dressed in formal enforcer ceremonial uniforms - the kind used for executions and official trials.

We're out of time.

Chapter 6

Wren

We're not alone. Viper's words hang in the silence. My fingers go to my waistband, seeking out the gun I took from him when we were shooting at the enforcers. It's not there. I must have left it in the van.

"Are you sure it wasn't Miles?" I ask, keeping my voice low. He gives me a decisive nod.

Ariel is still playing in the firetruck behind me. I jump up on the step to talk to her at eye level.

"I drive," says Ariel. She reaches for me. I bend over so she can wrap her arms around my neck. I press a quick kiss on her forehead when I pull away.

"We're going to play hide and seek," I whisper. "I'm going to close the door. I want you to stay on the floor so I can't see you through the windows. I'm going to hide. Miles is 'it.'"

I have no idea where Miles is. If unknown people are hiding in the back rooms, I hope he's alright. Ariel beams. She presses a finger to her lips in an exaggerated "shhh" motion that would be adorable if not for our current predicament. She crawls on the floor under the steering wheel and draws her knees up to her chest, making herself as small as possible.

"Max," I call. He raises his head from his paws. His ears perk up. "Guard," I order, pointing at Ariel. He gives me a small yip and crawls closer to Ariel. He won't let anyone near her until Grams, Miles, or I call him off. Max hasn't been a police dog for years, but he still remembers his training. He'll protect Ariel or die trying.

I gently close the door and pray the metal is thick enough to stop anything that could hurt my baby. I also pray it won't come to that. Viper has his weapon out. He's watching the door with apprehension. Glitch is standing at his side with a handgun I didn't know she had.

"I'll cover you," says Glitch. Viper nods once and jogs to the door, staying against the wall. I hop off the truck and approach Grams.

"Stay behind the truck. I'm going with Glitch and Viper," I tell Grams. I would have told her to join Ariel in the cab, but the step bar is pretty high. Grams is mobile for her age, but she struggles with stairs. Thankfully, she doesn't argue. Grams walks around the truck and stands behind the tire so her legs aren't visible.

When I'm sure my family is hidden as well as they can be, I take off after Glitch and Viper. I find them inside the kitchen. It's a proper setup with stainless steel countertops and plain cabinets. Everything is clean and well-maintained. It looks like it has been used recently.

"Let's check the basement," murmurs Glitch. She moves to open a door in the corner. I would have guessed it concealed a pantry. Viper wraps his fingers around Glitch's arm, stopping her. She raises an eyebrow, but Viper doesn't respond. He steps around her, taking the lead. Viper silently opens the door before flicking the light switch on.

Nothing happens.

He snatches a flashlight off the hanger beside the door, flips it on, and starts down the stairs. Glitch disappears after him. I pause by the knife block sitting next to the sink. I'm the only one without a weapon. If enemies are hiding in the basement, I don't want to be our weakest link. I grab a knife at random.

It's a cleaver.

I feel like the idiot in a horror movie who ventures into the creepy basement and ends up possessed or stabbed thirty-two times in the chest.

I've watched enough crappy movies to know you don't go into the basement of an abandoned building and expect it to end well.

My friends don't seem to have the same hesitation. I take a few deep breaths. I've always been weird about the dark. Maybe it's a childish fear, but I grew up in a neighborhood where bad things happen after the sun goes down.

Glitch shrieks.

Any hesitation is forgotten, overridden by my need to get to my friend. I readjust my grip on the knife handle and run down the stairs.

I come out swinging.

A firm hand latches around my wrist, stopping my knife mid-thrust. I panic, aiming a kick at my assailant's knee. I hear a grunted curse. Suddenly, a flashlight is shoved in my face.

"Would you stop," Viper growls. I squint against the beam. Viper is shaking out his right leg; a scowl etched on his face.

"Sorry," I mumble. The overhead lights click on, illuminating a much larger basement than I would have expected a building of this size to have. His eyes go to the knife still clutched in my right hand. I swear I see his lips twitch in amusement.

It takes me a moment to process the situation. Glitch is jumping up and down, hugging a woman I don't think I've seen before. It takes me a second to process that the shriek I heard wasn't one of distress.

It was one of recognition.

There have to be at least thirty people down here. Sleeping pads are strewn across the floor and bunk beds that look like death traps assembled out of garbage wood and scrap steel against the far wall. Overturned cardboard boxes with playing cards are situated in the middle of the space with pillows on the floor surrounding the setup. A wide variety of ages are represented from kids younger than Ariel to elderly folks. Many of them are armed, but their weapons are at their sides. They don't perceive us as a threat.

Glitch pulls away from the woman she's hugging. She's middle-aged, with gray starting to weave into her brown hair. Her hair is long, falling almost at her butt. She's wearing a t-shirt for a band I don't recognize and jeans that look newer than anything I own. Her eyes are warm and kind. Her skin wrinkled from the sun, and laugh lines around her eyes.

"Wren, meet Rose," says Glitch, stepping aside so the woman can offer me her hand. I transfer the knife to my left hand to accept her greeting. Her handshake is firm, her palms calloused from hard labor.

Viper. Glitch. Rose.

I wonder if it's a community custom to use an alias or a nickname? I make a mental note to ask Glitch about it later.

"Nice to meet you, Wren," Rose says. I release her hand and step back.

"Not to be rude, but who are you people?" I ask. Glitch laughs.

"This is the community Viper and I belonged to before we joined Miles at the Syndicate compound," Glitch explains. "Rose took us in after we lost our parents. She practically raised us."

Rose waves her off. "You were already grown. I just let you bum off my couch for a bit." She gives Glitch a warm smile that tells me Glitch's sentiment means more to her than she's letting on.

She steps around us and pulls Viper into a hug. I tense, expecting him to shut her down, but Viper surprises me when he hugs her back. The man is about as cuddly as his nickname, so I guess if he trusts Rose, then I'm probably in good company.

"We didn't recognize the car you showed up in, so I had everyone hide down here," explains Rose.

"Are you their leader?" I ask.

Rose shakes her head. "We don't have leaders in this community. We make decisions together."

I don't miss the way she emphasizes "this community." I wonder what makes Rose's community different from the other communities?

"She says that, but if anyone wants to do anything, they run it by Rose first out of respect," says Glitch. She says it like a jab, but I can hear the underlying respect in her tone. The fact that no one in the room objects speaks volumes.

Rose rolls her eyes. "What brings you here?"

"Enforcers attacked Syndicate headquarters. We needed somewhere safe to regroup," explains Viper.

"Were you followed?" Rose asks.

"No."

It dawns on me that these people could probably teach me a lot about hiding from the Enforcers and surviving outside the cities. I wish I had taken more of an opportunity to learn while staying at the Syndicate compound. To some degree, it never sunk in that I wouldn't be returning to my old life. Some part of me knew that was never going to happen, but it hurts to admit that part of my life is over.

"I better go get Grams and Ariel," I say.

"We'll come up with you," says Rose. "No sense hiding in the dark if there isn't a threat."

I climb the stairs first, with the rest of the community trailing behind me. I don't want to startle Grams or Ariel if I don't have to.

"It's okay," I call across the building. "You can come out now."

I'm greeted with silence.

I speed up, a growing sense of unease building with each step until I'm at a flat-out run. I skid around the side of the truck, but Grams isn't there. Jumping up on the step bar, I open the firetruck door. Max lets out a low growl before he realizes it's me. Ariel pokes her head out from under the steering wheel.

Thank God.

"Game over?" Ariel asks. It takes me a second to remember I told her we were playing hide and seek.

"No, stay hidden just a little longer. We fooled Miles this time," I say, trying to keep the fear from entering my voice. Ariel giggles and ducks back under the steering wheel. I glance around the room, but there's nowhere Grams could be hiding. I close the fire truck door and race to the exit. Pressing my back against the wall, I lean forward just enough to peer through the window.

There are three off-road vehicles and at least eight enforcers in front of the fire station. Grams is being led to the nearest truck by a man who towers over her by at least a foot. He has one hand wrapped around her upper arm and his other hand on his weapon. Grams is trying to pull away, but she isn't having much success. She stumbles. The man yanks her forward as soon as she regains her balance, so she stumbles again.

I see red.

I'm out the door before I realize what I'm doing.

"Stop!" I yell. The enforcers turn around, their weapons aimed at me. I pound to a stop.

The man holding Grams is Commander Harper.

I didn't interact with him much at the Academy outside of the recruit assessment in the virtual reality arena. His bald head is shiny with sweat, and his white uniform has dirt and blood spots on it, indicating they were involved in the assault on the Syndicate compound. He smirks when he sees me.

That's when I realize I'm facing down a firing squad with a cleaver.

Not my finest moment.

"I was wondering when I'd see you again," laughs Commander Harper. He tightens his grip on Grams' arm. I see her flinch and imagine what it would feel like to have my hands wrapped around his throat, choking the life from his body.

"Let her go," I growl.

He shrugs. "Why would I do that?"

"She's innocent."

"She's a Syndicate sympathizer. That's far from innocent."

"Only because I dragged her into my mess because she didn't have anywhere else to go. I'm the guilty one here. Take me instead," I say.

"Wren-" Grams interrupts.

"Deal," says the commander, surprising me. I didn't expect him to accept my offer, but I'm glad he did.

"Let her go first," I say.

The commander laughs. I grit my teeth.

"Same time then," I say, hating that I have zero power in this situation. I hope Glitch and the rest of the community can see what's happening outside. Maybe they'll be able to stop the enforcers before they get out of town. I take a step further out into the open. The commander seems to think about it for a moment.

"Fine," he says. He releases Grams's arm and prods her in the back with his weapon. "Start walking."

"Sir, our orders-" One of the enforcers protests.

"Shut up," the commander snaps. "I'm in charge." He pokes Grams again. "I said walk."

Grams starts forward. I start walking, matching her pace. I don't want to give the commander a reason to renege on his deal. There are so many ways this could end badly. I try not to think about it as I put one foot in front of the other. Grams and I cross paths in the middle.

"Get inside," I murmur. She stops walking.

"Don't do this," she says.

"Take them out," orders Commander Harper. I curse and shove Grams behind me. Of course, he would toy with us before giving the order to kill us. We're still too far from the firehouse door to make it to cover. I turn around and hurl the cleaver at the commander. It falls short, clattering to the ground.

We're so screwed.

A shot rings out in the silence.

I slam my eyes shut and wait for the searing pain of a bullet tearing through me, but it doesn't come.

I open my eyes.

More shots ring out. One by one, the commander's squad drop to the ground. I shove Grams in front of me.

"Get to the building," I shout. Grams moves as fast as she can, but it's not fast enough. A bullet shatters the glass in the door a few feet ahead of us. I yell, throwing myself forward just as Grams shoves the door open. We land in a heap inside. Miles jumps over us and races outside along with a few of Rose's people. I push up into a seated position.

"Are you alright?" I ask Grams. She gets up more slowly.

"I think so," she says. "Are you?"

"I'm fine."

"You shouldn't have come after me."

"I wasn't going to leave you," I say. Grams looks like she wants to say something but decides against it. Viper walks through the door with Miles behind him. There's a sniper rifle slung over Viper's shoulder.

"We're good for now, but we need to get out of here before others come looking for them," says Viper.

"How did they find us?" Rose asks.

"Drones," says Viper.

Drones. I didn't even think about that. It would have been easy for the enforcers to track our vehicle after we escaped from the compound. After we left the farmhouse, there weren't many trees concealing the road. We would have been an easy target to follow even if we did get a head start. Miles jogs around Viper and sinks to his knees in front of me.

"Are you hurt?" Miles asks, running his hands up and down my arms, searching for a nonexistent wound. I grab his hands and hold them in front of me. He's shaking. I look at Viper, taking in the sniper rifle and calm demeanor. He saved my life. He saved Grams' life.

"Thank you," I say. His face is expressionless, but he inclines his head to acknowledge my statement.

"That was a heck of a shot," I say.

"I've had some practice." Viper's expression darkens. I study him but decide against asking follow-up questions I know he won't answer. "Their leader got away."

My blood turns to ice in my veins. Commander Harper is still out there somewhere.

"He won't risk coming back here without reinforcements. We need to move out before he returns," says Viper.

"I need to check on Ariel," I say.

Miles puts his hand on my shoulder to stop me.

"What were you thinking? Running out there without a weapon was suicide."

"I had a cleaver," I say, getting defensive.

Miles snorts, but there's no humor in it.

"They had Grams," I press.

"Jesus, Wren." Miles scrubs his hands over his face. "The least you could do is pretend you care about your life even a little bit. Show even an ounce of self-preservation before you put yourself in danger."

I freeze. "What is that supposed to mean?"

"It means you put everyone else before yourself. You're the ultimate martyr. You don't have that luxury when you have a kid."

I stab him in the chest with my finger. "Just because you don't care about your family doesn't mean everyone else is as heartless. I wasn't going to sit back and let those enforcers take Grams."

Miles glares at me. I watch as his shoulders slump and the fight bleeds out of him. He takes a deep breath.

"I wasn't going to let them take her," he whispers. His hand comes to the back of my neck. "I haven't always been honest with you, but you can trust that I'll protect you. Always. You're my family, Wren. Ariel and Grams too. You're all I have left," says Miles, his voice breaking.

For the first time since Miles was arrested, I get a glimpse of my best friend.

Miles leans his forehead against mine and closes his eyes. I close mine too. No matter what happens, we will always be two kids from a grunt neighborhood who are just trying to make their way in the world. We argue. We drive each other crazy. We hurt each other. At the end of the day, we apologize and make things right.

Because that's what families do.

"I won!" Ariel crows before body slamming Miles and throwing her arms around his neck from behind. He laughs. I feel his warm breath on my lips as he releases my neck and pulls away.

"What did you win?" Miles asks.

"She thinks we were playing hide and seek," I explain. "You were 'it.'"

Miles smiles. He grabs Ariel's legs and stands up to give her a piggyback ride. Miles spins around in a circle and Ariel laughs. Grams watches them with a small smile, Max sitting beside her. I can't believe how close we came to losing her today.

"Rose and her people are packing up downstairs," says Glitch, approaching our group. "We need to leave before reinforcements get here."

"Are we going with them?" I ask.

"You can. I'm not," says Glitch. "I'm going to the city."

"I'll go with you," says Miles, setting Ariel down.

She raises an eyebrow. "I thought you were against our rescue attempt."

"We have a safe house there I can use to get in touch with my people," says Miles. "We have different goals, but we can help each other break into the city before parting ways. What about you, Wren?"

My eyes widen in surprise. This is Miles compromising. I look at Grams and Ariel standing off to the side.

"I can't. I have to make sure my family is taken care of," I say.

"They could stay with Rose and her community," says Viper. "They'll be safe with them."

"What about you?" Glitch asks Viper.

"I'm staying," he says. Glitch's face falls. "The communities have been neutral for so long they're out of touch with the rest of the world. I think a lot of people will want to join the fight that's coming. Besides, I can use the community resources to help you rescue Roy. It'll be beneficial to have someone outside the city walls."

Glitch frowns, but she doesn't question his response.

Grams steps in front of me and puts her hands on my arms. "Wren, you should go with your friends. I'll look after Ariel until you get back."

"We don't know these people," I say.

"Viper just saved our lives. Miles and Glitch trust them. We're safe with them," says Grams with a confidence I wish I had.

Ariel hugs my leg, and my heart cracks a little more. I missed so much of Ariel's life while I was working for the Enforcers. If I go with Glitch and Miles to the city, I have no idea when I will see her again. I can't do that to her. It isn't fair.

"I can't," I say.

"But you want to."

I swallow. Grams gives me a sad smile.

"You'll probably hate me for saying this, but you and your mom are alike in many ways. Neither one of you can stand to see other people hurting."

"What are you trying to convince me to do? Abandon you and Ariel so I can throw my life away trying to rescue Roy and Ash?"

"No, I want you to stop using Ariel and I as an excuse. I know you, Wren. You'll regret staying behind when your friends need you. We'll be fine. I can take care of Ariel."

She's right. Miles, Glitch, and I have our differences, but I still care about them. I can't let them walk into this situation alone. I mutter a curse before drawing Grams into a tight hug.

"Look after Ariel for me. I love you both so much," I say, my voice cracking and my eyes welling with tears. There was a time when I bottled up my emotions. I refused to let anyone see me cry, because I perceived it as a weakness. I've cried more lately than I have in my entire life. I guess I was long overdue.

I pull away and swipe under my eyes before I squat down to kiss Ariel on her head. "You're going to stay with Grams and Rose for a bit, okay?"

"Don't go," Ariel wails and my heart splits open. I hug her closer.

"I'll be back before you know it," I promise, blinking back tears. Grams takes Ariel from me. Viper is watching our exchange in silence. His mouth is set in a firm line, the sniper rifle still slung over his shoulder. "Promise me you'll watch out for them."

Viper extends his hand. "You have my word." I accept it and study his eyes, but I don't see any signs of deception. I have no reason to doubt him, but I'm still uneasy about leaving Grams and Ariel behind. Glitch wraps her arm around my waist and guides me outside. I don't look over my shoulder. I don't turn around because I know I'll never walk away if I allow myself one last glance.

"You can trust Viper," says Glitch. "They'll be alright."

"What's the plan?" I ask. If I have a plan to follow, I can focus on that. I won't have time to regret or second guess my choice of going back into a city where I'm a wanted fugitive accompanied by two people who have done nothing but lie to me.

I'm doing this to build a better world for Ariel. I'm doing this for Ash. I'm doing this for my friends and neighbors and those who are just like me - suffering at the hands of the Council and Jace Axton but powerless to stop it. People who have no choice but to join the Syndicate.

Miles walks ahead, navigating through the lifeless bodies of the fallen enforcers until he reaches the nearest shuttle. He opens the door and peers inside.

"We'll take one of the off-road vehicles into the city. They're registered with the Council and should be authorized with travel passes that will get us across the border," says Miles. "There aren't any extra uniforms inside." He winces, glancing at the bodies closest to him. It takes me a second to realize what he's getting at.

"We can't take their uniforms," I hiss.

"He's right," sighs Glitch. "We can't show up in an enforcer vehicle dressed like this. We won't make it past the security gate."

Miles goes to work, stripping the uniform off the guard at his feet. I hate everything about this, but I swallow the bile rising in my throat and mirror my friend's actions.

This is wrong on so many levels. Disrespectful. Cruel.

They were going to kill you.

The voice in my head might speak the truth, but that doesn't make this act any less disgusting. I button up the uniform over my clothes and get in the backseat of the shuttle. Miles gets behind the wheel and Glitch takes the passenger seat next to him. The interior design is similar to the Enforcer Pod I rode in with Ash during my training, but this vehicle has more seats and isn't autonomous. There is a tablet mounted to the dash in front of Glitch. She starts tapping on it, navigating through the various screens.

"The GPS is set for the border checkpoint we have a pass for," says Glitch. Miles starts the engine. A few of Rose's people stand outside the firehouse to see us off. Glitch offers a half-hearted wave. I scan the crowd, but Grams and Ariel are still inside. I'll have to do my best to end this as quickly as possible.

The sooner we bust Ash out and remove Jace from the director's seat, the sooner we can go home.

Chapter 7

Ash

“W hat’s this about?” I direct my question at Elle, but I raise my voice so the other guards can hear me. I don’t want them to know she’s still talking to me. It’s safer for her if everyone thinks I’m the ex-fiancée that wronged her. They believe I’m a traitor. She needs to put as much distance between us as possible to remain in good standing with the Council. It’s the only way she can stay on the other side of these bars.

“Turn around. Hands between the bars,” says Hawkins. “Both of you.” He nods over my shoulder at Liam.

Elle gives us a look that says to play this out, but I can’t shake the feeling that something is wrong. I’ve been escorted to the Axton mansion and events on Jace’s orders before, but I know this is different for some reason. There’s an almost somber mood among the guards - a level of seriousness that isn’t usually present. It has me on edge. Deciding to trust Elle’s judgment, I turn around and stick my wrists through the bars. Hawkins snaps on the cuffs and opens the door.

“It’s a bit early for dinner at the Axton mansion, isn’t it?” Liam asks.

One of the younger guards snorts. “You’re not going to the Axton mansion.”

Hawkins elbows her. "Shut up," he says. I nod at Liam, thanking him for probing for information.

Where are they taking us if we're not going to the Axton mansion?

And, more importantly, what aren't the guards telling us?

Usually, our escorts can't wait to taunt us. They're the first to bring up Jace's latest idea, wasting no time in their relentless mocking. It's uncharacteristic for them to stay quiet. I don't like this. Hawkins and another guard open our cell door. Across the hall, Trip and Roy are brought out too. Roy looks dead on his feet, but he manages to stand tall. I think sheer determination is the only thing keeping him upright.

The guards take up ranks around us, marching us down the corridor and into the lobby. The young enforcer at the front desk watches us with wide eyes as Hawkins punches the button for the elevator. We wait in silence. I wonder if Hawkins and the others are on their best behavior because Elle is here. The elevator doors open and we all crowd inside. It's a tight fit.

"Jeesh, think you could fit a few more guards in here?" Trip asks.

"Quiet," Hawkins snaps. Trip shrugs, his shoulder brushing up against mine in the close quarters. The elevator draws to a stop, and the doors slide open to the Council floor. Instead of taking a left to go to the Council meeting room, the guards turn right.

We walk past Byron's old office. The lights are turned off. From what I can see through the glass, it looks like Jace has renovated. The bookshelves and drink cabinet are gone. Now, there are large monitors mounted on the walls. Everything has been repainted white. Even the carpet has been replaced with white tile. It reminds me more of the Academy atrium - crisp, clean, and modern.

The guards lead us to the Council judgment chambers. I wonder if the Council finally woke up and decided to overthrow Jace, but I know that's just wishful thinking. We wouldn't be paraded through the building like prisoners if Jace were no longer in power.

Historically, the Council chambers are where the high visibility trials are held. It's where I thought my trial would be held. Any lingering hope dies when I see Jace standing in the center of the room without handcuffs.

The entire Council is present.

I didn't think it was possible, but they look more on edge now than at my trial. Whatever Jace is planning, it can't be good. The Council members are arranged in tiered seating in a semi-circle. Jace is standing at ground level along with a camera crew. Floor-to-ceiling windows line the wall facing the door providing natural lighting and a view of the city no one is admiring.

The cameras are already on, capturing our entrance. I throw my shoulders back and tilt my chin up. It's an instinct born from years of guidance from Byron when attending similar events. I guess I have the man to thank for something.

Confidence in the face of uncertainty.

Staring down your enemy with your head held high when you want to run.

The late director knew what he was doing. I wish I hadn't used that skill so often over the last three months. After all of this is over, I'm making my way to the coast, where I can sit on a beach, have a few drinks, and watch the sunset.

The world won't be ending.

No one will need me to do anything for them.

Just me, Wren, and Ariel enjoying the sand. I've never been to the beach, but I bet it's nice.

The guards lead us to a horizontal bar in the middle of the room with metal rings welded to the top. My cuffs are released long enough to feed them through the metal loop before they're secured again. I watch as Elle breaks from our group to climb the stairs to the first tier.

Whatever happens, don't agree to Jace's demands.

Roy is secured beside me, followed by Liam, then Trip. There are no chairs. I glance at Roy to see how he's holding up. He's leaning against the railing to support himself, but he's doing a decent job of masking how uncomfortable he is.

He's not an idiot.

He sees the cameras. He sees the Council.

Right now, showing weakness isn't an option.

"You good?" I ask quietly. Some of the Council members are talking, so I'm banking on that concealing our conversation. Roy nods.

"This room is smaller than it looks on TV," says Roy. I chuckle. He's not wrong. The first time I attended a trial in person, I had the same thought. Jace walks behind the camera crew. He says something to the camera operator. The red light clicks off, indicating they're no longer broadcasting. Jace crosses the room, stopping in front of me. He looks down his nose, trying to make me feel less than I am. I suppose it's meant to be intimidating, but Jace forgets I grew up with him.

I've seen that look almost daily since we were kids.

It doesn't phase me anymore.

"What? Do I have something in my teeth?" I ask. I make a show of poking at my front teeth with my tongue like I'm searching for a stuck piece of lettuce. Jace scowls, irritated I'm not taking this more seriously.

Good. Let him sweat a bit.

"You are going to agree with everything I say, or there will be consequences," Jace says.

"Like tossed into an Academy jail cell?" Liam asks with a yawn. "Been there, done that."

"It's not so bad, especially with the TV. Thanks, man!" Trip says. I didn't expect the surge runner to say anything, let alone team up with Liam to put Jace in his place. Jace has a vein popping out at his temple. He's glaring with such intensity I'm surprised he doesn't burst a blood vessel.

"Enough," he snaps. "You will admit to killing the director or I will start killing off your friends."

"Trip isn't my friend," I say.

"Hey!" Trip grumbles. I shrug, feigning a calm I don't feel. This is what Elle was warning me about. She doesn't want me to admit to killing the director on a live broadcast. If my trial video is as inflammatory as Roy made it out to be, I can see why. Admitting I killed the director would be a massive setback in gathering support to overthrow Jace. People will assume I'm just as bad as he is. Maybe even worse if you consider murdering the previous director and then lying about it. People will see it as a betrayal, and things will return to how they always were.

Elle is right. I can't let that happen, but I also can't ask my friends to die on that hill with me.

"Are we clear?" Jace asks.

I spit in Jace's face.

It's not an answer, but it's not *not* an answer either. I'm buying myself time until I can find a way out of this.

The Council gasps. Jace wipes my saliva off his cheek. He aims a punch at my head, but it's slow and sloppy. I dodge it easily, even with my hands tied to the pole. Jace stumbles forward, his balance thrown off by the missed hit. I take advantage of the opportunity to knee him in the gut. He topples over, but before I can get another strike, the guards rush forward to help him. Hawkins crashes into me, shoving me sideways into Roy. The cuffs cut into my wrists as my arms pull against them. I'm lucky I didn't break or dislocate anything.

"Stop. We need him to be in one piece for the broadcast," says Jace. He shoves the guard's hands off of him and straightens his suit as if nothing happened. I move away from Roy, returning to my place at the bar.

"Sorry," I murmur to Roy. I no doubt made his injuries worse by slamming into him.

"It was worth it," says Roy. He gives me a resigned, confident smile. "Don't admit to anything."

"He threatened your lives. I'm not going to let him kill you over this."

"I'm with Roy. If he wants us dead, we're dead regardless of what you say. Don't give him anything," whispers Liam. Trip looks at Liam and Roy before meeting my eyes.

He shrugs. "Screw it. Viva la Syndicate. I'm in."

My shoulders slump. I don't want to do this. I don't want so many people to rely on my image and ability to do better than the rest of my family. At the Axton mansion, Elle told me I needed to show people that I was better than Jace. She told me not to give them a reason to doubt me. If that includes letting my friends take a bullet for me, I don't want the title.

Let some other heartless fool be the martyr this country needs.

"Yesterday, the Enforcers raided the Syndicate headquarters. We killed their leader and ended their operations permanently," Jace starts. I blink. The cameras are back on and Jace is addressing the Council. I'm running out of time to make a decision.

"He's lying," says Roy, deciding for me. He yanks against the chains securing him to the bar. "The leader of the Syndicate escaped."

"Even if he didn't, the Syndicate is like a Hydra, man. You chop off one head, and two grow back in its place," adds Trip. I almost laugh. Watching TV endlessly gives you some good fodder for insults if nothing else. I have a growing appreciation for the guy. Jace grits his teeth. I'm surprised he didn't learn his lesson the first time he put me on the stand. I'm not the only one who is okay with breaking protocol to call him out.

"Jace is a liar. I witnessed him order Commander Harper, a high-ranking Enforcer official, to murder a twelve-year-old boy using Axton AI riot bots," says Liam, adding another nail to Jace's coffin.

"Do you still believe Jace?" I ask, addressing the Council members. I see a few of them shift in their seats, but no one speaks up.

How many wake-up calls will it take for them to do something?

More importantly, what is Jace holding over them to keep them in check?

"Enough with your lies," growls Jace. He is standing in the center of the courtroom with his hands behind his back. To the casual observer, he appears unphased by our accusations. I know better. I can see it in the vein by his right eye that becomes a little more prominent when he's irritated. I can see it in his strained smile.

He's pissed.

"Asher Axton interrupted his trial three months ago to tell you I killed the director. That was a lie, just as his friends are lying now. He gets one last chance to tell you the truth or I have no choice but to execute him." Jace turns and offers me the floor.

I swallow. Roy, Liam, and Trip all watch me expectantly. Roy gives me a slight nod. I sigh. I wish I could keep my head down and walk away from this, but the people deserve to know who their leader is.

Robbie's death has to mean something.

Wren and Ariel need to live in a safe world.

The only way those two things are going to happen is if something changes.

I've watched the Council remain idle through not one but two public hearings. They may not get a third chance. I take a deep breath and let it out slowly before I wrap a metaphorical noose around my neck.

"Jace Axton killed the director. He accused me of the murder. The others are telling the truth."

Short, simple, and to the point. As if anything is straightforward about this situation.

The Council members break out in chatter. I can feel the camera lens, but I refuse to look. I stand tall and watch Jace as he has a meltdown in slow motion.

Ah yes, the five stages of the breakdown. The first two have already happened: the tiny blood vessel by his right eye and his tense posture.

Third is the angry, stomping walk towards us.

Fourth is a snarl in preparation for a pointless tirade no one wants to hear.

Fifth is...wait, is that a gun?

Jace tugs a gun out of his waistband, aims, and fires.

Roy hits the ground beside me, a bullet hole in his chest. His arms hang limply above his head, still secured to the pole.

"No," I roar, ripping at my cuffs, but it's futile. I can't get to Roy. I'm trapped. The other Council members are either trying to sneak out the door or are yelling at Jace to stop. It's Elle who finally vaults over the first row of seats. She grabs Jace's gun out of his hands. She yells something at the camera crew and draws a hand across her neck, indicating they should stop filming. All of this is happening in the background, but I can't take my eyes off Roy. He's not moving. A puddle of blood on the floor is growing dangerously large.

"You're dead," I snarl. Jace ignores me and heads for the door.

That's when the windows explode.

I crouch instinctively, getting low to the ground and doing my best to shield my face without using my hands. There are three loud pops before the room starts filling with smoke. My eyes fill with tears, and I begin to cough.

Five figures dressed in black clothes with gas masks come towards us. I try to kick out, but my vision is blurry. I miss. One of the figures touches my hands. There's a cracking sound, and my hands are free. Someone tugs me to my feet and drags me towards the windows. I hear Council members screaming.

There's gunfire, but I don't know how anyone can see well enough to aim at a target. That's a scary thought.

My assailant guides me to the window. For a moment, I think they're going to shove me out. I struggle against them, but a coughing fit impedes my movements. My feet touch down on metal grating, and a cool breeze washes over me, clearing the air of smoke. I take a few deep inhales, trying to purge my lungs. My vision is quickly coming back to me.

I'm standing on a platform outside the window suspended from the top of the Academy by a steel cable. It's a window washing station. Two of the black-clad figures are already on the platform. As I watch, the remaining three come through the window, guiding a coughing Liam and Trip.

"We have to go back for Roy," I say. My voice is hoarse, and I immediately break into another coughing fit.

"He's dead." The voice comes from one of the masked figures, their voice muffled. "Hang on to the rail. We're dropping." I barely manage to wrap my arm around the metal handrail before the platform starts plummeting to the ground faster than any elevator I've ever ridden on. I snap my eyes shut, the wind roaring around me as my stomach drops. Liam yells something unintelligible. I can't tell if it's a curse, a prayer, or a little of both. The platform brakes hard enough for my feet to lift off the ground before it comes to a stop.

"Get in the van," someone shouts. I push myself to my feet and look up at the Academy. I can just make out the broken window on the top floor. I can't believe we did that. I can't believe Jace killed Roy. Jace usually stops at harsh words and temper tantrums. He killed the director to gain power. He killed the cameraman to keep it.

Killing Roy was meaningless.

I was hoping that Jace could be saved, but I was wrong.

You don't cure a rabid dog. You put it down.

Liam grabs my arm and tugs me towards the van. Enforcers are starting to stream out the front door of the Academy. I have no idea who these people are, but it still has to be safer than staying here. I climb into the van. It takes off before the door is fully shut, peeling away from the curb and barreling into traffic.

"Who are you?" I ask, taking in the five masked figures sprawled out on the van floor. Six of them, if you count the driver. The interior seats have been removed, so the space is empty. Our rescuers pull their masks. I recognize the blond woman immediately.

Rook.

"You," I snarl, launching myself at the leader of the surge crew. Trip intervenes, throwing his arm across my chest. His reaction startles me more than the hit, but it does its job. I stumble back and stare up at him. Rook looks at Trip as if asking permission. Trip nods. What is going on?

"I didn't kill Robbie, if that's what you're pissed about," says Rook. She tosses the gas mask on the floor and tucks her blond hair behind her ears. "Someone at the Academy overrode the controls. They came after my men too."

Liam shifts beside me. "We know."

"Did you kill the director?" Trip asks Rook, interrupting our standoff.

"Negative. He left the courtroom earlier than expected."

Trip curses. I look between Rook and Trip. Why would the leader of the surge crew personally rescue a low-level runner like Trip? It doesn't make sense. I picture the guy who has been spouting off history and animal facts for the last three months.

The joker. The idiot.

He's not exactly the picture of competence. He caved under interrogation to give me details about Robbie's capture and where the surge crew would be holding him. He's mediocre at best, utterly inadequate at worse. The van takes a sharp turn. I throw my arm against the wall to steady myself.

"Where are we going?" asks Liam.

"Surge stronghold. You'll have to lay low for a few days before we get you out of the city," Rook explains.

"I'm not leaving the city," I say.

Rook snorts. "Then you're an idiot. The director won't stop looking for you. You'll have to remain in hiding for the rest of your life. At least in another city, you may get a little more freedom."

"I have no intention of hiding. I have unfinished business with Jace."

Rook studies me for a moment before glancing at Trip. "Then you may be able to help us." The van comes to a stop. Someone bangs on the outside of the vehicle, indicating it's time to move. One of Rook's people opens the back door. Liam and I hang back while everyone is filing out.

"Can we trust them?" Liam asks. My friend has a slice across his right cheekbone. It's probably from when the window exploded in the courtroom. Otherwise, he appears unharmed. We're lucky.

"No, but we don't have a choice. Keep your eyes and ears open. The second we have a chance to run, we're taking it."

"You want to find Wren," he says, his expression softening.

"Roy said she escaped with Miles. I have to know for sure. This is the surge crew. I understand if you need to bail."

Liam grimaces but shakes his head. "I'm with you, brother. Whatever you decide, I'm in."

"You guys coming or what?" Trip calls from outside. I roll my eyes and make my way out of the van. We're parked in a back alley sandwiched between two brick buildings that look like they're leaning towards each other, their foundations shot. I watch as one of Rook's people pulls a metal gate across the driveway, effectively blocking the van from view. Two more people drape a tarp over the top of the van. It's smart. If Jace sends out patrols or drones to scan the area, the van won't be immediately apparent from the ground or air.

"This way," says Trip. He gestures for Liam and me to follow him into the squat brick building. Inside, we take a narrow stairway to the second floor. The building smells damp and dusty, like it hasn't been occupied in years.

I wonder if this is a temporary holding site until Rook can decide what to do with us. I wish I had my gun on me or some kind of weapon. There were six people in the van plus Trip, not including any other surge crew members hiding inside. Those aren't good odds if they try to start something.

The stairway opens to an apartment on the second floor. The bottom panes of the windows have been boarded up, but enough light seeps in through the upper panes to illuminate the room. There are backpacks and totes with supplies stacked against one wall. An old wooden table with four chairs sits in the middle of the room. There's a couch pushed up against one wall with some cushion foam exposed that looks more like a sanctuary for bed bugs rather than somewhere to relax.

It looks like someone took a cheese grater to the walls - the orange paint is peeling off in sheets revealing a previous coating of pale pink. Down the hall, I can just make out the corner of a kitchen counter and more doors that probably lead to bedrooms. There don't appear to be any other surge crew members here.

Trip pulls out a chair and plops down, kicking his feet up on the table. Rook sits next to him and gestures for Liam and me to do the same. I don't know where this is going, but I decide to play nice until I have more information. I sit down, and Liam follows my lead.

"What happens now?" I ask.

"We stay here until the initial manhunt dies down, then we move to a more secure location," says Rook.

"Why did you rescue Trip?" I ask.

"They missed my charming personality," chuckles Trip. He winks at me.

"Trip just happened to be in the courtroom. The real target was the director."

"I don't believe you," says Liam. Rook raises her eyebrows. "If you were targeting the director, there are better locations than the Council chambers. You were there for Trip. That was the first time he was removed from the Academy holding cells in three months. Why go after a low-level runner?"

Rook's expression remains impassive, but I don't miss the slight tightening of her jaw. Liam's instinct was spot on. She went in for Trip. The question is, why? That's when it dawns on me.

"Because he's not a low-level runner," I say. "Trip is the leader of the surge crew."

Chapter 8

Wren

I 've been sitting in a car for the last four hours, but my body hasn't gotten the memo. My heart is beating like I just finished a marathon while chugging a gallon of coffee. In short, I'm a nervous wreck.

Miles rolls forward as another car is allowed across the border and into the city. There are only two more cars ahead of us before we're at the front. I count five Enforcers on top of the wall with automatic weapons. Only two officers are checking the cars at the gate, but I'm sure there are more in the single-story, cinder block buildings next to the checkpoint to provide backup if required.

One lane over, I watch an autonomous cargo truck cross the border uninhibited. It's easy to see why we left the city in a shipping container the first time; the security measures are much more relaxed. I guess the Council trusts computers more than people. I would.

Miles and Glitch discussed sneaking onto a cargo truck before we reached the border, but they decided against it. Without access to the Syndicate computer system, they have no way of hacking into the manifests to reroute a truck. We would have had to hijack one on the main highway where the camera coverage is heavier. They decided it was less risky to cross the border in our stolen vehicle than procure a new one.

We got to the city in record time. If Commander Harper has reported back to the Enforcers already, there's a good chance we'll be arrested before we can cross. My eyes run over the sturdy fence and the armed guards.

We won't get a chance to run if they know who we are.

The guard checking identification raises his weapon gesturing for the driver ahead of us to get out of the car. The door opens and a teenager with a pockmarked face unfolds himself from the driver's seat. He's wearing baggy clothes that, judging by the severe wear and tear, have had a few owners before him.

He says something to the guard. I can't make out what. Two more Enforcers converge on the driver, hauling him into one of the cinder-block buildings. The kid is yelling, trying to throw them off, but he's outnumbered. Another guard gets in the kid's car and drives it off the road, around the back of the building.

"I'm beginning to regret this life choice," I mutter.

"Just this one?" Glitch asks sweetly, not looking up from her phone. I roll my eyes. She's too distracted to notice.

"We'll be fine," Miles grits out. "Something was wrong with the driver's documentation. We're in an official Enforcer vehicle. They're not going to look twice."

I hope he's right.

The guard gestures for Miles to move forward. I take a few deep breaths to calm my heart rate. I lean back and cross my right ankle over my left knee. I uncross my legs and then cross them again. I'm freaking out. We're just three Council-loving idiots on our way home after crushing the hopes and dreams of the masses. Nothing to see here, folks.

Why is it so hard to act naturally when you need to?

I throw my arm across the back of the seat for good measure. I spent enough time around the Academy to know anyone on their way home from patrol won't be alert. They'd be dead on their feet, ready to sleep in their compartments or spend a few hours relaxing at Intrepid. They'd be halfway through planning their evening, not stressing out about a border crossing they shouldn't be worried about. My borrowed uniform is slightly too tight, tugging uncomfortably at my knees and hips. Miles rolls down the window as he stops in front of the gate.

"Credentials," says the guard in a bored tone. Miles reaches across the console and takes a tablet from Glitch. I vaguely recall a lesson from Ash about security measures at border crossings. The tablet Miles hands the guard is paired with the vehicle and synced with the security system at the Academy. If the authentication number generated on the tablet doesn't match what the guard is showing on his device, we're screwed.

"Good patrol?" asks the Enforcer.

Miles shrugs. "Uneventful."

The guard nods and hands the tablet back to Miles. Miles accepts it with his other hand. That's when I notice the little drop of blood on my best friend's sleeve. I hold my breath and pray the guard doesn't see it, but we've run out of luck. The guard's eyes narrow.

"Sir, I'm going to have to ask you to step out of the car."

"What's wrong?" Miles asks, still oblivious to the blood stain that's putting our lives in jeopardy.

"Now," orders the Enforcer, raising his weapon.

"Okay, okay," says Miles. He turns off the car and opens the door slowly, keeping one hand raised.

I follow his lead, opening the back door and raising my hands. I scan the border wall and our surroundings, looking for...I don't know what.

A weapon? An escape route? A flying unicorn to lift us over the gate?

At this point, I'll take anything if it gets us away from here. The instant the guard scans Miles's chip implant, I know it's over. His profile pops up on the scanner. A flashing red bar across the top identifies him as a fugitive. More Enforcers swarm us. There's a lot of yelling and rough hands on my arms. Someone scans my chip implant, the red bar signaling my guilt.

"This one doesn't have a chip," says the Enforcer attempting to scan Glitch's implant. She tries a second time, but still can't get a read. Another guard takes the reader from her and tries again as if the chip will manifest itself by scanning the same location on her left forearm, in the same way, a third time.

"That's impossible," she says. She twists Glitch's arm back and forth, running the scanner across her skin like it will help them find something that's not there. I wonder how Glitch got into the Academy without having an implant. They're used for everything, so she must have some kind of identification implant somewhere.

Maybe it's just not in the Enforcer system. That's more likely. Glitch spent her entire life learning how to stay invisible. She wouldn't put something in her body that ties her with a public alias if it wasn't necessary. She's smarter than that.

"We'll figure it out later," says the guard. "We need to move them inside."

They lead us into one of the cinder-block buildings next to the road. My first impression is it's filthy with yellowing paint, linoleum tile, and shop lights tacked haphazardly to the ceiling. It doesn't look anything like the Academy. Then again, I doubt this building has ever been photographed or on camera. This is the side of the law no one sees.

A younger Enforcer sprints down the hall. He doesn't look much older than the teenage driver who was arrested a few minutes ago. "There's an emergency at the Academy. We have orders to report downtown to provide backup." His pupils are blown wide in terror. I'd bet good money he hasn't been through a real emergency since taking his post.

"What are we supposed to do with them?" One of our guards asks. The kid shrugs, his eyes flicking between us.

"The boss didn't say."

The guard leading Miles sighs. "We'll put them in lock up and figure it out when we get back."

Our group navigates down a few dimly lit hallways. The Enforcers we pass are rushing for the exits with weapons in tow. Whatever is happening at the Academy must be severe if they have orders to leave the border gate with minimal staff.

"What's happening at the Academy?" Glitch asks the young Enforcer.

"There was an explosion of some sort," says the kid, raking a hand through his hair.

"Shut up," snaps my guard. "Go with the others." The kid's face turns white. He whirls around and sprints down the hall, back the way he came. We're led down a side hall to an unmarked door. Inside, there's a heavy wooden table and two chairs. It looks like some sort of interrogation room. The guards close the door behind us. I can hear the lock engaging and muffled footsteps walking away. Glitch sits on top of the table, resting her feet on one of the chairs

"What do you think happened at the Academy?" I ask, sitting beside her. She has bruise marks in the shape of finger-prints beginning to form on her forearm where the Enforcers searched for her implant.

Under any other circumstance, I would be happy if the Academy went up in flames; however, I have no idea if Ash and Roy are being held there. I hope the explosion the kid mentioned wasn't targeting the holding cells.

Miles tries the door, but it doesn't move. He throws his shoulder into it a few times before giving up. He pulls out the second chair and sits in front of us. He rests his forearms on his thighs. It takes me a moment to realize he's staring at the tiny drop of blood just above his wrist that started this fiasco.

I nudge Miles's knee with my foot to get his attention. He scrunches his eyebrows, causing a crease to appear across his forehead. I've already decided I will not yell at him for getting us captured. What's done is done. Now, we just have to find a way out of this mess.

"Do you have any contacts in the Enforcers who can bust us out?" I ask. Miles shakes his head. Glitch stops pacing and crosses her arms, tapping her fingers against her left bicep.

"No one through the Syndicate, but if we're lucky, maybe someone from our recruitment class will recognize us and make a case on our behalf."

"They wouldn't risk it," I say.

Miles shakes his head. "That isn't a plan. That's hoping for a damn miracle."

"I'm just brainstorming here," Glitch grumbles.

The door to the interrogation room opens, and an Enforcer steps into the room. He closes the door most of the way behind him, leaving it cracked so the lock doesn't engage. His dark hair is buzzed close to his scalp. He has a strong jaw, kind brown eyes, and a dark skin tone. He looks familiar, but I don't know if I've seen him before or if I'm desperate enough to believe I recognize him that my mind is starting to manufacture a relationship that isn't there.

"We have to go," he says. None of us move to stand up. I exchange a look with Miles. The man has a rifle slung across his back. I wonder if we can overpower him and make a run for it...

"I'm a friend of Ash and Elle. My name is Joel," he says.

"Prove it," says Glitch. Joel sighs.

"How?" he asks. "What do you want to know?"

Miles stands up and stretches. "What's the worse he can do? Tell the Enforcers we're with the Syndicate? We're already living our worst-case scenario. Let's go."

He has a point.

"The facility is mostly empty. Everyone is on their way to the Academy. Follow me, keep your heads down, and don't stop for anyone," says Joel. He looks at each of us to make sure we understand before he opens the door into the hallway.

It's chaos.

As we jog through the facility, the Enforcers we pass are too wrapped up barking orders or following them to pay much attention to us. We're still wearing our uniforms. People will see what they want to see unless they expect otherwise. Lucky for us, not one of them is as vigilant as the guards at the gate. Joel leads us outside to a vehicle that looks a lot like the one we rode into the city. When I see a scratch above the back right wheel, I realize it is the exact vehicle we arrived in.

Joel tosses Miles the keys. "We're on the other side of the border wall. The parking lot gate is already open. Make sure you switch cars before you get to where you're going. We reinstated the tracking on this one."

"Why are you helping us?" I ask.

"Ash and Elle were in my recruitment class at the Academy. I was there when Ash was arrested. I've seen how Jace treats him. It doesn't take a genius to guess what happened to the late director." Joel shrugs. "You guys better go, I need to get to the Academy before anyone asks questions."

Joel leaves us, jogging across the parking lot to join a group of his colleagues preparing to leave. Miles gets behind the wheel. I take the passenger seat this time and Glitch sits behind me. He backs out of the parking space. I hold my breath as we pass through the gate leading out of the parking lot, but no one so much glances at us. Miles sighs as soon as we're clear.

Glitch cackles. "My idea was solid."

Miles and I stare at her.

"An Enforcer classmate rescued us," Glitch continues, spelling it out for us.

"Technically, it wasn't our classmate," I say. Glitch glares at me until I can't keep a straight face anymore. I burst out laughing.

"You guys suck," mumbles Glitch, but she's smiling too.

Miles drives about ten minutes into the city before parking the stolen vehicle on a street with no cameras. We strip off the uniforms to reveal the street clothes we kept on underneath and leave them in the car.

"Now what?" I ask.

"We're still a few blocks away. We'll have to walk to make sure we're not being followed," says Miles. He takes the lead, setting his pace at a brisk jog. I can't remember the last time I did this much physical activity.

My training with Ash made me a decent runner, but I haven't kept up with my training since I left the city. There's a stitch in my side and my breath is coming out in pants. Glitch and Miles aren't fairing much better, but we need to put as much distance between us and the abandoned vehicle as possible before the Enforcers realize we're gone.

I have no idea where we're going. We talked about it on our way into the city. Glitch was all for setting up shop in one of the Syndicate safe houses, but Miles wasn't sure which locations were still secure after the Enforcer raid at the farmhouse. He was worried some of the captured Syndicate members might have cracked under interrogation or traded information for entry into a rival crew.

So, we landed on hiding out with a "friend" Miles said we could trust. We stay with his friend until Miles can determine which of his safe houses are secure. It will also give him time to find out how many of his people made it back into the city. That's where our temporary truce ends. Glitch and I will decide how to infiltrate the Academy and Miles will work on rebuilding his inner circle. We'll be making it up as we go along. We turn another corner, and I stumble on the curb when I recognize the street. The familiar red awning of a long-closed take-out restaurant beckons to us.

I pound to a stop. "No way," I say. Miles stops a few feet ahead of me with Glitch at his side. "The store owner is your friend?"

"We can trust Otto," says Miles, watching my expression with a quiet intensity that says he's not sure if I'm going to bolt or go inside.

I'm not sure, either.

"I've barely had two full conversations with the man in the last five years that don't consist of grunts or head nods. What makes you think he won't turn us in?"

Miles presses his lips together, appearing instantly uncomfortable.

"Otto is with the Syndicate," says Glitch. Miles shoots her a sharp look. "What? It's not like that's the biggest secret you've kept from Wren. She deserves to know what we're getting into."

Grams, Miles, my mom, my dad...is there anyone in my life who isn't Syndicate leadership or protecting someone who is? I'm glad Glitch stepped in to call Miles out, but how many times has she let his lies slide? Just like that, the fragile trust Miles has begun to earn back disintegrates.

I push past Miles and shove open the flier-covered door to Otto's shop. It looks the same as the last time I was here. The take-out menus above the counter are cracked or missing entirely. The shelving units are still stacked precariously with supplies. Even Otto is where I left him last, sitting behind the counter scrolling through his tablet.

If I had to guess, I'd say Otto is in his seventies. He wears wire-framed glasses that appear oddly delicate on his hooked nose. His trademark polo has every button at the collar undone, showcasing a plume of chest hair that makes everyone uncomfortable except for him. He has his hand under the counter, probably reaching for his stashed weapon. I'm about to tell him to calm down when I see a tower of canned goods at the end of an aisle comprised of tuna, peaches, and asparagus.

I pick up a can of peaches and slam it down on the counter in front of Otto.

"Where were these when I ate beans three meals a day?" I growl. Otto removes his hand from under the counter and offers me a lazy shrug that only makes me want to throttle him more.

"Wow, I've never seen someone so worked up over canned goods before," whispers Glitch behind me. I hear Miles snickering, and I just about lose it. Maybe it's unreasonable to be this upset, but I don't care. Otto seems to take in Glitch and Miles standing behind me for the first time. He frowns.

"You bringing trouble with you?" Otto asks.

Miles shakes his head. "No one followed us."

Otto grunts. "This way." He gets off the stool behind the counter. It lets out a squeal as it swivels back into the forward-facing position.

"We're not done talking about this," I snap, snatching the can of peaches off the counter to take it with me.

What? I earned it.

Otto raises an eyebrow but doesn't tell me to put it back. He walks around the counter to the back of the store and unlocks a door I haven't noticed before revealing a narrow stairwell.

"You guys go ahead. I need to close the store, and then I'll be up," says Otto.

The stairwell is claustrophobia-inducing. I'm not a large person, but even my shoulders almost brush up against either side. When Miles opens the door at the top of the staircase to reveal a fully furnished apartment, I wonder how Otto managed to get the full-sized couch up here. Did they lift it in with a crane before they put the roof on?

In complete contrast to the chaos of the general store below, Otto's apartment is immaculate. The carpet and walls are coated in fresh white paint. The windows are adorned with bright pink curtains. A pink couch with frilly armrest protectors is the focal point of the room. It's not what I expected from Otto.

I follow Miles further into the room. On the end table, there's a picture frame with Otto standing beside a beautiful woman with raven hair. He has his hand wrapped around her waist, his fingers resting on her hip. They're both beaming at the camera. I wonder if that's his wife.

"Yes, she died ten years ago," says Otto, appearing in the doorway behind us. I realized I spoke my thoughts aloud and blush.

"Sorry."

"It's life." He shrugs and walks to the kitchen.

Okay then...

"Coffee?" Otto asks. I guess we're back to communicating with grunts and one-word answers now. Everyone says yes to the coffee before taking a seat on the frilly pink disaster that is the couch. Glitch grabs the remote and turns on the TV.

"I want to see what's going on at the Academy-" Glitch's voice breaks off. Ash, Liam, and Roy are on the screen. They're handcuffed to a horizontal bar in the Council courtroom. Aside from the Axton mansion and the Academy atrium, it's one of the most recognizable government rooms. Glitch turns up the volume so we can hear the voice-over.

"...earlier today. Please watch with caution. The following broadcast contains graphic images that may disturb some viewers," says the reporter. The camera zooms in on Jace Axton in the center of the courtroom.

"Yesterday, the Enforcers raided the Syndicate headquarters," says Jace. "We killed their leader and ended their operations permanently."

"Didn't know I was dead," mutters Miles. Glitch shushes him.

"He's lying," says Roy. "The leader of the Syndicate escaped." The camera pans to him, yanking against his restraints.

He looks terrible. One of his eyes is swollen shut. The rest of his skin is a mottled mess of cuts and bruises. Glitch lets out a choked noise, covering her mouth. I drape my arm around her shoulders and pull her against me.

We watch in rapt silence as Trip, Liam, and Roy call Jace out in front of the Council. All the while, Jace appears to grow more livid by the minute. Ash gives the Council a chance to intervene, but, as always, they disappoint. What is it going to take for them to step up?

"Jace Axton killed the director. He accused me of the murder. That's the truth," says Ash.

That's when Jace loses it and pulls a gun.

I see Roy go down, and Glitch screams. I hold her even tighter. I can't take my eyes off the screen. People start rushing out of the room. The camera is jostled a few times before it freezes. It's clear that the camera operator is no longer at their station.

The floor-to-ceiling windows lining one wall explode inwards. I watch as Ash shakes Roy, trying to get him to wake up. I know it's futile. I don't see Roy lying there lifeless; I see Robbie. Tears stream down my face, but I wipe them away with the hand that's not holding Glitch. I have to see what happens.

Smoke starts filling the courtroom and black-clad figures appear through the broken window, heading towards our friends. The broadcast switches back to a news desk. "The assailants were identified as Syndicate extremists targeting Council members. Luckily, no Council members were harmed. "

The Council-funded anchor continues to spout whatever lies he has been told to say on live air, but it doesn't matter. Jace Axton killed Roy. An unknown group of people broke into the most secure room in the world. I have no idea what happened to Ash, Liam, or Trip.

"What was that?" Miles asks, sounding as shell-shocked as I feel. Otto clears his throat. He sets three cups of coffee on the table in front of us. Glitch is wailing. Her head is tucked into the crook of my neck, and her tears are soaking my shirt. I just feel numb.

"I recognize that gear. The smoke bombs and the equipment used by those masked people. I sold it to them," says Otto.

"What do you mean?" I ask.

"Otto doesn't just run a corner store," explains Miles, his voice sounding as lifeless as I feel. "He manages a big portion of the Syndicate supply chain. If you need weapons, ammunition, or smoke screens, then Otto is your guy. Who did you sell that to?"

Otto studies Miles, his eyes flicking to the door behind him. For a second, I wonder if he will make a run for it.

"Look, I sold that gear before I knew what she did to you and Marcia," he trails off.

Miles's eyes narrow. "You sold it to Rook."

Otto reluctantly nods. Miles curses.

"Can you arrange a meeting with her?" I ask.

"I guess so. I can't promise she'll respond," says Otto.

I came to the city to rescue my friends, but that goal changed when Jace killed Roy. A man like that cannot be in the director's seat. As much as I want to get back to Grams and Ariel, I have to find Ash. I have to convince him to go after the director's seat. It's the only way I'll ever be able to bring my daughter home.

Chapter 9

Ash

Trip is the leader of the surge crew. I didn't see that one coming. After he dropped that bomb on us, Rook's phone rang. Trip followed her into one of the rooms off the main living space and they shut the door. I hear them talking, but it's too faint to make out the words.

It makes sense that Rook would want to get some things squared away after losing her boss for a few months. I wonder how much administrative work running a drug operation takes? I'm not sure I want to know the answer to that question.

Liam sits on the couch with his feet on the coffee table. He's wearing a borrowed black tank top and ripped, dark wash jeans tucked into thick combat boots. It's a stark contrast to the Enforcer uniform he normally wears. Before he disappeared with Rook, Trip threw a pile of clothes and towels on the kitchen table. He told us to lose the prison jumpsuits and take a shower. I ended up with a combat green t-shirt, black jeans, and boots identical to Liam's. I took the leather jacket as well. I think it was meant for Liam to wear over the tank top, but his shoulders are too broad.

Liam may look relaxed to an outsider, but I know him too well to fall for the ruse. The last time he was around the surge crew, he ended up locked in a cage before being tortured and then pumped full of the drug sharing the crew's name. That's not something you get over. I can tell Trip's lack of transparency is making Liam's anxiety worse.

We talked briefly about leaving the safe house while Trip was distracted, but it didn't take long before we realized that was not an option. We haven't exactly been told we're prisoners; however, I doubt the guards downstairs would let us walk out the front door without alerting Trip.

I have no idea where we would go if we did manage to sneak out. After Don's betrayal, I'm sure my secret apartment isn't much of a secret anymore. The Enforcers are probably swarming the city looking for us, so it's not like we can drive around until we find a new hideout.

Trip opens the door to the living room with Rook right behind him.

"We're leaving," says Trip.

"Where are we going?" asks Liam, getting off the couch.

"The Iron Maiden."

"What's that?" Liam asks.

"Ask your friend. He's been there before," says Rooks, gesturing at me. It takes me a minute to understand what she's referring to.

"You mean the bar where you held a gun to Wren's head?" I ask with a scowl. Rook doesn't flinch, but I see a muscle near her eye twitch. When I took Wren out on her first Enforcer patrol, Rook and a handful of surge crew members lured one of our riot bots into an alley. Rook and her goons threatened us. She ordered Wren to dismantle the tracking on the lead riot bot. I don't have fond memories of the place.

"Yeah, that's the one," she says. "Our crew owns it. I've set up a meeting with some old friends of yours."

That gets my attention.

"What friends?" Liam growls.

"Miles O'Reilly," says Trip.

So, Miles escaped the Enforcer raid on the Syndicate head-quarters. Why would he come back to the city? More impor-tantly, did he bring Wren with him? If he did, he's an idiot. This is the worst place for her to be. Everything about this situation screams at me to run the other way. If I were smart, I'd listen to my gut.

If Trip meets with the current Syndicate leader, it's safe to assume a fight will break out. I doubt Miles will play nice with Rook. She was there when Robbie was killed. Even if Liam can confirm it wasn't directly her fault, I don't think he'll write it off and move on. I wouldn't. Rook is the reason Robbie was there to begin with. Even so, if there's a chance Wren is with Miles, then I have to be at that meeting.

"I'm going," I say. I shove my chair back and shrug into the leather jacket. I glance at Liam.

"I'm in," he sighs.

Trip leads the way downstairs and into the alley. We pile into a beat-up, four-door car parked next to the van we ar-rived in. Trip starts the engine and waits for the guards to roll back the fence before gunning it onto the street.

"Don't we have to worry about drones?" I ask.

"My people have been tracking them. They went down this street five minutes ago. We have a few more minutes before they make another round," says Trip. I lean back, readjusting the seat belt to get more comfortable. That's when I notice something in the pocket of my borrowed jacket. I pull out a half-empty pack of cigarettes and a lighter. I stare at them for a moment before Liam snatches both of them out of my palm. He rolls down the window and chucks them outside.

"We need to stop for chewing gum," says Liam.

Trip raises an eyebrow at us in the rearview mirror. "We don't have time."

Liam curses at Trip. Rook opens the glove box and scrounges around. She tosses a pack of cinnamon chewing gum into my lap. "Sorry about that," she says. "I quit a few years ago. I should have told my guys to check the pockets before they brought you clothes."

"Thanks," I mumble. She shrugs, returning her eyes to the road. I open a stick of gum and shove it in my mouth. Trip turns on the radio and cranks the volume up, effectively drowning out the argument Liam is trying to start.

This is going to be a long night.

At one point, we catch a glimpse of a drone a few streets over. Luckily, we spotted it before it spotted us. Trip turned in the opposite direction, making a big circle back to our original route to avoid intersecting it. Before long, we pull up in front of The Iron Maiden.

I recognize the flickering neon sign on the front door advertising a beer I haven't heard of. The windows are barred, and the glass is cracked underneath. A large red awning hangs over the front entryway...I think it used to be red. Now, it's more of a pale pink with illegible gold font. Trip gets out of the car without turning off the engine. A kid runs over to open Rook's door for her.

"Bring the keys to me after you park it," says Trip, stepping aside to let the boy into the driver's seat. The boy nods eagerly, taking the keys from Trip. Trip sees me watching the exchange. "We keep the cars in a garage a few blocks away, so we don't draw too much attention."

The front door is closed, but the music inside the bar is so loud I can make out the lyrics from here.

"You're not worried about the music drawing attention?" I ask.

"Enforcers don't care about a bunch of poor grunts drinking and listening to music. If they start seeing cars or anything expensive, then they get interested. If you own a car, chances are you're important enough in the Syndicate to get paid well." Trip shrugs and walks ahead of us. He's right, but I'm surprised by his insight. He holds the front door open for Rook before gesturing for Liam and me to follow her. I stumble on the crooked concrete step on my way inside.

The place is an absolute madhouse compared to the last time we were here. There are people packed shoulder to shoulder next to a makeshift stage I don't think was there before. The lead singer belts the lyrics to a hit I recognize from about a decade ago. It almost sounds like the original.

Rook leads us to a red-vinyl booth in the corner. It's currently occupied, but as soon as they recognize Rook, they get up to offer us their seats. A waitress sets a round of beers on the table without being asked. Trip passes us both a drink before taking one for himself. I leave mine untouched in front of me.

"Where is Miles?" I ask.

Trip shrugs. "We're a bit early. Just enjoy the music. I'm sure he'll be here soon."

I scowl, crossing my arms and leaning back against the booth. I don't want to enjoy the music. I want to know why Miles is back in the city and I want to know if Wren and Ariel are with him. Neither of those questions involves sitting here drinking with these idiots. The band gets impossibly louder, the crowd singing along with them.

"Do you think it's frowned on to unplug their amp?" asks Liam, following my gaze. I laugh and turn to say...I had no idea what I was going to say.

Every coherent thought exits my brain the second Wren walks into the room.

Her wild brown hair is in a messy bun on top of her head. Despite her disheveled clothes, she's standing tall with her shoulders thrown back - ready to conquer the world. I practically crawl over Liam to get out of the booth. I shove through the crowd. People curse and give me dirty looks, but I couldn't care less. I wrap my arms around Wren and pull her against my chest in a bone-crushing hug.

"Hey, back off." Miles forces himself between us, shoving me away, so I stumble back a few steps. I didn't see him. My focus was entirely on Wren. He looks healthier than the last time I saw him - more alive. He steps in front of Wren and sizes me up. "Who are you?" My eyes widen. I can't believe Miles doesn't recognize me. Then again, why would he? The last time I saw him, I had recently had a haircut. A decent meal. A shower.

At this point, I'm almost rocking a full-grown beard.

I hope I didn't freak Wren out. She probably thought I was some psycho rushing up to her.

I shouldn't have worried. Wren steps around Miles and wraps her arms around my waist. I hug her back, holding her so closely I swear I can feel her heart beating. After the dinner party at the Axton mansion, I was terrified she had been killed in the raid. I say a silent prayer of gratitude to the universe for protecting them. After a few seconds, she pulls away far enough to prop her chin on my chest. She looks up at me with her arms still around my waist, her deep green eyes filled with warmth.

"Hi," I say because I've lost the ability to speak like a normal human.

Hi? Jesus.

"Hi," she says with a grin. She reaches up to brush a stray strand of hair out of my eyes but stops at the last minute. I see her hesitation, her uncertainty. It's not unwarranted. I kissed her and then bailed to go back to the Academy. We said our goodbyes when Robbie was killed. I haven't had a chance to apologize, and it's not like we've had an opportunity to have the what-are-we conversation. That's her decision. Whatever the verdict is, I'm here for it.

I weave my fingers through Wren's, so we're holding hands before I offer a handshake to Miles. "Sorry for startling you, man," I say. Miles stares at my extended hand before looking pointedly at my other hand, which is still intertwined with Wren's.

"Where's Rook?" Miles asks, ignoring my attempt to make peace between us. I sigh.

"She's in the corner booth." I point over my shoulder with my thumb at the booth in the corner. Miles pushes past me, knocking his shoulder into mine. For the first time, I notice Glitch. She was standing behind Miles. I only had eyes for Wren when they walked in, so I missed her the first time. Her eyes are puffy and red from crying. She looks wrecked.

"I'm sorry," I say. Glitch's eyes come to mine. "About Roy. It was my fault. I should have given Jace what he wanted."

Glitch shakes her head. "You did the right thing, but do me a favor. Don't talk to me for a bit, yeah? I need some time to process it. When I look at you, I see him."

Ouch.

My heart cracks at her words, but I nod and step aside so Glitch can walk in front of us to the booth. I wonder if Wren feels the same way about Robbie and me? Miles is leaning over the table when we get through the crowd, his fingers clawing at the wood surface. He's in Rook's face. They've been here five minutes, and things are already going south.

"There's plenty of time to yell at each other later. Sit down before my guys drag you out of here," demands Trip. Miles looks like he's going to throw a punch, but he huffs and plops in the seat next to Liam. The three of them scoot around the bench to make room for us. The waitress brings more drinks. Wren sits beside me, sliding so close that her thigh rests against mine. I'm glad. I need the reminder that she's here - that she's not just a figment of my imagination.

"Give me one good reason why I shouldn't kill you," growls Miles. He's glaring at Rook like he already has his hands around her throat.

"I can give you three," says Trip. He holds up his fingers to tick them off. "One, you were searched when you came in here. I know you don't have a weapon, and Rook is trained in hand-to-hand combat. You would be picking a fight you can't win."

"Two," interrupts Rook, "I didn't kill your brother. Someone overrode my control of the bots. They were firing at me too. Why would I have the bots aim at my people if I could order them around?"

"Three," Trip adds without missing a beat, "this is a surge crew bar. You're outnumbered, so sit down and shut up."

Liam clears his throat. "She's telling the truth. Commander Harper had me arrested and took control of the bots on Jace's orders."

Wren places her hand on Miles's bicep. He glares at her. "Let's hear them out," suggests Wren.

"You do a lot of talking for someone who isn't in charge," mutters Glitch, observing Trip.

"He's the leader of the surge crew," I say.

Trip glares at me. "I suggest you lower your voice before I have my men drag you out of here."

I roll my eyes. Miles starts laughing, but Wren continues to study Trip. She sees what Miles doesn't. She has met Trip before. She's seen the quiet calculation behind his joking demeanor. The more you think about it, the more sense it makes.

The surge crew is massive. They have operations in every major city in the country. That also means they have enemies in every city. Wherever there is power, there are people who want to take it. By playing a runner, Trip could easily keep his ear to the ground within his operation to weed out the competition. Giving Rook the leadership title gave him the freedom to do whatever he wanted under the radar.

"What does that make you?" Glitch asks Rook.

"His second in command," Rook says.

"Who knows about your true identity?" asks Miles, his laughter fading. I think he's slowly realizing Trip is serious.

"Outside of the people at this table? No one," says Trip.

"Why?" asks Glitch.

Trip shrugs. "If you act like an idiot, people don't expect anything else," says Trip. "They tell you things they wouldn't say otherwise. They drop their guard."

"Then why trust us with your secret?" Liam asks.

"Because we need your help to take out the new director," says Trip. He clasps his hands and sets them on the table. "A few months ago, Jace Axton approached Rook about setting up a meeting with Marcia Navarro. In exchange, he would give her a seat on the Council and leadership of the Syndicate."

Wren blanches.

"Who's Marcia Navarro?" I ask, squeezing Wren's hand under the table. The name sounds familiar, but I can't place it right away.

"She was the leader of the Syndicate," says Trip.

"My mom," Wren says at the same time.

Wren's mom was the leader of the Syndicate? I look at Wren from the corner of my eye, but she's still watching Trip. She squeezes my hand in a discreet plea for my silence.

"Did you know when we were working together?" I whisper. Wren sighs and looks at me with a frown. I know it's not the most sensitive question to ask right now, but I need to know if Wren played me the whole time. Was there anything between us that was real?

Wren seems to understand what I'm asking and her eyes soften. She shakes her head. "No, I found out after we left the city. I didn't know Miles was her partner or that he developed the 8-Bit app. Grams and my dad knew. It turns out there are a lot of things I was clueless about." She shoots an angry look at Miles.

Miles ignores her, continuing his conversation with Trip. "The leadership seat wasn't Jace's to offer."

Trip shrugs. "It was the best shot I had at taking it."

"Family drama aside," Liam clears his throat to interrupt the conversation before it can turn into a fight, "why are you okay with painting a target on your back as the leader of the surge crew?" he asks Rook.

Rook shrugs. "It's a necessary sacrifice."

"You make it sound like you're doing this city a favor by protecting that idiot." Liam inclines his chin at Trip. "What's in it for you?"

Rook claps her hands on the table and leans forward. "Look, I know you hate the surge crew. You have every right to. Trip and I weren't around when you were captured a few years ago, but some of the older members were. I'm not naive. I know what the old surge crew stood for, but I'm not them."

Liam's expression darkens. He takes the first sip of his drink, his eyes glazing over with the memory of horrors I can't begin to fathom.

"What Rook is trying to say is that we don't lock anyone in cages and torture them for information. We're looking to get out of the surge business altogether," says Trip.

"Why would you stop producing your most profitable product?" Glitch asks.

"Because I care about the grunt sectors. I grew up watching the Syndicate become the only option for people like me. The Syndicate was great at first, but then Marcia got greedy. She started rewarding crews for being rich, strong, and powerful. The problem was, it didn't matter how they got that power. The surge crew became as bad as the Council and Enforcers, just in a different way. I joined when I was old enough and quietly worked my way to the top because I knew the only way I could go up against Marcia was to have a platform too large to ignore."

Rook nods. "Our goal was never to run a drug operation. We wanted to force the Council and the Syndicate to talk. When Jace Axton contacted us, we decided to negotiate with him because Marcia wasn't willing to listen to us. Jace asked for a meeting with Marcia and I agreed."

"It was a trap," says Trip, his expression darkening. "Jace killed Marcia and Rook barely escaped."

Rook looks at Wren. "I'm sorry for your loss. I didn't know Marcia had a family. If there were any other way to reason with her, I would have taken it. I didn't think Jace would kill her."

Wren looks like she's barely holding it together. She doesn't respond to Rook's apology. She just continues peeling the corner of the label off of her beer bottle. I glance between Rook and Trip, thinking over everything Trip has said. I wonder if he's playing us like he did when he sent Wren and me on a surge delivery that ended with us facing a firing squad. He's impossible to read. I think he's telling the truth, but I've been tricked so many times I can't believe him.

"I have a proposal," says Wren. Trip gives her a small smile. He offered Wren a job a year ago as a mechanic for his crew. That means more now that we know Trip is in charge. Instead of sending Rook or another of his people, Trip personally went to Jimmy's Auto to seek out Wren. That speaks volumes of her skill. It's easy to see he respects her. "I want your help to remove Jace from the director's seat."

My eyebrows shoot up.

"Not what I expected you to say," chuckles Trip. "Why would I do that? I failed once." He leans back in his chair, amusement tugging at his lips.

"Because Jace promised you something he couldn't deliver on. You'll do it for revenge."

Trip's mouth tilts up in a smile. He leans forward, so his forearms are resting on the table. "Revenge is nice but unnecessary. I meant what I said. My goal is to get the Council and the Syndicate to talk to each other. If you can promise I'll get that chance, I'm in."

"I can't promise you that," says Wren.

Trip points at me. "He can. Ash is the rightful heir to the director seat. In essence, he is the Council."

"What are you getting at?" I ask.

Trip meets my gaze. "I want Miles to turn over leadership of the Syndicate."

"You're insane," growls Miles.

"Let him finish," Wren snaps, glaring at her friend. Trip just looks amused.

"Make me the Syndicate's leader, and I'll help you overthrow Jace. Once Ash is in power, I get a seat on the Council. The Syndicate and grunts will finally get a voice. Miles can be one of my advisers. He will still manage the 8-Bit app but report to me."

"Let me get this straight. You'll help us stage a coupe, and then you'll be fine with accepting a Council seat while Ash has the director title?" asks Liam.

"Like I said, my goal isn't to sit in the director's seat. My goal is to unite the Syndicate and the Council to create a better system for grunts," says Trip.

"Then why not let me stay in charge of the Syndicate?" asks Miles.

"People don't trust you. They need a leader to rally behind," says Glitch. Miles's mouth drops open with a look of betrayal and disbelief.

"She's right," says Rook. "After headquarters was raided, a lot of Miles's people joined the surge crew. The grunts will support a leader they believe can protect them. Miles isn't that person right now."

"Do you think we're going to buy that?" Liam asks.

"I agree with the pansy," snarls Miles.

"Can you and Rook give us a minute?" I ask Trip.

Trip studies me for a moment before sliding out of the booth. Rook follows him. They walk to the bar, far enough away that the music will mask our conversation. I lean across the table anyways.

"We need to get on the same page," I say.

Liam crosses his arms. "I don't trust them, but we need their resources to overthrow Jace. I say we agree to Trip's terms, but watch our backs."

"Look, I came back to the city to bust Roy out of prison. I'm planning to leave the first chance I get. This isn't my fight anymore. I'm out," says Glitch. Her shoulders sag, a far cry from the spitfire recruit who was wreaking havoc at the Academy.

"I can't believe you're considering this," says Miles. He looks at Liam with an arched brow. "Aren't you an Enforcer? What happened to law and order?"

Liam snorts. "You're one to talk."

I cut them off before their conversation can devolve into bickering. "Let everyone say their piece before we discuss."

"I agree with Liam," says Wren. She glances at Miles but doesn't look apologetic about her decision. "Jace has to go, and Trip's offer is the best we'll get."

Miles slams his palm on the table. Wren jumps. "I can't believe you're siding with the pansies. Think about Ariel and Grams."

So much for waiting.

"I am thinking about them," Wren growls, matching his tone. "I know how this plays out if we don't do anything. The city becomes a war zone. There are more bots in the streets killing innocent people like Robbie. The grunt neighborhoods become uninhabitable. I can't bring Ariel and Grams home to that."

Miles scowls, but he doesn't rebuke what she's saying. Wren has a point, and he knows it.

I nod. "I'm with Liam and Wren."

Miles slams his open palm down on the table so hard the bottles rattle. "So, that's it then? I just hand over the Syndicate to that thug?" He points at Trip, who takes that as his cue to return to the table. "Let me out," snarls Miles. We slide out of the booth to let Miles out. As soon as he's free, he takes off through the crowd heading for the door.

"We have a deal," I say, offering Trip my hand. He accepts my handshake.

"Miles doesn't seem like he's willing to give up the Syndicate leadership seat," says Trip.

"I'll talk to him," says Glitch somewhere behind me. She takes off after Miles, disappearing into the crowd on the dance floor.

"Then it's settled," says Trip. "There are guest rooms above the bar you can stay in. It's late. We can discuss this more tomorrow." He gives us directions on how to get there and tells us which rooms to take before disappearing into the crowd with Rook.

"I'm going to head upstairs," says Liam.

"Okay," I say. "I'll be right up."

I watch Liam head for the stairway Trip directed us to. I'm alone with Wren at the table. Well, as alone as you can be with another person in a crowded bar. She grabs her left elbow with her right hand. She looks nervous. I don't think she knows how to act around me anymore.

"I should go talk to Miles," she says. Her voice is so low it's hard to hear her over the music, so I lean closer. Despite her words, she makes no move to chase after her friend.

"I'm glad you're alright," I say. "Are Ariel and Ms. Parker with you?"

Wren shakes her head. "They're safe outside of the city."

"That's good."

"Yeah."

I don't remember things ever being this awkward between us before. Even when we were yelling at each other, it was better than pretending to be two strangers meeting for the first time. The band breaks into a haunting, slow melody that has the entire room swaying on their feet. I offer my hand to Wren.

"Dance with me?" I ask.

"I don't know…" Wren starts, trailing off. There are a million ways to finish that sentence: I don't know where we stand. I don't know that I can trust you. I don't know if this is a good idea.

All are fair points, but it doesn't matter.

I'll work to dismantle every hesitation she has until she has no choice but to give me a second chance.

"We'll figure it out together," I say.

Wren gives me a small smile. "The dancing or the mess Byron left behind?"

"Both."

I grab her hands before she can object and place them on the back of my neck. I drop my hands to her waist. To my surprise, Wren wraps her arms around my neck and closes the distance between us. I breathe her in. Her fingers toy with the hair at the base of my neck as the singer goes on about unfulfilled promises and a relationship that was over before it began. He talks about what ifs, the road not taken, and second chances. Wren leans her head against my chest and lets out a contented sigh that I feel down to my bones.

Being here with Wren feels like coming home.

Chapter 10

Wren

I can't believe this is real. I rest my head on Ash's chest to hear his heartbeat. I didn't think I'd ever see him again when I left the city. I need the reminder that he's here and he's alive.

That this isn't a dream.

Ash doesn't look like the polished Enforcer he was when we first met. His hair, buzzed short on the sides and cut longer on the top, has started to grow out. The top is long enough that a single strand falls over his forehead. Somehow, it still works for him.

He's wearing ripped black jeans, a dark green shirt, and a leather jacket that smells faintly like cigarette smoke. He looks edgy and nothing like himself. I bet the clothes are borrowed. I doubt he had a chance to go shopping after breaking out of the Academy.

As the song ends, Ash leans back to see my face, but we don't break contact. His hands are still on my waist, his thumbs brushing over my hips. My hands are still loosely around his neck, my fingers toying with his hair.

"I haven't had my hair this long since I was a kid," Ash chuckles.

"It's...different," I say.

"I'm cutting it at the first available opportunity."

"Thank God," I say with faux relief.

"Hey, it's not that bad!"

"Really? Are you sure you're not here with the band?" I ask, allowing my hands to trail down his chest to the leather jacket. I tug on the sides as if straightening the material.

"Positive. I'm completely tone deaf," he tries to sound serious, but his voice comes out breathless instead. Ash brushes a stray piece of hair out of my face, tucking it behind my ear. He must see something in my expression that makes him pause. "Is this weird?" he asks. He's close enough that I can feel his breath on my lips.

"It should be, but it isn't," I whisper. Ash's eyes flick to my lips. For a second, I think he's going to kiss me. I *want* him to kiss me. Ash brushes his lips against my forehead instead. When he pulls away, I try not to let my disappointment show.

"I need to find Miles," I ramble. I can't meet his eyes. "Talk to you later."

I bolt.

Talk to you later? Seriously?

I literally run for the door.

What is wrong with me?

I should be focused on staying alive, but Ash's lukewarm reception bothers me. My feelings for him haven't changed, but I wonder if he still feels the same. As the band kicks into a fast-paced dance song, I tighten my ponytail and shove through the hoard of gyrating bodies.

We're going to war.

Grams and Ariel are counting on me, so dying isn't an option. If toppling a government doesn't get either of us killed, then Ash will take over the director seat. He'll be busy negotiating with the Council and the Syndicate. I'm not sure where Ariel and I fit into that picture. Besides, Ash left my apartment after Ariel talked to him about her new toy dinosaur during our video call. Maybe he doesn't want to be with someone with a kid?

If that's the case, screw him.

By the time I push through the front door of the Iron Maiden, I'm thoroughly irritated. I should have gone after Miles as soon as Trip left us, but I wanted to spend a few more minutes with Ash. I take a deep breath of cool night air. A few people are smoking on the sidewalk and chatting in small groups, but for the most part the party is contained inside. I spot Miles and Glitch down the street. Glitch is gesturing wildly, and Miles looks like he's a second away from storming off again.

"I can't give Trip what he wants," hisses Miles. "Marcia sacrificed everything to make the Syndicate what it is today. I won't allow him to destroy everything she built."

"I hate to break it to you, genius, but you don't run the Syndicate anymore. Trip does. Asking you to give up the leadership title was a formality. He did it to be respectful, but he didn't need to," says Glitch.

"I can't believe you're defending him! His partner killed my little brother," roars Miles.

"No, she didn't!" Glitch snaps back, matching his volume. Miles has a whole foot on her, but she somehow manages to get in his face to make herself heard. "Liam confirmed an Enforcer commander was responsible for Robbie's death. Stop blaming Rook for something that isn't her fault. Trip and Ash have a once-in-a-lifetime opportunity here to unite the country. The timing and the people aren't ideal. I get it. You don't have to like them, but can you at least see the value in letting this play out?"

Miles opens his mouth to shout at Glitch, but I make myself known before he can get the words out.

"Glitch is right," I interrupt. Miles rounds on me. His hair is tied back, but it's starting to come loose. Tendrils of blond hair escape from his hair tie, framing his face. He's no longer rocking the lumberjack beard he favored when we worked at

Jimmy's Auto. After we left the city, he shaved it off. It makes him look younger. I study his cerulean eyes, watching the anger slowly drain out of them.

"The Syndicate is Marcia's legacy, Chickadee," he sighs. "Are you sure you trust Trip?"

Chickadee.

It's the first time Miles has called me by my old nickname since I found out he was lying to me.

"I think it's worth the risk," I say. "When Marcia...mom created the Syndicate, it was exactly what people needed to survive. I think the world has outgrown it. We're ready for something new."

Maybe I should feel bad about breaking up the organization that cost my mom everything. She gave up her family and identity to build it, but I know it's the right decision. My mom died when I was twelve and Marcia, the Syndicate leader, died a few months ago. I can't see them as the same person.

I refuse to hold on to the dream she created for the sake of preserving her memory. It's not pragmatic. More importantly, it's dangerous. It would mean leaving Jace in power. It would mean turning a blind eye to the bots terrorizing grunt neighborhoods. I can't do that.

"I'll let Trip know," says Miles. His shoulders sag in defeat. He leaves, heading for the front door of The Iron Maiden.

"Do you think you two will ever get back to normal?" asks Glitch, standing beside me.

"I'm not sure I remember what normal is anymore," I sigh.

"He loves you."

"I know. I love him too," I say.

"You know that's not what I meant." Glitch gives me a pointed look.

I cringe. Before we received the call about Robbie, Miles kissed me. So much has happened since then. The hurdles kept piling up and I haven't had the mental capacity to deal with any of them.

"Yeah," I sigh.

"And you don't feel the same way," says Glitch, reading between the lines.

"Why do I have to be so messed up?" I ask, scrubbing the heels of my palms into my eyes. "Miles and I make sense. We grew up together. He's been there for me my entire life. Ariel loves him and he's good with her. Being with Miles should be easy."

"But it's not. You like the pretty enforcer with a bad attitude," she smirks.

"Is it that obvious?"

"Only to anyone with eyes."

"I don't think he feels the same way," I mumble. I'm not sure why I'm admitting all of this to Glitch. I have bigger problems, but it feels good to get everything out in the open to start processing it.

Glitch rolls her eyes. "Please. The guy confronted the director and started a revolution to make things right after someone you loved died. He has feelings."

"Don't we have more important things to worry about?"

"Stop dodging my questions. What is it about Ash that makes you run for the hills?" Glitch asks. I wonder if she saw my race for the exit after dancing with Ash. I doubt it, but her words couldn't be more accurate. I think about her question. Sure, there's the fact that we're going to war. I'm also worried Ash won't love and accept Ariel into his life, but he hasn't outright said that and I haven't asked. I sigh.

"I guess I'm scared to give Ash a chance because I get hurt every time I open up to someone. I'm not sure how much more I can take before I become a complete basket case. On top of it, I feel terrible for not reciprocating Miles's feelings. I just don't want anyone to get hurt." The words pour out of me like they were planned. I didn't realize that's how I felt until Glitch forced me to verbalize my hang-ups.

"I've known Miles longer than I've known you, but that doesn't mean I take his side by default," says Glitch. "We're friends too, Wren. That means you're entitled to my unsolicited advice and unfiltered opinions just as much as he is. You're not a terrible person for prioritizing your long-term mental health over what you think you want at this moment. It's okay to give yourself time to think, but you need to talk to them. *Both* of them. Let Miles off the hook and tell Ash you need time to figure things out. You don't get to decide who gets hurt, but you can lessen the blow by being honest and not dragging it out."

I think about Glitch's advice. She's right. I'd rather face down Jace and the Council than have a long-overdue conversation with Miles, but I've already been avoiding it for too long.

The second-story window above the red awning opens. I see Liam poke his head through, resting his arms on the sill. He closes his eyes, allowing the breeze to wash over his face. I remember Ash talking about his time with the surge crew and the patches I saw on his arms to help stem his addiction. Even if Trip and Rook promise to lead the surge crew differently than their predecessors, working with them can't be easy for Liam. He opens his eyes, noticing me for the first time. I give him a lame two-finger wave. Liam smiles and waves back.

"I'll talk to them," I say. I can't think of anything I want to do less.

"Good," says Glitch.

"Are you sure about leaving?"

"Yeah, I meant what I said. This isn't my fight. I was born in the community, and it has been years since I went back. It's time for me to go home. Don't worry. I'll get you a conversation with Grams and Ariel before I leave. I'll keep an eye out for them while you're doing whatever you're going to do with Trip and the team here. Miles handles his issues by lashing out at everything that moves. You bottle it all up inside until you explode. I process things by talking to others. I think spending time with my family is exactly what I need right now."

"For what it's worth, I'm sorry."

"I am too," Glitch clears her throat. "I'm going to go to bed. I'll work on contacting Viper in the morning."

"Sure," I say. Glitch lifts her hand and awkwardly pats me on the shoulder before she heads inside. I sigh, taking a seat on the curb. I drape my arms over my knees and watch the people coming and going from the bar. It has to be after midnight, but the band doesn't seem to be winding down. If anything, more people are arriving.

"If I could change what happened to him, I would." I jump. I was so wrapped up in my thoughts I didn't see Trip approaching. He plops down beside me, leaving a respectful two-foot gap between us. He mimics my posture, cradling his knees with his arms. Liam is watching our exchange. I know he can't hear what we're saying over the pumping music. He doesn't trust Trip. I think he's keeping an eye on me to make sure the surge leader doesn't do anything shady. I decide to ask the question that has been nagging me since I found out who Trip is.

"Did you try to recruit me from Jimmy's Auto to get to Marcia?" I ask.

Trip shakes his head, watching a particularly rowdy group cross the street. For the first time, I try to picture him as the leader of the most powerful Syndicate crew. It's easy to see why he picked Rook to front his operations. With his tousled, ash-blond hair and casual style, he looks more like a surfer bro than someone who shoulders the responsibility of such a large operation. Where his accent is jagged edges, Rook's is smooth lines. Where Trip is easy to talk to, Rook is intimidating. It's easy to see how they complement each other.

"Turns out, you were Marcia's best-kept secret. Some of my guys were talking about Jimmy's Auto. We needed to hire a mechanic to service our runner vehicles, so I reached out to you. That's it. My request was honest," says Trip.

"Miles agreed to your deal. The Syndicate is yours, so long as you hold up your end of our deal. You don't need to babysit us," I say.

"I wasn't babysitting you. I wanted to apologize for the fake surge run I sent you on that almost got you killed. In my defense, I thought the Enforcers would arrest you and Jace would spin some story to get Ash detained. I didn't think he'd actually try to kill you."

The apology is unexpected. I think about the Enforcers attacking us in that tunnel. I decided to rush the line, not realizing they were firing live rounds. Ash knew. He pulled me off Indy, my motorcycle, and we managed to escape. I left my bike in the tunnels. It's probably still down there.

"You owe me a new bike," I grumble.

Trip chuckles. "I'm good for it."

Whatever comeback I was going to make dies in my throat when I see a blur of movement at the end of the street. The lighting isn't the best, so it takes me a second to process that I'm seeing a squad of crowd control bots headed straight towards us. They stand just over six feet tall with clear, plexiglass shields mounted to a platform with wheels. I know from my training at the Academy that a standard squad has five bots plus a lead bot controlled by the tech team. I wonder if anyone monitors the bots now that Jace is in control or if they're just programmed to kill anyone without the correct chip implant.

Either way, Trip and I are fugitives. We have to get off the street.

"We have to go," I say, scrambling to my feet. Trip follows my line of sight to the approaching bots. He curses.

"Let's go inside," says Trip.

"No," I say, panicking. "The bar is packed. What if the bots fire on the crowd?"

Trip glances between the bar and the bots before his gaze returns to me. "Then we run."

"Liam, clear out the bar!" I yell, pointing at the incoming bots. "We'll lead them away."

I don't wait for his response. I scoop up an empty bottle and hurl it at the approaching machines. My aim is spot on. It smashes against the lead bot shield. The lights on the base turn red before the bots change course.

Assaulting an Enforcer bot is grounds for arrest. I just made certain they would follow us to buy Liam some time. Trip and I take off at a sprint. I'm unfamiliar with this area, so I let him pull ahead slightly to lead the way.

The bots are gaining on us.

I push myself to run faster, but I'm already tapped out from our jog earlier today. I don't know how much longer I can maintain this pace. As if reading my mind, Trip grabs my arm and pulls me into an alley. He tries the handle of the first door we come to. Luckily, it's an unlocked stairwell. We take the stairs at a breakneck pace. Trip slams open the door at the top and we rush out onto the roof. I run to the edge and peer over. The bots are spreading out around the base of the building. We're completely surrounded and there aren't any buildings close enough to jump to. I curse.

"They're programmed to keep us here until reinforcements arrive," I say. "Is there another way down?"

Trip shakes his head. A low buzzing sound filters up from below. His eyes widen.

"Drone?" Trip asks.

"Drone," I confirm. There isn't anywhere to hide on the roof, so I start backing toward the stairwell. Enforcer drones are equipped with surveillance equipment and tranquilizer darts. If we stay in the open, we'll be unconscious before we can figure out how to escape.

I remember a discussion with Ash regarding how the drones scan for chip implants before firing to ensure they don't hit innocent civilians. It's why they're the preferred method for hunting down individuals in crowds or elite neighborhoods. They're more discreet than the riot bots and far more accurate. Trip ducks into the stairwell beside me, closing the door until only a sliver of light filters through.

"Give me your jacket," I say. Trip starts shrugging out of his jacket. I raise my eyebrows, surprised that he's complying without asking questions. He shrugs.

"It sounds like you have a plan. That's more than I have right now."

"I'm going to try to catch the drone."

"What now?" Trip asks. I throw open the door before I can talk myself out of it. Trip curses behind me. A drone is circling overhead. It descends to line up a shot as soon as it spots me. I shake Trip's jacket out, feeling a lot like a matador. I'll have to wait until the drone is about to fire before I make my move. That's the only way it'll be low enough for me to reach it. I grit my teeth, holding my ground as the drone gets closer and closer.

I throw the jacket at the last second.

A tranquilizer dart hits the heavy fabric before falling to the concrete. The drone keeps firing, but the flimsy darts fall to the ground harmlessly. Trip runs past me and jumps on the drone, bringing it to the ground.

"Don't break it," I say, squatting beside him. I pull out my pocket knife, flicking open the blade. It's not the most sanitary, but it's sharp. I turn the knife around and offer it to Trip. "My chip implant is in my right forearm." I draw a circle around my arm where I remember the chip being placed when I turned sixteen. I just hope my memory serves me right. I don't want to have to do this twice.

"I would cut it out myself, but I'm right-handed. I don't think I can hold the knife steady enough to remove it myself," I say, shaking the knife when Trip fails to take it. The drone continues to buzz under his arms like a hornet's nest. I don't know if it's out of darts or if it's on pause. If it's the latter, I don't want to release it without a plan.

"You want to attach your chip to the drone to throw off the bots," says Trip catching on. He sets his foot on the drone to keep it in place before rolling up his shirt sleeve. "Use my chip instead." He points to a similar spot on his right forearm.

I blink. "What?"

"My chip has already been flagged and recorded by the Enforcers. After our stint at the Academy, it should be more than enough to draw the bots away. It's a sacrifice I'm willing to make to stay on your boys' good side." Trip winks.

"They aren't my boys," I grumble.

"Could have fooled me," snickers Trip. I dig the knife into his forearm. He winces. "A little warning next time would be nice."

I twist the blade gently until I feel it catch on the capsule. At least, I think it's the capsule. I say a silent prayer that I'm not about to nick anything important. Trip lets loose a colorful string of curses as the capsule comes free. I pick it up off the ground while Trip puts pressure on his arm. He keeps his boot on the drone while I inch the jacket off enough to find a place to attach the capsule. I manage to wedge it behind the camera. It's not perfect, but it should stay there for a few miles. Hopefully, that will be enough time to get away.

"You ready?" I ask.

Trip nods. "When I let the drone go, put on my jacket. The sleeves are RFID-blocking. That way, your chip won't confuse the drone."

I blink. Well, that's brilliant. With the prevalence of chip scanners, it's nearly impossible to move through the city without being identified. It's a simple but effective solution.

"Okay, let's do this," I say. Trip removes his boot, and I yank the coat off the drone. I sprint for the stairwell, tugging on Trip's coat as we go. We run down the stairs until we get back to the alley. I open the door a sliver before shutting it again.

"The bots are still there," I hiss. "The drone hasn't moved. We must have broken it when we brought it down."

"The bots and the drone are connected, right?" asks Trip.

"Yeah...what are you getting at?"

"As far as the bots are concerned, we don't have chip implants. They aren't going to recognize us. If we walk out the door right now, what are the chances the bots will stop us?"

"They could hold us for not having chip implants," I reason.

"But there has to be some sort of hierarchy. They won't take off after two random people after cornering a known fugitive, right?"

He has a point. I have no idea if that's how the bots work, but we're out of options. It's either wait until the enforcers arrive or take our chances with the bots.

I sigh. "This is a terrible idea."

"Never said it wasn't." Trip takes a deep breath before pushing open the door and stepping into the alley. "They're not moving. I think we're okay," he whispers.

I step out beside him. Sure enough, the bots remain immobile. We practically tiptoe to the alley entrance. Trip was right. The bots stay put. As soon as we exit the alley, we start jogging back toward the club. I keep glancing over my shoulder, but the bots aren't following us. We're a block away from The Iron Maiden when the first Enforcer Pod turns down the street. Trip snakes his arm around my waist and tugs me against his side, taking me by surprise.

"I'm hiding my arm under the coat. If they see me bleeding, someone may stop and ask questions," he whispers. I nod and try to keep my eyes focused on the sidewalk in front of us. Pod after Pod passes us, heading towards the building surrounded by riot bots. I force myself to keep a steady pace when I want to run.

Somehow, we make it back to the bar without being stopped. Trip opens the front door to the Iron Maiden. I walk ahead of him, but he keeps his arm around my waist so we end up edging into the building sideways. The band is packing up and only a few patrons are milling around. Liam must have spread the word. A kid runs up to Trip and hands him the keys to his car.

"Your car is out back. They're waiting for you," he says.

"Thanks, kiddo." I swear the boy blushes at the praise. I'd almost think it was hero worship if I didn't know who Trip was. We walk through the bar and down the hall behind the counter. I haven't seen any bots or drones inside, so I shrug out of Trip's jacket and hand it to him.

"Thanks," I say.

"Sure," says Trip. He opens the back door. Just as the kid said, there's a car idling in the alley. Rook, Ash, Liam, and Glitch are standing beside it. All of the doors are open, but not one of them is inside.

"Chickadee!" Miles is the first to spot us. He starts forward, but Ash pushes in front of him.

"Are you okay?" Ash asks, the panic evident in his voice. He runs his hands over my arms and back. I'm confused until I remember Trip's wound. I'm probably covered in his blood. Ash is trying to find an injury. I grab Ash's hands before he can continue looking for a nonexistent wound.

"Ash, it's not mine. I'm fine," I say. I squeeze his hands until his eyes come to mine. He yanks me forward so I slam against his chest, pulling me in for a bone-crushing hug.

Trip clears his throat. "Hey, where's my hug?"

I look up just in time to watch Rook dump an entire bottle of antiseptic on Trip's arm. There's a first aid kit sitting on the hood of the car. Trip yelps, pressing his fist against his mouth to cut off the sound. Rook tosses the bottle into the kit and snaps the lid closed before throwing it in the backseat. "Get in the car, you moron."

Trip gives her a crooked smile. "Love you too, Rookie."

Rook flips him off and gets behind the wheel.

Chapter 11

Elle

No one has ever accused me of being a pushover. It's taking every ounce of willpower I have not to tell Jace to jump off the nearest bridge whenever he orders me to do something. I'm not opposed to authority. I agree that there's a time and place for structure. The Enforcers and the Council would fall apart without protocols and respect for the hierarchy of command.

The Council's past orders have aligned with my personal beliefs. I never questioned them because I agreed with them. I knew their end goal and was happy to be a part of making it happen.

That changed when Jace took office.

The last few months have been a trial in restraint. Jace knows I'm close with Ash and Liam, so he's going out of his way to test my limits. He wants to see how far he can push before I break down and become his malleable little soldier.

He'll be waiting for eternity because I don't give up. Ever.

It's not in my DNA.

So, I bite my tongue during Council meetings and pretend to be the good little elite heiress my parents taught me to be while I watch Jace play his games with weaker minds and wreak havoc on our vulnerable nation. I'm biding my time, identifying the Council members and Enforcers who disagree with the world Jace is trying to build.

It's a slow process. Some of them hope things will improve and Jace will grow into the role. Most of them know he's a lost cause, but they're too afraid to take a stand. It's not unwarranted. Jace has sentenced more than one Council member to death for expressing a contradictory opinion. At first, he was discreet about it - carrying out the verdicts in private and delivering some made-up excuse to the public via the Council news channel. After Ash's trial, he stopped caring.

He shot an Enforcer recruit, Roy Bishop, on the live broadcast.

Until a few months ago, I lived in a black-and-white world. There was no gray area and I was perfectly fine with that. Ash cracked the door to show me how the world truly operates outside of the Academy, then Jace blew it off its hinges when he fired that shot.

I joined the Enforcers because I wanted to make a difference. Ash was born a grunt. He moved into the Axton mansion when his mom married the late director. My best friend's life is a classic rags-to-riches tale - the sort of thing fairytales are made of. At least, that's what it looked like from the outside. I know better because I saw what he went through.

I watched the elites tear Ash apart. He was ostracized and treated as a lesser person by the people I spent my entire life looking up to. Maybe I should have followed the crowd and treated him the same way. Things would have been easier for me, but I couldn't do it. It seemed ridiculous to follow a set of unwritten social rules around him just because of where he grew up.

People were accepting of our friendship when we were younger. I was applauded for my philanthropy and willingness to help the poor grunt fit in with elite society. I think my parents allowed it because it gave them social credit with their affluent friends. They thought I would outgrow our friendship and develop a more appropriate social circle. They told me as much.

Appropriate. Boring. They're the same thing in my book.

I couldn't bring myself to care enough to get to know the Penny Bronxtons of the world. You know the type. Social media harpies that feast on the flesh and blood of those they deem unworthy. Cats with claws they use to climb the social ladder and teeth they sink into anyone with the money and means to give them what they want. The human dolls that aren't allowed to have a coherent thought, because they're being trained to live life as the arm ornaments of powerful men.

Yeah, forget that.

I'll make my own way to the top, thank you very much.

It doesn't help that my "dream man" is a "dream woman." By the time I admitted that to myself, I knew enough about my parents' expectations to keep my mouth shut and my faith in humanity low. Ash and Liam are the exceptions. They're the only people in my life I'm completely transparent with. There isn't a hidden agenda or a mask to maintain. They know everything about me and accept me for who I am, just as I accept them. We trust each other.

I betrayed that trust when I arrested Ash.

When Ash let Wren and Miles go, I didn't know what to do. I know Ash. I know he never does anything without a logical explanation. Still, I couldn't reconcile my Syndicate-hating best friend with the man who allowed the leader of the same organization to escape. The Enforcers would be able to trace Miles's escape to Ash. I knew I had to keep myself distanced from the situation so I could help him make his case to the Council.

So, I arrested my best friend.

I'm the reason Ash was locked in the Academy basement for three months after being convicted for a murder I'm sure he didn't commit. I'm the reason he was humiliated in front of the Council time and time again at Jace's bequest. I'm the reason the rightful director is a fugitive and Jace is in charge.

If I had trusted Ash from the beginning, I have no doubt the three of us would have found a way around this. Instead, I had to watch the surge crew break into the most secure room in the Academy and escape via a window washing station with Ash and Liam in tow.

That has to be the first time in the history of the Enforcers anyone has ever written that in a report.

"Why are we going through this footage?" asks Zoe, drawing me out of my thoughts. "It's already in the archives. I can't change it without someone knowing it was altered."

Zoe is leaning over Liam's computer reviewing the footage from the drone Wren and Trip incapacitated. When the Enforcers arrived on the scene, they found the drone hovering above the roof with Trip's chip implant shoved behind the camera. It confused the bots and allowed the two of them to escape.

We met Zoe during our first year at the Academy. She was in our recruitment group. Where Ash, Liam, and I clicked immediately, Zoe was more of a peripheral friend. She's tiny - a foot shorter than I am and just over a hundred pounds soaking wet. She wears her auburn hair in a messy bun on top of her head.

Joel is standing behind her. He was also in our graduating class. With his strong jaw, buzz cut, and bulging muscles he looks every bit the enforcer he has trained to be. When Joel lets you into his circle, you realize he has the personality of a golden retriever - loyal to a fault and extremely friendly.

To be honest, I think it's one of the reasons we were never close. Growing up among the elites, it's dangerous to be transparent. To survive, I had to surround myself with people who understood how to play the game. Zoe and Joel aren't the friends you want to attend a political dinner with, but they're the people you want in your corner when you're staging a coup against the director...which explains why we have been working together lately.

"If I didn't know better, I'd think this chick has a death wish," mutters Joel. We're watching the drone feed of Wren throwing a jacket over the drone. "Two run-ins with the authorities in one night. That's either bad luck or she's knowingly putting herself in the line of fire."

Joel told me he helped Wren, Miles, and Glitch escape after they were detained crossing the city border. I'm glad he recognized them and was in a position to help.

"I want to make sure there's nothing in it that could lead Jace to Ash and Liam. If there is, I want to be ahead of it," I say.

"How do you know Ash and Liam are with them? They could have left Trip after they busted out of the Academy," says Joel.

"Call it a hunch," I say. I leave it at that. I've never seen Ash look at a woman the way he looks at Wren. Sure, he's dated before, but those were flings. He's never been with anyone long enough for it to be considered a relationship. He certainly never pursued anyone.

Wren is different.

Ash was willing to put his vendetta against the Syndicate on hold for her. That's something Liam and I couldn't get him to do. I would have had you committed if you had told me a few months ago that Ash would let the Syndicate leader walk away for a girl. I'm happy for him. I really am. I just wish he would have fallen for someone with less baggage and fewer obstacles to navigate. It would have made my life easier. At the same time, I know Ash would never settle for ordinary. I wouldn't either. So, I'll do what I can to ensure Wren is safe.

Besides, this revolution would have happened with or without their relationship acting as a catalyst. The tensions between the grunts and the elites have been getting worse by the year. With the introduction of the 8-Bit app, the grunts became more organized. That's something they don't tell you at the Academy but is apparent to every enforcer: There are more grunts than there are elites. If they decided to rise against the Council, there's very little we could do to stop them.

They have the numbers. We have the firepower.

The elites have become more complacent. Most of them lived a life of luxury before Axton AI and the Council. I suppose, in some ways, nothing has changed for them. They don't realize they should be worried. The only thing that keeps the grunts in check is fear. We keep them starved to the point where they can only focus on survival. When you spend your days searching for food, medication, and shelter, there isn't much time to worry about changing the world. All your energy goes into surviving.

I wonder if Bryon Axton ever thought about the grunts in those terms.

Love him or hate him, the man was a visionary. There was a time when I believed in his eloquent speeches at the Ascent Day events. The images he verbally painted of building a world where humans and technology coexisted to create a better existence for all people, regardless of status. It was a beautiful sentiment, but that's all it was.

A sweet nothing whispered in the ears of the elites.

A broken promise delivered with pomp and circumstance to the grunts once a year on Ascent Day.

The Ascent could have been what this city needed. A lottery for eligible eighteen-year-olds to get a shot at a legal job could have leveled the playing field. Ash's mom was on the right track when she proposed it, but she died before she could see her dream come to fruition. I wonder if she would even recognize the bastardized publicity stunt it has become over the years.

I wonder if things would have been the same if she was still alive. Losing her made Byron double down on his efforts to eliminate the Syndicate. It made him ruthless, creating a Council that was biased against grunts. It led to the need for the 8-Bit app and ultimately sent more people into the arms of the Syndicate.

My phone lights up with a notification. I swipe it off the desk and open the text. I let out a long, agonizing sigh.

"What does Jace want?" Joel smirks, reading my screen.

I pinch the bridge of my nose, trying to fend off the headache that's beginning to form. "He wants me to come to his office. This can't be good."

"I'm sure it's nothing. You know he's been panicking since the trial." Zoe stops typing and turns to face me.

"Do you want me to go with you?" Joel isn't asking because he thinks I'm incapable of handling Jace on my own. He means exactly what he says. His personality is like slow moving water that gradually smoothes rough stones. I take a deep breath.

"I've got this. Just keep digging into the footage. I'll be back soon," I say. Zoe nods, returning to her task while Joel watches over her. I leave Liam's old office and close the door behind me. The officer assigned to replace Liam already had an office on this floor, so Liam's has remained vacant. It's the perfect place for the three of us to meet without drawing too much attention. I push through a few IT people who give me a wide berth. Anyone with eyes can see I'm on Jace's bad side. They're smart to keep their distance. I'd do the same.

I get in the elevator and hit the button for the top floor.

I never used to hate the Council chambers and executive offices housed on the top floor of the Academy. There was a time when I almost found the meetings peaceful. They were a retreat from the chaos; they allowed me to find peace in a monotonous process that resulted in justice.

Now, being summoned to the top floor makes me want to put my fist through the drywall.

The door slides open and I step into the hall. Jace took over his father's office the day after he died. As I approach,

I hear voices inside. I knock once before opening the door without waiting for an invitation. Jace is standing in front of the floor-to-ceiling windows that make up the back wall of the office.

When this space belonged to Byron, there were shelves lining both walls overflowing with books. The man always preferred reading paper over tablets. Even the Council reports and meeting notes were printed and given to him to review. The books have since been cleared out, and the walls have been painted white. The mahogany desk is also gone, replaced with a solid white table. Even the floor has been tiled in marble.

Jace's black suit contrasts with the blank canvas, making him the focal point of the room. I wonder if the sterile environment makes him feel clean when no amount of soap can wash the blood from his hands. Carl Bronxton and his daughter, Penny, are sitting in front of him. Carl was Byron's business partner at Axton AI. Since Byron's death, Carl has been running Axton AI on his own. I have no idea why Penny is here. The girl is more interested in reality shows and designer brands than in Council dealings. She wouldn't be caught dead on this floor because someone might wrongly assume she has half a brain cell.

Penny is stunning. Her long, brown hair has red undertones that give it more of a copper color. She wears just enough makeup to hide the freckles on her nose. We grew up in the same social circles. In other words, I knew her when she still had a soul. We went to the same school and, if my parents had their way, I would have given Penny the best friend title over Ash. We were friends in elementary school, but we grew apart. She traded her soccer ball for stilettos and I joined the Enforcers. I wonder how she felt about the marriage Byron and Carl were trying to arrange between her and Ash. I always thought she had a thing for Jace. Given the scowl plastered on her face now, I'm not so sure I read that correctly.

"Are you going to come in?" Jace asks. I realize I'm still standing in the doorway with my hand on the handle. I step further into the room and close it behind me.

"What is she doing here?" Carl asks. I note the dark circles under his eyes and the lackluster color of his hair. He's wearing his usual suit, but the tie is loose around his neck and his shirt is wrinkled. We're talking about a man who shines his shoes to lounge on the couch. Okay, maybe that's an exaggeration, but still. Carl is typically the picture of class. Today, he looks more like an overworked research assistant who just lost his grant funding.

"I thought you might need a little push," says Jace.

"What's this about?" I ask. "Sir," I add as an afterthought. Like most leaders who haven't earned the respect of their people, Jace demands it instead.

"I've ordered Carl to give the Enforcers full control of the crowd control bots and drones Axton AI provides us with," says Jace.

"I thought the Enforcers already controlled them?" I ask. "We have an entire floor of techs dedicated to surveillance. We have trained bot operators on site."

Jace looks at Carl with a bored expression. "Explain."

"Jace wants the Council and Axton AI to merge," Carl sighs.

"That's 'director' or 'sir' to you," scowls Jace. I stop myself from rolling my eyes.

Carl looks like he's about ready to shove Jace through the window behind him. I probably wouldn't arrest him if he did. Carl takes a visible breath before continuing.

"When Byron and I created the Council, we kept Axton AI separate. Axton AI sells crowd control bots, drones, and chip implants that are used and governed by the Council. Everyone knows that. Right now, Axton AI owns the servers and the intellectual property that makes this possible. Ja...the director proposes that Axton AI be absorbed into the Enforcer operations. Axton AI wouldn't be collecting a paycheck from the Enforcers. It would become a part of the Enforcers."

My face pales. Byron and Carl kept Axton AI separate from the Council to create a check on the director's power. If Axton AI decides the Enforcers crossed a line, they can shut down the bots remotely. They can limit what the bots can do.

Jace is asking for complete control over the most powerful surveillance technology in the world.

"Respectfully, I told him no," says Carl, studying my expression.

Thank God.

"I wasn't asking you. I was ordering you. I'm the director. When I ask you to turn over Axton AI property, you do it," seethes Jace.

Carl shakes his head. "The Council and the director have no right to order Axton AI to turn over intellectual property without payment. We get to decide which products we sell when and to whom."

Jace clasps his hands behind his back. "You're right. You don't have to do anything." He inclines his head at me. "Arrest Penny Bronxton."

Penny blanches, but she doesn't say anything. Carl shoves his chair back to stand. It topples over from the force.

"You can't do that. My daughter hasn't done anything wrong."

"Maybe not, but I can hold her as a suspect for being involved with the Syndicate," says Jace.

"She's never been involved with the Syndicate," Carl booms.

Jace shrugs. "We won't know that until her trial. That could be months from now. Maybe years. She can stay in the Academy holding cells until then."

"This is blackmail!"

"It's fine," says Penny. She puts her hand on her father's arm to get his attention. "I'll go with Elle." Penny hugs him, whispering something in his ear that I can't make out. She kisses him on the cheek before approaching me. "Let's go."

Carl is still standing in front of Jace's desk. He looks torn between grabbing Penny and leaving the country or beating Jace to a pulp. I hope he makes the smart decision and bides his time. Neither of those options will get him anywhere. I step aside to allow Penny to walk through the door first.

"Cuff her," orders Jace. I freeze with my back turned toward Jace.

"She's not resisting arrest. That isn't necessary," I grind out, trying to keep a professional tone.

"It's fine," Penny says, giving me a sympathetic smile. She offers me her wrists. Her nails are hot pink and she's wearing a diamond golf bracelet. I pull the cuffs off my belt and secure them loosely around her thin wrists.

"Let's go," I say. I take Penny's arm to lead her away before Jace objects to how I handle a peaceful arrest again. Carl is a frayed thread away from snapping. I know I have to get Penny out of here before he does something he can't take back that puts her in more danger. I lead Penny to the elevator and press the button for the Academy basement. As soon as the doors slide closed, Penny's shoulders slump. I release her arm.

"Shit," she mutters. I raise an eyebrow. I've never heard her cuss.

"Pretty much sums it up," I sigh. The elevator stops on the IT floor. I'm preparing to tell whoever it is to get the next one, when the doors open to reveal Joel. I watch his eyes go to the cuffs on Penny's wrists and my hand on her arm. I clear my throat to get his attention. "Can you tell Zoe to give me a few minutes? I'll be with her shortly," I say, hoping Joel delivers the message and Zoe can guess what I'm really asking for. There's only so much I can say because the elevator is monitored.

Joel frowns, but he nods and steps back to allow the doors to close. The elevator continues to the basement without another stop. The guard behind the desk in the processing area is a Council loyalist. I wonder if Jace changed around the schedule knowing he would push Carl to turn over Axton AI today. Maybe he thought I would try something.

"I need a cell assignment," I say.

"Eight," says the man. He doesn't bother looking at the computer screen, confirming my suspicion that this was planned ahead of time. The man frisks Penny, pulling her phone out of her back pocket and setting it on the counter. It's the only thing she has on her. I decide to let her keep the golf bracelet. They'll probably confiscate it later, but I don't trust Jace's man not to steal it if I hand it over now. I lead Penny through the side door into the block of holding cells.

Eight.

The same cell Ash and Liam were being held in.

I swallow. Jace knows how to mess with your head better than anyone I know. Penny steps inside her cell and I remove her cuffs. Inside the cell, I watch the red light on the security camera mounted in the corner blink out. I say a silent "thank you" to Joel and Zoe for correctly interpreting my message in the elevator.

"We can talk without anyone listening for a few minutes, but we have to be quick," I whisper, securing the cuffs back on my belt. "Why doesn't Jace take Axton AI by force? What does Carl have that he needs?"

There has to be a reason Jace doesn't force his way into Axton AI. He has the firepower. He has the Council. The only explanation is that Carl has something he needs to make his plan work.

Penny's eyes widen. "My dad suspected Jace would try something like this, so he created a secret kill switch that's separate from the rest of the Axton AI infrastructure. So long as Jace doesn't know the location and how to get through the encryption, we can still shut down the bots and drones remotely."

"How did Jace find out about the kill switch if it's so secretive?"

Penny shrugs. "I think Jace suspects it exists, but I don't think he knows for sure. He's probably threatening dad to make him show his hand."

"Does anyone else know where the kill switch is?"

Penny thinks about it for a moment. "There are a few Axton AI employees they trusted to set up the site. They might crack under interrogation, but I doubt Jace could figure out which employees were involved. I don't even know. As for the encryption, only my dad and I know how that was done. We have to make sure my dad doesn't give Jace what he wants," says Penny. There's steel in her words, reflected in her eyes that I didn't know she was capable of.

"If he doesn't, you could be stuck here a long time," I warn. I won't sugarcoat it. She needs to know what she's getting herself into.

"I'll take one for the team," she says.

The irony isn't lost on me that I spend more time breaking people out of the holding cells than trying to keep them in. Carl Bronxton will break under interrogation. I'm sure of it. The only way Ash and the Syndicate have a fighting chance is to ensure the bots are out of commission. I have to buy us enough time to come up with a contingency plan. Removing Penny from the equation is the best way to do that.

"I'm breaking you out of here," I say.

For the first time, I think I understand what Ash was going through when he chose to let the leader of the Syndicate escape. It wasn't because he wanted to. It was because it was the least terrible choice out of a sea of bad options.

Chapter 12

Ash

I thought I escaped my boredom when Rook and her people busted us out of the Academy, but it turns out that revolutions involve a lot of sitting around. After the incident at the Iron Maiden, Trip moved us to another safe house. Since then, we've been stuck inside. We risk being identified by a drone or security camera if we leave. The city has been crawling with Enforcer patrols since our escape.

It's not worth the risk.

Jace is pouring all of his resources into finding us. I wonder why he thinks I'm still inside the city walls? I would be halfway across the country if I had half a brain cell. Maybe Jace knows me better than I think he does. I won't leave. Whether it's out of a misplaced sense of duty or because I owe it to Byron and Robbie to try to end what I started, I will stay until I have no other choice.

Who am I kidding? I'll stay because Wren asked me to.

The building we're living in is a single-story house on a street of identical homes. It has white siding with peeling paint, a grimy bay window with a rotting window sill, and two feet of side yard that butts up to a privacy fence. It looks like the type of working-class neighborhood Byron talked about growing up in before he lost his father in a factory accident.

Trip, Rook, Glitch, Wren, Miles, and I are staying here until we decide our next steps. A few surge crew members rotate in and out for extra security and meetings, but they sleep somewhere else. I'm thankful because the house is over capacity as is. There are only two bedrooms, one of which looks like it was originally a closet. It's so tiny the dresser touches the side of the bed. The living room is a makeshift bunkhouse with cots and sleeping bags on the floor.

We'll have a little more space when Glitch leaves. Rook and Trip are trying to organize transportation out of the city for her. After we escaped from the Academy, additional security measures were implemented at the borders. It will be nearly impossible for her to slip out on a truck like she did the last time. It will be interesting to see what they come up with.

Wren and Miles tried to convince her to stay, but she's determined to return to the community. I don't blame her. Not only are we preparing for a war we probably won't win, but we also have to sleep on the floor while we do it. I've heard of the communities before, but I assumed they were comprised of a few rogue grunts who rejected modern day society. From eavesdropping on Glitch's conversations, I'm beginning to think they're larger and more organized than the Enforcers suspected.

I cross my arms behind my head, my cot creaking with movement. I study the yellow water stain on the ceiling. It's beside an outdated dome light with dead bugs trapped between the light in the glass. The stain is just under the only bathroom in the house. I try not to think about that too much.

Trip and Rook have been meeting with people all day. They're gathering information and strengthening alliances with other Syndicate crews. Liam and I sat in a few meetings, but our presence hurt more than it helped. The other crew leaders didn't want to talk about numbers and resources with two ex-enforcers in the room. I might have stood up to Jace, but that doesn't make me their ally. It makes me a wild card. People don't know what to think yet.

So, I've been chilling on my cot and trying to act like Wren's active avoidance isn't bothering me. I know she's in a weird place right now. I'm trying hard not to let it get to me. I want to pick up where we left off. Go back to the friendship we shared before I wrote her that note and left for the Academy while she was on the phone with her family. Maybe she needs more time. I get it. I don't have to like it, but I get it. I'll give her all the time she needs. I just hope at the end of it, she'll give me a second chance.

The back door slams. I don't hear shouting from the security team, so I assume they're friendly. Miles stalks into the room a few seconds later, confirming my theory. He flops down on his cot with a groan, throwing his arm over his eyes. I open my mouth to ask what's wrong, but I close it again. Miles and I aren't friends. He has a thing for Wren. That much is obvious. It doesn't matter if she reciprocates his feelings, because he will see me as a threat to their relationship either way. I won't have a shot at peace until that changes.

"You're staring," grunts Miles. He doesn't remove his arm from his face.

"Do you want to talk about what's bothering you?" I ask. I sit up, swinging my legs off the side of the cot. Miles drops his arm to his side, his eyes focused on the ceiling.

"Nope."

"Cool." I shrug, content to drop it. I can't force Miles to open up to me, but that doesn't mean I won't stop offering him an olive branch. After a few minutes, Miles drops his eyes from the ceiling with a sigh. "I went to check out the backup servers for 8-Bit. When the Enforcers raided the farmhouse, we destroyed the servers to prevent them from accessing anything important. I had backup servers in the city just in case."

"Had?" I ask.

"The Enforcers found all of my hidden locations. Every single one of them is under active surveillance."

"Do you think they got anything important off your equipment?"

Miles shakes his head. "The machines would have wiped themselves without proper authorization when booted up. They're probably waiting to see if anyone comes back for them. I have to find another way to get the 8-Bit app up and running."

"Aren't there more important things to focus on? You know, like overthrowing Jace and making sure we don't die."

"While we're focused on taking out Jace, people still rely on that app to feed their families. Not everyone can or wants to be part of this fight. The longer the app is down, the longer people go without necessities," Miles snaps.

His answer surprises me. The guy has been hostile to the surge crew and me since we started working together. He has been outright nasty to Rook. Until Trip fulfills half of the bargain, Miles is technically the leader of the Syndicate. We should be enemies. I expected him to be an egotistical hothead, but I should have known better. If Wren trusts him with her friendship, that should have been an adequate vetting process. She doesn't let anyone in unless they deserve it. Maybe I should give the guy a chance.

"Do you have another backup?" I ask.

Miles sits up. He rests his forearms on his knees and studies me with a curious expression. "Yeah, but it's impossible to get to."

"Where is it?" I ask.

"My old apartment building," says Miles.

"Jace would have had the place ransacked," I say. "He knows your identity."

Miles shakes his head. "He wouldn't have found my equipment even if he stripped the place to the studs. It wasn't in my actual apartment unit."

"Where is it?" I ask.

Miles gives me a look that says, "Like I'm going to tell you."

"Fair enough," I sigh. "You know, it might still be possible to access it. Jace would have ordered an initial sweep. He may not have enforcers stationed there permanently. If he does, there will only be a handful of them and they'll be focused on your unit. We could sneak in and out before they realize we're there."

"We?" Miles asks, raising his eyebrows.

I shrug. "8-Bit is important to you and you're important to Wren. Not to mention, I can see how this will impact millions of people positively."

Miles fake gags. "Seriously, why are you helping me?"

I roll my eyes. "Despite the differences you and Wren have had in the past she's giving you a second chance. I can either get between you or I can get on board. This is me choosing to get on board. Don't talk me out of it."

Miles studies me like he's looking for something hidden beneath my words. He won't find any. I meant what I said and I plan to see it through. He stands up and stretches before walking to the door. I think he's rejected my offer for help until he glances over his shoulder and says, "You coming, pansy?"

"What? Right now?" I ask.

"No time like the present."

"Shouldn't we tell the others where we're going?"

"We'll be back before they notice we're gone," says Miles.

"You're just worried Trip will say you can't go."

"Trip doesn't tell me what to do. Until we overthrow Jace, I'm still the leader of the Syndicate. Technically, I outrank Trip."

I don't justify his comment with a response. I shove my feet into my boots and stand up. On my way to the door, I see Glitch and Wren sitting on one of the beds looking at a laptop. Glitch was going to get in touch with Viper so Wren could talk to Grams and Ariel. I hope she's successful.

I've never been more terrified than when Wren showed up covered in blood at The Iron Maiden after her run-in with the bots. We haven't had any time alone to talk since we got to the safe house. It's not like the building is large enough to offer any amount of privacy. I'm not sure Wren would want to talk even if we had the chance. She has been avoiding me and she's not exactly great at sharing her feelings. I think about telling Glitch and Wren we're heading out, but I decide against it. I don't want them to worry.

Like Miles said, we'll be back before anyone realizes we're gone.

Miles is already talking to a surge crew member in the narrow driveway beside the house when I open the back door. The guy is leaning against the wall with a gun in one hand and a lit cigarette in the other, looking like the poster child for poor life choices.

I'm surprised the smoke doesn't phase me. There was a time when I would have salivated at the smell, but I guess I'm past that now. Now that I think about it, I haven't had cinnamon chewing gum since Rook gave me a stick in the car.

"We're running an errand for Trip. Which car can we take?" Miles asks, lying flawlessly. I cross my arms but I don't call him out in front of Trip's man. Miles will find a way to get to those servers with or without my help. I'd rather be there to watch his back than explain to Wren that I knew about his plans and did nothing while he was captured or killed by the Enforcers. That doesn't mean I have to like his methods. The surge crew member removes the cigarette from his lips long enough to point to a gold sedan parked along the fence.

"That one has fuel. Keys are in the ignition."

"Thanks, man," says Miles. He opens the door to the driver's side and gets in. I walk around the front of the car to the passenger door. Miles starts the ignition while the guy with the cigarette opens the gate at the end of the driveway.

"How pissed is Trip going to be that we stole one of his cars?" I ask.

"First of all, we're borrowing. Not stealing. Second, I don't care about what Trip thinks. Besides, we'll be back before he realizes we're gone."

"You keep saying that. It doesn't mean it's true," I grumble.

Miles pulls out in the street. In the rearview mirror, I watch Trip's man close the gate behind us. The sun set about an hour ago and the roads are dark. There aren't streetlights in this part of town. I see some lights on in the buildings we pass, but all the curtains are drawn and the windows are closed. No one is out walking. I see a scrawny dog sniffing around some bushes behind a house that looks abandoned. I wonder if his owner is in the area or if it's a stray. Rook said the grunt neighborhoods have been quiet since Jace launched more frequent bot patrols. She wasn't kidding. People are scared. They're only leaving their homes if it's necessary.

"Are you going to tell me where the servers are hidden before we get there?" I ask.

Miles doesn't respond.

"Okay," I say, drawing out the word into multiple syllables. "Can you tell me anything at all before I risk my life to do you a favor?"

Miles scrubs his hand over his face. "We need to get to the roof."

"The servers are on the roof of your apartment?" I ask, incredulously.

"Yeah, let's go with that."

Wow. It's like pulling teeth getting any information from this guy. It doesn't sit well with me, but what can I do? I already agreed to come and it's not like I can turn around. Miles is driving. I'll just have to watch my back and hope for the best. Miles parks a few blocks away from his old apartment building. He kills the engine and gets out of the driver seat.

"You sure we're okay to leave the car here?" I ask.

"It's not my car. If anyone messes with it, that's Trip's problem."

Miles starts down the sidewalk, making no move to hide or be discreet. I follow a few feet behind, watching the windows for any movement. I have that tingling sensation you get when someone is watching you, but I don't see anything that looks suspicious. I shove my hands in my pockets and take a deep breath. I'm probably just being paranoid.

Miles strolls up to the front door of the apartment building like he's returning from a day at work. He starts to climb the stairs to Wren's level before stopping on the landing. I catch up to him, putting a hand on his shoulder.

"Slow down. There may be enforcers here. We need to be careful," I hiss. Miles shrugs off my hand and throws open the door, the exact opposite of being discreet. Luckily, there aren't any enforcers in the hall.

"What are you doing?" I whisper shout.

"You said the enforcers probably aren't here anymore," says Miles at full volume. "I'm just following your advice, pansy."

"I said 'probably.' That doesn't mean I'm certain. We need to be careful. I thought we were going to the roof?"

"There's something I need to check first," says Miles.

We pass the elevator doors that are cracked open, revealing the dark elevator shaft. Wren told me the elevator has been out of commission for years and that the tenants have been using it as a trash shoot. I make a wide arc around the opening to avoid the trash that didn't quite make it to its intended destination.

Miles stops in front of Wren's apartment door. He tries the handle and the door swings inwards. Someone left it unlocked. I stand in the doorway as Miles enters the unit. I half expect a swarm of drones to come buzzing out of the bedroom, but that doesn't happen.

The enforcers tossed the place.

The contents of kitchen drawers are strewn across the floor. The couch cushions are ripped open, the material spilling out onto the carpet like mangled entrails. I'm glad Wren isn't here to see this. Miles navigates through the mess and opens the bathroom door.

"Now really isn't the time to take a dump," I say, still standing at the front door. I lean back to look down the hall, but we're alone for now. "We need to get out of here before the enforcers decide to come back for another security sweep."

I hear a cabinet door slam shut and he reappears holding a wrench. "This belonged to Wren's dad. She's upset that she left it behind. I thought since we were here risking our lives anyways, I might as well make another stop."

He shoulder checks me on his way out the door and heads for the stairwell. I grit my teeth and force myself to remember why I'm being nice to the guy. I shut Wren's apartment door and jog after Miles. I appreciate that he's trying to do something nice for Wren. Anyone can see that their friendship is strained right now.

Glitch gave me the thirty-second summary of everything that transpired since Wren and Miles left the city. I can't blame the guy for trying, but he has an uphill battle. At the same time, I'm jealous of the history they have. Miles was there for her when she needed him the most. Where I've known her for a few months, they have a lifetime of shared experiences. Miles has time on his side. She will choose him. Always.

It's not that I inherently dislike the guy. I just don't trust him.

There's the obvious fact that he's the developer of the 8-Bit app and the leader of the Syndicate, but it goes deeper than that. I try to imagine what it would be like for me to keep a secret of that magnitude from Elle or Liam for years. I probably wouldn't last a week. Miles doesn't operate in the same reality the rest of us do. It makes it hard to anticipate what he will or will not do. That makes him dangerous. Miles opens the door at the top of the stairwell and we exit onto the roof.

Miles crosses the roof, tugging his hair back and knotting an elastic around it as he walks. He's heading for a squat, brick enclosure housing an elevator. Miles retrieves a crowbar hidden behind a beat-up air conditioning unit. He slams the bar in the crevice between the elevator doors to pry them open. Inside the elevator, a single metal case is tucked in the corner. Miles pops the clasps and opens the lid. He grins.

I whistle. "The elevator was never broken, was it?"

"No." Miles rises to his feet.

"Wren's going to be pissed when she finds out you made her walk four flights of stairs multiple times a day for no reason."

Miles ignores me. Inside the elevator, a single metal case is tucked in the corner. Miles pops the clasps and opens the lid. He grins.

"They didn't find it. Everything is here," he says.

"Seems a bit small for a server," I say.

"That's because it isn't a server," he says slowly as if he's explaining something to a child. "These are hard drives. It's not the latest version of the 8-Bit app, but I backed it up recently enough that it's a good place to start. It's more than I had before." He puts the clasps back in place and tucks the case under his arm. We're halfway across the roof when the buzzing starts. Miles and I freeze.

"Drones," I mutter. Miles pales. We sprint to the stairwell door, but I can already hear people approaching.

"It's too late. We're boxed in," I say.

"How did they find us?" Miles asks.

"The apartment must have had motion sensors or hidden cameras," I say.

"I might be able to get the elevator working," says Miles. "Buy me some time?"

"I'll do my best," I say.

Miles takes off to tinker with the elevator just as a drone appears above the edge of the building. I glance around for a weapon. There's a single brick on the ground. Someone probably used it to keep the door propped open. I don't think. I grab the brick and hurl it at the drone.

My aim is true. The brick slams into the drone. It careens wildly before dropping out of sight. Grabbing the door handle with both hands, I put my feet against the wall and lean back with all my weight. The enforcers reach the door and try to tug it open. I manage to hang on, bending my knees to help take some of the strain off my arms. We're playing a game of tug of war I know I won't win. There are more of them and the second they think to send another drone up here, I can't cover my back and hang on. The door handle will probably break off before that happens.

"Any day now would be great," I yell. Risking a glance over my shoulder, I see the interior lights of the elevator come on. Miles steps inside. He gives me an apologetic look.

"Don't you dare," I shout.

Miles presses the button and the doors close, carrying him to safety and cutting off my only means of escape.

The bastard left me behind.

I take a deep breath as the door slams into my shoulder again. I can make out three or four individual voices in the stairwell, but there could be more than that. I won't be able to hold them back much longer. My shoulder is throbbing and my sweat is making the handle slippery. I hear a low buzzing that indicates more drones are on their way.

I'm out of time.

That's when the handle snaps off. I hit the ground on my back, the force driving the breath out of me. I roll over and push up to my feet just as the door flies open. I send a kick into the ribs of the enforcer leading the attack. He howls, his weapon clattering to the ground. The next enforcer through the door aims his rifle at me, preparing to fire. I grab the barrel and jerk up just as he squeezes the trigger. I feel a breeze on my right cheek from the passing tranquilizer dart.

It was that close.

The rifle pulls the enforcer's fingers in an unnatural direction. He releases the weapon with a scream, clutching his hand. I slam the butt of the rifle into the face of the third enforcer and duck into the stairwell before anyone can stop me.

I kick the door shut. It bounces off the frame, the mangled handle failing to keep it closed. Cursing, I take the stairs three at a time. There aren't any more enforcers in the stairwell, but it's only a matter of time before more arrive. The call would have gone out for reinforcements. I just hope there aren't any other patrols in the area.

When I get a few floors down, I hear footsteps in the stairwell below me. Any hope of delayed reinforcement disappears. I throw open the door on the next landing, hoping I can cut across to the stairwell on the opposite side. If the enforcers haven't blocked that one yet, then I have a chance of making it to the street. I sprint down a hall that looks identical to the one Wren's apartment is on. It's an exact replica down to the dingy, trash-covered carpet and yellow walls. The only difference is the gold apartment number plates nailed to the doors.

I'm halfway down the hall when the stairwell door bursts open. The enforcer leading the pack lets out a surprised yell. I practically trip over my own feet trying to reverse direction. I pick up speed, pumping my legs to get back to the stairwell I just came from but that door opens as well. More enforcers pour into the hall.

I'm boxed in.

I skid to a stop. The enforcers realize I have nowhere to go, so they stop running. They can take their time to follow protocol. I'm no longer a threat. I know what they're doing, because I was one of them once. I know what their strategies are. I know how they were trained.

"Drop the weapon," someone orders. I glance at the rifle hanging loosely at my side. I didn't even bother to raise it. I'm so outnumbered it wouldn't make a difference. I look around, my eyes landing on the open elevator shaft. I can just make out the thick cables hanging in the center.

I have a terrible idea.

I know the cables are secure. Miles just took the elevator down. I didn't hear a loud crash or see any fireballs when I was on the roof. Granted, I was a bit preoccupied, but I probably would have heard something...right? Wren is going to be pissed when she finds out Miles let her walk four flights of stairs multiple times a day for no reason.

"I said, drop the weapon!" The enforcers are closing in, as if they know something is about to happen.

Here goes nothing.

I toss the rifle at the enforcer barking orders and take off at a sprint. As expected, they open fire. I throw myself into the void, free-falling for a story before I manage to catch one of the cables. My shoulders scream as my body jerks to a stop, my momentum turning the cable into a pendulum that slams my body into the back well. I don't know how I manage to hold on. I loosen my grip and slide down the cable, my hands burning as the skin is stripped from my palms.

I scream.

The hall lights from each floor are just enough to illuminate the shaft. I can't see perfectly, but it's enough to make out the top of the elevator box below. I manage to slow my descent just enough that I don't break both of my legs.

It still hurts.

Cursing, I get on my hands and knees. There's an access panel on top of the elevator. It isn't locked, but it takes me three tries to pry it open. My hands are slick with blood and the lighting at the bottom of the shaft isn't the best. When

I manage to get the panel open, I swing my legs over the edge and drop into the box. It takes me a precious second to process what I'm seeing. The sliding doors are open, but the box must have gotten stuck in between two floors. There's a two-foot opening at my feet. I sit down and shove my feet through the opening, using my arms to control my motion. When I feel something solid under my toes, I allow myself to fall to the floor.

Or what should have been the floor.

Instead, I'm laying on top of a mountain of trash. The stench makes me gag. I try to breathe through my mouth as I crawl over the bags that have burst open, spilling their rancid contents filled with maggots. My only consolation is that I know Miles must have crossed through here when he got out of the elevator.

I hope he smells like a bloated swamp monster.

I manage to make it out of the building just as another Enforcer Pod arrives. Spinning around, I run through the alley to the street behind the apartment building. I'm sure Miles took the car. I don't have a plan and my body is in rough shape. I won't be able to run for much longer.

I don't care if he's Wren's best friend.

If I make it out of this alive, I will kill him.

Chapter 13

Elle

I'm going to run, and all it will cost me is my career and my family. No big deal, right? I take a deep breath to center myself. I've stayed at the Academy for as long as I can. Jace is starting to get suspicious. How long will it be before he has me arrested? Or, worse, orders me to do something I ethically won't do?

My parents will disown me. Even if I could explain, my mom won't care. She'll be more concerned about the hit to her reputation than supporting her child. I'll be written off as a disappointment. My name will become taboo at the dinner table, and life will continue. Dad may be more open-minded, but I doubt he will go to bat with mom to make his feelings known. I sigh.

If I leave now, at least I get to trash my reputation on my terms.

I couldn't find a way to break Liam and Ash out of the Academy without burning bridges. Leaving is a lot easier when you don't care about damaging your reputation. I'll set fire to every bridge I've ever built if it means locking Jace out of the Axton AI servers. My reputation is a small price to pay to protect the city. I take Penny's cuffs off and swing the cell door open.

"What are you doing?" Penny asks.

"I told you, I'm getting you out of here," I say. She steps into the hall, and I close the cell door behind her.

"I didn't think you meant right now," Penny hisses.

"We have to leave before Carl caves and gives Jace everything he's asking for." I glance at the camera in the corner. The red light is still out. I pull my phone out of my pocket and dial Zoe. She picks up on the first ring. "I'm leaving the Academy with Penny. Can you give us a clear route?" I ask. Zoe lets out a startled noise. There's a crash followed by some static before the sound of frantic typing comes through the speaker.

"Yeah, I can do that. I'm securing the back stairwell now. There's a guard in the lobby. Get past him, and you're clear until you get to the parking garage."

"I'll handle him. Thanks."

"Is there anything else we can do?" Joel asks. Zoe must have put me on speaker.

"Make sure the enforcers loyal to us are ready. I'll get in touch when we have a plan."

"Copy that," says Joel. I hang up the phone and look at Penny.

"I need you to stay here for a minute," I say.

"I thought you said we are getting out of here."

"We are, but I have to get rid of Jace's dog first." I point over my shoulder towards the lobby. "Unless you know how to take down a man twice your size, I need you to stay out of the way."

Penny taps one perfect pink fingernail against her bicep. "Fine."

"Great," I say, shoving open the door. I stroll to the front desk and rest my forearms on the counter. The guard doesn't look up from his phone. I wonder what he's watching that's so interesting. He knows I could write him up for it. The fact that he's making no attempt to hide his phone is concerning. It means he doesn't think I'm a threat. It means that he sees Jace as the ultimate authority. I clear my throat to get his attention. He gives me an annoyed look.

This guy.

"Jace called," I growl. I'm trying to keep my cool, but it's a struggle. "He asked you to transport an incoming prisoner from the atrium."

The man looks up with a startled expression. He leaps to his feet and bolts to the door, tucking his phone into his pocket as he goes. I blink.

Jesus, I expected at least one follow-up question. I guess blind loyalty does have its perks.

I open the door for Penny. "We're taking the stairs up. Stay close and do exactly as I say."

Penny rolls her eyes but doesn't complain. We jog up the steps, putting as much distance between us and the holding cells as fast as possible. Penny manages to keep up, but she's breathing heavily. If we're going to get out of here, we can't do it on foot.

I lead us out the back door and into the parking garage. There are a few enforcers milling about, but I walk confidently into the open with Penny at my side. No one has sounded the alarm yet. So far as they're concerned, we're just taking a stroll. Penny's head whips back and forth as if she's expecting Jace to come running after her.

"Keep your eyes forward. You look like you just robbed someone," I whisper out of the corner of my mouth. Penny's eyes snap ahead of us, and she scowls.

"Excuse me, I haven't done this before," she hisses.

"Neither have I. Just act natural."

Penny huffs, but she slows her pace and keeps her eyes forward. As we cross the garage, I force myself to maintain a steady, confident gait. All I want to do is run, but that would only draw unwanted attention. I take a few deep breaths to settle my nerves. It doesn't work. I discreetly take my phone out of my pocket and drop it on the ground, kicking it off to the side. I don't want Jace to track us.

A floor-to-ceiling chain-link fence blocks off the back corner of the parking garage. It's where we keep impounded vehicles that are part of ongoing investigations. Most of them will be transported to a larger lot on the outskirts of the city. Unfortunately, there aren't many options. I spot a truck with a flat tire sitting on the rim and a bright red convertible that would draw too much attention. Tucked in the corner is a beat-up motorbike with more rust than paint.

"Hello, you beauty," I mutter. I'm not sure the bike even runs. As we approach, it looks like one side is completely scraped up, as if the owner slid out on it. As the least conspicuous option, it will have to do.

The gate guarding the impounded vehicles is locked with a biometric scanner that only authorized personnel can access. We don't station guards here. Enforcer leadership didn't think civilians would be stupid enough to break in. Lucky for us, I'm one of the trusted few with permanent access. I press my palm against the biometric scanner mounted beside the door. It flashes red with an "Access Denied" banner appearing across the top.

"My access must have been revoked." I read the screen in disbelief before shaking the gate. It doesn't budge. So much for that plan.

Penny pulls two bobby pins out of her hair. Her bangs flop over her eyes. She snaps the first one in two, discarding one piece on the ground. She sticks the other piece in her mouth, biting down on one end. She rakes the metal through her teeth and spits before holding the metal strip up for inspection. The little raised ball on the end is gone, leaving a smooth metal tip in its place.

"What are you doing?" I ask.

"Picking the lock," she says as if it's the most natural thing to do when encountering a locked door. She takes the second bobby pin and bends it at a ninety-degree angle. Penny squats in front of the door, inserting her makeshift picks into the lock. "Most doors with biometric scanners also have old-fashioned locks. The idea is if the electricity goes out or the battery backup fails, you can still open the door."

Her tongue pokes out the side of her mouth in concentration. It's kind of cute. I chastise myself for the thought. Penny Bronxton is a knockout. Anyone with eyes can see that, but now isn't the time to check out the pretty elite socialite.

"I didn't know that," I grumble.

"Clearly," Penny snorts. She grabs the handle and pulls the door open with a satisfied smirk.

"Where did you learn how to do that?"

Penny tosses the mangled bobby pins aside. "Please. My dad owns half of the world's most advanced technology and security firm. It would be weird if I didn't know how to pick a lock."

"Huh," I say. Honestly, I'm at a loss for words. Penny always struck me as the kind of person who values appearances over intellect. I didn't think she had it in her. I slide the gate back until there's a motorcycle-sized gap. There's a key rack mounted to the concrete wall. The motorcycle key is smaller than the others, so it stands out. I snatch it off the hook, my eyes going to the security camera in the corner. The Enforcers will know I stole the bike and escaped with Penny, but there's nothing I can do about it.

I swing my leg over the bike and say a silent prayer that I can get it running. It starts on the first try. I grin, revving the engine and backing out of the parking space. Penny is still standing by the door, wearing an apprehensive expression.

"Do you even know how to drive that thing?" she asks.

"Yes." I roll forward until I'm idling next to Penny. I rest my hand gently on her arm. "I know this is a lot. You can trust me."

Penny stares at me for a moment before getting on the bike behind me. She wraps her arms around my waist, keeping as much distance between us as possible.

"You ready?" I ask.

"No." Penny lets out a nervous laugh. I smile and rev the engine, pulling out of the parking space. I don't gun it, but the sudden movement makes Penny yelp. She bands her arms around my stomach, closing the distance between us. A few Enforcers give us curious looks, but no one says anything. I've always played by the rules. They have no reason to doubt me.

I leave the parking garage and pull out into traffic. It has been a long time since I operated a vehicle and even longer since I rode a bike. My dad was a massive collector of antique cars. It was something we bonded over. He had a few bikes. It wasn't really his thing, but he taught me how to drive them. My mom complained that it was uncouth for "a young woman of our social standing" to drive, so my dad sold his collection.

It broke my heart.

The wind whips my ponytail over my shoulder, the breeze tickling my face. It takes me a few miles to get a feel for the bike, but after that, it's like I never stopped riding. Penny is silent behind me, her face pressed against my back. I can't tell if she's trembling or if it's the vibrations from the engine. I try to drive as smoothly as possible.

I told her she could trust me. I'm not going to give her a reason not to.

Once we're a few miles away from the Academy, I make the decision to go to Wren's old apartment building. The last time I went there, I was able to get Joel's video of Ash's trial to Glitch for distribution. I wish she could have seen the tantrum Jace threw when she posted it on the official Council website. The girl certainly has a flair for the dramatic. I don't know if Glitch or her people are still monitoring the apartment, but it's worth a shot. I left the Academy without a plan. Now, I'm just winging it and hoping for the best.

I need to find somewhere for us to lay low. Once Carl realizes Penny isn't in danger, he'll be more likely to resist Jace. If he's smart, he'll use the window we gave him to eradicate the riot bot technology. The riot bots and drones are useful to the Enforcers, but at what cost? Giving Jace unlimited access to Axton AI technology is like giving a toddler free rein in a candy store - nothing good will come of it.

I stop at a red light. Most of the vehicles surrounding us are civilian Pods. There are a few manually operated vehicles intermixed with the traffic, but they're becoming rarer. The Council has been talking about eliminating the traffic signals downtown. They'll stick around until someone can develop a safe alternative for pedestrians crossing the streets.

The Academy is located in the city's center, only a few streets away from the wealthy elite shopping districts. You can buy anything online, but many elites prefer to try the latest trends in person before placing their orders. The shops are glorified showrooms, but they've become a staple of the elite lifestyle. The store on my left has a massive window that runs the length of the first story. In the reflection, I see a black enforcer Pod stop a few cars behind us. I adjust the mirror mounted on my handlebar to get a better look. There's a second Enforcer Pod crawling to a stop behind the first. I thought Joel would be able to buy us more time, but I guess the enforcer I sent away from the lobby desk sped things up. I should have come up with a better excuse.

"Hold on," I say.

Revving the bike, I gun it through the intersection before the light turns green. I'm banking on the Pod sensors being responsive enough to avoid a collision. Penny shrieks as a Pod stops a foot from the side of our bike. Her arms tighten around my stomach, making it difficult to breathe. My instincts were spot on. As soon as we're clear of the intersection, I open up the throttle, and the bike shoots forward.

I'm surprised we're able to pick up speed so quickly. Some-one put some love into maintaining this bike despite how it appears. I glance in my mirror and see the Enforcer Pods cross the intersection. They're quickly gaining on us. The motor-bike is no match for the newer electric engines in the Pods. Coupled with the navigation system that allows the Enforcers to map the most efficient interception path through traffic, we might as well be parked.

I turn the corner. On the side of the building is a multi-story digital display showing an advertisement for a women's cloth-ing store. It flickers out, replaced by a black screen. My name appears in strobing white letters: "ELLE....ELLE...ELLE."

I swerve, narrowly avoiding a Pod going a third of my speed. As I look at the display again, it changes to a large arrow pointing to the right. I can either follow a stranger's directions or wait for the Enforcers to arrest us.

I follow the sign.

As soon as I round the corner, I spot another digital banner in a coffee shop window that changes from advertising daily prices to another set of arrows pointing straight ahead. I keep driving, and the arrows keep popping up. We weave through the city with an invisible guide, staying a few blocks ahead of the enforcers.

The next sign I see doesn't have arrows. It just reads: "Shoot the gap."

I don't like the sound of that.

The traffic light in front of me turns red, and I suppress a groan as cars flood the intersection. My invisible navigator clearly wants me to cross the street, but I'm not sure I should try my luck twice in one day. My guardian angel might decide I'm too stupid to protect anymore. The Enforcer Pods are so close that they take up the entire rearview mirror.

I punch it.

I hear the crunch of metal colliding. I keep my eyes focused, refusing to get caught up in whatever is happening around me.

I risk a glance over my shoulder when we make it through the intersection. Civilian Pods are blocking the intersection altogether. Some are even parked on the sidewalk to prevent the enforcers from steering around them. Whoever is helping us must have hacked into AVA, the app civilians use to book Pod transport. I just hope there weren't any innocent bystanders injured in the chaos.

I don't slow down. It's only a matter of time before the enforcers find a way around the Pod-barricade. We have to leave the downtown area where the cameras and monitoring software are the densest. The further we get into grunt territory, the easier it will be to lose them.

I head for Wren's apartment, taking as direct a route as I dare. I don't think Jace will guess where I'm going, but I'm not taking any chances. I've underestimated him before. I won't do it again. There were enforcers on surveillance duty the last time I went there, but Zoe was able to send them away. Without her help, I can't risk approaching the building head-on. I plan to get in the general vicinity and off the street. We can find a hiding place and figure out our next move once I see what the surveillance situation is like. Maybe I can find a way to get in touch with Zoe or Joel.

The rest of the trip to Wren's neighborhood is blissfully uneventful. I'm a street over and three blocks away when I see an Enforcer Pod cross the intersection ahead of us, roaring toward Wren's apartment building. I slam on the brakes and turn the bike down a narrow alley between two storefronts before killing the engine. I hold my breath, waiting for the Pod to reappear. The shadows will only do so much to conceal us, but I hope it's enough. Penny is silent behind me, her arms still wrapped around my waist despite the bike being parked. I wait for what feels like an eternity, but the Pod never appears.

They didn't see us.

I let out a breath. If enforcers are searching the area, we can't stay here. At the same time, I don't want to hole up too far away from the apartment. We have to get in touch with the Syndicate if we want to survive, and it can't just be anyone from the Syndicate. It has to be someone we can trust.

A man races across the street at a dead sprint, heading away from the apartment building. He's about six feet tall with black hair and an athletic build. He's wearing civilian clothes, but I would know my best friend anywhere. I'm about to call out to Ash when the black Pod reappears. Ash spots it. He runs towards the alley across the street from us, but he's not going to make it. The Pod is moving too fast.

"Get off," I order with more bite than I meant to. Penny releases my waist and clambers off the bike. I fire up the engine and peel out into the open. I jump the curb and accelerate toward my best friend, but I know I'm too slow. The enforcers are going to reach him before I do.

A car barrels into view, turning the corner on two wheels. There's a ramming bar mounted to the front bumper. It picks up speed on the straightaway heading for the black Pod. Ash ducks in the alley, throwing his hands up to protect his face from broken glass. Enforcers stumble out of the Pod, but they're disoriented from the impact. The car fared better. The front windshield is cracked, but the mounted bar did its job. It still looks operable - the frame and engine compartment are intact.

Trip gets out of the driver's seat and takes out two enforcers with a rifle. Liam gets out of the passenger side and Wren from the back seat. They make quick work of the enforcers inside the Pod. I'm surprised by their efficiency, given Liam has been off field duty for years, Wren hasn't completed her training, and Trip is a Syndicate lackey. They work well as a team. I can see the little orange plumes on the ends of the tranquilizer darts. The enforcers will wake up dazed, but they'll all go home.

It's more than they would have done for my best friend.

"Elle?" Ash asks, walking out of the alley. I get off the bike and put down the kickstand. Ash crashes into me, pulling me into a bear hug that I return. Ash and I don't have an overly affectionate friendship. Neither of us is a hugger - that's more Liam's speed, but I couldn't care less. My best friend is alive.

"You smell like a dumpster," I laugh, pulling away. His clothes are covered in grime. There's something that looks suspiciously like a squashed banana on his shoulder.

"Is it that bad?" He makes a show of sniffing his shirt, but he doesn't have to fake the following gag. "Yeah, point taken."

"Ash!" Wren sprints around the car. I step back a few steps to give her room. "Are you okay?" She stops in front of him, but Ash loops an arm around her waist and draws her in. He kisses her forehead before resting his chin on her head, wrapping his arms around her waist. Wren turns her head, so her ear is pressed against his chest. She closes her eyes, her hands balling into the material as if she's worried he'll disappear if she lets go.

I smile. I've never seen Ash so...content. It's a good look for him.

"I am now. Thank you," he sighs.

"Where's my hug?" Liam asks, a fake pout on his face. Ash flips him off behind Wren's back. I chuckle, hugging Liam just as I hugged Ash.

"I missed you guys," I say.

"We missed you too," Liam chokes. He's probably surprised I initiated the hug.

Wren gasps. "What happened to your hands?" Ash's hands are bloody, the skin torn from the palms.

"I jumped down the elevator shaft and used the cable to slow my fall," says Ash.

I wince. I've burned my hands on rope before, but that sounds like a different level of torture.

Trip clears his throat. "Hate to break up the family reunion, but we need to get out of here."

"Is that...Indy!" Wren races over to the motorbike I just dismounted. She runs her hands over the frame and the handlebars as if it's made from fine porcelain. "Where did you find her?"

"I stole her from the Academy impound. Speaking of which..." I glance at the alley where Penny is hidden and gesture for her to come over. She emerges hesitantly from the alley, looking both ways before jogging across the street. Her hair is windswept, and her shoulders are hunched in fear. I wince. I shouldn't have yelled at her to get off the bike. I owe her an apology.

"Is that Penny Bronxton?" Ash asks.

"It's a long story. I'll tell you when we get somewhere safe," I say. Ash accepts my answer with a nod.

"Can I take the bike?" Wren asks. She's trailing her fingers over the seat like she's petting a cherished pet.

I shrug. "Sure. It's yours."

Trip gets behind the wheel, and Liam joins him in the front seat. I take the back seat with Penny and Ash. It's a tight fit. The car has three seats in the back, but the middle seat wasn't designed for a full-sized adult. Our shoulders and legs are touching. Trip backs up and does a three-point turn before he guns it down the street. Wren starts up the motorbike and follows us. Ash glances out the back window and grins.

"You just made her day," he says.

"I busted it out of the Academy impound. I hope it made her whole damn *month*."

"Welcome to the dark side," says Ash, only half joking. We both know I can't go back to the Enforcers after this.

Penny is unusually quiet. She's staring out the front window and twirling the simple silver band she wears around her thumb. She looks nervous. I debate striking up a conversation with her, but Liam turns on the radio in the front seat. He's bickering with Trip over something. I haven't been paying enough attention to know what they're arguing about, but I can tell Liam is annoyed. When Trip tries to speak up, Liam cranks the volume louder until Trip gives up on their conversation.

Thirty minutes later, we arrive at a single-story house on a street of equally run-down, cookie-cutter homes. Trip gets out of the car and jogs to Wren. He says something to her before she follows him around the side of the house, probably to stash the bike. It's a good call. As soon as the Enforcers realize it was taken, they'll have drones scanning for it. Parking it in the driveway is the equivalent of setting off a beacon broadcasting our location. Liam, Ash, Penny, and I slide out of the car. Ash puts his arm on my elbow, stopping me, then drops it before anyone can see. Penny stops, too, wondering why I'm not following her into the house.

"I'll be inside in a second. I want to catch up with Ash for a minute," I say.

She looks between us, wearing a nervous expression. I almost groan. I forgot the rest of the world thought Ash and I were engaged before he went rogue. It was a fake arrangement we made to get Ash out of an arranged marriage proposal between her father and his. I wonder if she feels snubbed? Or maybe she's embarrassed. It's hard to tell. Either way, she probably still thinks something is going on between us. I'll have to clear that up sooner rather than later. Penny closes the door behind her. Ash leads Liam and me a few paces away from the house. He turns around, so his back is to the windows, not wanting anyone to read his lips.

"I think Miles just tried to get me killed," he says, keeping his voice low. He explains what happened on the rooftop of the apartment building.

"That bastard," Liam growls. He starts towards the house, but Ash stops him.

"He's Wren's best friend," says Ash, as if that explains everything.

"Which is why she deserves to know the truth," I say.

"I'm not suggesting we lie to her," says Ash, a pained expression on his face. "I'm suggesting we give him the benefit of the doubt. We were in a tough situation. He might have panicked and been too scared to do anything to help me. I can't fault the guy for that. We've had training for those kinds of situations. He hasn't."

I'd be willing to let it drop, but there's no part of Ash's explanation that sits well with me. The expression on his face tells me he doesn't believe what he's saying, either. Miles was the leader of the Syndicate. I can guarantee he has been in challenging situations before. Which means he intentionally left Ash for dead.

"First things first, we need to get your hands cleaned and wrapped," says Liam. "Then, we can figure out what we're going to do about Miles."

"We're not going to do anything," says Ash. "We wait. We watch, and we intervene if he does anything sketchy. In the meantime, watch your backs." I thought getting Penny to the Syndicate meant we'd be safe. I was wrong. We're not safe. We just swapped one dangerous idiot for another.

Chapter 14

Wren

"**I**s there anything I can say to get you to stay?" I ask. Glitch and I are sitting on the bed in the smallest bedroom. It's the only room in the safe house that offers some semblance of privacy. I swear this house was built before modern insulation was standard. The walls are paper-thin. Anyone in the living room can hear what we're saying, but I guess it's the thought that counts.

That said, it's nicer than the apartment I grew up in. The plumbing doesn't leak. I haven't seen any bugs. It doesn't look like the kind of place that has been kept vacant. Trip must have had people maintaining the building. I'm glad we have somewhere we can stay while we figure out our next steps.

"I came back to the city to bust Roy and Ash out of the Academy. Now that that's off the table, it's time for me to go home," says Glitch. I watch as she navigates to the video call on her laptop before handing the device to me. Viper hasn't logged on yet, so we're faced with a blank screen.

Glitch clasps her hands in her lap, staring vacantly at the wall. She has always been the ray of sunshine in the dark. Glitch has somehow managed to remain an optimist, whereas everyone else is jaded. She's the life of the party, even if the party is terrible. She doesn't let anything phase her.

Watching her mourn Roy is heartbreaking. Her grief is chipping away at her personality like a pickax to stone. It isn't happening all at once, but bit by bit, her sunny disposition is crumbling under the constant assault. I wish there were something I could do or say to make it all go away, but the truth is I'm just as messed up as she is. Any advice I offer would only make me a hypocrite.

Personally, my mood fluctuates by the day. I don't think there's a one-size-fits-all cure to feelings of grief, betrayal, or pain. It's not a linear graph that goes from laying in bed to being ready to take on the world. I picture the line plots I've seen of radio waves with peaks and valleys, oscillating with the pitch and tone of voices.

Depression is like that.

There's an ebb and flow. It's hard to see it when you're in the middle. You always feel like you're at the peak. Ash told me once that he got through a hard time by having a goal. Maybe that's the answer. Maybe I just need to focus on taking down Jace and returning to my family.

"We need your help," I say.

"You have Miles. He's a better hacker than I am." She doesn't sound bitter about it. She says it as if stating a fact. "I'm sure he can find some of Trip's tech-savvy people as well. You don't need me to overthrow Jace."

I want to push her to stay again, but I know it won't change anything. Glitch has made up her mind. She needs time to process. If she thinks taking that time with the community she grew up in will help, who am I to judge? It's not like I'm a model for healthy coping mechanisms. There's a ping, and Viper's face appears on the screen. He tucks his dark hair behind his ears. Glitch gives him a big smile.

"Hey there, boo," she says with a wink.

Viper frowns. "How are you holding up?" he asks. Glitch stares at him. I can't blame her. The question is out of character for her stoic friend. If Viper is commenting on Glitch's mood, then she's worse than I thought.

"I'm just peachy," she snaps. Viper doesn't look offended. He just waits for her to continue. "Wren wants to talk to Grams and Ariel. Are they around?"

The frown doesn't leave Viper's face, but he doesn't push it. He glances at someone over his monitor and gestures for them to come closer. Grams appears on the screen.

"Hey, Grams," I say. Viper gets out of his chair and offers Grams the seat. He shows her where to look in the camera.

"When you're done, let me know," says Viper. Grams squeezes his forearm in thanks and takes a seat. Viper disappears from the frame.

"I'm going to let you guys talk," says Glitch.

"You aren't leaving right now, are you?" I ask.

Glitch shakes her head. "I'll wait until you're done, and then I'll head out. I need my computer," says Glitch.

"Glad to know saying goodbye to me ranks below your precious computer," I say dryly.

"Of course. A girl has to have priorities," jokes Glitch. She gives me a smile that doesn't reach her eyes before leaving the bedroom and closing the door behind her. Satisfied she's not going to sneak out of the house without saying goodbye, I return my eyes to Grams. She looks better than she did the last time I saw her. The dark circles under her eyes are less pronounced, and the color has returned to her cheeks. Her hands are resting on the desk in front of her comfortably. She has on a bright blue dress, the same color as a clear summer sky, with little white flowers on it. It looks newer than anything she has ever owned.

I'm glad living with the community agrees with her.

The wracking guilt that has been my constant companion since I left Grams and Ariel behind nags at me. Rose and her people are providing for my family better than I ever could. I should be there with them. Instead, I'm hiding in a safe house, waiting for a riot bot to bust down our door. If that doesn't happen, I'll be risking my life trying to bulldoze my way into the Academy.

We haven't decided on a plan, but I have no doubt we'll eventually be taking this fight to Jace. Whether that means storming the Academy or the Axton mansion remains to be seen. They're both risky. I know we won't stand a chance if the Enforcers find us before we're prepared. The numbers aren't on our side. We have to be smart about this.

"How are you, my girl?" Grams asks, tugging me from my thoughts.

"Surviving," I say.

"Viper told us about Roy. I'm sorry."

"Yeah."

"But you found Ash?"

"I did."

"Then you're coming back?" she asks.

I swallow. Usually, I would be ecstatic to get the chance to speak to Grams and Ariel, but that question is the reason I've been putting it off.

"Not yet." I feel so selfish for saying that aloud. What right do I have to stay here and fight a battle when my family needs me? I should be packing a bag right now to leave with Glitch.

"You want to help take down Jace," says Grams. I raise my eyebrows. "Don't give me that look. You forget I changed your diapers. I can practically read your mind, so don't bother lying."

"You disapprove?" I ask.

"No. Yes." She pauses for a moment to collect her thoughts. "I'm worried about your safety, but that's nothing new. I've worried about you since you started running Jimmy's Auto. I think if you don't do this, you'll regret it. I disapprove of the danger, but I know it's necessary."

"I want to be able to bring Ariel home without worrying about her safety," I say. "Where is she anyway?"

"She's with Rose and a few of the other community members. Viper has been helping me keep an eye on her. There's a lake near where we've been staying for the last few weeks. He's teaching Ariel how to swim."

"You let him take Ariel to a lake without you?" I yelp.

"Relax, Wren. This isn't the first time Ariel has been out swimming. I've been there every time except for this one. I trust them, Wren."

I try to calm my breathing, staving off a panic attack. "Is she doing well?" I ask.

Grams grins. "Really well. She could paddle from one person to another on her own yesterday. She's getting the hang of it."

I never learned to swim. It's not like there are lakes in the city or many public pools open. I'm glad Ariel can experience things I cannot give her. "I'm sad I can't be there to watch her," I say quietly.

"Maybe you can come here before we go home. Ariel can show you what she has learned," says Grams.

"Yeah, I'd like that," I give her a small smile.

"Wren," says Grams with a sigh. "I wanted to apologize for hiding Marcia and Miles's roles with the Syndicate. That wasn't my place. I hurt you, and I'm sorry."

I start to interrupt her. I want to tell her to leave the past in the past. Whatever anger I held onto died when Commander Harper tried to take her from us. It was a stark reminder that life is too short to hold grudges. Grams holds up a hand before I can say anything.

"Hear me out, please. It was wrong of me to keep that from you. I thought I was keeping you safe at the time, but I know better now. Roy told me a little about what you were going through at the farmhouse. I know I was a part of those feelings, and I apologize. If there were a way to take it all back, I would. Can you forgive me?" she asks.

I stare at the camera. This conversation has been a long time coming. The truth is, Grams tried to corner me for weeks after we arrived at the farmhouse. I wasn't in the right frame of mind to listen. Now, I'm back in the city and separated from my family. I'm getting ready to overthrow the director, and Grams is taking care of Ariel. We've had our differences, but the truth is Grams is my family. Somewhere along the way, I started trusting her again. I'm not sure I ever entirely stopped.

"Yeah, I forgive you."

Grams tears up. She swipes a finger under her eye and sniffles. My own eyes well with tears.

"Stop that," I say with a small laugh. "You're going to make me cry."

"I love you."

"I love you too."

Someone says something off-camera, and Grams nods. It sounds like Viper. "I have to go, but I'll try to call back when Ariel gets in."

"That sounds good," I say. We say our goodbyes, and I hang up the call, closing the laptop lid. I tuck it under my arm and open the bedroom door. Glitch is lounging on the only couch in the living room.

Couch is generous.

Glitch is sitting on the center cushion. Her weight is causing the stuffing to stick out on either end, making the couch look more like an overstuffed breakfast sausage. She's halfway through a prepackaged sandwich. Liam is sitting on the floor on the other side of the coffee table. Both of them have playing cards in their hands. She smirks at her cards before taking another bite of the sandwich. Liam is too focused on his hand to notice.

"What are you playing?" I ask.

"Poker," says Glitch aroumd a mouthful of sandwich. I cross the room and set the computer on the coffee table next to their game. She finishes the last bite of the sandwich and licks a stray drop of mustard off her index finger just as Liam swears and tosses his cards in the center of the table.

"She's a damn card shark," says Liam, sounding more amused than offended. He gathers the cards into a pile and straightens them into a neat stack.

Glitch shrugs. "I used to play with people in the community. I have a lot of practice." Liam taps the deck on the table to get the cards to line up and sets the deck off to the side.

Glitch leans back against the cushions and scrubs her eyes. "Trip is organizing a transport out of the city. I'll be gone in a few hours."

I nod slowly.

Glitch's phone buzzes. She reads the text on the screen and curses.

"I need my computer," she says, getting to her feet. I hand her the laptop, and she disappears into the bedroom, slamming the door behind her. I stare at the closed door.

"What was that about?" I ask.

"No idea," says Liam.

I hear the gate open outside and a car idling in the driveway. Someone yells something, but I can't make out the words through the walls. Liam and I share a look. He gets off the couch just as Miles runs into the room with Trip on his heels. Miles's shirt is soaked with sweat, and there's a manic expression on his face I haven't seen before.

"What's going on?" I ask. Miles steps behind me, placing his hands on my shoulders.

"Stop using Wren as a human shield," growls Trip. I'm glad Miles sought me out as soon as he walked into the room. I've never seen Trip so pissed off.

"Someone better start talking," says Liam. He glances between Trip and Miles, his gaze settling on me. He raises one eyebrow as if to say, "Are you okay?" I give him a slight nod. Liam presses his lips into a fine line and crosses his arms. I didn't get to know Liam during my time at the Academy. After spending a few days with him at the safe house, it's clear that Liam is protective of his friends. I guess I fall into that category now.

"That idiot stole my car and was stupid enough to get spotted by enforcers. He's lucky no one followed him back here," snarls Trip.

"I told you it was important," says Miles. His fingers dig painfully into my hips.

"Why?" Liam asks.

"I had to get the 8-Bit backup," says Miles.

"Did you get it?" I ask.

"Yeah, it's in the trunk."

"Wait, where's Ash?" I ask, looking around. I just realized he's not in the room with us. With the amount of noise Trip and Miles were making, it's uncharacteristic that he wouldn't come to check it out. Miles tenses behind me. I grab his hands and remove them from my hips so I can turn around. He runs a hand through his hair, looking anywhere but at me.

"I'm sorry, Wren," murmurs Miles. "The enforcers surprised us, and we had to run. When I got back to the car, I realized he wasn't behind me. They must have arrested him." He tugs something out of his back pocket.

It's my dad's wrench.

The last time I saw it, I had tucked it under the bathroom sink in my apartment when I was changing my clothes. I take it from Miles with both hands, not fully believing it's real until I feel the cool metal. I never thought I would see it again.

Liam shoves Miles away from me. He stumbles a few feet before his back crashes into a wall. Liam follows him, pinning Miles against the wall with a forearm to his throat. I tuck the wrench in my pocket and lunge at Liam. I grab his arm and try to pull him away from Miles, but I might as well be a mouse trying to move an elephant for all the good it does me. Trip lets out an exasperated sigh. He loops his arm around Liam's neck in a choke hold, cutting off his air supply.

"Knock it off," snarls Trip. "I'm all for beating up Miles, but take it outside." Liam grabs Trip's arm and tries to pull him off, but the surge crew leader is stronger than I gave him credit for. "If I let you go, will you trash my safe house?"

Liam shakes his head, and Trip releases him. He gasps, rubbing his throat where Trip's arm was digging in.

"We have to go back for Ash," I say.

"You can't. There are enforcers everywhere. They're probably transporting him to the Academy already," says Miles.

"We have to try," says Liam. He looks at me. "I'll go with you."

"How are you going to get there?" Trip asks, crossing his arms. "Last I checked, neither one of you has a car."

"We're borrowing yours," says Liam.

"Like hell, you are," Trip snaps. "I'm not compromising our safety by allowing you to drive into an enforcer-infested neighborhood."

"We had a deal," I snarl. "Ash is your ticket to a seat on the Council."

"Maybe I've reconsidered. I have the surge crew. Maybe I should call off our deal and quit while I'm ahead," says Trip. I hope he doesn't mean that.

"We have bigger problems," says Glitch. There's something in her tone that makes everyone shut up and listen. She's standing in the doorway to the bedroom with her laptop in one hand. "Elle busted someone out of the Academy. I managed to help her get away from the downtown area, but we need to get to her before they send more."

Liam grabs a rifle lying against the wall and drapes the strap over his shoulder. "Do you know where she's headed?"

"I can guess. The last time Elle contacted me, she went to Wren's old apartment building. She's probably going there."

"That's where I just came from," says Miles. "It's swarming with enforcers."

"We can't let her walk into that without backup," I say.

"We won't," says Liam. He looks at Trip. "I need to borrow your car."

"You aren't borrowing anything," says Trip.

"Chickadee, it's dangerous," says Miles.

I snort. "When has that ever stopped me?"

"You don't owe that pansy anything," says Miles.

"You told us you wanted to make the Council and the Syndicate talk to each other," I say, addressing Trip. "That your goal is to make this city a safer place. How do you expect to do that if you allow the future director and a high-ranking enforcer sympathetic to your cause die because you refused to take a risk?"

Trip studies me. "We could all end up in jail."

I scoff. "How is going after Ash and Elle more likely to result in jail time than running the surge crew or breaking out of the Academy? We're risking everything hiding out in this safe house instead of getting as far away from the city as possible."

Trip sighs, the fight leaving him. "Fine."

"I'm coming with you," says Miles.

"You've done enough," I growl. Miles blanches.

Glitch clears her throat. "Miles, I could use you here. We need to help Elle lose the enforcers following her."

Miles nods, refusing to look at me. I duck around him and head for the door with Liam and Trip trailing behind me.

***

We return to the safe house with Ash, Elle, and Penny a little over an hour later. It feels good to be on the back of my bike again. The last time I saw Indy, I laid her down in the tunnels when we were running from the Enforcers. I'm surprised the damage wasn't more severe. The body is more scraped up than it was before. I doubt anyone but me would notice, she was in pretty rough shape, to begin with, but I spent hours combing over every inch of this bike until she was road-ready. Trip parks in front of the safe house and gets out of the car, jogging towards me. I roll to a stop, bracing the bike with my legs.

"I'll show you where to park. I don't want to keep all the vehicles at one house," Trip says. "Follow me."

It makes sense. With the drones patrolling, we don't want the safe house to draw attention by creating a makeshift parking lot in the backyard. No one is well-off in this neighborhood. A handful of people would have the resources to buy a vehicle, but no one would be able to afford multiple. It would be a red flag.

Trip takes up a pace that's fast enough that I can keep the bike rolling without having to walk it forward. He goes a block over and two streets down before stopping in front of a house with peeling red paint and a crooked mailbox. It has a covered porch that was probably nice at one time, but the roof is leaning precariously to one side as it loses its battle with gravity.

Trip unlatches a black security door between the house and a one-stall garage. It's a tight fit, but I manage to maneuver the bike through. I park it behind the house and kill the engine. The backyard is a tiny ten-foot square with a sketchy wooden pergola covering the whole thing. Vines are weaving through the beams, the leaves so dense they block out the sky. I wonder if the entire structure would collapse if you removed the vines. It doesn't look like there's much left of the wood. I'm hesitant to leave Indy underneath it.

In the center of the tiny backyard, there's a stone fountain that's taller than I am and looks like it weighs more than Trip's car. It dwarfs the backyard. Whoever installed it would have had to remove the black wrought iron fence and security gate to get it behind the house. The water sitting in it is murky. It's probably a collection of the last few storms we've had. There are bugs and leaves floating in it.

"What is this place?" I ask.

"Another safe house," says Trip. "I have a few in this neighborhood. They're spaced out just in case the Enforcers come looking."

I blink. "You're telling me you have more than one safe house when all of us have been crammed into the other for a week?"

Trip shrugs, appearing not at all apologetic. "I trust you guys, but that doesn't mean I want you to know all my secret hideouts."

"If we're working together, that's exactly what that means," I say, putting my hands on my hips.

Trip sighs. "I'll let the others know about this safe house. It may still be a tight fit. Once we have a plan for attacking the Academy, I'll need to bring in more of my people." I don't miss that he says *this* safe house and not all of his safe houses. I decide not to push him.

"Until then, we can spread out," I say.

"Are you feeling claustrophobic, little bird?" he asks with a wink.

"Don't call me 'little bird.'"

"My bad, I forgot you prefer 'Chickadee.'"

"Don't call me that either."

"Why not? That's what your friend calls you."

"The key word being 'friend.' You don't fall in that category."

Trip places a hand over his heart. "You wound me."

"You'll get over it."

Trip grins. "So, you're saying if we become friends, then I can call you Chickadee? I'll add that to my list of life goals."

"No, I hate that nickname." I frown, crossing my arms. Trip's eyebrows shoot up. I clamp my mouth shut and shove past him. I don't know why I admitted that to Trip, of all people. I'm so physically and emotionally exhausted that I let my guard down more than I realized. I hear the gate to the backyard close behind me.

"Hey," says Trip, drawing up beside me. "I didn't mean to offend you. If you don't like your nickname, you should tell Miles. You have a right to decide what people can and can't call you."

I glance at Trip, but his apology appears to be sincere. I sigh, letting my shoulders droop.

"He's been calling me Chickadee for years," I say. "I can't correct him now." We turn the corner, and I see Ash standing in front of the house, talking to Elle and Liam. Liam says something, and Ash throws his head back and laughs. He's tragically beautiful. The kind of unconventional beauty that makes you do a double-take. Like an abstract painting where the meaning is up for interpretation - breathtaking because of its ambiguity, not despite it.

We don't make sense.

I have a daughter. He has the director seat. Our lives and goals couldn't be further apart.

It's a truth that's painful to admit. But then I think about the dance we shared at the club or how he took me into his arms when we rescued him from the enforcers earlier today. He didn't feel like someone that was out of reach. He felt like home. Trip clears his throat, and I jump. I'm still standing on the sidewalk, staring at a closed door. I forgot. Trip was here watching me creep on Ash. I blush.

"It's okay to change your mind, Wren." He glances between me and the closed door to ensure I know he's talking about more than my preferred nickname. Trip leaves me on the sidewalk, disappearing into the safe house. There's just one problem with his advice.

Changing my mind would imply I know what I want to begin with.

Chapter 15

Ash

Miles is sitting on the couch when I walk into the safe house. He glances up at me and winces. I open my mouth to...I don't know. Call him out? Describe, in elaborate detail, what a garbage human he is?

It doesn't matter.

The words die in my mouth when Wren walks in behind me. Her hair is windswept from riding her bike, the curls taking on a life of their own. Her emerald eyes shine with a life that wasn't in them when I left this morning. She looks high on life. She glances between Miles and me as if honing in on the source of tension in the room.

It would be so easy to throw Miles under the bus. He deserves it. We both know it, but I can't do that to Wren. So, I take a deep breath and plaster a smile on my face. I notice Miles doesn't relax. His shoulders are still taught as if he's preparing to run for the door at the first sign of trouble. I'm glad he can see my smile for the loaded gun it is. Maybe he'll think about it next time before he does something stupid.

"I take it you were responsible for helping us outrun the Enforcers?" Elle asks. She's addressing Glitch, who's sitting on the couch with her computer on her lap. Glitch glances up from her screen, closing the laptop lid. She gives Elle a sly smile.

"That depends. Are you going to arrest me?"

Elle snorts. "I'm not in a position to arrest anyone."

Glitch smiles. Elle offers her hand, and Glitch shakes it. "I'm glad you made it out."

"Thanks."

"No offense, but who are you two, and why are you in my safe house?" Trip asks, crossing his arms. Rook shoots him a look, but Trip ignores her. His eyes bounce between Elle and Penny as if evaluating the potential risk of letting them stay here. Penny is leaning against the wall. She has her arms crossed and shoulders hunched like she's trying to make herself as small as possible. I've never seen her look so unsure of herself. It's a far cry from the social butterfly who paraded around at elite events. It makes me wonder how much of her effortless confidence is a mask.

"Elle is my friend," I say. "Penny is..."

"She's with me," says Elle, saving me from trying to guess why she brought Penny here, of all people.

"Why did you leave the Academy?" I ask. Penny tucks her dark hair behind her ears. She uncrosses her arms and stands up a little straighter, years of training overriding her insecurities.

"Jace ordered Elle to arrest me. She got me out instead," says Penny.

"Why?" Liam asks.

Penny shrugs. "He wanted my father to move the Axton AI servers to the Academy so he could have full control over our monitoring technologies - drones, bots - you name it. Jace sent enforcers to the main office to seize the servers, but my father expected it. He had them moved off-site weeks ago."

"Mr. Bronxton was...upset that Jace had involved his daughter. I thought he could withstand questioning better if Jace didn't have Penny as leverage."

Penny cringes, and Elle gives her a sympathetic look. I don't blame her. Elle basically admitted that she took Penny from the Academy so her father would be able to buy us more time by withstanding torture. Even with Trip's small army, we wouldn't stand a chance against uninhibited Axton AI monitoring technology. Elle was saddled with a terrible decision. I would have made the same choice as she did.

"Who knows the server location?" I ask.

"Just Dad and I," Penny sniffles. "We packed up everything and moved it after hours this week. It was like he knew something was going to happen."

"Do you think Bronxton will break?" Trip asks, raising an eyebrow. Penny winces. Elle wraps an arm around her shoulders and glares at Trip. He shrugs. "What? We need to know what we're up against."

"I think he'll hold out for as long as he can," says Penny, trying not to lose it.

"Then we need to move fast. Get to the servers before he can," says Liam. There are murmurs of agreement.

With Penny's help, we map out a plan to hit the server location the next day. I wanted to leave tonight, but I was outvoted. There are a few factors that are working against us. The others wanted more time to prepare for. The servers are hidden downtown, so we'll be in an area heavily patrolled by enforcers.

We need to move as soon as possible, but we also need a solid plan. Trip and Rook are calling in some of their reinforcements as well. All the moving pieces take time to organize, so we agreed to wait until tomorrow. We're aiming to hit the server location in the middle of the day. It's risky, but Jace won't expect us to be so bold.

"Does this mean you're staying?" Wren asks Glitch.

Glitch shrugs. "The second I tried to leave, everything went to hell. I can't trust you guys alone. It would be like leaving a puppy in a kitchen unattended. I'm not an idiot."

"I take offense to that," says Trip.

"Why?" asks Rook, sitting next to her partner. "It's accurate."

Glitch, Rook, Wren, and Liam trade insults making the surge crew members around them laugh. I watch Miles sneak out the back door while Wren is preoccupied. About an hour later, people start calling it a night until Trip, and I are the only people left in the living room. He kicks his feet up on the coffee table and weaves his fingers together, resting them on his stomach.

"What are the chances we'll be arrested tomorrow?" Trip asks, leveling with me.

I think about it for a moment. If everyone else were here, I would tell him not to worry. Everything would be fine, and we'd have it in the bag, but I decide against it. Trip and I have a strange relationship. We were enemies when we met. He sent me into a trap that almost killed me, and I beat him up in an interrogation room. We've both wronged each other, but our hate has transformed into mutual respect somewhere along the way.

"If we get to the servers before Jace does, I think we have a decent shot," I say cautiously.

"And if we don't?"

"I'll buy you a beer in the afterlife."

Trip smirks. "I'll hold you to it."

I yawn and stretch my arms over my head. "I should go to bed."

Trip nods, then frowns. "You should talk to Wren."

I freeze with my arms above my head. "Why? Did she say something?"

Trip rolls his eyes. "She didn't have to. It's so painfully obvious you're into each other. You should make the first move and put you both out of your misery. The angst is killing me, and I'm just a bystander."

I scrub my eyes with the heels of my hands. "It's complicated."

"So un-complicate it."

"That's not a word."

"It is in my dictionary. You said it yourself. We may not make it out tomorrow."

I don't respond. I could tell him that I won't make the first move. That Wren has a past with men forcing things on her against her will. I'd love to be with her, but I won't make that decision. It has to come from her.

"Goodnight," I say instead, shoving open the front door.

The second safe house is just around the block, so it doesn't take me long to reach it. I open the black wrought iron gate into a dilapidated courtyard. It's secluded, tucked behind the building, with a vine-covered terrace concealing it from drones. Wren's bike is parked next to the fountain. I'm glad Elle was able to reunite Wren with Indy. Maybe the universe decided it had taken enough from Wren and decided to start giving things back to her. She deserves it. I open the side door and step inside.

"Did you tell her?" Miles asks before I even shut the door.

I guess tonight is the night for awkward conversations.

"Tell who what?" I ask, even though I know damn well what he's talking about. He can spell it out for me if he wants to have this conversation.

Miles narrows his eyes. "Did you tell Wren?"

"That you tried to get me killed? Of course not."

"Why?" Miles asks, appearing genuinely surprised.

"You're her best friend." I shrug as if to tell him I can't see why that's the case.

Miles sags against the kitchen counter. "Thank you."

"I didn't do it for you. I did it for her. Wren has had her heart broken enough. I'm not going to be the one to break it again. You need to do better."

"I know. I will. It's just hard."

"Hard to stop lying to everyone, including yourself?" I snort. "Look, man. I know you don't like me, but you love Wren. I get it. I'm the outsider here, but I'm not going to step aside or apologize for how I feel about her. If she's willing to give me the time of day, that's her decision. If she chooses you, then I'll respect that choice too."

"You'd tell me you'd willingly walk away if Wren chose me?" he asks.

"I would. I wouldn't like it, but I would respect her decision," I say.

"Hate interrupting whatever this is, but why don't you just ask her?" Penny yawns, stretching her hands above her head as she walks into the kitchen. She's wearing an old t-shirt that lands mid-thigh, and her brown hair is flat on the back like she was lying against a pillow. Her freckles are visible across the bridge of her nose. I haven't seen her without makeup in so many years I had forgotten she had them. I avert my eyes, looking out into the courtyard.

It's strange seeing her in such casual attire. The Bronxtons came to the Axton mansion for dinners, balls, and charity events. We've existed in the same circles for years, but this is the first glimpse I'm getting at the Penny behind the fancy gowns and cultivated persona.

"How long have you been listening?" I ask.

"Long enough," Penny shrugs. She addresses me. "For the record, I had nothing to do with the arranged marriage. I didn't mean to get between you and Elle...although, now I'm beginning to think I misread that situation." She studies me curiously.

"You definitely misread it," I agree. "Jace told me what Carl and Byron were planning. Elle did me a solid."

"You still owe me one, by the way," says Elle, breezing into the kitchen past Penny.

"Seriously, is everyone in the house eavesdropping on this conversation?" Miles asks. He scrubs a hand over his face.

Elle ignores him. "Make that two. I sent you money for a Pod when you needed it," she adds.

"You're keeping track of the favors I owe you? I thought we were friends," I say with a small smile.

Elle scoffs. "Right. I'm your friend, not your bank account."

"Harsh," snickers Penny. She offers her fist for Elle to bump. Since when did those two become friends?

Elle puts her hands on her hips. "So, to recap, you both have the hots for the badass, beautiful Syndicate mechanic, and you're sabotaging each other to better your chances. That about sum it up?"

"Hey, there was no sabotaging on my part. That was all, Miles," I say. Miles gives me a what-the-heck look. I shrug. "They already know you left me on the apartment roof."

"I thought you said Wren doesn't know," he grits.

"She doesn't. I wasn't lying."

"You should talk to her," says Elle. "Both of you."

"I'm trying to give her some space," I say.

Elle snorts. "Please. The woman has had three months of space trapped at a Syndicate cult compound in the middle of nowhere with Tweedledee." She points at Miles. "Meanwhile, she has had a few weeks in a safe house with nothing to do but talk to Tweedledum." She points at me.

"Hey!" Miles and I both say. He glares at me.

"What are we bonding now?" he asks.

"In your dreams." I roll my eyes. Elle snaps her fingers in front of my nose.

"Focus. If you two pay attention, you'd see what's going on."

"Which is?" Miles asks, hanging on to her every word. I would say I'm above that, but I'm just as eager to hear what she says next.

Elle fills a glass of water and holds up a finger. She drinks the whole thing in one go while we wait for her to respond. When she finishes it, she drags the back of her hand across her lips before setting the glass on the counter.

"I don't know. I'm not a damn mind reader. Talk. To. Her," says Elle, emphasizing her last three words. She steps around us, disappearing into the other room. Penny snickers, following her newfound friend through the door. I hear a talk show come on and a muted conversation.

Miles offers me his hand. "I'm sorry I left you on the roof. Can we call a truce?"

"Are you serious?" I ask. Miles shoves his hand in his pocket. "We're a long way from being friends. Don't try to kill me again, and I'll think about it."

"Fair enough," sighs Miles. He pours himself a glass of water and leaves the kitchen. I turn on the faucet and splash some water on my face. A light tapping comes on the back door, and I freeze. I can't hear anything outside. Elle breezes into the room and flings open the back door without a care in the world.

"Are you trying to get us killed?" I snap. Elle rolls her eyes. She holds the door open wider, and Wren walks past her.

"Chill out. I texted Wren and told her to stop by to watch a movie with us."

"Thank you for inviting me," says Wren.

"You're welcome," she says. "Penny is in the living room. You can join us after you talk to Ash."

Wren looks at me curiously. When she turns around, I shoot my best friend a furious look: Elle, the eternal meddler. Of course, she texted Wren.

"Sure thing," says Wren. Elle disappears into the other room with a two-finger wave, leaving us alone.

Eternal. Meddler.

Wren clears her throat. "So, what did you want to talk to me about?" she asks. The movie starts in the other room. Elle cranks up the volume to give us some privacy. I'm going to kill her.

I sigh. "Can we talk outside?" I ask.

Wren nods, but I can tell she's on edge. Why wouldn't she be? I'm acting like a total creep. I follow her into the courtyard, shutting the door behind me. The light from the kitchen window illuminates the backyard enough that we won't trip over anything. She walks over to Indy, running her hand over the body. I've never seen anyone who loves machines the way she does.

"I'm glad Elle was able to bring her back to you," I say. Honestly, I had forgotten Elle knew how to ride. Her dad had a huge car and bike collection back in the day. I wonder if she misses it. Wren and Elle probably have more in common than they realize.

Wren smiles at me. "I am too. I missed her." She turns the key in the ignition so the electrical switches on and presses something between the handlebars. Music starts to play softly in the background. It's a familiar, melancholy tune I recognize from The Iron Maiden.

"It's our song," I grin.

"Since when is this our song?" Wren asks.

"We had our first dance to this song. That makes it ours."

"That seems like a coincidence."

"Then dance with me."

"Here?" Wren whispers, glancing around.

I offer her my hand, giving her a playful smile. "Once is a coincidence, but twice? That makes it our song."

Wren chuckles, accepting my hand. "You're stubborn. You know that, right?"

I tug at her hand. She makes a startled noise, falling forward and putting her hand on my chest to steady herself. "That's better. You were saying?"

Wren laughs, a beautiful blush spreading across her cheeks. I place her hand on the back of my neck, half expecting her to pull away. I know I should put some space between us. I meant what I said to Trip and Miles. I want to give Wren the space she needs to make her own choice. If that's being with her best friend, then I'll respect that.

But Miles isn't the guy she's dancing with right now.

"I was saying you're the most stubborn, bull-headed pansy I've ever met," she says seriously before resting her cheek on my chest. I wrap my arms around her waist, so we're closer to hugging than dancing.

"Don't forget cocky, self-deprecating, and charming."

"The vote is still out on the 'charming' bit."

I chuckle. "Tough crowd."

"What is this?" Wren asks. My heart skips a beat in my chest. She doesn't look up, her eyes and nose buried in my shirt. I rest my chin on top of her head.

"What do you want it to be?" I whisper.

Wren is silent for so long I wonder if she's asleep on her feet. The cicadas buzz around us, adding a unique bass line to the song as it draws it to an end. Another song comes on the radio, and then another, but I keep swaying gently to the rhythm. I can't risk breaking the spell that has come over us.

"You make it too easy to fall for you," says Wren, so quietly I almost miss her words.

"Then fall," I say, pressing a kiss into her hair.

"I can't."

"Why not?"

"Because I have to think about Ariel," Wren sniffles. She takes a step back. I allow my fingers to trail gently to her hips, giving her space but refusing to let her go. There are tears in her eyes, her irises like lily pads floating on a pond.

"What?" I ask, thoroughly confused. Wren shuts her eyes. When she opens them, the tears are gone. I watch her walls go up in real-time and know I'm losing her again.

"You made it pretty clear you have no interest in getting to know Ariel when you completely bailed on my life. When they called us at the apartment, Ariel asked you to play with her. You heard that and bolted. I get it. Kids aren't for everyone."

Wren rubs her nose. "I can't be with someone who doesn't want my daughter in their life. We're a package deal. Always will be."

Wren starts heading for the gate. My feet are frozen. I'm completely shocked by her admission. That's what her hesitation is about? I jog a few steps and block her path.

"You're wrong," I say, holding my hands placatingly. "Give me a chance to explain. Please." Wren looks like she's one wrong word away from bolting, but she gives me a hesitant nod. This isn't going as smoothly as I hoped it would. I take a deep breath and let it out, deciding to roll with the cluster of emotions running through my head because they're the unfiltered truth. My truth.

"I told you I was raised by a single mom. We were broke, so toys were few and far between. The day I left you at the apartment, Ariel showed me her stuffed T-Rex," I say. Wren stares at me like I've grown a second head. Maybe I have. I don't recognize the bumbling idiot standing here trying to form coherent sentences.

"She asked for a T-Rex because she thought it was my favorite dinosaur," I rush out. "Ariel wanted us to be able to play together," I say.

"You didn't want to play with her, so you freaked out and ran," Wren interprets.

"No, I never said that. I had to leave after that call because I knew if I stayed any longer, I wouldn't be able to."

"Why?" Wren asks.

"Because that was when I realized I'm in love with you, Wren Parker." Wren inhales sharply. I continue before she can decide to bolt or punch me. "I love Ariel too. I know you're a package deal. You didn't have to tell me that. It's obvious. I'm okay with that. More than okay. Ecstatic. Because not only did I find the woman I want to spend the rest of my life with, I found a family. I'm not asking you to choose between Ariel and me. I would never do that. I'm asking you to give me a chance to be there for both of you."

Everything is out in the open now. I wait while Wren stands there with an expression somewhere between wonder and fear. She has my heart in her palm. I don't know if she will crush or protect it. I proposed to Elle in front of the nation. I stormed a Syndicate stronghold to rescue Liam. I've done some crazy things in my life, but I've never been more terrified than I am right now.

That's what Wren does to me.

She takes every defense I've built over the years and crumbles them with a single look.

"You don't have to make a decision right now. I'll give you all the time in the world. If you decide I'm not it, I'll be heartbroken, but I'll get it. I'll walk away."

Wren throws her arms around my neck, jumping to wrap her legs around my waist. I stumble back a few steps in surprise before my hands go under her thighs to support her. She lays a kiss on my lips that steals my breath. She tastes like strawberries, sunshine, and everything good in this world. It's intoxicating. She's intoxicating.

She's my new favorite vice - an addiction I never want to be free from.

"I love you too," she whispers against my lips.

"Are you kidding me?" Wren leaps out of my arms with a yelp. Her foot catches on one of the uneven paving stones, and she lurches forward. I grab her arm before she can fall, steadying her. Miles is standing on the back porch step. The light from the kitchen spills out where the door is left open behind him.

"Miles..." says Wren softly. Her face is pale, and she looks so guilty it guts me.

"No," chokes Miles. "Just...no." He disappears inside, the screen door slamming behind him. Wren groans and covers her face with her hands.

"Hey," I say gently, "you didn't do anything wrong. He'll come around."

"He loves me."

"I know." She peeks over the top of her hands with a questioning look. "He told me to stay away from you." Wren buries her face again.

"Why does this have to be so hard?"

"Most things that are worth it are."

"I should go talk to him," Wren says.

I gather her in my arms and hug her. "You should."

"You're not mad?" she asks incredulously, peering up at me.

"No," I say. "Miles was in your life before I was. You care about him. I think it's important for you to fix things with your best friend."

Wren rests her ear against my chest, snuggling into my warmth. "You're better than I deserve."

"I could say the same about you."

"Maybe that's what this is," Wren whispers. "Two unworthy people finding a home in each other."

"I like that," I say, holding Wren against me. "I like that a lot."

Chapter 16

Jace

"**Y**ou're a monster."

Those were Carl Bronxton's last words before I slit his throat. Maybe I am. People use the word "monster" to describe something they don't understand. Something they fear. It doesn't matter. You don't have to understand someone to obey their orders.

Besides, monsters get results.

Now I know where the backup Axton AI servers are being stored.

I wet a paper towel under the faucet and dab the single drop of blood that splattered onto the cuff of my white dress shirt. It doesn't take out the stain. It dilutes it, so I'm left with a light pink blob. I frown. This is a new shirt. It was a new shirt—what a waste. I hate knives. They're messy and uncivilized. I prefer the efficiency of guns, but Commander Harper recommended against using firearms for interrogations. He said blades are more effective.

He was right.

I shrug off my ruined dress shirt and stuff it in the trash can before pulling out my phone to ask Don to bring a replacement to our meeting. The man has been insufferable since he betrayed the location of the Syndicate compound.

I wonder if he feels guilty for turning on his son. He shouldn't. Miles O'Reilly doesn't deserve a second thought. He joined the Syndicate. He led the Syndicate. He doesn't deserve the time it takes to think his name let alone to be the subject of another man's conscience. Bryon and I had our differences, but he always had my back. That didn't stop me from shooting him when he became an embarassment.

Maybe Don and I are more alike than I thought.

I roll my eyes, watching my reflection in the mirror. Don may have betrayed Miles, but it was only because he missed living in the Axton mansion. I have his loyalty because he fears me. I have his loyalty because I can offer him more than the Syndicate. We're not friends. Don is a simple creature with simple failings. He's easy to control and even easier to predict. That's his greatest attribute.

It doesn't hurt that the man also knows how to press and iron a shirt like a pro.

I turn the water off and grab a paper towel. I wonder if Don thinks working hard to gain my favor will somehow balance the past. Whatever his reason, he's useful for now. I'll change my stance when he gives me a reason to. People will always disappoint you. It's just a matter of how long it takes them to do so.

I dry my hands and toss the paper towel in the trash before picking up my suit jacket from where it lays folded on the counter. I shrug it on over my undershirt and open the bathroom door. The top floor of the Academy is mostly deserted. When Byron ran things, Council members used to mingle in the halls or try to get an audience with the director to state their case. Now, they avoid this floor unless they're summoned.

My father was a slave to the Council.

It never made sense to me - how he listened to what they had to say, bowing to their every whim. He built Axton AI from the ground up and then created a society we could all be proud of. He didn't need to listen to anyone. He chose to. Not one of the Council members had as much experience as my father in building the future. He shouldn't have taken their advice.

It made him weak.

It got him killed.

I won't make the same mistake. My father was a visionary but lacked the leadership skills necessary to defend the throne to the kingdom he had built. He married a grunt nurse after my mother died. Worse still, she had a grunt son she brought along when they moved in with us. I'll never understand his affection for that woman. Anyone with eyes could see she was a mooch. She was willing to say anything or do anything she needed to ensure she and her son were taken care of. She never loved my father. She was using him.

Byron was blind to it. He disregarded every warning I gave him. He called me selfish, entitled, and a disappointment. He told me he was ashamed of me. He wanted me to be more open-minded towards grunts because they outnumber us. He believed he could only stay in power because the poor allowed him to.

I snort. A shepherd is outnumbered by his sheep, but that doesn't mean he lets them wander to any pasture they want to graze in. The shepherd commands them and, in doing so, protects them from the wolves. He knows what is suitable for his flock. He gives them what they need, not what they want. The analogy isn't perfect, the grunts aren't as helpful as sheep, but the logic stands - they are not in control. I am.

I think my father's intentions were more altruistic than appeasing the grunts to keep the director title. He thought he was making a difference. That he, Byron Axton, could change the world for the better so there won't be any kids who grew up like him: orphaned due to a factory accident.

That dream blinded him.

For years, I watched Asher's mother whisper in my father's ear, poisoning him against me. She gave him the idea for the Ascent Day lottery, paving the way for other grunts to dilute the elite professions with second-class citizens. Even after she died, my father wouldn't listen to reason. He decided to divide his kingdom, my birthright, between his lawful son and the bastard she left behind.

Asher.

Asher moved in with us when he was thirteen, and I was fifteen. It's not like I had a great home life before we added two grunts into the mix. After my mother died, Byron threw himself into work. I saw him maybe once a week. I think it was a coping mechanism more than anything. If he was too busy to think, then he was less miserable - something like that.

Things changed when Asher and his mom moved in. Byron started coming home for dinner. He tried to organize family activities for us to get to know each other better. Asher and I hated it. In the beginning, my stepbrother seemed willing to make things work. I think it was more for his mom's sake than anything. We both knew going into this that we had nothing in common. We're not related. Asher will never be my brother. It just took him a few years longer than me to figure that out.

Eventually, Asher and I stopped entertaining Byron's requests. I actively tormented Asher, and he avoided me. He started spending more time at Elle's house. Soon, it was as if he wasn't living at the Axton mansion. I thought the distance would force things back to normal in the Axton house, but I was wrong. If anything, Byron pushed me further away and tried to draw Asher closer. It didn't work. Both of us hated him for it.

So, there you have it. Byron was a failure to the Council, the country, and his own family. He would have destroyed everything he built if I hadn't killed him first. I saved the life he made for us. The Council may not see that yet, but they will.

I huff out an annoyed breath, opening the door to my office. My stepbrother has been a nuisance since the day I met him. I have to admit. He's harder to track down than I thought he would be. I should have killed him at his trial instead of the camera operator. It doesn't matter. He won't be able to hide once I have complete control over the Axton AI servers.

Byron tried to keep Axton AI, the Enforcers, and the Council as separate entities. It put him at a disadvantage. I feel that once I take the training wheels off of the Axton AI monitoring systems the Enforcers currently use, we'll be able to find anyone anywhere at any time. We can automatically scan for identification chips and arrest grunts without chip implants. We can turn every camera, delivery drone, and Pod into monitoring devices. There will be nowhere for grunts to hide when they disobey the law.

When not *if.* It's only a matter of time before every one of them reveals their true colors.

Once the country is crime-free, the Council and the elites will see what I have done for them. They will wonder why they doubted me in the first place. I sit in my chair and prop my feet on the desk. When Byron occupied this office, the walls were lined with bookshelves crammed with actual paper books. Rich, mahogany undertones dominated the space, and an old-fashioned drink cart was in the corner.

I made a few changes when I moved in.

The bookshelves and drink cart are gone. The walls are now white, with large displays mounted on swivel arms. I had the carpet torn up and marble tile installed. Even my desk is white. I stripped the room of everything that had a trace of Byron's personality to wipe the slate clean. Presentation is everything, and I wanted everyone to know that I'm a different type of ruler than Byron. Commander Harper and Don O'Reilly appear outside the glass office door. The commander knocks, even though it's unnecessary. I respect his need for boundaries. I gesture for them to come in.

"Have you found Elle yet?" I ask. Commander Harper takes the seat across from me. Don stands nervously off to the side with a white dress shirt on a hanger. I extend my hand, and he almost trips in his rush to hand me the shirt.

Commander Harper shakes his head. "No, sir. Someone hacked the AVA app and caused a series of Pod accidents downtown that blocked the streets. I promise we'll find her soon."

I remove my suit jacket and shrug on the fresh shirt. "Put someone else on it. I want you to move the servers from the location Bronxton gave us into the Academy tonight. Don can help you."

Don inclines his head in respect. He's been a loyal servant, turning in his son to solidify his position in my inner circle. It's time I rewarded him with increased responsibility. Don may be a grunt, but he has spent decades as an attendant in the Axton mansion. He knows how to act around elites. Our manners have rubbed off on him enough to ensure he's not a complete abomination in social situations. I could never elevate him to a leadership position in the Council, but there may come a time when he's not folding clothes and dressing elites. After all, I have to give the other grunts something to strive for.

"Very well, sir," says Commander Harper.

"If Penny knows where the servers are being kept, and she takes that information to the Syndicate, I don't want there to be anything for them to find. Am I clear?"

"Yes, sir."

Movement outside of my office catches my attention. I recognize the man, Trent Richards, as one of the Council members. He opens the door without knocking. I frown.

"Can I help you?" I ask, not bothering to mask my irritation. Trent stands frozen inside the door. His tie hangs loosely around his neck, and his shirt is untucked. There's a stain on his suit jacket lapel, and his shoes are scuffed. There are dark circles under his eyes and a sickly pallor to his skin that doesn't look natural. His hair is askew. As I watch, he rakes his fingers through it.

"Do you want me to remove him?" Commander Harper asks, rising. The commander looks more amused than worried. Trent isn't a large man. He wouldn't stand a chance against the experienced enforcer. Don remains seated, his eyes flicking between Trent and the commander. I have no doubt Don would bolt if there were a clear path to the door. I shake my head, crossing my arms behind my head and tilting back further in the chair.

"Speak," I order, looking down my nose at Trent. He's a Council dog. It's only fitting I treat him like one. I watch Trent clench and unclench his fists as he tries to reign in his fury.

"You arrested my family. I want them released," he snaps.

I raise an eyebrow. "I didn't hear a 'please' in that ask."

Trent takes a deep breath. "Please."

Trent confronted me during a Council meeting a few days ago. He disagreed with my decision to execute Roy Bishop on the stand. He said the Council chambers are a place of law and order. He argued that my actions directly contradicted our legal process and what that room stands for. I could see that some of the other Council members agreed with him, but they didn't say anything. Either way, it's best to fix cracks in the glass before the window shatters. I had the Enforcers arrest Trent's wife and teenage son. They're probably in the Academy basement as we speak.

"I want you to retract your statements to the Council. Then, I want your resignation on my desk."

Before this, I hadn't interacted with Trent at all. I know Byron valued his opinion. When he opposed me in the Council meeting, I did some research. Trent worked in the medical field before joining the Council. He married and advanced into administrative roles that allowed him to spend more time with his wife and newborn son. When Byron asked him to join the Council as a public health adviser, he readily agreed. The better hours and higher pay would have made sense at the time. I wonder if he regrets his decision now.

Trent scowls but nods in compliance. "I'll make a statement during the Council meeting tomorrow. I'll hand in my resignation afterward. Release my family. Please."

"No deal," I say.

"What?"

"I said 'no deal.'" I repeat, using the same bored monotone. "You barged into my office and demanded me to take action. A statement to Council and your resignation are the apology I require for not detaining you. You'll have to offer me something better."

"I have nothing left," Trent booms. "You made sure of that."

"That's not my problem." I remove my feet from the desk and pick up my tablet. "You're dismissed." I scroll on the screen. There's nothing I need to do right now, but Trent hasn't earned my attention.

"You don't want to do that, Trent." Commander Harper's authoritative voice draws my attention back to my unwelcome guest. Trent has a gun in his hand. It's an antique revolver that looks like it was pulled off the wall of a museum. I wonder if it even fire. His hands are shaking. I doubt he'll be able to hit anything if he doesn't calm down. I have to say, I'm surprised he had it in him.

"Release my family," he orders.

"No." I smirk. The commander looks at me, silently asking me to shut my mouth. Too bad. I want to see what happens when I poke the bear. Trent lets out a furious scream. The gun goes off, and my ears ring in the confined space. I can't believe how loud it is. Commander Harper tackles Trent to the ground, wrestling the gun away from him and tossing it aside. He has the man's arms pinned behind his back, and his cheek pressed into the marble tile in under ten seconds.

Don is slumped over my desk, a pool of blood forming under his head. I was right about Trent's aim. If he was trying to shoot me, he missed by two feet. I watch as the trickle of crimson flows over the side of the desk, creating a slow-moving waterfall that stands out stark against the white surface. I stand up before I ruin another shirt.

"Arrest him and send someone up to deal with this mess," I say, gesturing to Don's limp form.

Commander Harper nods, hauling Trent to his feet. "I'll have the servers moved by the end of the night."

I nod. The commander drags Trent out of my office. He's thrashing and yelling obscenities, but the door closes and cuts off the sound. The antique revolver is lying in the corner of my office. I walk towards it, drawn by some invisible current to the weapon that was meant to end my life. When I pick it up, the handle is smooth in my hand. I tuck it in my waistband. By the end of the night, the servers will be moved to the Academy, and any risk I might have faced from the Syndicate or the Council will be gone.

Chapter 17

Ash

I didn't talk to Miles last night. I left Ash in the courtyard and chased after my best friend. Elle told me he ran out the front door. By the time I got outside, he was long gone. I went to the first safe house where Glitch and I were staying. He wasn't there, so I started walking around the block.

After half an hour, Trip asked me to come inside. He was worried I would blow our cover with all the drone patrols flying in the area. I wasn't happy about it, but he promised to send someone "more discreet" to look for Miles.

Whatever that means.

I was up most of the night tossing and turning, worried that Miles had done something reckless. I sigh, leaning my head against the driver's side window. I regret not getting much sleep last night. It would be nice if someone else could drive, but I know I'm the best option. Most of the surge crew members staying here don't know how to drive or haven't been driving for long. I have more experience than the majority of them.

We're taking two cars downtown. They are older models that can't be traced easily, but they appear well-maintained. It also means they don't have any autonomous features. I'm one of the best drivers they have, so it makes sense for me to be behind the wheel. I'm already nervous. Everyone is here and ready to go, but Miles is still missing.

If you had asked me a few months ago, being a hothead is the last thing I would have accused Miles of. I still think of him as the calm and methodical computer technician I worked alongside at Jimmy's Auto. So many things have changed in the last few months that I would be stupid to rely on the character traits I once took for granted. To be honest, I'm not sure what Miles is capable of anymore.

He's lost a lot this year, and that kind of loss changes people. The Miles I know today isn't the Miles I knew growing up. It's not that I dislike this version of my best friend, but it is new. He's harder to read. More withdrawn. A bit more jaded. How can I judge him for changing when I've changed too? I'd like to get to know the new Miles, but I haven't given him a chance. I've pushed him away at every opportunity. I should have talked to him sooner.

A part of me fears he won't forgive me for choosing Ash. I hope he can understand that it was never a competition. I love them both, just in different ways. Maybe that's the problem. I can't love Miles the way he wants me to love him. It would be easier if I could, but I can't. Maybe if I had never met Ash. Maybe if he had confided in me over the years instead of lying to me.

Those are two big maybes.

I hope he can forgive me. I hope he moves on and finds a girl or guy that can love him back. Miles deserves to be happy. I rest my forehead on the cool leather of the steering wheel. I wish I had found him last night. I hate being at odds with my best friend, especially when I don't know what the day will bring.

Surge crew members gathered at the safe house overnight. Glitch told me Trip and Rook have been up for hours finding places to house the extra people. She said they're expecting more later today. Even though the surge crew leader has amassed a small army, only ten of us are going to the server site. It took a lot of discussions to find the right balance. Too many of us will draw unwanted attention, but if too few of us go we can't defend ourselves.

Our group is split between the two cars. I'm driving the first car, and Trip is driving the second. I have three surge crew members I haven't met before, chattering away in the backseat. They seem content to ignore me, and I haven't felt the need to engage them. Glitch is staying behind to support us on the technology side. Elle recommended it after experiencing the benefits of her skills firsthand when she escaped the Academy. If this goes poorly, Glitch is our best option for making it out alive.

Liam decided to stay behind with Glitch. He wanted to come with us but was worried about leaving Glitch with the surge crew. Despite living under the same roof for the last week, he doesn't fully trust Rook, Trip, or their people. I can't say I blame the guy. They've given him a lot of reasons not to trust them. I'm grateful she has someone to look out for her. Liam is a good fighter and a great guy. She'll be safe with him.

Rook also stayed behind to ensure the surge crew members arriving throughout the day have supplies and a place to stay. I wonder how many safe houses they have in this neighborhood? She didn't seem worried they'd run out of space. It always shocks me just how well Trip and Rook run their operation. They're more organized than I gave them credit for. They always seem to have backups for their backups. It's impressive.

The passenger door opens, and Miles takes the seat next to me. I stare at him, but he keeps his eyes locked on the car ahead of us, intentionally avoiding my eyes. I want to talk about last night, but we're surrounded by people. He's wearing the same clothes as yesterday and looks like he has barely slept. This is all my fault.

Trip taps on the window. "Miles, you're with me. We're getting ready to head out."

"No," growls Miles. Trip looks like he's going to argue, but Ash puts his hand on Trip's shoulder.

"It's okay. I'll ride with you."

Trip shrugs and gets in the driver's seat of the car ahead of us. Ash takes the passenger seat. I can see Elle, Penny, and another surge crew member in the backseat. I start the engine, and my passengers fall silent as if the reality of our situation is just now beginning to sink in.

We're about to break into an Axton AI server room.

From what Penny told us, it is one of the most secure locations in the world. Without her help, this mission would be over before it began. Miles crosses his arms and sinks lower in his seat, his eyes focused on the passing houses. I think about starting a conversation a few times, but there's nothing I can say that won't devolve into an argument. I doubt Miles wants me to air our grievances while we have three strangers in the backseat. We'll have to talk later.

Trip guides us on a roundabout route that ends in one of the primary elite shopping districts. I'm not familiar with the area, but I went over the map so many times with Glitch I'm getting a weird sense of deja vu. At the next traffic light, Trip takes a left, and I continue straight. Last night, we decided we didn't want to approach the server location together. Splitting up makes it harder for Jace and his men to identify and track us. Additionally, if one of the groups is stopped, the other group can continue to the target. It also makes sense to park our two getaway vehicles in different locations. We want to give ourselves the best chance to get out of here alive if everything goes south.

It's peak shopping hour in one of the city's busiest areas. I thought it was crazy when Penny recommended we break into a server room in the middle of the day, but now I can see why she wasn't concerned. The streets are jammed with people. The crowds are our camouflage. Following Glitch's instructions, I make my way into an underground parking garage three stories down before finding a space near the elevator.

"I don't like this," grumbles Miles. He straightens in his chair and readjusts the seatbelt, so it's not biting into his neck.

"I don't either," I agree. If we have to make a fast getaway, it will be challenging to make it three stories up to street level without someone blocking the exit. Glitch told me why she picked this garage. It's close to our target with enough cars to provide some anonymity. It doesn't have interior cameras, and the exit opens on the street, making it easy to get out of downtown quickly. Our plan is solid. This is a good location. I know that, but it doesn't stop the anxiety from creeping in. I don't think it's unwarranted. There are a lot of ways this could end poorly for us.

"We should park somewhere else," says Miles, somehow reading my mind.

"Stick to the plan," says one of the surge crew members in the backseat. "We follow Rook's orders."

"We'll be fine," I say, but I'm not sure if I'm trying to reassure Miles or myself. The three surge crew members get out of the car. I watch them check their weapons and stash them under their clothes. The guy who told us to follow Rook's orders offers us two handguns.

Miles takes one. He checks the chamber and tucks the handgun into his waistband. He executes the motion with such ease that I know he's done it before. I mentally chastise myself for being surprised. He's a high-ranking Syndicate member. Of course, he would know how to use a weapon. I take the other gun, make sure the safety is on, and shove it into my waistband. I readjust my shirt, thankful it's baggy enough to hide the outline.

Miles hits the call button for the elevator. It arrives almost immediately. Inside, the overhead speakers are playing opera, and the walls are mirrored. I check out our reflection, making sure we didn't miss anything obvious. I don't see any of our weapons sticking out, but we still look like we're going to rob somebody.

Or maybe we look inconspicuous and I'm just projecting because I'm freaking out.

The elevator doors open into a hotel lobby with high ceilings, a forest green accent wall, and white furniture. It's chic, modern, and expensive looking. A few employees are behind the desk talking with customers and a security guard standing by the door. I freeze, but Miles waltzes into the open without a second thought. I half expect the security guard to make a scene. Maybe tackle Miles to the floor before arresting him, but the guard doesn't give us a second glance. I take a deep breath before following Miles across the lobby and outside via the revolving door.

I could see the crowds from the car, but seeing and being a part of it are two different things. People are rushing by, pressing in on all sides. My heart hammers as my claustrophobia kicks in. I haven't had any issues since I went dancing at Intrepid with Glitch and Roy. Then again, I haven't been around any crowds since then.

Miles interlaces his fingers with mine. I glance up at him. "Are you good?" he asks.

I nod, swallowing. "It's just a lot of people."

Miles leads us through the shoppers dressed in all manner of clothes, from fancy formal wear to t-shirts and jeans. Holding Miles's hand calms my nerves. The crowd is still there, but having that connection to something familiar grounds me. Now that I can separate the people from the crowd, I realize the hotel guard's lack of reaction makes sense.

We blend in.

I was the one making us stand out with my mini panic attack. Miles leads the way through the crowd, picking a path to a mid-sized building with floor-to-ceiling windows. It's connected to the adjacent building with a skywalk on the third floor. The bottom floor houses some sort of clothing boutique. Miles navigates his way through the crowd, careful not to shove anyone lest it draw unwanted attention. He never once releases my hand.

When we enter the clothing store, I immediately spot Elle and Penny. They pick through a dress rack, pretending to be interested in the patterns. A moment later, I spot Trip and Ash on the other side of the room next to a table with folded t-shirts. Our team is here. Everyone made it.

That's when one of Trip's men bumps into a security guard, nearly knocking him over. The breath stalls in my lungs. He apologizes profusely, helping the guard back to his feet. The guy looks livid.

"Just get out of here," the guard snarls. Trip's guy puts his hands up in a display of innocence and heads for the door. His path takes him by Trip. The hand-off is so smooth that I almost miss it. I knew someone had to swipe a key card from one of the guards, but I didn't expect it to be like that.

"That was impressive," Miles murmurs beside me.

"No kidding," I say.

Miles winces. "You can stop strangling my hand now."

"Sorry." I drop his hand. I didn't realize how tight my grip was. Trip heads for the elevator at the back of the store. Glitch explained that the guards are here to prevent shoplifters. They don't watch the stairwells or elevators because they require key card access. We all converge on the elevator when the doors open, sliding in as quickly as possible. Trip taps the button for the fourth floor and pounds another button to force the doors to close.

No one seems to notice us.

I let out a breath I didn't know I was holding. When I look up, Ash is watching me. I give him a weak smile that he returns. We all pull out our weapons as the elevator makes its way up. My hands are trembling slightly. I take a few deep breaths to calm down. It won't help anyone if I'm shaking so badly I can't aim straight. We're operating on a skeleton crew as it is. I can't be the weakest link. My friends rely on me to keep them safe.

The doors slide open into a white-walled lobby that reminds me of the Academy atrium. There's a desk pushed against the far wall, but there aren't any logos or pictures to indicate what this place is. Behind the desk is a steel door that appears out of place and utilitarian in the otherwise designed space. It looks exactly as Penny described, with one important deviation.

There are no guards.

"Something is wrong," says Penny. We fan out into the room, but my initial assessment appears correct. The place is abandoned. Penny told us Axton AI would hire private security guards to keep an eye on the site. Carl knew he needed security, but he didn't want to involve the Enforcers for obvious reasons.

"Check in," says Trip, tapping his earpiece. He pauses to listen to the responses. His pickpocket is outside, acting as a lookout just in case Glitch misses something on the cameras. Trip lets out a string of curses. "We've been made."

Elle marches past Trip and tries the door to the server room, but it doesn't budge.

"We have to leave," says Trip.

"We're already here. We have to destroy the servers," says Elle. "Try the scanner." She steps aside, allowing Penny to press her hand against the biometric scanner. It turns green, and the door opens. Elle goes into the room first, leading with her weapon. We're all waiting to see what happens.

That's when the elevator dings.

I whirl around.

The doors slide open revealing Commander Harper and a squad of enforcers. The commander's eyes widen as he scrambles for his weapon. They weren't expecting anyone to be here. Ash pulls me behind the desk before I can fully process what's happening.

"Keep your head down," he barks, but I don't listen. I peek from behind the desk just in time to see Miles and Trip shoot into the elevator. The commander shoves one of the enforcers in front of him. I watch in horror as his body is punctured with bullets. The elevator doors close, the commander still very much alive.

"Where are we at with the servers?" Trip yells, checking his remaining rounds.

"They got here before us. Everything has been cleared out," says Penny, leaving the server room with Elle. Her face is stark white. I've never seen her look so scared before. One of Trip's men is lying lifeless on the floor, taken down by the commander. I avert my gaze.

"How long do we have before Jace has control of everything?" Ash asks.

"There's no way to tell. He may have been here hours ago, or they may have just left," says Penny.

"We need to leave. Now," says Elle.

"Everybody, clear out," orders Trip. "We're taking the stairs."

The remaining surge crew members follow his order, disappearing into the stairwell. Elle and Penny follow. Miles is still standing in the middle of the room, staring at the closed elevator door. His gun is hanging loosely at his side. He's shutting down. Was that the first time he killed someone? Trip was shooting too, but I'm not sure that detail matters. I can't imagine what I would be feeling if I were in his place.

I touch his arm gently, and he jumps. "We have to go," I say.

Miles nods, but he doesn't say anything. I grab his hand and tug him towards the stairwell. Ash takes up the rear covering our retreat. Someone fires a gun in the stairwell below us.

"Enforcers in the stairwell. We have to find another way out," Trip yells. I try the first door we come to, but it's locked.

"Stand back," Ash says. Miles, seeming to wake up from his stupor, guides me to a corner shielding my body with his own. Ash shoots the handle and forces the door open. We exit the stairwell as more gunfire erupts below us. He slams the door shut. I hope the rest of our team is alright.

We're standing in a high-end clothing boutique. Unlike the store on the ground level, this place is a bit more exclusive. There are serving bots delivering glasses of champagne to wealthy patrons. The clothing racks are spaced out and sparse, the wasted floor space screaming that this is an expensive store. I can see the skywalk entrance outside of the store.

A few of the elite customers gawk at us, our presence announced by the firefight in the stairwell. Someone drops a champagne glass. I expect the serving bot to drive over the spill to vacuum it up, so it surprises me when the bots start rolling toward us instead.

"What..." Ash says.

"Jace must have had control of the servers for longer than we thought," I say. We can't let the bots surround us. "This way." I take off for the skywalk at top speed. I can hear the whir of the bots following us. Can we outrun them? What is the maximum speed on a serving bot? It's not like they're the armed riot bots the Enforcers use, but I have a feeling if they hit us at full speed, they'll do some damage.

The skyway opens into a high-end restaurant...with more serving bots.

I groan, pounding to a stop as the machines swivel in our direction.

"The kitchen," says Miles. He takes the lead, shoving a confused customer out of the way in his haste to get to the back of the restaurant. Ash and I follow him, tearing through the restaurant as more serving bots join the horde chasing us. Miles throws open the double doors leading into the kitchen.

At the far end, I spot a red, illuminated "Exit" sign indicating a stairwell. We're running as fast as we can, but the bots are faster. Out of the corner of my eye, I watch one on the other side of the counter speed up so it can cut us off before we reach the stairwell. We stumble to a stop so we don't crash into the bot blocking our exit. Miles curses and raises his firearm at the machine.

"Don't. It'll ricochet," Ash says, shoving his arm down.

"What do you want me to do? We're surrounded," Miles yells. The bot stays in front of us, immobile. I wonder if they're simply holding us here until reinforcements arrive. I look around, trying to find something we can use to attack the bots without injuring ourselves.

My eyes land on a roll of aluminum foil sitting on the counter.

I set my gun on the counter and snatch the roll from the cardboard carton. I drop it, allowing gravity to unwind it faster than I could by hand. I tear off a generous strip and start wrapping it around my forearm. Ash and Miles look at me like I've lost my mind. "It'll block the RFID signal from your chip," I explain. I toss the box at Miles, pressing the foil, so it forms to my arm. He follows my example, wrapping the foil haphazardly around his forearm before offering Ash the box to do the same. The bots still haven't moved.

"How do we know if this will work?" Miles asks.

It's a good question.

Trip's jacket was RFID-blocking. That was how we confused the bots the last time, but I have no idea if kitchen-grade aluminum foil will be as effective. It's a shot in the dark. Either we take a chance with my sketchy plan or sit back and wait for enforcers to arrive.

It's an easy decision.

I reach the counter and crawl across the other aisle without a bot blocking the path. The bot doesn't seem to notice I'm no longer with my friends. I drop to the floor and walk to the back of the kitchen, holding my breath. The bots stay where they are. It's just like when Trip and I snuck out of the building when we were surrounded after leaving The Iron Maiden. Miles and Ash follow my lead, crawling over the counter.

The bots stay where they are.

I open the stairwell door as quietly as I can manage. Ash and Miles tiptoe around me. As soon as I close the door, we start sprinting down the stairs. Miles and Ash are taller than me, so I have to take the stairs two at a time to keep up. The door at the bottom opens into an alley with dumpsters.

"Slow down," says Ash, grabbing Miles's arm before he can run out onto the main street. "Running will draw attention. The streets are packed," says Ash, offering me his hand. I take it, ignoring Miles's scowl. Ash looks at Miles. "Just maintain a normal pace and walk with purpose."

We exit the alley and join the crowds on the sidewalk. I catch my breath and try to look like I didn't just run for my life. Enforcers are everywhere, but they're struggling with the sheer number of people on the street. They haven't closed the shops, but I can sense an urgency in the crowd that wasn't there before. People are rushing to get away from the enforcers. We take advantage of the crowd's momentum, allowing the shoppers to carry us away from the shopping district and the watchful eyes of Axton AI technology.

"We have to get back to the car," I say.

"Too dangerous," says Miles.

"He's right," says Ash, glancing around.

"I've got this," says Miles. He pulls his phone out of his pocket and taps a girl on the shoulder. She looks like she's in her mid-teens. She has her phone out, taking pictures of a display in a shop window. "Excuse me, would you mind taking a picture of my friends and me?" Miles asks with a smile so wide I'm surprised it doesn't break his face. The girl gives him a once-over before deciding he's worth her time.

"I guess," she says, taking Miles's phone. He pushes between Ash and me, throwing his arms around my shoulders.

"Smile, dick head." He elbows Ash in the ribs while the girl messes with the camera settings.

"What are you doing?" Ash hisses.

"Just shut up and smile," Miles repeats out of the corner of his mouth. Ash grumbles something unintelligible and pastes a fake smile on his face. The girl takes a picture and hands the phone back to Miles. "Thanks," he says, already walking away. Ash and I follow him, but Miles has his eyes firmly on his screen. I grab his arm to keep him from walking in front of a Pod.

"What are you doing?" I ask. Miles glances up from his screen and looks around. A Pod pulls up to the curb in front of us. He scans his phone, and the door slides open. Ash and I share a look.

"Let's get out of here," says Miles, taking a seat in the Pod. I get in, scooting over to make room for Ash. The Pod door closes, and we're whisked away.

"Why aren't the enforcers stopping us? They would have been notified the moment you used your account," I say.

"I didn't use my account," Miles says smugly. He turns his phone around. The AVA app is pulled up, but the profile picture shows the girl who took our picture. Not Miles. Ash whistles.

"How did you pull that off?"

Miles shrugs, clearly proud of himself. "To log into an AVA account, you need a fingerprint and a chip implant. When she took our picture, my phone scanned her fingerprint. It was also close enough to create a copy of her chip signal."

I clear my throat. "Won't she get in trouble?"

Miles shakes his head. "Her phone location won't match the route this Pod is taking. If the enforcers arrest her, they'll be able to tell she was hacked." Miles nudges Ash's shoulder. "Come on, Pansy. Aren't you just a little bit impressed?"

Ash tears his eyes from the window and scowls at Miles. "You made me smile for no reason."

"I just wanted to see if you'd do it." Miles grins.

Chapter 18

Wren

We meet up with the others in a parking lot between the shopping district and the safe house. Elle, Penny, and Trip were the only ones who made it out. The rest of the surge crew members who accompanied us are either dead or missing. Trip is hopeful they're laying low until the enforcers stop searching. We'll know more later. Miles sends the Pod away, and we all pile into Trip's car.

As Trip drives us back to the safe house, the only break in the silence is the click of the turn indicator and Penny's sniffles. She's sandwiched between Elle and the window, watching the buildings pass with vacant eyes. Four of us crammed into the back seat, but we couldn't risk going back for the other car. The Pod we were riding in could eventually be tracked. He didn't want to lead the enforcers to the safe house. We could have waited for Glitch to send another ride, but we voted to keep moving.

We failed.

The longer we stay out in the open, the greater the chance that the enforcers will find us with the help of limitless Axton AI technology. Ash and Miles discussed the implications of Jace's new reach while we were in the Pod. Axton AI has its fingers in everything from the service industry to the military.

The company is more powerful than most countries. Byron and Carl kept their business segmented, realizing the implications of the technology their company developed. It'll take Jace time to bring it all together, but we're talking days.

In one day, he turned service industry bots into his army.

I don't want to think about what he'll do in a week, a month, or even a year from now.

Penny sniffles again, and Trip hands her a crinkled fast food napkin from the front seat. She takes it from him, wiping her nose. If Jace found the servers, it means Carl broke. I don't want to think about what Jace did to make that happen. Elle takes Penny's hand in both of her own. She strokes small circles over the knuckle of her index finger with her thumb in a comforting gesture. She doesn't bother with words. There's nothing she can say that will make this better.

When we return to the safe house, Miles throws open the door and hits the pavement at a jog. I ask him to stop, but he doesn't look back. He picks up his pace, disappearing around the corner toward the house with the crooked covered porch and the courtyard. I get out of the car and follow him. I'm sure the others will meet to discuss our next steps. Someone will have to catch me up later. I need to talk to my best friend.

I round the corner and slow down when I see Miles talking to a couple of surge crew members. They look familiar, but that's not unusual. Trip and Rook have been calling in reinforcements over the last few days. It takes me a second to place them. I recognize them because I met them at the farmhouse.

They used to be Miles's men.

I'm glad some of his people escaped the compound. I wonder how many were arrested and how many joined the surge crew. Maybe some sought a third option, like joining one of the communities. The opportunities aren't as limited as I once thought they were. Miles has a forced smile on his face. I can tell he wants to be alone, but he doesn't want to be disrespectful to those who were once loyal to him. I clear my throat as I approach the group.

"Sorry to interrupt," I say. "Rook called a meeting."

Miles raises an eyebrow, but he doesn't question my made-up excuse to get them to go. The surge crew members shake Miles's hand before leaving us alone.

"Thanks," mutters Miles under his breath.

"No problem," I say.

Miles's shoulders droop, the weight he carries showing itself now that he's with a friend. "We need to talk. Follow me?"

"Sure," I say. His words put me on edge. Of course, we need to talk. That's why I chased after him when we got home, but that doesn't make me any less nervous. We walk side by side to the safe house across the street. Miles opens the gate to the courtyard and continues to the back door like I did the last time I was here. I start to toe off my shoes.

"Leave your shoes on," he says, shutting the door behind us. He walks through the kitchen and up the stairs. I follow him to the second floor and down the hall to one of the bedrooms. Miles strides over to the window and unlocks it.

"What are you doing?" I ask, standing in the doorway.

"Sitting on the roof," says Miles, as if it's the most normal thing in the world. He slides the window open and throws one leg over the sill, folding his body nearly in half to squeeze through. "It's a lot nicer than being stuck inside."

Miles disappears around the corner. I cross the room. The bedroom window opens on top of the covered porch. From the ground, you can see that it slants to one side. You can't tell when you're standing inside, but it's not a fact I'm likely to forget.

"You know I don't do so well with heights," I mutter.

"We're like eight feet from the ground at most. You won't die if you fall. You'd probably just break a leg."

"That doesn't help." I eye the shingles suspiciously. "What if it collapses? It looks like I could put a foot through it." Miles rolls his eyes. He jumps up and down a few times. "Stop!" I practically yell.

"It's sturdy. You're not going to fall through. I've got you. Now, get on the damn roof."

"Bossy idiot," I grumble, sticking one foot out the window and the other. The shingles are easier to walk on than I thought they would be, the soles of my feet quickly gaining purchase. I force myself to look at Miles so that I won't look at the ground. I walk my hands down the wall until I'm sitting right in front of the window with one arm gripping the sill like a cat clawing its way out of a bathtub.

"Come down here," says Miles, trying to hide his amusement. He pats the roof beside him. Miles is sitting in the middle of the roof, a few feet from the window. Logically, I know it's a safe vantage point, but my fear is telling me he's dangling his feet off the edge. I gulp.

"Nope, I'm on the roof. That's good enough. Don't push your luck."

Miles chuckles. He crawls back up the roof, sitting next to me. He bends one knee and props his arm on it, leaving the other extended. He leans his head against the siding and sighs.

Miles has always been my anchor.

I could have had the worst day at work, gotten a flat tire on the way home, eaten canned beans for two weeks straight, and been late on Syndicate protection fee payments. None of it mattered. So long as I had Miles and my family by my side, I could make it work. I could find enjoyment in surviving.

I didn't realize how much I relied on our friendship until it was taken away. It was like a cornerstone of my life disappeared overnight. It forced me to figure out who I am without Miles by my side. Maybe that was a good thing. I found I could stand on my own, but I don't think I prefer it.

Sometimes letting someone in is worth the risk of destruction.

"I'm sorry," I say, breaking the silence.

"For what?" he asks.

"Everything. Let's just make it a catchall. I have a lot to apologize for."

"Ditto," groans Miles. "I'm an idiot. I let my dad into the Syndicate compound. It's my fault Robbie is dead, and I messed up my relationship with my best friend by lying to her for the better part of her life. Then, I tried to kiss her because I was afraid of losing her. If we're making catchall apologies, I want in."

I lift my head from his shoulder so I can look at him. "You're not an idiot, Miles."

He makes an irritated, disbelieving noise in his throat. "Trust me, I am."

"You're doing the best you can with a terrible situation."

"Terrible situation, huh? That's putting it mildly." Miles lets out a dark chuckle that turns into a groan. He scrubs his hands over his face. "I killed someone today."

"Was it..."

"The first time? Yeah." Miles drops his hands from his face. "I've lied about a lot of things, Wren, but I'm not a murderer. At least, I wasn't before today. Maybe that's what my life is reduced to. I've alienated everyone I've ever cared about. My family is gone. I lost the Syndicate. Maybe it's my job to be the exterminator, so no one else ends up like me. Or maybe Trip's bullet killed the enforcer, and I managed to mess that one up too."

He rakes his hands through his hair, pulling the hair tie out, so it falls loosely around his shoulders. I wonder if he did it out of habit or to hide his face.

How did I miss it? All this time, I've been angry at Miles. I was so blinded by rage I didn't see what was right in front of me. My best friend is hurting. He was hurting long before the enforcers arrested him. Rather than helping each other through our pain, we pushed each other away. I'm just as much at fault as he is.

"You're a good person, Miles," I say, wrapping my arms around his shoulders in an awkward side hug. "I was pissed off that you lied to me, but I understand why you did. It has taken me a long time to get here, but I know every decision you've ever made was to protect your family. I'm sorry I wasn't there for you when you started working for the Syndicate. I can't imagine going through what you did alone with no one to confide in. I'm sorry I haven't been there for you while you grieved Robbie...and my mom. I promise I'll be there for you now. Whatever you need."

Miles tucks his hair behind his ears. His blue eyes are a storm of emotions, a tsunami threatening the shore. "Can we start over?"

I squeeze his shoulder. "I think we've known each other too long to start over, but we can forgive each other. No more secrets, no more lies."

"I can do radical honesty, Chickadee." Miles gives me a small smile.

I cringe. "If we're being honest, I hate that nickname."

Miles's eyes widen. "What? I've been calling you that for years! Why didn't you tell me?"

I shrug. "I didn't know it would stick. It became our thing, and I didn't know how to tell you I was over it."

"Well, from now on, you need to tell me if you hate a nickname. I feel like an idiot."

"Not your fault. I should have said something."

"Yeah. I guess that's the good part about a blank slate. We can get everything out in the open and move past it."

We watch as the sun sinks behind the taller buildings painting the sky pink. The temperature starts to drop, and I shiver. Miles climbs back in the window and grabs a blanket off the bed, bringing it out on the roof. He drapes it around my shoulders.

"Is someone going to be pissed we stole their blanket?" I ask.

"It's Ash's. I don't think he'll mind," he says.

"Thank you," I say, wrapping the blanket around me in a warm cocoon. Miles sits beside me, draping his arms loosely around his legs.

"I can see why you love him," he says.

"What?" I raise an eyebrow.

"We're doing the radical honesty thing, remember? You know I'm talking about the pansy." Miles says "pansy" playfully, like a nickname. There's no malice in it like there once was. "I didn't see it at first. I thought you were too different. To be honest, I was scared you would get hurt. I thought he was taking advantage of you. I was afraid I was losing my best friend.

"I thought I was in love with you, Wren. After I was arrested, I was worried I would never see you again. I didn't expect you to rescue me. The enforcers changed you. Ash changed you. You stand up for yourself now. You don't let anyone cut you out of the truth because they pity you. Those are great changes, but I didn't know how to act around you anymore.

"I got scared and it made me an idiot. I made my insecurities your problem and I'm sorry for that. Don't get me wrong. I do love you. But I think my fear convinced me that my love for you as a friend was something that it wasn't.

"Ash is good for you. It's hard to admit that, but it's true. He fights for you when you don't fight for yourself. That's important. You put everyone else first. You're so selfless that it overrides self-preservation, and that's dangerous. You need someone who will look out for you."

I stare at Miles, dumbstruck. As far as apologies go, that takes the cake. Someone knocks on the window sill behind us and clears his throat. I turn around to see Ash standing inside the room with an uncomfortable smile.

"I'm sorry for eavesdropping. I thought you guys saw me walk up to the house...." Ash trails off, tugging on the back of his neck. He's right. We would have seen him if we weren't so engrossed in our conversation. Miles shrugs as if completely unphased that the man himself heard his heartfelt acceptance.

Miles pushes himself to his feet. "It's cool. I was just leaving. I'll stay at the other safe house tonight. Glitch can catch me up on the plan for handling our little bot problem." He claps Ash on the shoulder as he crawls through the window. "Just so we're clear, I'll kick your ass if you don't treat her right." He throws out the threat with a disarming smile that doesn't match the venom in his words.

"Miles," I groan, but Ash just chuckles.

"I'd think less of you if you didn't."

"Good," he says. "See you tomorrow, Wren." Miles heads for the bedroom door, and Ash crawls out on the roof beside me. He's wearing the same battered leather jacket he wore when I danced with him at The Iron Maiden. Mixed with his dark hair and charcoal eyes, he looks like a fallen angel or maybe a demon flirting with redemption.

"Am I going crazy, or did that sound like Miles approving of us?" Ash asks.

"You're not crazy." I smile.

"Are you two going to be alright?"

"I think so. This conversation has been a long time coming. I think we both needed to get some things out in the open."

"That's good. How is he...handling everything?" Ash forces out the question, grimacing at the awkward phrasing.

I chuckle. "That question sounded painful to ask."

"It was," Ash snorts. "Miles is a dick, but you care about him. That makes him my problem." I roll my eyes, but I can't help the small smile that tugs at my lips. I'm glad Ash and Miles are starting to get along in their own, messed-up, way.

"I think he's still in shock, honestly. He'll talk about what happened downtown when he's ready. I don't think either of us will ever be the same with Robbie gone. That's not something you can get over and move past. The best we can hope for is finding a new normal. It sucks, and it's painful. I just hope we get there." I watch Miles cross the street and disappear around the corner. "So, what's the plan for handling Jace's new status as king of the bots?"

Ash sighs, letting out a sound that ages him a decade. "We've decided to attack the Academy tomorrow. Our only option is to take out Jace before he gets even stronger."

My mouth drops open. I knew we would have to retaliate soon if we wanted to stand a chance, but I didn't expect it to be as soon as tomorrow. "Wow," I manage, closing my mouth.

"Yeah," sighs Ash. He goes into the details of the plan we'll be following tomorrow. It's surprisingly robust, considering the amount of time they've had to pull it together, but there are plenty of opportunities for things to go wrong.

"Rook will talk to Miles about contacting some of his people. Trip isn't worried about tipping Jace off this time. We have to throw everything we have at him."

"Has Glitch reached out to the communities? They may be willing to send people."

"She's going to, but she doesn't think they'll get involved. The communities have been neutral since they were founded. Glitch doesn't see them going against years of tradition to send reinforcements now. I have to agree."

I think of Viper, Ariel, and Grams safe outside the city. I'm surprised Viper hasn't tried to get in on the action considering he's close with Glitch, but I'm glad he's with my family. It makes me feel better knowing they have someone watching out for them, especially if things go south at the Academy tomorrow.

"They want me to take the director seat once we overthrow Jace," Ash detachedly says.

"I thought that was the agreement we made at The Iron Maiden? You get the director title. Trip gets a seat on the Council, and Miles hands over control of the Syndicate."

"They want me to *stay* in the director's seat."

I'm silent for a moment until it dawns on me. "You thought it was temporary," I say.

Ash nods. "I never wanted to be the director. I agreed to Trip's terms because I thought it was best for the city, but I'm not sure. The Council and the people will see me as another dictator. I'm not a politician, Wren. Elle has always been better at that than I have. I'm an enforcer. I don't know how to do this."

"Then surround yourself with people who do. Elle isn't going anywhere. She'll be by your side. We all will. You don't have to do this alone. The option to step down is always on the table, but I don't think you should until you're certain the person replacing you will be better than Jace."

Ash sighs. "Jace didn't have to be alone, and neither did Byron, but they chose to be. Will taking the director title isolate me from everyone I care about? Before I met you, I may have considered it. I can't put you and Ariel in that position. There will be people who want me dead - both grunts and elites. We'll be surrounded by enemies. I can't ask you to stick around through that."

"Hey," I say, grabbing his hand and interlacing our fingers. "It's not like I lived the safest life before we met. In case you've forgotten, I was a Syndicate mechanic. Whatever happens, we'll get through it together. We'll make that decision together if you take the director's seat. If you decide to step down, we'll talk about it. We're a team, pansy, don't forget that."

"Pansy?" Ash chuckles. "We're regressing to name calling, grunt?"

"Only if you're back to keeping things from me. What's next? Are you going to leave me a note and run back to the Academy?" I say, only half joking.

His expression darkens. "You'd be safer if I did."

"But I wouldn't be happier," I bring his hand to my mouth and ghost my lips over his knuckles. "When I said I wanted to be with you, Ash, I meant it. Every piece of it. The good.

The bad. The complicated. All of it." Ash's expression softens. He presses a gentle kiss to my lips, his hand cradling the back of my neck. It's not heated like the kiss we shared in the courtyard. It's slow and intimate - like we're testing the depths of our new bond.

Someone wolf whistles below us. Ash breaks our kiss to glare at them. Several surge crew members are standing on the sidewalk with drinks. They're laughing and joking as they continue down the street, already forgetting about us. I'm sure Trip will tell them to get inside soon. We can't risk a drone catching a glimpse of our forces ahead of tomorrow. Jace would have us wiped out before we had a chance to get downtown.

"We should probably get inside before Trip starts locking people in houses for breaking his curfew order," says Ash, reading my mind. He climbs back through the window. I untangle myself from his blanket, handing it to him before stepping inside. Ash closes the window and locks it.

"I want to stay here tonight," I say. I internally slap myself for how eager I sound, but I'm too drained to have any game right now. "I mean if that's okay with you?"

Ash smiles. It's a mischievous, boyish grin I haven't seen in a long time. "I'd like that," he says, tossing the blanket on the bed. He rubs his hands up and down my arms, replacing the heat he stole when he removed the blanket. He leans in to kiss me but draws back. "I don't want you to feel like I'm pressuring you into anything. We can just sleep."

"I'm not tired," I say.

Maybe that was too bold but screw it. It's not like I can take it back now.

I know what I want, and I'm done fighting it. For just this once, I'm going to be selfish.

I close the distance between us, crashing my mouth against his. Ash freezes for a second before kissing me back, his lips parting to deepen the kiss. He tastes like intoxicating familiarity, like sinking into a warm bath after a long day.

Ash's arm bands around my waist, pulling me against him. Setting my hands on his chest, I push him gently until he gets the hint and backs up. His legs hit the edge of the bed, and he sits before losing his balance, his mouth never leaving mine. Ash pulls me onto his lap. I go willingly, running my hands under the jacket. I drag it over his shoulders. Ash breaks our kiss with a chuckle, shrugging off the jacket and tossing it aside.

His fingers ghost under the hem of my shirt. He pauses and looks at me for consent. I nod, biting my lip. Ash tugs the shirt over my head. Or tries to. It gets caught in my hair, and I have to help him. I laugh when it's finally free and toss it on the floor.

"I'm a mess," I say.

"You're beautiful," corrects Ash. The way he looks at me, I believe him. Ash's fingers trail up my ribcage, making me shiver. He pauses on my stomach, and I tense. I know he sees my stretch marks.

I panic, worried the jagged lines of lighter-colored skin will repulse him. I don't have a normal body for someone my age. I've had a kid. I'm muscular from working in the shop. I'm not soft and delicate like many elite-born women. I know that. I thought I was at peace with it, but being vulnerable with Ash makes the insecurities resurface. Ash must see something on my face because he gently takes my chin between his thumb and forefinger. He lays a gentle kiss on my lips.

"Beautiful," he repeats with a sincerity that leaves no room for doubt to creep in. My nerves disappear as I fall in love with him a little bit more. I didn't know I could be this comfortable around another person. Ash has knocked down every wall I ever built. Any fear left over from previous experiences, he washes away simply by being him.

I trust him.

I love him.

I didn't know falling so hard so fast was possible. I thought that was the kind of stuff that only happened in movies, but I guess even the most far-fetched fictions have a foundation in reality. Nothing about us makes sense. We just fit.

Chapter 19

Ash

I wake up to pins and needles in my arm, but I refuse to move. Wren's back is pressed against my chest. She's using my left arm as a pillow, and my right arm is draped over her waist. Her hair is loose, spiraling out from her face in natural ringlets.

Wren looks peaceful in her sleep. Her face is relaxed. She doesn't have the tightness in her jaw or the little crease between her eyebrows she gets when she's upset. I hope there's a time when the peace she finds in sleep carries over to when she's awake. It's sweltering hot under the blanket. Cuddling with Wren is like sleeping in front of a fire in the middle of the summer, but even that isn't enough to convince me to move. I don't want this moment to end sooner than it has to.

The alarm goes off.

Wren groans, shifting against me. I feel blindly for my phone on the bedside table, dropping it twice before I manage to shut it off. I curse. When I turn around, Wren has her head buried under the pillow to block out the noise and the light streaming through the window. It's more than a little endearing.

"You can come out now. I've taken care of the evil alarm," I say, snickering. Wren shoves the pillow off her face. It falls on the floor beside the bed. She scrubs her eyes and yawns.

"Good morning," I say, grinning at her. She stretches her hands above her head, arching her back. She's wearing my gray t-shirt. It's so big on her that it fits more like a dress.

"Good morning," she grins back. I see the moment she starts to put her walls back up, her nerves intruding on our perfect morning.

"I can hear you overthinking things from here. Don't."

"Am I that obvious?" Wren grumbles.

I grin. "Yep. We're going to enjoy this little snippet of peace before the chaos. We deserve that much." I kiss Wren, and she sighs against my mouth, melting into me.

Someone knocks on the door.

"Go away," I yell, returning to our kiss.

"We're heading out in ten minutes," Elle calls from the hall, sounding amused. "I'm leaving some Enforcer uniforms by the door." I break our kiss with a groan, resting my forehead against Wren's.

"She knows I'm in here," sighs Wren. It's not so much a question as a statement.

"Probably."

"She's going to give me crap when I leave, isn't she?"

"Definitely," I snicker, pressing a final kiss to her forehead. I throw the covers off and swing my legs over the edge of the bed. I crack open the bedroom door to ensure Elle isn't in the hall before opening it to pick up the uniforms. I kick it shut behind me.

"I wish we could stay here the rest of the day," I say, dumping the uniforms at the end of the bed. "Would it be so bad to let Jace have the whole damn country? We could always find a new place to live. Maybe find a beach somewhere with some fruity drinks and colored paper umbrellas.

"You know we can't do that," Wren says, flopping back down on the bed.

"But paper umbrellas," I fake pout.

She laughs. "I think the paper umbrellas will still be there tomorrow."

"Fine," I sigh. "You win. You can take the first shower," I say. Wren doesn't argue. She gets out of bed with the blanket wrapped around her like a burrito. She grabs one of the uniforms and disappears into the bathroom, shutting the door behind her.

A few minutes later, I hear the water turn on. I lay down, throwing my hand over my eyes to block the sun. I know running away to the beach isn't an option so long as Jace is in power. There isn't anywhere in the country where I could guarantee Wren and Ariel's safety. Jace will hunt us for the rest of our lives. Even if there isn't a practical reason to search for us, he'll do it out of spite. We either confront him today or leave the city for good. When the situation is framed like that, it's an easy decision.

I shower after Wren, changing into the Enforcer uniform. I use the bath towel to clear the fog on the mirror so I can see my reflection. After months in the Academy basement, it feels strange to be in uniform again. I hardly recognize myself. When Rook busted us out, I traded my prisoner jumpsuit for civilian clothes. The rough material feels foreign against my skin. The neckline feels high and restrictive.

I feel like an impostor.

I finger-comb my hair and toss the towel over the shower curtain rod before exiting the bathroom. Wren is sitting on the bed with her phone against her ear.

"I'm getting ready to head out. Can you tell Ariel I love her?" Wren asks. She winds the bed sheet between her fingers. Her voice is steady, but I can tell she's nervous.

"I love you too," says Wren. She hangs up the phone.

"How are they?" I ask. She drops the phone on the bed and sighs.

"They're good. Ariel is out swimming with Viper again. She can't get enough of it."

"You didn't tell her we're attacking the Academy today," I say.

"No, I didn't." Wren wipes a tear from under her eye. I sit next to her, wrapping my arms around her.

"You can talk to her when we get home tonight," I say, pressing a kiss to her temple.

"We should get going before Elle comes looking for us again," groans Wren.

She's right. I know she's right, but I don't want to leave. I give Wren's shoulders a final squeeze before I stand up. I offer her my hand, and she takes it, interlacing her fingers with mine. Whatever happens today, we'll face it together. Outside the safe house, a crowd has gathered since last night. There are at least thirty civilian Pods lined up along the street. There have to be hundreds of people out here. Everyone is dressed in Enforcer uniforms. I have no idea how Trip and Rook procured that many at the last minute. I have a feeling I don't want to.

Wren spots Glitch and Elle. She grabs my hand and leads the way through the crowd. Elle's eyes lock onto my hand in Wren's. If she didn't know we were an item before, she does now.

"Wren, you're in the last Pod," Elle says, pointing down the street. "The rest of your team should be there. Ash and I will be in front."

"Thank you," says Wren.

I frown. I hate that this plan requires Wren and me to split up. I'll lead the primary attack on the Academy with Elle and Liam. Glitch, Miles, and Wren will split off from the leading group to sneak up to the technology floor, where Joel and Zoe will be waiting for them.

Our plan is simple. Take down the servers. Stop the bots. Arrest Jace.

What can go wrong?

We don't know how many enforcers will switch sides when the attack begins. Elle thinks she has a handful of people who are loyal to her, but I'm not going to count on them. There are a lot of things that can go wrong today. I don't want to rely on help that might not come.

"I'll see you later tonight," I say, trying for the confidence I don't feel. "Maybe we can talk about that beach on our way to see Grams and Ariel? We need a vacation after this."

"I've never been on vacation before," says Wren.

"Then it's settled. After today, it's all sangria, sand, and sunshine."

Wren smiles. "That sounds nice." She starts to release my hand, but I tighten my grip and pull her towards me. I kiss her. I pour everything I want to say into the kiss that I don't have the words for. Wren breaks the kiss, a faint blush spreading on her cheeks.

"I'll see you later," I say. She bites her lip, nodding. She gives my hand a final squeeze before starting towards the car Elle directs her to. I expect Glitch to follow her, but she and Elle stare at me.

"So, you and Wren?" Glitch asks, waggling her eyebrows. She grins.

I groan. "If you give her a hard time, recruit, so help me-"

"Recruit?" Glitch's eyebrows shoot up, and she laughs. "That's adorable. Look at him pulling rank to protect his girl."

"He gets formal when he's embarrassed," Elle supplies.

I glare at her, but she just laughs. "I'm not adorable," I grumble.

"I'm happy for you," says Glitch, smiling. "Wren is the nicest person I know. She deserves to be happy."

"Thank you," I say, unsure how else to respond. Elle takes out her phone and types something before shoving it back into her pocket with a sigh. Glitch's phone vibrates with a notification a few seconds later. "What was that?"

"Elle and I had a little wager on when you two would get together already," says Glitch.

"Seriously?"

"You just won me twenty credits." Glitch winks.

"I wasn't far off," says Elle, rolling her eyes. "I said you would get together after we stormed the Academy. I was within twenty-four hours."

"I'm going to pretend I didn't just hear that," I say. Glitch snickers. She tucks her phone in her pocket and heads for her Pod. I follow Elle to the front row. The last few stragglers are sorting themselves into vehicles. We need to leave before the drone patrols do another sweep. Miles and Glitch made sure the Pods weren't tracked, but that doesn't mean anything if the Enforcers realize what we're doing before we get to the Academy. Surprise and luck are the two things we have working for us today.

Liam, Trip, and Rook are already seated in the first Pod when Elle and I arrive. Trip tried to convince Rook to ride in the center of the pack or toward the back, where she would be safer, but she refused. So far as the surge crew knows, she's their leader, and they need to see their leader on the front lines. In her words, "how can I expect them to do something I wouldn't do?" I gained a lot of respect for her with that comment.

Trip reluctantly agreed. Not that it would have mattered. Rook could order Trip to be detained, and no one would question it. In leading from behind the curtain, Trip also out-sourced his power. I wonder if he realizes just how little say he has if Rook decides to cut him out of her decisions altogether. He's only the leader of the surge crew if Rook allows him to be.

"We good?" Liam asks. He has a tablet on his lap. While Elle and I are leading the fight, Liam will be responsible for communicating with Wren's team.

"Let's roll," says Elle. Liam taps something out on the tablet, and the Pods creep forward. Trip starts drumming his fingers against the base of his rifle, creating a rhythmic clicking sound. Rook captures his fingers.

"Could you not?" she asks through her teeth.

"Sorry," Trip shrugs, sounding not at all apologetic. He stops for a moment before his foot starts tapping instead. Rook glares at him.

"Sorry," he repeats, throwing up his hands. "Can we play some music or something?"

"No," Liam and Elle say at the same time.

"Jeesh, you guys are party poopers."

I snort. Liam and Elle straight up laugh. Even Rook cracks a smile. Trip scowls and looks out the window, but I can see a smile in his reflection. He pushes everyone's buttons to give them something else to focus on. In a stressful situation, he's the comic relief. I think I'm beginning to understand him a little bit better.

Liam relents and puts on some music to fill the silence, and everyone relaxes into their seats. We talk. It's all light nonsense. We haven't forgotten where we're going or what we are doing, but it's more productive than sitting here stewing in our anxiety and fear. That won't help anyone.

I wonder what Wren and the others are talking about in their Pod? I hope she's doing alright. She decided not to tell Grams and Ariel about the attack on the Academy. Viper is aware of what we're doing and will let them know how today turns out. Wren didn't want them to worry. I would have tried if I thought I could have convinced her to leave the city. It would have been futile. Wren has decided to be here. There isn't anything I can say or do to change her mind.

Liam turns down the music. "We're two minutes out. Everyone, strap in." I buckle my seatbelt, listening to Liam count down until we breach the Academy. His announcement is being transmitted to the other Pods, so they know we're close.

Our Pod veers off course, jumping the curb outside of the Academy and propelling itself onto the sidewalk. Pedestrians scatter, watching in horror as the Pods behind us follow in a close line. We pass under the metal arches crisscrossing above the entrance. I close my eyes.

Liam's voice cuts off as the Pod jerks violently. I hear glass shattering as we crash through the doors at the front of the Academy and continue into the lobby. There are a few Enforcers milling about, but it looks like we've taken them by surprise. They yelp and dive out of the way. Some of them scramble for their weapons, but most are unarmed. They were utterly unprepared for our makeshift battering ram. The Pod continues until we reach the back of the atrium by the waterfall. The other Pods fly through the doors behind us, picking up speed now that the path is cleared.

So far, so good.

We jerk to a stop beside the lip of the pool at the base of the waterfall. Elle is already unbuckled and on her feet when the Pod doors open. I follow her, taking out an enforcer to Elle's left as we push forward to secure the lobby. Everyone in the assault team, myself included, is armed with tranquilizer rifles. It was something Elle, Liam, and I insisted on. Most of the enforcers we will be fighting today follow Jace's orders. They deserve a second chance to choose the right side. Our attack force grows as more Pods filter into the atrium. I watch the last enforcer drop to the ground and hear a few cheers from our squad.

"Bots," yells Elle. I spot a string of riot bots streaming into both sides of the lobby. They're working to surround us. Elle slings her rifle over her shoulder, opting for the handgun strapped in her waist. She sends a few bullets toward the approaching riot bots, but they bounce harmlessly off the shields.

We drastically underestimated the bot response time. They're not supposed to be here for another five minutes, at which point we should have cleared the lobby enough to get Wren's team to a stairwell or an elevator. Jace must have lined the halls branching off from the atrium with units because they rush into the space spreading out to cover the exits. I watch in horror as they wrap around the lobby, linking together to create a barrier between us and the entrance.

"Redirect the other Pods," I order. Liam nods, tapping furiously on his tablet. A few seconds later, I watch an incoming Pod take a sharp right to avoid the atrium entrance. It careens off the sidewalk and out of sight. I see the Pods behind it changing direction as well. I let out a breath. Wren was somewhere toward the back of the line. She should be safe outside.

"Take cover," Elle yells, ducking behind the nearest Pod. I follow her lead. The riot bots fire and the shots slam into the metal exterior of the Pod in a deadly hailstorm. They don't let up. There are screams as our soldiers are caught in the crossfire. I cover my ears.

"Can you bring the Pods in closer? We need more protection," screams Elle.

"They're not responding. Someone is jamming the signal," Liam yells back, swiping on his tablet. A stray bullet slams into the tablet, tearing it from Liam's hands. He curses, scrambling for cover.

"We need a plan," says Elle.

"I've got an idea, but you're not going to like it," says Rook, sliding down beside Elle.

"Spit it out," snaps Elle. Rook points up at the ceiling before returning her attention to the firefight. I risk a glance up. We're standing right under the chandelier of broken glass that the Academy atrium is known for. The pieces of glass are hung from thin cords that are practically invisible from the ground, but they all tie into a large glass mirror on the atrium ceiling.

"That's a big target," I say. I'm not sure if we can bring it down by shooting at it. I have no idea how it's secured. Elle, catching onto the plan, starts barking orders. She's trying to get everyone to take shelter in the Pods.

"We should give the enforcers a chance to surrender," I say.

Elle scoffs. "They've had plenty of time to surrender. Why would they? They're winning. Are you going to stick your neck out to ask nicely?"

"I have to try."

Elle sighs. "Okay, then you can be the one to take the chandelier down. Our people are clear. Ask once, then shoot. Don't hesitate."

I nod. Taking a deep breath, I switch my weapon to fire live rounds and hold it above my head in surrender. "Don't shoot!" I yell. I take a deep breath before I step around the Pod, half expecting to meet a bullet before they give me time to explain myself. There are five enforcers directly in my path. I see a handful of bots and more reinforcements arriving as we speak. They keep their weapons trained on me. I recognize a couple of recruits.

There's a young kid with red hair and wide, green eyes. He's shaking so severely that his rifle is bobbing up and down. This is probably the first time he's pointed it at something other than an immobile target. I don't see Jace anywhere. Not that I expected him to join the men he orders to fight on his behalf. He's too much of a coward for that.

"Drop your weapon, traitor," a man growls. It's Hawkins, the guard assigned to me at the Axton mansion when I was forced to serve food. The guard that tased Liam. I clench my fists. Of course, he had to be one of the enforcers. I'm risking my life to offer a second chance.

"Jace is the traitor. Everything I said at my trial was true," I say, trying to reason with him. Hawkins actually laughs. "Look, you have ten seconds to clear the atrium, or you're dead. That's a promise."

"You're a little out-gunned to be trash-talking," says Hawkins. I shrug and look at the kid. His eyes widen when he realizes I'm watching him.

"Run, kid. You shouldn't be here," I say.

I don't know what causes the kid to listen to me, but he lowers his gun and takes off.

"Hey, get back here," my ex-guard orders. To my relief, the kid doesn't listen. He's already long gone. I see a few more enforcers leave down the side halls. I'm thankful a few of them took my warning, but not nearly enough. I take a deep breath.

"This is your last chance to get out of here. Please listen to me," I practically beg, but the other enforcers don't move. I wonder what Jace has done to drive such unfounded loyalty.

"Arrest him," orders Hawkins, scowling.

The enforcers start closing in on me. I grab the gun from my waistband, aim at the chandelier, and fire. I dive for the Pod behind me, not bothering to see if my shot was accurate. Searing pain rips through my left shoulder. I scream, hitting the ground and rolling under the vehicle. I shut my eyes, but that does nothing to stop the sound of screaming and glass hitting the atrium floor.

Something sharp hits my face, and a small trickle of blood makes its way from my forehead to my jaw. I use my sleeve to wipe it away. I roll out from under the Pod when the screaming turns to moaning. My uniform is torn on the left shoulder. Blood starts soaking my uniform from a gash, dying the white fabric red. A bullet must have grazed me when the enforcers started firing. The bots roll forward, unimpeded by the glass shower.

"The bots are still online," I call, jogging back to my team.

"Any update from the other team?" she asks Liam.

"My tablet has a bullet hole through it. I can't exactly check," snaps Liam. Elle's eyes widen when she sees my shoulder, but there's nothing we can do about it. We don't have time. The bots are still rolling forward, the red laser targeting system creating a pattern of dots on my chest. They're going to blow away our entire army. I believe that Wren, Miles, and Glitch will find another way. I just have to stall.

That's when inspiration strikes.

"Jace, I know you're here," I yell. The riot bots stop rolling. I was right. Jace is watching this play out, probably from somewhere in the building. "I'll publicly renounce my claim to the director title, but you have to let my friends go."

"You can't do that," growls Rook. I hold up a hand to silence her. Her eyes narrow. I'm sure we'll have words about this if we survive. I need Jace to bite. I have no intention of denouncing anything, but he doesn't need to know that. I just need him to entertain the idea long enough to give Wren and her team time to break into the server room. The bots roll to a stop a few feet away. The intercom comes to life with a crackle of static that makes me wince.

"I'll talk to you if Elle and Liam come with you," says Jace in a bored tone. I hesitate. I consider lying to him - tell him my friends aren't here, but there are bots everywhere, and they haven't exactly been cowering inside the Pods. People have seen them. Jace will know I'm lying right away.

"We're going with you," says Elle. I glance over my shoulder. She's already loosening the strap on her rifle, swinging it above her head. Liam hands his tablet to another surge crew member before joining us.

"Okay," I say. "We agree to your terms." I feel like an idiot addressing a faceless voice. A few enforcers exit one of the side halls leading out of the atrium. They're probably obeying additional directions from Jace delivered through their headsets. I don't resist as they pat me down for other weapons before escorting us across the atrium. I see Hawkins lying on the atrium floor with glass shards sticking out of his chest. I look away, swallowing the bile that rises in my throat.

He didn't deserve that. None of them did. Okay, maybe Hawkins deserved it a little bit, but the others were just following orders. I try not to count the bodies on the ground. If we make it out of here today, I'll have to come to terms with the lives I took. I expect the enforcers to take us to the top level, where the courtrooms and the director's office is, so I'm surprised when the elevator stops on the floor that houses the virtual reality arena we use for training.

The locked cages that line one wall are empty, and the training weapons have been removed from the racks. The walls and floor are devoid of color. The windows have been blacked out to keep natural light from filtering in. Jace is standing in front of an army of riot bots. They're parked in even rows with a minimum gap between units. There have to be at least a hundred in the room. He has a tablet in his hand, and as he swipes his finger on the glass, a few of the bots roll forward to surround us.

"You can leave us," says Jace, flicking his wrist to dismiss the enforcers. They disappear into the elevator, leaving the three of us surrounded by Jace and his army. I have at least three red dots from their weapon-targeting systems on my chest. There are probably more on my back. The riot bots have linked their shields together, pinning us in.

I glance at Liam, but he shakes his head. We haven't heard from Wren and her team yet. We're flying blind.

"Asher," growls Jace. He takes a few steps forward, so he's on the other side of the riot shield, directly in front of me.

"Hey there, sunshine," I say with a wink. I don't know why I'm provoking him. I think it's a habit more than anything. I know I need to keep him talking until the lights at the base of the riot bots turn from green to red, indicating they're offline.

"Tell me, do you ever get tired of playing the hero?" Jace asks with a bored yawn.

"I don't know. Do you ever get tired of being a jackass?" I counter.

Jace frowns. He swipes something on the tablet screen. Liam howls behind me. I whirl around. My friend is writhing on the floor, his body convulsing with electricity. Jace instructed one of the bots to tase him. Elle kneels beside him, but she can't touch him or risk hurting herself.

"Stop," I roar.

"Then apologize," snarls Jace.

"I'm sorry," I say. Liam falls quiet. His body is still convulsing with electricity, but he's unconscious.

"That didn't sound sincere. Get on your knees and apologize again," says Jace. He smirks, clearly enjoying having me at his mercy.

"You're killing him," screams Elle. Liam is in rough shape. We don't have time for this. I have to get him help.

I drop to my knees. "I'm sorry!"

Liam stops convulsing. Elle crawls over to him to check his pulse. She gives me a slight nod. He's still alive, just unconscious.

"Make the announcement, or I'll keep hurting your friends. Your choice." Jace watches me as I get to my feet. His eyes are filled with disgust and hatred. I wonder what I did to make him hate me so much.

"Ash," Elle hisses. I glance at her, but she's looking at the bots. That's when I realize the red dots on my chest have disappeared.

The bots are offline.

Chapter 20

Wren

We're within a hundred feet of the Academy entrance when our Pod brakes hard and changes direction. I lurch forward in my seat, the seatbelt biting into my skin.

"What's going on?" I ask.

"The atrium is overrun with bots," says Miles, swiping on his tablet. Glitch is doing the same. Her eyebrows are drawn together, her tongue poking out the side of her mouth in concentration.

"I thought we had more time," I say.

"I thought so too," grumbles Miles. Fear settles in my stomach as I think of Ash and the rest of my friends in the first Pod. I hope they're safe. We have to find another way in. Glitch, Miles, and I have a mission separate from the others. I read through the details Glitch emailed me this morning. We reviewed the plan on our drive here.

We were supposed to arrive last and find a way to sneak up to the technology floor while the others distract the bots. Zoe, Elle's contact, is waiting for us to deliver a program that will disable the servers. Miles started writing this program a few years ago when the riot bots became problematic. He finished it with Glitch last night. Ash said they had a bunch of technical reasons for why they couldn't deliver it virtually. He didn't fully understand it. The bottom line is we need to get the program inside the Academy to deactivate the servers.

Miles picks up his phone and calls someone. "We need another way in." He pauses while the person on the other end says something. He leans forward to look out the window. "Stop the Pod in front of that building," he says, addressing Glitch. Miles points to an office building advertising website development services. "Yeah, we're stopping."

"Who are you talking to?" I ask.

"Zoe," says Miles. "Elle gave me her number."

"Are you sure we can trust her?" I ask.

"It's too late to worry about it now." Miles shrugs, unbuckling himself from his chair as the Pod rolls to a stop. He has a point. When we get out of the Pod, Glitch orders it to leave before we follow Miles into the lobby. A human secretary is sitting behind a big desk against the back wall. Zoe must have directed us to this building because she knew a bot didn't guard the front entryway. The guy isn't much older than I am. He has electric blue hair and an earring dangling from one ear. When we get closer, I can see that his white collared shirt has a pattern of tiny oranges.

"Can I help you?" he asks, eying our uniforms with apprehension.

"We need access to the roof," says Miles.

"It's locked. I'm not authorized to open it."

"Not a problem. If you can buzz us in, we'll do the rest," says Glitch, giving him a warm smile.

The man grumbles something about entitled enforcers, but he messes with something on his desk, and the elevator doors glide open.

"Take the elevator to the top floor. When you get off, go right. The stairs are at the end of the hall. You'll have to take those the rest of the way up."

"Thanks," says Miles. We crowd into the elevator, and Miles hits the button for the top floor.

"What are the chances he calls his boss to ask why a group of enforcers need access to the roof?" Glitch asks.

"If he's good at his job, he'll be on the phone now," says Miles.

Glitch curses. "I hope whatever Zoe has in mind doesn't take too long."

Miles grunts in response. We follow the secretary's instructions, and a few minutes later, we find ourselves in front of the locked roof door. It has a keypad on it.

"Are you going to hack it?" I ask.

"Nah, that takes too long." Glitch pulls a thing, a square plastic card, out of her pocket. She shoves it between the door and the frame, swiping down quickly. The lock disengages, and Glitch pulls the door open. When I step outside, the first thing I see is the Academy. We're directly across the street from it and just above the raised patio that runs the length of the third floor that's connected to the cafeteria. The front doors are smashed open. I hear weapons going off inside, but it's faint up here.

"We're here," says Miles. I turn around. He has his phone pressed to his ear again.

"You've got to be kidding me," I say. I watch as a row of delivery drones change course, rising until they're even with the ledge of the cafeteria balcony. They're spaced out like garden stepping stones, creating a path through the air.

"Wait a minute. You want us to walk across those things?" I ask, my voice betraying my fear.

Miles puts the phone on speaker so we can all hear Zoe's response. "No, I want you to *run* across them. The drones are strong but weren't built to support a person jumping on them in mid-air. You'll have to be fast. I would recommend choosing the lightest person to make the trip."

Glitch and Miles look at me.

I blanch. Miles is already shaking his head. He knows I'm terrified of heights. Glitch isn't large by any stretch of the imagination, but she's taller than I am.

"No," says Miles. "There has to be another way."

I take another step towards the ledge and over. My vision swims.

That's a long way down.

"Then tell me what it is! You think I don't realize how stupid this is?" Zoe asks. I hear her inhale sharply. She clears her throat. "Sorry. I'm a little stressed out, in case you didn't notice."

Glitch snorts. "Join the club."

I know Zoe's right. Ash and everyone else inside the atrium is dead if she can't override the building security. The only way to do that is to get the program my friends created to Zoe.

I sigh. "Give me the program."

"You're not considering this," groans Miles.

"We both know it's our best option. Give me the program," I repeat. Glitch digs in her pocket and hands me a flash drive. Miles shoots her a dirty look, but she's too busy working on her tablet to notice. I stare at the relic sitting in my palm. I can't remember the last time I used one of these.

"Are you sure the Academy computers even have a port for this?" I ask.

"Yes," says Zoe.

I tuck the flash drive in the zippered pocket in my vest before stepping onto the ledge. I don't look down this time. I try not to think about how high up I am. I wouldn't hesitate to take the challenge if these drones were on the ground.

I can do this.

I step off the ledge and walk to the other side of the roof. Taking a few deep breaths, I say a silent prayer to anyone listening. I launch into a sprint, picking up speed until I push myself past the ledge. My foot lands on the first drone off-center. It rocks violently to the side. I push off, throwing my body weight in the other direction. I over-correct, and my foot nearly slips off the next bot.

Cursing, I windmill my arms to regain my balance. By the time I manage to right myself, the drone is a foot lower than the others and sinking fast. Zoe wasn't kidding when she said they weren't made to take our weight. I push off the drone and make the following three steps without falling to my death.

I guess that's a win.

Because fate has it out for me, I'm two drones from the balcony when the cafeteria doors open. An enforcer walks out with a tray of food in his hands. Why he's at the cafeteria when there's a battle going on in the atrium is beyond me. He shouts in surprise. Dropping his tray, he scrambles to bring his weapon around.

I consider turning around but disregard the idea as soon as I have it. I don't know if the drones are still behind me. If I stop now, I might not make it. I double down and pick up speed, kicking off from the final drone to propel myself through the air. I bring my rifle around and fire a tranquilizer dart at the enforcer.

My aim is true.

The enforcer slumps to the ground, unconscious. I hit the roof with an impact that rattles my teeth. I tuck into a roll, trying my best to avoid injury before landing on my back. I take a few deep breaths. A drone buzzes overhead, casting a shadow on my face before it disappears.

I laugh.

"Are you okay?" Miles asks, his voice sounding panicked in my earpiece. I sit up, giving them a small wave. He sighs with relief. "Thank God. We lost sight of you after you tackled the enforcer."

"I'm fine," I reply, still laughing.

"Okay...patching you into Zoe now. She'll be able to give you directions. As soon as Academy security is down, we'll come to find you," says Miles.

"Copy that," I say.

Zoe's voice comes through the earpiece. "Go through the cafeteria to the back stairwell."

"Is it empty?" I ask, crunching up into a seated position.

"No, but it doesn't matter." A male voice that sounds somewhat familiar comes through the line. "The alarms just went off. They're directing everyone to the atrium to provide back-up. You're dressed like an Enforcer. Everyone will be too distracted to notice you."

"Who is this," I ask, getting to my feet.

"It's Joel. We met at the border crossing."

Joel. The dude with the buzz cut, bulging muscles, and strong jaw who busted us out of our holding cell. If I listen for it, I can faintly hear the alarm he's referencing. I take a deep breath before tugging the door to the cafeteria open. I wince. I can't believe how quiet the alarm was outside. The sound is so intense I feel like my chest is vibrating.

It's absolute chaos inside the cafeteria.

Enforcers are abandoning their food and rushing for the elevators and stairwells to obey the commands issued over the intercom. I guess they didn't know we were coming after all, but the bots mobilized so quickly that it didn't matter. Jace has had access to those servers for over a day and can hold off a full-scale assault on the most vulnerable part of the Academy. Given more time, I'd hate to see what he's capable of. I have to get the program to Zoe.

I join the horde of enforcers converging on the stairwell. Once inside, I have to fight against the current to go up. I hug the inside and force people to go around me. Some of them give me dirty looks. They probably think I'm neglecting my duty and will find someplace to hide while the battle rages on without me.

Whatever.

So long as they don't try to stop me, I don't care what they think.

The crowd thins out the higher I go. I'm sweating and gasping for breath when I reach the technology floor. I can't remember the last time I ran that many stairs.

"I'm here," I say, shoving open the door. A petite woman is standing in the hall with her phone pressed to her ear. When she sees me, she waves and ends the call. Her auburn hair is piled on her head in a messy bun. Joel is standing beside her with his arms crossed. He has a foot on her and easily two hundred pounds. He stands at her back, watching over her more like a bodyguard than a coworker.

"Hey, I'm Zoe," she beams.

"Wren," I say. I pull the flash drive out of my zipper pocket. "Where does this go?"

Zoe's face lights up. She reaches for the flash drive, but I pull it back. "No offense, but I went through a lot of trouble to deliver this. I want to be there when you upload it," I say.

"Right. Sure. Of Course," says Zoe. She sounds hurt, but she quickly conceals it with a smile. "This way."

I follow Zoe to an office in the back corner. There's an embossed name plate outside the door that reads "Liam Richards." Joel follows us into the room, closing the door.

"The Axton AI servers are set up in the room next door, but I don't have access," explains Zoe.

I groan. "So, we're screwed."

"Not necessarily." She grins. Zoe tries to move some boxes on the floor behind the desk, but she's struggling. They're almost as big as she is. Joel rounds the desk to help her move them. When they're out of the way, I see a hole cut through the drywall.

"I cut the hole last night when Elle reached out. I planned to cut through the drywall on this side and leave the other side intact just in case anyone looked before you got here, but I accidentally punched all the way through." She squats to the side and gestures for me to join her on the ground so I can see through the wall.

"I told you to wait for me to help you," Joel grumbles.

Zoe either doesn't hear him or doesn't care enough to respond. She grabs a pair of glasses from the desk and slips them on her face, pushing them up her nose. "There's a server wrack pushed up against this wall. They didn't bother with cages, so I could access the ports from here." She beams at me. "Pretty nifty, right?"

"Yeah. Nifty," I say, half understanding what she's saying. This is outside my area of expertise.

"If I can have the flash drive now, I'm going to plug it into my computer and upload it to the server." She offers me her hand palm up instead of reaching for the flash drive as she did before. I place the device in her hand.

"Cool beans, I'll have those bots down in a second."

Cool beans. Nifty. How old is this chick?

Zoe goes to work, grabbing her laptop off the desk so she can sit cross-legged on the floor. She hums as she works, trying to lighten a mood that's dark for a reason: Joel's phone buzzes, and he curses.

"Someone just tripped my sensor. Shut the security gates."

Zoe's face pales, but she doesn't look up from her computer. "I can't. We're still locked out. The program is running, but it hasn't brought down all of the firewalls yet. There's a manual override at the end of the hall. If you hurry, you can get there before they do."

Joel unsheathes his weapon and flicks the safety off.

"I'll come with you," I say, taking my weapon out. Joel looks like he's going to argue but decides against it. We don't have time.

"Lock the door behind us," he tells Zoe. We step outside. Joel waits until he hears the lock click before taking off. The hall is carpeted, so it muffles the sound of our footsteps. I lag behind, Joel's longer strides carrying him forward faster than I can run.

When Commander Harper strides around the corner with his rifle raised, Joel is directly in the line of fire. A shot goes off. I return fire and dive to my left. The doors lining the hall are offset slightly, creating some cover. I press my back against the wall. Joel throws himself around the corner, crashing into me. He regains his balance, leaning around the corner to fire twice.

"Are you hit?" I ask.

"I got lucky," he says.

I curse. "We're too late."

"Maybe not. Do you see the button on the right side of the hall about two feet up from the floor? It looks kind of like a fire alarm." Joel asks. I poke my head out long enough to see what he's talking about. A bullet slams into the light fixture behind us, shattering it. I flinch, ducking back into the doorway.

"Yes," I say.

"That's the manual override for the security gate. If we hit that, the hall behind us will be blocked off. They won't be able to get in until someone with access clears them. If we're lucky, Zoe will be through the firewall by then. She can keep it locked down until your team takes the Academy."

He doesn't have to say what will happen if we're unlucky.

"We're going to have to make a run for it," I say. Joel winces, but I can see he agrees with me. We're the last line of defense against the bots. If we fail, the battle is over.

"On the count of three," says Joel. "One."

I take a deep breath and close my eyes.

I kept my head down when I took over Jimmy's Auto. I worked hard and kept my client list clean. I refused Trip's offer to join the surge crew and made neutrality a way of life. It didn't matter. I lost my home, my shop, and the trust I shared with my family. Maybe I'm beginning to understand a little bit of what my mom was going through. It was messed up to fake her death to run the Syndicate, but I think I get why she did it.

"Two."

Byron Axton and the Council were punishing the people she cared about. As a police officer, she believed in the law. I wonder if she tried to do things legally first. I'm sure she did. When the system failed her, she found another way. It's the same reason I stayed in the city after we rescued Ash: I have a responsibility to my kid to make this a better world for her to grow up in.

My mom created the Syndicate and, indirectly, gave me a way to provide for our family. She kept food on our table, and the brawlers kept us protected. We were happy. I don't pretend that I would make the same choice if put in a similar situation, just that I hate her a little less than I did before.

How can you despise someone for making an impossible decision? You can't.

"Three."

Joel and I throw ourselves into the hall. I fire as I sprint towards the commander, never once laying off the trigger. Joel yelps and stumbles. I don't look. Most of the enforcers have disappeared around the corner to avoid the firefight, but Commander Harper stands his ground.

My rifle clicks, indicating an empty clip. I curse, tossing the gun aside. There are a handful of decisions in life that define us. Sometimes it's easy to recognize what those decisions are when we're presented with a choice. Sometimes they might seem small and insignificant. Sometimes they might not seem like a choice at all.

This isn't one of those times.

I know I will die before the commander takes his first shot.

I keep running, pushing myself forward. My palm slams into the button to bring down the gate. At the same time, a burning pain slices through my abdomen. I collapse on the ground. An alarm blares, and the gate descends behind me. It's too fast for the commander to do anything. He curses and smashes the button a few times, trying to get it to open again.

I did it. We won.

I smile. The pain is there, but it's a dull throb. Background noise. Insignificant static.

I close my eyes.

Someone is shaking me, but I want them to stop. It's warm here. I wonder if this is what sunbathing on the beach will feel like when I run away with Ash tomorrow.

"I'm sorry," I mumble, but I don't know why. The reason escapes me like a paper boat dissolving in the waves before reaching its destination.

Chapter 21

Ash

Jace tries to get the bots to respond by slamming his finger on the tablet. When he realizes there's nothing he can do, he throws the tablet on the ground. The device bounces a few times, the screen shattering on impact. I rear back and send a front kick into the riot shield of the bot closest to me. My aim is true, my foot landing in the center of the shield. Without the electronic stabilization to counteract the force from my kick, the machine topples over with little resistance.

"Stay with Liam," I say. Elle nods. Liam's head is in her lap. She's trying to get him to come to.

When I turn my attention back to Jace, he's holding a gun he must have hidden under his suit jacket. I curse and reach for my holster before I realize it's still downstairs with the enforcers who frisked me. His hand is shaking, his ordinarily perfect hair falling into his eyes as his sweat eats away at the hair gel.

He doesn't look like the same man who killed Byron Axton in his study. I suspect a full-on assault on the Academy wasn't something Jace was prepared for. I'm sure he thought we wouldn't dare confront him once he had control over the Axton AI servers. He thought he was invincible, so he let his guard down.

That was his first and final mistake.

"Jace," I say in the calmest tone I can manage. I raise my hands, showing him I'm not holding a weapon. "Let's talk about this."

I know that reasoning with him is futile. His pupils are blown out with fear, his breath coming in short pants. He's panicking. There isn't anything I can say that will get through to him right now, but I have to try. For the first time in my life, I have something I can lose.

Jace doesn't get to kill me now.

The gun is an antique revolver I don't recognize. I wonder how many bullets are in the chamber. A gun like that will have more kick than the Enforcer issued weapons. If I rush him, will he be able to shoot with accuracy?

"There's nothing to talk about. The Council will kill me," says Jace. He drops the barrel of his gun an inch. I stake another step forward, but Jace brings the weapon back up. "Stop."

I stop moving. "You don't know that. I can tell them you surrendered peacefully and that you cooperated with us to shut down the servers."

"But that's a lie."

"They don't know that," I say quietly.

"Why would you do that?"

Because Byron would have wanted me to.

I almost speak the words aloud, but I know Jace wouldn't respond well to them. For whatever reason, Byron let me stay at the Axton mansion after my mom died. Maybe it was out of love for the wife he lost. Maybe it was out of pity. He didn't have to. He could have sent me back to my old neighborhood. I owe him one. Maybe giving Jace a second chance is how I pay that debt.

The truth is, Jace is my stepbrother. We've spent most of our lives ignoring that fact when it's a reality we can't escape from. I've known Jace longer than I've known Liam and Elle. I don't have to like him. He's family.

I sigh. "I'm offering you a second chance. Take it."

His arms start to lower. He's considering my words. I can tell he's a second from giving in.

The elevator doors slide open and Trip barrels into the room backed by a group of enforcers. Jace whirls around, his hand tightening on the trigger.

"No," I scream.

A shot goes off. The window shatters.

I throw myself to the ground, acting on instinct. Jace shrieks, clutching his hand. It takes me a second to process what I'm looking at. Jace's gun is on the floor with his finger still sitting on the trigger.

As in, the finger isn't attached to his hand.

Jace is holding his right hand against his chest, blood dripping onto the floor. My stomach roils.

"Sniper, take cover," yells Trip. There are limited options in the open room. It occurs to me that I should take cover as well. Sitting out in the open with a sniper in the area doesn't bode well for my longevity. I should probably be behind the riot bot shields or even a little concerned, but I'm not.

The sniper wasn't aiming at me.

Whoever made that shot was accurate enough to relieve Jace of his finger from a substantial distance. If they wanted me dead, I'd be dead. I kick Jace's gun toward Elle so it's out of his reach before going to the window. We're far enough up that the wind rushes through the opening, whipping my hair back from my face. Across the street, I see a dark clad figure standing in a busted window with a sniper rifle slung over their shoulder.

I wave. They wave back.

It has to be in the top five strangest interactions of my entire life.

"Who is that?" Trip asks from somewhere behind me.

"I have no idea," I say.

The person is wearing a mask, and they're too far away to assess height or gender accurately. They're completely anonymous. The figure backs up, disappearing inside the building.

"What do you want us to do with him?" Trip asks. I turn around. Jace is sitting on the ground, clutching his hand and appearing utterly defeated.

"I'm sorry," Jace pleads, tears streaming down his face. He's clutching his injured hand to his chest. "Please, don't kill me." I could tell him to get on his knees, to ask me nicely a second time. I could stoop to his level, but I'm not going to. Elle told me once I needed to be better than Jace because this city deserves a better leader. I guess that starts here.

"That's up to the Council," I sigh. "Lock him in the director's office."

"You don't want him in the holding cells?" Trip asks.

"Take the enforcers who didn't surrender to the holding cells. They're going to be pissed at Jace. I don't want them to kill him before he can stand trial."

Trip nods and starts doling out orders. Elle appears with Liam's arm slung around her shoulders. He's conscious and upright, but he's deathly pale.

"Are you alright?" I ask, even though I know it's a stupid question.

"Never better," Liam gives me a pained grin.

"Has anyone been able to reach Wren, Miles, or Glitch?" I ask.

Liam looks around. "You'll have to find someone to check. They took my gear when they frisked me." He frowns. "I know you probably don't feel like it, but we need to make a statement to the people. Preferably now. The unrest is spreading to the other sectors. We're about to have a full-blown riot on our hands. People are scared. You need to tell them what's going on. They need to hear from the director."

It takes me a second to realize he's referring to me.

"Director," I try out the word. This can't be real life.

"Yeah, just don't let it go to your head," smirks Elle.

"Yeah," I say, numb. "Sure."

A surge crew member runs over to support Liam to free up Elle. She transfers his weight to the other guy. She orders one enforcer to check on Wren and her team and another to bring her a phone or a tablet. Thirty seconds later, she has her phone in her hand.

"I'm going to start a live stream," she says.

"What?" My eyes snap back to her in panic. "Now?"

"We can do something more formal later. Liam's right. You need to get the message out there as soon as possible so we control the narrative." She turns around and yells, "Everyone clear out or shut it!"

It takes a few minutes for the room to empty. Soon, I'm alone with the riot bots and my friends. Elle positions me in front of the window furthest from the one the sniper shot out. She wants anyone watching the video to know we're inside the Academy. It will be easy for anyone to identify where we are from the view behind us.

"Shouldn't I clean up or something?" I ask. The pain in my shoulder has dulled from a sharp stabbing to a steady throb. Someone wrapped a tight bandage around it. I have no idea when that happened. I've been a little out of it since Liam called me the director, and Elle told me I had to address the nation. I'm still wearing my Enforcer uniform. I know I have blood on my face from a cut, and there's still broken glass in my hair from the chandelier.

Elle lowers her phone and studies me. "You stormed the Academy to overthrow Jace because you wanted a different future for this country. I think it's important you don't look like he does."

I think back to all the times Jace had an entire camera crew at his disposal. My trial. The courtroom during Roy's assassination. He always wore a suit or the terrible Enforcer dress uniform. He was always one to put on a show. Meanwhile, I announce that I'm taking control of the country over a damn social media video. I chuckle before raking my hands through my hair. I wince when I cut my palm on a piece of glass.

"This is insane," I mutter.

"You've got this, Ash." She says it with such conviction I feel like I have to believe her. Elle holds up her phone with her finger hovering over the button. She gives me a silent countdown with her fingers.

Five. Four. Three.

I'm live.

Wait, where did those last two seconds go?

I stare at the camera, the gravity of what I'm about to do making it hard to get the words out. Elle clears her throat, her eyes flicking to the phone screen in front of her.

Right. I have to say something, even if it is complete garbage.

"I'm not the best at giving speeches, so bear with me," I say. I scrub a hand over my face, the exhaustion from the day overriding my adrenaline at the most inconvenient time. "I never expected Byron...Director Axton," I correct when Elle blanches behind the camera, "to make me his designated successor. If he had told me ahead of time, I would have refused. That's probably why he sprung it on me in a Council meeting."

Elle throws her hands out in a "what the heck are you doing" gesture. I know I'm probably giving her a coronary with my lack of public speaking skills. Byron tried to teach me over the years, but I never developed a knack for it. I always thought Jace would be the one in the spotlight, so I didn't bother practicing.

I wish I had paid more attention.

I clear my throat and continue. "That being said, I saw what Jace Axton did to this country. I saw what it meant to sit back and do nothing. I watched the murder of a twelve-year-old boy by Axton AI riot bots controlled by an Enforcer commander. I watched Council members be executed for voicing their opinions. Before that, I watched the Syndicate flourish because the government wasn't doing enough.

"Byron failed you, Jace failed you, and I failed you. For that, I'm sorry. But we all let this happen. Our neutrality and indifference towards policy got us here. It wasn't one decision or one lousy leader that put us on this path. It was a long road with lots of warning signs we chose to ignore.

"Luckily, we have a chance to fix it now. That's why I'm stepping down as director and relinquishing power to the Council." I press forward, ignoring the incredulous look Elle is giving me, becoming more confident in my words as I go. "They will keep the seat open until we can organize elections for the public to vote. In the future, the Council seats will also be up for election. The director won't appoint them. They will have limited terms and be forced to step down after a set period.

"We've been at each other's throats for too long. The Syndicate versus the Council. The grunts versus the elites. The rich versus the poor. We're caught in an endless cycle of violence with no way out. The new Council will be more inclusive. Let me be clear: I don't care if you're a mechanic for the Syndicate or a member of an elite family. You get to decide who will lead you.

"That is how we break the cycle. That is how we build the resilient society that Byron Axton spoke of. Think of it as an Ascent Day where everyone is eligible - a final Ascent. The opportunity for any citizen to be elevated to the most prominent seat of power. The choice is yours."

Elle presses the button to stop filming. She drops her phone to her side and stares at me.

"Well?" I ask.

Elle gives me a small smile. "That was a hell of an announcement."

"Do you think it will change anything?" I ask.

"I think it's a good place to start," she says. Her phone vibrates in her hand, and she looks at the screen. Her knuckles go white, and she gasps, her other hand covering her mouth.

"What is it?" I ask, my stomach sinking. When Elle looks up from her phone, there are tears in her eyes.

"There was an accident. Wren was shot. They're taking her to the hospital now," Elle chokes. I just stare at her, the words failing to process.

Accident.

Shot.

Wren.

I wobble on my feet. "I have to go," I say.

"Of course, I'll have someone meet you in the lobby to drive you. I can hold the fort for a few hours. I'm sorry, Ash. I'm so, so sorry."

***

Wren got out of surgery an hour ago. I'm standing outside her hospital room, waiting for the doctors to allow me inside. Miles is pacing the hallway. The nurses watch us with apprehension. They recognize me. After my announcement today, I'm the most recognizable person in the country.

After my broadcast, I left Elle to deal with the fallout from my broadcast. She assembled the remaining Council members. They're working through what our interim government will look like. I know I'm expected back, but I won't leave the hospital until I'm sure Wren will be alright. Trip appears around the corner. He's still wearing his Enforcer uniform, blood stains and all. The medical staff gives him a wide berth as he walks toward us.

"What's wrong?" Miles asks. He stops pacing. Trip shakes his phone at us.

"I tried to call you," he says.

"I turned it off," I say.

Trip sighs, tucking his phone back in his pocket. "It's not good. The Council has voted to hold the sniper accountable."

That wasn't what I expected him to say.

"That sucks, but why...?"

"Why did I have to come here to tell you that in person?" Trip summarizes. I nod.

"I thought the sniper got away?" Miles asks.

Trip frowns. "He did, but the Enforcer tech team managed to identify him using footage from a security camera he passed on his way out of town. It was Viper."

Miles whistles.

"Who's Viper?" I ask, looking between the two of them.

"He's a community member. Viper and Glitch grew up together. I hired them both to help develop 8-Bit," Miles explains.

"How does a hacker know how to make a shot like that?" I ask.

"He used to be a hired gun for the communities," says Miles.

I stare at him. "The communities have hired guns?"

Miles looks at me like I'm too stupid to live. "The communities have everything. If you require an illegal skill set, they have someone who can help you."

"Okay, so it's a dick move to arrest this Viper guy for helping us out, but I don't see the problem. If the Council has decided he needs to be held accountable, then that seems like a small price to pay to gain their compliance," I say.

"It's not that simple," says Trip. "After the enforcers arrested Viper, the communities contacted us. Wren's grandmother and daughter are staying with them. They're holding them hostage until we release him."

I curse, sending a kick into a trash can. It topples over, spilling its contents across the hall. One of the nurses gives me a dirty look, so I apologize and start cleaning it up. "We have to release him," I say, scooping questionable-looking nachos back into the upended bag.

"Then we lose the support of the Council," sighs Trip.

"What if someone else was responsible?" Miles asks thoughtfully.

"They have evidence pointing to Viper," says Trip.

"Evidence can be faked," says Miles.

"What are you suggesting?" I ask, righting the trash can and standing up.

"Let's say Glitch miraculously discovers new footage that shows me firing the shot that hits Jace. They'd have to release Viper."

"They would arrest you," I say.

Miles rolls his eyes. "That's the idea, genius."

"Is Glitch capable of faking the footage?" Trip asks. I can't believe he's entertaining this idea.

"Definitely. In fact, she's so good she could convince them that I doctored the video placing Viper at the scene," he grins.

"Would she be willing to do that?" Trip asks.

"Glitch and Viper are close. I think she'd be willing to do just about anything for him," says Miles.

"This is crazy," I say.

"Crazy is what they want. I am...was the leader of the Syndicate. I created the 8-Bit app. Is it that far stretch to think I'd try to kill Jace? I don't think so."

Well, when he puts it like that...

"That was an expert shot carried out by someone with years of training. How do you explain that?" I ask.

"He was shot in the hand. Tell them I was aiming for his head," Miles snorts.

"This isn't funny," I growl.

"No, it's not." Miles levels with me. "Wren needs you. The whole damn country needs you. In this scenario, I'm the expendable one. Let me do this for her." I don't see fear, only determination in his eyes. He *wants* to do this for Wren. Honestly, I can't see another way to free Viper promptly. If the community wasn't holding Ms. Parker and Ariel, we would have more time to find an alternative.

I sigh. "Are you sure about this? You'll have to leave the city."

"Yes, and I'm aware."

"Wren is going to kill me."

His expression softens. "She won't when you tell her why."

"You can't," interrupts Trip. Miles and I balk. "You can't," Trip repeats, "because anyone we tell about this is in danger. Between the three of us, Viper and Glitch, there are already too many people in the loop. That's five different ways this cover up can go south. The fewer people who know, the better."

"I lost Wren once by lying to her. I won't do that again," says Miles.

"Then leave before she wakes up," says Trip, crossing his arms.

"Trip," I snap.

"What? I'm just stating the truth."

"He's right," says Miles, interrupting our brewing argument. "I'll pack a bag and meet Glitch at the Academy. I'll be out of the city in four hours."

Miles offers me his hand. "Watch out for her while I'm gone. When she wakes up tell her...I'm sorry."

I shake his hand. As I watch Miles and Trip walk away, I know I'm making a mistake.

I hope Wren will forgive me.

Chapter 22

Ash

T he curtains are thrown open, shining a light into the room that's the equivalent of a supernova. I groan and tug the comforter over my head, but it's immediately ripped off. I blink up at Ms. Parker. She shoves a cup of coffee at me.

"Elle called. Jace's trial is today. She wanted to let you know," she says. Her voice is gentle despite the rude awakening.

"I thought you said it was going to be held in a month," I say.

"Yeah, I did say that. A month ago." She tugs the comforter off the bed and tosses it far enough away that I can't reach it without getting up. I glare at her. "Elle is sending a car. It'll be here in half an hour."

She shuts the door behind her. I scrub my eyes and take a big mouthful of coffee.

A month.

I can't believe it has been that long. After the doctors allowed me to see Wren, they told me the surgery went well and that she would wake up soon. That it was only a matter of time.

She never did.

The love of my life is in a coma, and the doctors can't do anything about it. At first, they told me to be patient. That she will wake up when she's ready. Then, they stopped reassuring me. Eventually, they stopped coming by altogether other than to carry out the necessary tasks to keep her alive.

I only left the hospital when Grams practically forced me to return to the apartment to shower and change clothes. I still spend most of my days at the hospital, but I leave to sleep, eat, and shower, so I don't have Grams or my friends breathing down my neck about taking care of myself.

Elle and Liam have kept me in the loop. They organized a makeshift Council that would hold power until elections could be scheduled. I asked Liam to pack up my compartment at the Academy. He had everything moved into my apartment. It's not like the location is a secret anymore, but it doesn't matter. Everyone I was trying to hide from is either dead or behind bars. There's no one left to hurt me.

No one has been able to find Glitch.

After Miles left the hospital, he went to Glitch to create a convincing video depicting him as the sniper. Glitch made the video, but used her image instead of Miles's. She let Viper out of the Academy holding cells and locked Miles inside so he couldn't follow her.

When she released the video, the Council wiped Viper's record. When they found a fuming Miles in the Academy basement, they let him out and put out a warrant for Glitch's arrest. The community kept its word and released Ms. Parker and Ariel. The Council has people searching for her, but they haven't found anything. I'm sure she's using her community relationships to get as far away from the city as possible. If Viper and Glitch are as close as Miles thinks they are, he's probably helping her hide.

Ms. Parker and Ariel moved in with me when I extended the offer. I have plenty of space, and it didn't seem right to ask them to go back to an apartment that had been tossed by enforcers. The grunt neighborhoods are still in upheaval. The only difference is the elite sectors are too. It feels safer to stick together.

The first week was the worst. I still had hope that she would wake up at any moment. I slept in the chair in the hospital room with the TV on. I couldn't even tell you what was on, just that I needed the noise to distract myself from the what-ifs that, if explored, would lead me into a downward spiral I know I wouldn't recover from.

On week two, Ms. Parker told me to get out of bed. She said she was going downtown to help Elle set up her campaign for the director, and she needed me to watch Ariel. I was initially surprised, but the more I thought about it, the more I realized Elle was the perfect candidate. She's well-spoken, direct, and - more importantly - fair. She will build a Council that equally represents the grunts and the elites. She has enough experience with the old Council that it would be a seamless transition. Or, at least, as seamless as it could be given the massive changes we're making.

Ms. Parker's involvement with the campaign meant she was spending more and more time out of the apartment, leaving me to babysit Ariel. Looking back, I think she did it on purpose. Babysitting Ariel was the only thing that kept me going. I'm pretty sure I would have died in that hospital chair if it had been up to me. Soon, I began spending more time at the apartment than at the hospital. Don't get me wrong. I'm still there every day. I'm still glued to my phone. That hasn't changed, but at least now I have a reason to get up in the morning.

I roll out of bed and take a quick shower. I grab the Enforcer dress uniform Liam brought from my compartment but pause before I take it off the hanger. I'm not an enforcer anymore. I don't know where I stand with Elle and Liam, but you don't go AWOL and expect things to be the same when you get back. I hang up the uniform and opt for a pair of black dress pants and a blue button-down shirt instead. I put on a tie but immediately take it off. I don't need to dress up for this.

I open the bedroom door and head out to the kitchen. Ariel sits at the counter with a bowl of breakfast cereal, racing a toy car around the rim. Max is lying at her feet. He perks up when I walk into the room, flicks his tail, and then settles back down.

Ariel makes a loud *vroom* noise before jumping the car over the milk. I watch Ms. Parker grab her hand with lightning speed just before Ariel dunks the car into the bowl. I chuckle, the sound drawing Ms. Parker's attention. She smiles when she takes in my outfit. It's a far cry from the sweatpants and t-shirts I've been wearing lately.

"You clean up alright, pansy," says Ms. Parker. She has always called me a pansy, but there isn't any malice in her tone. It's more like an affectionate nickname at this point.

"Sorry I've been such a slob," I mumble.

"Nonsense. Now eat your eggs before they get cold." She plops a plate next to Ariel stacked with enough eggs to feed three people. I pick up the fork and start shoveling down the food. A quick look at the time on the microwave tells me I have less than five minutes before Elle's car gets here.

"Do you want me to come with you today?" Ms. Parker asks. "I could find someone to watch Ariel-"

"No, that's okay. You shouldn't have to see him again," I say.

"And you shouldn't have to do this alone." She puts her hands on her hips and gives me a pointed look. The action reminds me so much of Wren it's painful.

"I won't be alone. Elle and Liam will be there," I say.

Ms. Parker nods slowly. "I'll have a big dinner ready tonight. We can watch the new dinosaur movie Ariel wants to see."

"Yay, dinosaurs!" Ariel crows. The car flies from her hand and plops right in the center of her cereal bowl. Ms. Parker lets out an exasperated sigh, but the smile doesn't leave her face. I finish the eggs and pick up Ariel's bowl to wash it out in the sink. I scrub the car with soap before rolling it across the counter toward her. My phone buzzes.

"The car is here," I say, shoving my phone back into my pocket. I clear my throat. "Thank you for...everything, Ms. Parker. I know I haven't been the easiest person to be around."

"Call me Grams."

My eyes shoot up. She gives me a small smile. "I'll see you when you get home, pansy." She goes back to cleaning up breakfast without a word. I make my way downstairs. A white civilian Pod is parked along the sidewalk. I climb inside, and it takes off. My knee bounces up and down. The streets in the elite shopping district are surprisingly quiet. People have been staying in and avoiding public spaces after the Academy raid.

They don't feel safe.

The country is holding its breath, waiting to see what will come out of the new elections. I'm sure many of them expect more of the same. Another Byron. Another Jace. Another dictator. Their opinions won't change overnight, nor should they. It will take time for the Council to regain the trust of the people they betrayed. I just hope it happens eventually.

The Pod pulls up to the front of the Academy. A few of the windows are missing. Crews are dangling off the side of the building, repairing the glass. One of the arched steel beams that used to cross over the entrance is broken in half and blocking the front door. Excavators are clearing the debris and dumping the remains into the back of trucks to be hauled off.

Elle is out front talking to a woman wearing a hard hat. She points to something on the tablet. The woman nods before going to speak to her team. Elle's blond hair is tied back in a high ponytail. She's wearing slacks and a blouse, a far cry from her usual uniform. I take a deep breath and get out of the Pod. Elle approaches me, but she stops a few feet away.

"Hi," I say lamely, not quite meeting her eyes.

"Hey," says Elle.

"It has been a while," I say.

Elle raises an eyebrow.

"Since when do you do small talk?" Elle watches me for a moment, but I have nothing to say. She sighs. "Where's your uniform?"

"Where's yours?" I counter.

"I'm not an enforcer anymore," she says.

"Neither am I."

"Says who?" Elle asks.

"I left the Academy a month ago without permission and haven't checked in. You know that's grounds for dismissal," I say. More like arrest, but I'm not going to remind her.

Elle shrugs. "Anyone who had the power to say anything either died in the battle for the Academy or is behind bars. You're still an enforcer, Ash. So long as you want to be." I swallow before giving her a nod. "I had Liam move Jace to an interrogation room to give you some time to talk alone. You don't have to speak to him. It's up to you."

"I'll talk to him," I say.

Elle nods. She seems to want to say something more, but I don't think she knows how to interact with me. I follow her around the fenced-off construction site and through the front doors of the Academy. The last time I took this entrance, I was entering a battlefield. The atrium is immaculate, as it always has been, with white tiles, white walls, and white furniture. The only indication that something happened here is the missing chandelier.

"So, you're running for the director," I say, trying to break the uncomfortable silence.

"Yeah," says Elle. "There are many things I want to fix in this city. I spent enough years with the Enforcers being ignored, so I thought if I went higher, someone might listen."

"Who's going to run the Enforcers?" I ask. As Elle said, most high-ranking members were killed in the battle. To my endless dismay, Commander Harper managed to escape. Elle has people looking for him, but they haven't found anything. While that's convenient if I want to return to the Academy, it doesn't put the Enforcers in a good place when choosing a new leader. Elle stops in the atrium and turns to face me.

"I was hoping you would."

"Me?" I choke. "What about Liam?"

"Liam is working on something else," says Elle.

"I have no experience with Enforcer leadership. I've been training recruits for most of my career and leading squads in the field. I'm not exactly the sit-behind-a-desk-and-give-orders type."

"Which is exactly why you're the perfect fit," says Elle. "Look, I don't need you to give me an answer right now, but I want you to think about it. The grunts are still uncomfortable with the Enforcers as a concept. They've had nothing but negative experiences with them. We need to recruit and train more grunt-born citizens. We need to run outreach programs and work on our transparency. We need to build trust. You started out hating the Syndicate and the grunts before fighting alongside them. People know your story, Ash. Like it or not, what you did made you a celebrity. Your opinion matters. People trust you. I could use you on my team."

"I'll think about it," I say. Elle nods and continues leading me to the basement. The enforcers we pass stop and salute us both. It's strange to be back in the world of white uniforms and protocols. I shove my hands in my pockets and keep my eyes trained on the floor. I don't know what Elle was thinking. I'm the least qualified person for the job. Liam is waiting for us in the lobby when we get to the basement.

"Hey man," I say, offering him my hand. Liam takes my hand and pulls me into a bear hug that has me gasping for air. He sets me back on my feet after a few seconds.

"Don't disappear on us again, yeah?"

Guilt punches me in the gut. I've been dealing with a lot, but so have Elle and Liam. They're rebuilding the country. My losses are huge, but so are theirs. I should have been there for Elle when she decided to run for director. I'm her best friend. That's what you do. I should have been there for Liam when he sorted out the mess with who to arrest and who to pardon. Instead, I crawled under a rock and let my friends handle my responsibilities for me.

"I'm sorry."

"We can make apologies later," says Elle. "You have ten minutes with Jace before we have to take him up to the courtroom." Liam and Elle share a look. With the way they're acting, they must think I'm a few minutes away from having a mental breakdown. I wish I could say they're wrong.

I take a deep breath and open the door to the interrogation room.

Jace sits behind the desk with his hands cuffed in front of him. He's messing with the chain strung through the loop welded to the table in front of him. Jace is well-groomed and appears to have had enough to eat, unlike when he held Liam and me here. I'm sure he has Elle to thank for that. She's a much better person than I'll ever be. I shut the door, and Jace looks up, dropping the chain. There are a million things I could ask him now, but it all boils down to a single word.

"Why?" I ask.

I half expect him to tell me to pound sand or give me some snarky response instead of an honest answer. Jace brushes a strand of hair out of his face. He usually keeps it pinned back with hairspray, but I doubt Elle was that accommodating. His dark eyes are so similar to Byron's that I feel like I'm staring at a ghost. I wonder what it's like to look in the mirror every day and see the eyes of the man you killed.

"Do you know what it was like having you as a brother? Imagine losing your mom to the Syndicate...actually, that's not much of a stretch for you." Jace smirks. I bite the inside of my cheek, so I don't respond to the jab. "Then, your dad marries someone associated with the people responsible for her death - a grunt. If that wasn't bad enough, she has a son."

"Do you want me to apologize for taking away your status as an only child?" I ask, rolling my eyes.

"Yes," says Jace.

I blink.

He's actually serious.

"The worst part was, Byron loved you as a son. So much so that he was willing to split up my birthright to give you a legacy. A name. A purpose. He was always asking why I couldn't be more like you. There was nothing I could do right in his eyes."

"He said the same thing to me," I say. "Byron wanted me to be more like you."

Jace's eyebrows shoot up, but he then lets a soft chuckle. "I guess good old dad played us both."

"Yeah, I guess so."

Jace and I will never see eye to eye. We've both taken so much from each other. A crack may have formed when Byron pitted us against one another, but we widened it to a chasm on our own. There are so many emotions that well up inside me I don't know which to express.

Anger. I want to sink my fist into Jace's face.

Regret. My stepbrother felt just as alone as I did but never said anything.

Pain. For losing my entire family and realizing there's nothing I can say or do that will bring them back.

Pity. That Jace lost himself to the same desire for vengeance.

Hate. For what was done to Wren.

I wonder if things would have been different if Jace had friends like Elle and Liam in his life. Someone to care enough to show him that there was another way - that there are things worth putting aside our differences for. I unclench my fists and stand up from the table.

"You need to apologize to the Council for your actions," I say.

"I'm not sorry for what I did," says Jace. "The grunts ruined this country, and Byron let it happen. I did nothing less than what was necessary."

"If you say that, they'll execute you," I say.

"So be it," says Jace. He claps his hands in front of him, appearing resigned to his fate. He's not the same man who begged for his life in the virtual reality arena. Then again, he's had a month to process everything. Even if he did apologize to the Council, I wonder if they would take the change of heart seriously.

I sigh. "I guess this is goodbye, brother."

"You're not my brother," Jace snaps. I exit the room and close the door behind me. I lean my head back against the wood and stare at the ceiling. That took a lot more out of me than I thought it would. I'm not sure what I expected to gain from that conversation. Closure? An apology?

Whatever it was, I didn't get it.

I shouldn't have talked to him.

"How did it go-" I storm past Elle and Liam, cutting off her question. I take the stairs two at a time until I reach the atrium. A few enforcers recognize me. They shout a greeting and ask me to join them, but I'm not in the mood to listen. I'm in a Pod and halfway across town before I realize where I'm going.

Jimmy's Auto looks the same as it always has - a squat, cinder-block rectangle with boarded-up windows. The sign outside with the shop name looks like it's tilting more than it was the last time I was here. I get out of the Pod and jog around to the back door, but it was locked. I don't have a key.

That's when I remember the first time I met Wren.

I run around the block to the side of the fabrication shop. There's a broken window at about chest height. I take off my jacket and toss it over the glass stuck in the bottom of the pane before hauling myself up and over. I feel the glass slice into my shoulder where I misjudged the gap, but I couldn't care less.

Dropping to the ground, I cross the shop until I come to the hatch Wren cut into the back of the building. I tug it aside and make my way into Wren's shop. No one bothered to close up the hole. I try to turn on the lights, but the room stays dark. I take out my phone and turn on the flashlight. It takes me a moment to realize I'm standing in the office at the back of the shop. The desk is clean, and there aren't any fast food wrappers on the floor. It's unrecognizable from the last time I was here.

There's a picture on the desk of Wren's family. Wren is just slightly older than Ariel in the picture. It's incredible how much the two resemble each other. A man and a woman are holding her, pressing a kiss to either cheek. Besides them, I recognize a younger version of Ms. Parker. I assume the man next to her is her husband.

A drop of water lands on the glass, distorting the image.

She took my advice and cleaned out her dad's desk. She accepted the shop as her own. She moved on.

That's when I finally lose it.

I sob uncontrollably in a way I haven't since I lost my mom. Tears stream down my face, soaking my shirt. My nose is plugged, and my breath is coming in chest-wracking gasps. I hear the back door opening, but I can't bring myself to care. The lights come on, and Miles appears in the doorway, leading with a gun. I have no idea where he got it, but I can't say I'm surprised. When he sees it's me, he sets the weapon on the desk and approaches me.

"Hold on," he says. He takes his phone out and types something before sliding down the wall to sit next to me. "I texted Elle and Liam. They'll be here soon."

"How did you get the power on?" I ask, my voice coming out nasally and gross. Miles reaches up and snatches a paper towel roll off the top of the filing cabinet beside him. He tears off a square and hands it to me. I blow my nose with a long honk. Of course, he has to be here to see the one time I lose it.

"The breaker tripped. I reset it. What are you doing here?"

I take another paper towel and blow my nose again.

"I talked to Jace."

He winces.

"It went about as well as you think." I wad the papers up in my hand and toss them at the trash can by the door. It bounces off the rim and onto the floor. "What are you doing here?" I ask him.

"I put sensors on the doors. I get a text message if anyone enters the building."

"I didn't use the door."

"I know," says Miles with a small smile.

"Why?"

Miles sighs. "I haven't heard anything from Glitch. She knows I have a go-bag stashed here, so I thought she might stop by. It was wishful thinking. She probably left the city the day we arrested Jace."

He looks guilty. The video Glitch made was exceptional. No one questioned the authenticity. Her actions may have freed Viper and Wren's family, but it was a death sentence for her. Glitch decided to take his place, but Miles blames himself.

"She wouldn't have stuck around," I agree.

"How are you holding up?" he asks.

"I should be asking you that," I say.

He shrugs. "I guess I feel...lost. That's the best way to describe it. What about you?"

I lean my head back against the wall. "Lost is a good description. I've always had a plan or a goal. Something that I could work towards. Wren gave me a second chance to drop my vendetta against the Syndicate and choose to live instead. Then, that second chance was taken from me all over again." I pause, then decide to say what I've been thinking every day for the past month but haven't dared to speak aloud. "What if she never wakes up?" Miles doesn't say anything right away. What can he say? He can't see into the future. Anything he says right now would be a lie meant to soothe me. "No one should have to rebuild their world twice in their twenties. It's not fair."

"No, it isn't," Miles agrees.

"Meanwhile, I'm taking care of Ariel, and even that feels like I'm betraying Wren. She should be here to share all of Ariel's milestones with her, not me. Like reading her first chapter book or watching her use the swing at the playground for the first time by herself. I'm trying my best to hide that I'm falling apart. I can't do this. I can't do anything."

Miles is silent for a moment.

"We can be there for Ariel," he whispers. "Your world is falling apart, Ash, but hers is too. You, of all people, know what it's like to lose a parent."

"She's not gone," I snap.

"No, she's not," Miles agrees. He sighs. "Ash, you don't have to be perfect. You just have to be present. Start with that."

He's right.

I know he is, but saying the words and carrying them out are two separate concepts. I'm not convinced I'm what Ariel needs.

"What if I screw up?" I ask.

"Then Wren will have to wake up, so she can kick your ass," says Miles.

I snort, a giant snot bubble coming out of my nose. I grab a paper towel and wipe my face, chuckling at Miles's disgusted expression.

"She would do it, too," I say.

"Oh, absolutely," Miles grins back.

"I'll talk to Grams about letting you visit Ariel. She misses you," I say. Grams blames Miles for letting Wren get hurt. She banned him from the apartment and hasn't let him visit Ariel.

I let her do it, mainly because I was too wrapped up in my own grief to see how unfair that was to Miles. Miles and I have had our differences, but I know Wren's injuries weren't his fault. She would have found a way into the Academy with or without him. Miles has been a part of Ariel's life since she took her first breath. It's wrong to keep him away from her when we're all hurting.

"I appreciate it," says Miles.

Miles and I trade stories about Wren. The good, the bad, and the ones an ex-enforcer shouldn't hear. It's therapeutic to share memories of Wren with someone who knows and loves her.

When Elle and Liam arrive after Jace's trial, they sit with us on the floor and listen while Miles and I tell stories. I don't ask what the verdict was. I don't want to know. They chip in here and there, but for the most part, they're here to be with me. When we get too stiff sitting on the floor, Liam suggests we get some food. Liam, Elle, and Miles leave the office, giving me a minute to myself.

I prop the picture of Wren's family on the desk, my fingers trailing over the glass. The gold Axton seal ring I put on this morning reflects on me.

You don't have to be perfect. You just have to present.

Before joining my friends outside, I take off the ring and leave it beside the picture frame. I can't change the past, but I can leave it where it belongs. I lock the door and follow my friends outside. My phone buzzes in my back pocket.

It's Wren's doctor.

I nearly drop my phone in my haste to answer it.

"What's going on?" I ask as soon as the line connects. As the doctor talks, I hear a noise between a laugh and a sob. I sink to my knees.

"Ash....Ash!" I realize Elle and Liam are calling my name. They've probably said it more than once from the way they're shouting. "What's wrong?"

"That was the hospital. Wren woke up."

Epilogue

Wren – Six Months Later

I drum my fingers against the steering wheel as a crowd gathers on the steps of the Axton mansion. There are photographers holding cameras with huge telescopic lenses ready to snap pictures as soon as anyone important shows up. Luckily, they haven't recognized us. Why would they? I'm driving a beat-up Toyota Corolla a few decades past its prime.

It has character.

That sounds better than saying it has a suspicious suspension rattle, and the ceiling material is pinned up with a collection of buttons advertising obscure '80s bands.

A black Rolls Royce pulls up to the curb. The photographers raise their cameras, the flashes pulsing through the group, making them appear more like fireflies than humans. A woman in a crisp black pantsuit emerges from the car. She stands tall, her lithe figure framed with dark brown hair hanging in braids at her shoulders.

It's Elle.

Elle looks confident. Happy. Somehow more complete than she did when she first took office. I know there's one person, in particular, we have to thank for that. She reaches into the car to help her wife, Penny Bronxton. Elle proposed on air when she started her campaign. She said the city could choose all of her or none of her.

It turns out that the world was more open-minded than she thought.

It took Ash and Liam a second to get over the initial weirdness but seeing them together erased any concerns they may have had. Elle treats Penny like a goddess and Penny looks at Elle like she hung the stars. Penny waves at the camera and takes Elle's hand. I lean forward and rest my forehead on the cold leather of the steering wheel.

After Jace was executed, a lawyer approached Ash with the deed to the Axton family home. With Jace gone, he was the only Axton left. He got everything: the shares in Axton AI, the house, and the money. Ultimately, he couldn't bring himself to sell it or visit it. He said it felt wrong to move into a mausoleum of memories, so he gave Elle the deed as a campaign contribution.

"You don't have to do this. We can turn around and go home," says Ash from the passenger seat. He takes my hand, planting a kiss on the inside of my wrist before interlacing his fingers with mine.

"That's okay. I feel like I need to," I say. Ash nods. I can tell he disagrees with my decision, but he respects my choice as he always has. It's one of the biggest things I love about him. If it were up to him, we'd spend the day at home watching cartoons with Ariel. To say he's protective after I spent three months in a coma is an understatement.

"Are we there yet?" Chirps Ariel from the backseat. I turn around and force a smile that instantly becomes genuine. Ariel sits in a booster seat, eating French fries from a fast-food bag. She's wearing the dress Grams got her for her birthday a few months ago. It's white with a rainbow unicorn on the front.

"Yeah, we're here."

A big dollop of ketchup falls in slow motion from her mouth and onto her dress. She looks at me with wide eyes. "Uh oh."

I lean over the console and try to wipe the ketchup off Ariel's dress with a fistful of napkins. The red smears into the fabric, painting the unicorn red. Grams is going to kill me. Ash chuckles.

"I'll get it." He gets out of the car and opens the back door so he can clean up the mess.

The last few months have been an adjustment period for us all. Ash accepted Elle's proposal to become the head of the Enforcers with the stipulation that all bots be retired immediately. Elle agreed. He's been working to recruit more people from grunt neighborhoods, leading outreach programs, and building back the trust that was lost. It's slow going, but the country is in a better place than it was a few years ago. People are beginning to have faith in the Council again. More jobs are available, and we're slowly raising the poverty line. We're headed in the right direction.

Ash turned over his Axton AI shares to Liam. He said he wasn't qualified to run a technology company and couldn't think of anyone more suited to the job. Liam took some convincing, but eventually, he came around. Carl's shares went to Penny, so the two of them are deciding how Axton AI will be managed in the future.

As for me, I'm back at Jimmy's Auto with Miles. In his free time, he works with Liam and Penny to incorporate elements of the 8-Bit app into Axton AI services and products. We both get to do what we love, and we don't have to worry about being arrested. It's a dream come true.

After Elle was elected, Grams stepped away from the campaign. She decided to move back into her old apartment a few months ago. She said the old place made her feel closer to Jimmy. Against my protests, Ash used some of the Axton money to fix the place up. Grams wouldn't let him do much. She wanted to keep it exactly the way it was. I decided to stay with Ash downtown. Ariel starts preschool in a few months. The programs downtown are still better than the school district Grams lives in. It's something I'm working with Ash to change.

Glitch and Viper disappeared the day we stormed the Academy. After I woke up, Ash told me evidence had surfaced proving that Glitch had tried to assassinate Jace by firing a shot across the street. The story checked out - the rooftop was the last place I saw my friend. A few weeks later, I received an email from an address I didn't recognize. It just said, "I'm sorry." I knew it was from Glitch. When I tried to respond, the email bounced back undelivered. I wish I knew where she was. I wish the Council would drop the charges against her so she could come home. I miss her.

Ash helps Ariel from her seat and scoops her into his arms. She's getting a bit too big to carry around, but I know we'll keep doing it for as long as we can. He hip-bumps the car door shut. I get out to join him.

"I don't think I've seen that cartoon character before, but 'bloody unicorn' could be a new bestseller." I turn around just in time for Miles to throw his arms around me in a bone-crushing hug. He releases me and peppers a kiss on Ariel's cheek. Ariel laughs. "I missed you, baby girl."

"I'm not a baby anymore." Ariel frowns and crosses her arms. Miles pulls back and grins. "You're right. You're practically a grownup!"

Ash sets Ariel down, and she takes Miles's hand, tugging him towards the people crowded on the front steps of the Axton mansion.

"Hey," calls Liam. He's crossing the circle drive with Gram's hand resting on the crook of his elbow. I knew Grams wanted to be here to see Elle's announcement. Ash spent the morning with the Enforcers finalizing security details and ensuring things were handled so he could watch her speech from the crowd. I got things settled at the shop. I barely had time to shower and get us both ready. Thankfully, Liam agreed to pick up Grams.

"Grammy!" squeals Ariel, dropping Miles's hand and racing over to Grams. She hugs her around the waist. Grams grins, hugging her back. When Ariel pulls away, Grams looks at Ariel's ketchup-stained shirt and raises an eyebrow at Ash.

"She wanted French fries," Ash shrugs, giving her an apologetic smile.

Grams pauses for a beat. "Well, I'm sure it's nothing some stain remover won't fix," she says, letting us off the hook. Ash lets out a breath.

"If I didn't know better, I'd say you're scared of her," whispers Liam loud enough for everyone to hear.

"You're damn right I am," Ash whispers back.

"Smart man," mutters Miles. Liam snorts.

"Good afternoon," says Elle, drawing the eyes of the crowd. She's standing at the top of the stairs behind a podium with Trip and the rest of the Council on the steps behind her. She waits for everyone to quiet down before continuing. Ash picks up Ariel and puts her on his shoulders so she can see.

"You're probably wondering what this surprise press conference is about. The last six months have been eventful." There are a few chuckles from the crowd. "We disbanded the Council and joined forces with the Syndicate. We have actively rejoined the rest of the country and worked to find a balance between the old and the new. In the past, technology grew faster than the legislation we had to govern it. We all know the result." Her eyes find us in the crowd.

"For all his faults, Byron Axton recognized a problem few saw and tried to fix it. His solution didn't work, but that doesn't mean we should stop trying. Technology will always be a part of our lives. Without innovation, we stagnate. We regress. We've opened Pandora's box, and there's no going back. That is why I am establishing Overwatch." The cameras light up, and the crowd starts shouting questions. Elle holds up her hand, waiting for the noise to dissipate.

"Overwatch is a new initiative consisting of members elected annually by the people to be their advocates on critical technological issues. They will be the watchdogs. The canaries in the coal mine. The whistleblowers. They will serve as a reminder of what happens when we grow complacent.

"I chose to announce this here, at the Axton mansion, for a reason. A good friend once described this building as a mausoleum. I took that to heart. We have transformed the Axton mansion into a memorial dedicated to those who lost their lives fighting for change."

A banner floats down behind Elle with "Overwatch" scrawled beneath a large geometric bird.

A wren.

I stop breathing. I knew Elle was announcing the creation of Overwatch today, but I hadn't seen the logo yet. Elle's eyes meet mine. She gives me a small smile. More questions are asked, and pictures are taken as Elle cuts the ribbon and shakes hands with everyone as they walk inside.

Someone coughs off to the side, drawing my attention.

Glitch is standing by the fountain in the center of the circle drive. She glances left and right as if she expects someone to tackle her at any moment. It isn't unwarranted, she's the most wanted woman in the nation now. Six months a fugitive and she shows up on the front steps of a government building.

She looks better than she should. She's wearing civilian clothes and her faux hawk has been tamed down. Glitch gives me a shy smile. I run to her, throwing my arms around her in a bone-crushing hug that has her staggering back a few steps. "You're an idiot," I mumble into her shirt, my eyes welling with tears.

"I missed you too," she chuckles. Ariel tries to run to her, but Ash wraps his arm around her before she can get too far.

"You shouldn't be here," says Ash. I release Glitch from the hug, but I refuse to let go of her hand, afraid that she might disappear for another six months if I don't keep a close eye on her. Ash discreetly glances at the security guards surrounding the perimeter. A couple of them are pointing at Glitch, talking in hushed tones.

"Trust me, I have a good reason," says Glitch, gritting her teeth.

"Why can't I talk to Glitch?" Ariel asks, struggling against Ash's hold.

"Glitch is in trouble," says Ash, struggling to find a way to explain the situation to Ariel. The security guards are already pushing their way through the crowd, converging on Glitch.

They know who she is. She isn't walking out of here.

"I'm so sorry I was gone for so long," Glitch says, her eyes going from me to Miles. Miles is frowning at her, his arms crossed.

"It's not your fault," I say.

"You don't even know the full story-"

"Doesn't matter. You're family and families forgive each other."

"We'll talk after the ceremony," Ash promises. "You know I have to take you into custody, right?"

Glitch nods and offers up her wrists. She knew she would be arrested for coming here. Ash secures her wrists and gestures for the security guards to approach. They jog over to our group, taking Glitch between them. She doesn't fight them.

"Take her to the Academy holding cells," Ash says.

"Yes, sir."

I watch the enforcers lead Glitch away. She glances over her shoulder. Ariel gives her a small wave. Glitch smiles before returning her eyes ahead.

"Why did she come back now?" Miles mumbles.

Ash shakes his head. "I have no idea."

That's when the panic kicks in. "The Council will try her for attempted murder."

"We have a different Council today than we had when the verdict was made. She'll get the chance to tell her story. We don't know anything until we talk to her." Ash takes my hand in his and reaches down to grab Ariel's hand as well.

"You're right," I sigh, taking a deep breath and letting it out slowly.

"We'll figure it out, together." Ash gives me a smile so sincere it washes away any apprehension I had. Things will work out. They always do.

"Is that who I think it is?" Elle asks, strolling up to our group. She raises an eyebrow at the enforcers loading Glitch into a Pod across the courtyard. There are cameras everywhere. Elle will have to make a public announcement sometime today before the gossip channels run with whatever story they think will sell the best. She squeezes my arm, before nudging me towards the entrance of the Axton mansion. "Come on, I have something to show you."

We walk up the stairs as a group. Ariel hides behind Ash's leg. She's not used to being around this many people. I stop on the threshold, causing Ash to stumble into me. He puts his hand on my shoulder to steady himself. He starts to comment, but it dies in his throat when he sees what caught my attention.

A floor-to-ceiling, black and white portrait of my mom.

I walk further into the room as if drawn by an invisible string. It takes up the entire wall of the foyer. It's the first thing anyone sees when they walk in the door. I don't know when the picture was taken. She has a smudge of dirt across the bridge of her nose. Her curly hair runs wild, disappearing off the edge of the canvas as if captured by the wind. Her eyes are focused on something outside of the shot. She appears serious and focused. Not unhappy, but unsmiling. Like what she sees off-camera is something that gives her hope. The title of the exhibit - The Face of a Revolution - stretches out on the wall beside the canvas in scrolling font. The entire foyer is lined with pictures, some of which are familiar.

"The enforcers found Roy's camera at the Syndicate farmhouse," says Elle. "I had some of the images printed."

I can't believe she did this. More importantly, I can't believe it has been almost a decade since I saw my mom and six months since she passed away. I hate that phrase – "passed away." As if Marcia Navarro was simply a blip in the universe that faded without leaving a mark.

People told me it would get easier. That time heals all wounds.

What a load of shit.

Losing her hurts as much today as it did then. The pain is still there, but the rest of the world has moved on and they expect me to do the same. It hasn't crossed their minds that I don't know how. I don't even know if I want to, because moving on means accepting those we love are gone.

The only thing that has faded are my memories. It's getting harder to remember the sound of her voice. The smell of her favorite perfume. Her smile.

Ariel tugs my hand. "Daddy, what's wrong with mommy?" she asks with a frown. She's looking at Ash. I stare at her in disbelief. It's the first time she's called Ash that. It doesn't feel foreign or scary, but I wonder how he'll take it. I shouldn't have worried. Without hesitation, Ash scoops her up and plants a kiss on her cheek.

"Nothing, sweetheart," he says. I smile as Ash snuggles her close. "These are happy tears."

"You're weird," she says, shoving Ash away. He sets her down and she takes off for the courtyard to play with the other kids.

"Are you okay?" I ask. Ash gives me a lopsided smile that takes my breath away just like it did the first time.

"I'm on top of the world." He presses a kiss to my forehead and swipes his thumbs under my eyes to wipe away the tears.

When my mom left us, she took a piece of my heart with her but she left behind the tools I needed to patch it. I'll never get the pieces to fit quite right and it will never work as it once did, but I'm beginning to think that's alright.

My mom didn't pass away. She left the world with the subtlety of an atomic bomb, tearing down a system no one wanted to admit was broken and forcing us to rebuild. This was always her inevitability, her watchful eyes immortalized in black and white in a world that is anything but.

Acknowledgements

As always, I couldn't have done this without the support of my husband, Michael. Thank you for being my person.

A very special thanks to my mom who encouraged me to follow my dreams. You will always be my biggest cheerleader and most honest beta reader. The two sort of cancel each other out, but that's okay. You once told me to wipe excess lipstick on the inside of my sock (who wears socks and lipstick?!) so I know your advice is solid.

To my dad for helping with our soffit. You're the real MVP.

To my beta readers - Katelyn and Abi - thank you for helping me to tell Wren's story when the grammar and plot fairies failed me. You are truly superheroes.

To my readers - thank you for taking a chance on Wren and Ash.

About the Author

April Orion loves to write about near-future worlds and the technologies that will impact how we live and love. She is a data scientist by trade and a sommelier at heart. She is a lover of coffee, all things science fiction, and annoying her husband by singing off-key (and very loudly) to punk rock anthems.

Visit aprilorion.com for the latest book news and giveaways.

f facebook.com/aprilorionauthor/

⊙ instagram.com/aprilorionauthor/

Also By